Books by Susannah Stacey

Goodbye Nanny Gray
A Knife at the Opera
Body of Opinion
Grave Responsibility
The Late Lady
Bone Idle
Dead Serious

Published by POCKET BOOKS

DEAD SERIOUS

A Superintendent Bone Mystery

SUSANNAH STACEY

POCKET BOOKS

New York London Toronto Sydney Tokyo Singapore

This book is a work of fiction. Names, characters, places and incidents are products of the author's imagination or are used fictitiously. Any resemblance to actual events or locales or persons, living or dead, is entirely coincidental.

POCKET BOOKS, a division of Simon & Schuster Inc. 1230 Avenue of the Americas, New York, NY 10020

Copyright © 1995 by Jill Staynes and Margaret Storey

First published in Great Britain by Headline Book Publishing

ISBN: 0-671-00118-3

First Pocket Books printing November 1997

10 9 8 7 6 5 4 3 2 1

POCKET and colophon are registered trademarks of Simon & Schuster Inc.

Front cover illustration by Paul Bachem

Printed in the U.S.A.

For Rosamund Jenkinson
with gratitude and affection

THE PEOPLE IN THE STORY

Superintendent Robert Bone
Grizel, his second wife
Charlotte, his daughter by his late wife Petra
Inspector Steve Locker
DS Patricia Fredricks and other police personnel
Dr Ferdy Foster, pathologist

In Biddinghurst:

Graham Barnholt, late owner of Bidding Manor
Nigel Wells, television and film actor
Barbary Wells, television and film actress, his sister
Henry Purdey, a journalist
The Rev. Edmund Purdey, Rector of Biddinghurst, his
  brother
Kat Purdey, the Rector's daughter
Reggie Merrick, a pensioner
Phil Merrick, his grandson
Laurie Scatchard, garden designer and gardener
Fleur Scatchard, his daughter
Justin Rafferty, his assistant
Noah Pike, the sexton
Dolly Pike, his wife
Mrs Heather Armitage, a widow
Dave Hollis, an organizer of the fête
Midge Hollis, his wife
Lucy, their daughter
Tim, Kevin, etc., other and foster children of the Hollises
Darren Bartholomew, a teenager
Charlie Iden, owner of the Bidding Arms
Edie Iden, his wife
Jonathan Cade, a psychic investigator

In London:

Dr Beth Dillon, a visiting psychiatrist from the USA
Damien Winter, TV and film producer

PROLOGUE

'I still don't believe they sing at this time of year. And it's very dark. Don't they prefer moonlight?'

'The moon's only behind cloud. Your eyes will get used to it. This is where I heard it yesterday. Take my arm. You don't want to exert yourself too much—or to make a noise and disturb it.'

It was not disturbed. Whether the moon inspired it or whether it was mere coincidence, when the cloud passed and the white radiance poured down, the nightingale sang. Both men stopped their stroll and, one still leaning on the other's arm, listened. The sound might have been the moonlight itself singing. Behind them the old house, half-timbered, the leaded windows glittering, was also a silent witness. In the mind of one of the men was the thought that the house must have heard generations of nightingales during the long centuries it had stood there. In the mind of the other were very different thoughts, though concerned, too, with the house.

'Listen. What's that?' The older man gripped the arm that supported him. Another sound had crept in under the serene notes of the nightingale, scarcely heard at first: the sound of distant galloping hoofbeats. They drew nearer, louder, overwhelming the sound of the nightingale. No rider, no horse appeared with the hoofbeats as they thundered on, but the creak of the saddle and harsh breath could be heard as the rhythm altered a little and then quickened for a jump; there was a pause with only the fierce breath of effort as the horse cleared a jump, the impact of its landing and the hoofs again, louder.

'My God! Listen . . . !' The speaker let go his friend's

1

arm to press his own across his chest as if to quieten the beats within.

'Graham—are you all right?'

The hoofs passed, it seemed, within a few feet of them, and rapidly faded into the distance beyond the house. Both men let their breath out, audibly, and Graham staggered.

'Let me take you into the house.'

'No no. I shall be all right. For the moment, anyway. You heard it, didn't you?'

The nightingale's song now faded. In the moonlight, the younger man's face showed incomprehension. 'Heard it? Of course I did. I brought you out here to hear it. Beautiful, wasn't it?'

'Not the nightingale, the *horse*.'

'The horse? Where was the horse?' The young man looked all round, as if to find a horse in the shadows.

'It doesn't matter . . .' Graham once more gripped his friend's arm. 'Here it comes again.' He stood rigid, listening, in the night quiet, to a sound, while his companion stared at him, bewildered. 'Of course you don't hear it. I was the one intended to hear it, not you. You'd better go. It's late and I need my bed. Need it more than I knew. No. Don't come in. I can manage. I'd rather be by myself.' He turned at the great door with something like a smile. 'Thank you for giving me that moment of beauty tonight. It's like you to think of it, and you know how grateful I am.'

He touched the younger man on the arm and went in, shutting the door.

The moon had gone behind cloud again, making it difficult for the younger man to search among the bushes for what he had to remove. He was still crouched, one hand extended, when he heard the hoofbeats again. The rider took the leap over the gate and passed him, so close that he heard the scattering of leaves that did not lie here this summer night. He did not need to turn his head. He knew he would see neither horse nor rider if he did.

2

1

'Had a quiet night, then?' Charlie Iden, polishing glasses, was solicitous for his guest's comfort. Even at the height of summer, a village inn off the beaten track must please its customers if it hopes for a profit; though this particular customer was probably going to stay.

'Unfortunately—yes.' Jonathan Cade was rueful. 'Perhaps your beds are too comfortable. I was set on staying awake and when I looked at my watch it was all but midnight, so I thought I'd make it. Next thing I knew, it was morning.'

'So no footsteps?'

Jonathan grinned. 'Well, someone did go past my door soon after eleven-thirty, but it sounded like a woman. She was humming something from "Sunset Boulevard".'

The landlord admired the gleam on the row of glasses. 'That'd be the wife. She's been up to London to see it three times already and she's going again once the fête's over.'

'The fête is—Sunday?'

'Sunday. You've picked a bad time for a visit to Biddinghurst. It's all sixes and sevens. I reckon it'll scare any ghosts away.'

Jonathan shook his head and replied cheerfully. 'They don't live in our world, remember? If they take any notice of this one it's to come back on anniversaries or at times connected with their own experiences here. And of course to give the odd warning now and then; they keep in touch as far as that.'

'Warning! You want ghosts that give warning, you've come to the right place.' Charlie leant his arms on the

3

bar and said with relish, 'You ask anyone about the warning poor Mr Graham Barnholt got a week ago. Right, Edie?'

Edie Iden, the admirer of Andrew Lloyd Webber, was built on the same substantial lines as her husband. She came through from the shut public bar to take up position leaning on the bar beside Charlie, and rest her bosom on her forearms. Jonathan Cade, drinking his coffee a yard away in the empty lounge, pictured Mr Punch bobbing up beside them to crack a cudgel across their heads. Edie even sounded, with her breathy squeak, like someone in a puppet show. 'Poor Mr Graham Barnholt! He knew then, all right. Not that he'd have seen it.'

Jonathan pulled in his long legs and sat up straight. This was interesting. This was new. 'Just what was it he didn't see?'

'The horseman up at the manor—' Husband and wife turned to each other in mutual interrogation. Who would tell the story? Edie won, and took up in a lowered squeak. 'It came for him, you see. Comes along the road to the drive, and jumps the gate. Captain Barnholt, in the war, he heard it when he was on leave, just before he went back and got killed at Tobruk.'

Jonathan was fishing in his pocket for a Biro. His notebook was ready on the table.

'The family knew: the owner of the house gets the warning.'

Jonathan wrote fast. He believed what she said because her voice was perfectly matter-of-fact. He thought he was well able by now to detect the dramatic note, or the covert amusement, of someone having him on.

Charlie took up. 'It's Squire Garrett, that broke his neck in 1775. You can see the date on his tomb in the church. He goes for that gate every time an owner of the house is going to die. Nigel Wells was with Mr Barnholt that night; he told us that Mr Barnholt heard it.'

Jonathan's busy hand stopped writing. 'Then this Mr Barnholt . . . ?'

4

Charlie and Edie exchanged glances of mingled pity and satisfaction.

'Dropped dead, poor soul, inside his own front door. The doctor said he might have been going to open it, or just have shut it. Buried only Monday.'

'Oh . . .' Jonathan retracted the Biro point and sighed, less for the dead man, more for a lost interview which had promised to be rewarding. Only later it occurred to him that to ask a man about his own death omen might not be rewarding at all.

Edie, sensing disappointment, mistook its cause. 'Yes, if you'd been here Monday you could have gone to the funeral. Everyone was there, the whole village. Of course we were wondering who the manor belonged to now. Graham Barnholt didn't have any children.'

'Yes, if you'd been there, you'd have seen Nigel and Barbary Wells. Nigel came specially from London where he was filming. They do say Mr Barnholt left him the Manor.'

Jonathan realised at this he was expected to know who the Wellses were, but as he mostly spent his evenings writing and reading when he was not out on research, he knew very little about the stars of small screen or large. He saw that to admit ignorance would not just lower the Idens' estimation of him, but would also offend their pride in these Biddinghurst luminaries, so he muttered something that might be regret and Edie was quick to console him.

'Oh, you'll see them in the village. Ever so friendly they are, Nigel in particular, doesn't put on any airs, and they come into all the shops—'

'Nigel has his pint here with the rest in the evenings.' Her husband wanted to show the condescension extended to his premises as well. Jonathan had by now decided that he was not likely to find the Wellses—he saw them as a glamorous couple, swanning in and out of the shops, doing everyone a favour simply by living—

5

as attractive as the villagers did. He would try to avoid them during his stay.

'Barbary Wells's cottage was haunted, now, till that nice lady came—'

'She was a medium.' The Idens, like many couples, had perfected the art of interrupting each other, altering or contradicting what had been said. Charlie picked up his duster and polished his wife's elbows off the counter. 'A medium called Playboy or something.'

'Don't be daft! Playboy!' Edie good-naturedly reinstated her elbows. 'Play*fair*. She was Play*fair* and she wasn't a medium, she came with the cats.'

Jonathan's patience was not tried. He had long ago grasped that to hurry people is to confuse them, and he waited to see why the woman who had come as a side order to cats should apparently have stopped a haunting. Charlie was now upholding his certainty that this Playfair woman had been called in on purpose.

'Of course she was, dear.' Edie smiled at them both, indulgently. 'She was asked there to bring the cats. Then—' she overrode her husband's protest—'*then* she saw the old couple, in the doorway it was, and after that they were gone—pouf!' Edie heaved her arms wide and blew. 'They never heard them again.'

'You mean they'd heard them but not seen them?'

'That's right, but she saw them, right away in the door.'

Jonathan was writing fast again. The Playfair woman must in some way have released the ghosts by enabling them to appear. He wondered what she had actually done to help them to go. He would have to talk to Nigel and Barbary Wells after all—it sounded as if the couple had parted, as the cottage was referred to as Barbary's and Nigel had 'come down from London'.

'You'll have to ask Barbary and Nigel about it. I'm sure they'll be ever so helpful if you ask. They're to open the fête on Saturday, you know, so they're still here. Would you like us to give them a ring?'

'That's very kind, but I think I'll get around to seeing them a bit later on. From all I've heard, you have plenty here in Biddinghurst to keep me busy for a long while.' Jonathan consulted a list in the back of his notebook. 'If I've got it right, there's a coach with a headless coachman that goes down the street—is that past here?'

Charlie, busy winding the clock behind the bar, looked over his shoulder and forestalled his wife, who was about to answer. 'No one's seen that for donkeys', and it sounds silly to me. Headless coachman!' He snorted into the clock.

'Not so silly, when you think how he lost his head.' Edie tossed hers, indignant that any village amenity should be ridiculed. She leant further over the counter to confide in Jonathan. 'The horses went out of control, the coach hit a tree back at the crossroads and the poor coachman's head was caught in the fork of a branch and pulled right off.' She struck herself lightly across the throat and, taken by surprise, coughed.

Jonathan had read about this in *Kentish Ghosts,* a research book that had brought him here; headless coachmen were common all over England, but such a sensible explanation of their headlessness was uncommon indeed. What interested him was the driver's effort to control his horses without a brain, with only his will surviving death, to direct them.

'But when it comes, it passes this house?'

The telephone in the bar rang at that moment, drowning Charlie's reply; and Edie, reminded perhaps that there were other duties besides the pleasant one of chatting to guests, waggled her fingers in valedictory mode at Jonathan and vanished into the shadows at the back of the bar as skilfully as any spectre. Jonathan put away notebook and Biro, and took a mouthful of, by now, cold coffee.

It was time to go out and explore. He was here because the place was—after Pluckley which could rally thirteen ghosts in and around it—the most haunted village in Kent. Jonathan intended to devote at least one chapter to it in his *The Supernatural in Rural England*. Although he had missed the footsteps last night, for which the Bidding Arms were famous, he might be lucky any night to come.

There was plenty left, besides the headless coachman in Front Street, last testified to, not very reliably, by some revellers in the fifties who might have been legless themselves, and the now vanished couple at the Wells cottage. His list informed him of something in the church up the street from the Bidding Arms, a possible apparition in one of the antique shops across the street, a horseman on the Dover road, a poltergeist in one of the houses in a row rather impolitely called the Warren, and now, of course, the horseman at the Manor. He deeply regretted that he had not been here, say, a month ago, to question Graham Barnholt about the ghostly horseman who came to give the Manor's owner warning. It couldn't be expected that he would ride again—for that, presumably, another owner of the Manor would have to die. Jonathan thought guiltily that he was being callous, yet still he made a note to ask whether anyone was yet sure of Graham Barnholt's heir; and while he was on the subject, what had Graham Barnholt died of? The Idens would certainly have mentioned it if he had met a violent end.

A horseman who regularly broke his neck might be supposed to have a natural affinity with sudden death and be able to materialise when one was due. Jonathan, despite his interest in ghosts, was not a morbid or malicious man but, as he issued into the hot sunlight of Biddinghurst Front Street, he could not help wishing that, in another, shadowy world, Squire Garrett was saddling up.

2

Spoilt for choice as Jonathan was, he decided to start with the most handy bit of supernatural. Charlie Iden had told him who had the poltergeist, so he asked at the petrol station which house was Reggie Merrick's. The answer was a, 'Huh! Last house at the end of the Warren there,' with a briefly pointing hand and a look that suggested he was inquiring for trouble.

Poltergeists were not Jonathan's prime interest, and he did not expect to hear anything of significance. Doubtless there was some teenager in the house, whose psychic energies were causing the manifestations.

Reggie Merrick's house stood in a like row of council houses, red brick, set back from the road behind small, sloping front gardens divided by white paling or low hedges. If anything of his character could be inferred from this particular front garden, Reggie Merrick was a man of precision: he had lined up his plants in the beds bordering the front path in a way that admitted of no nonsense such as falling over or failing to flower. A magnificent hollyhock held its spine with military straightness beside the front door and, after ringing the bell, Jonathan was admiring the plant when the door jerked open and a man was glaring at him as if he had caught him in the act of severing the hollyhock's stem.

'Yes?' The glare took in Jonathan's clipboard and was not softened. 'I don't buy at the door, nor do I waste my time with market surveys. Good-day to you.'

The clipped voice, and the skull-like head barely softened by thin grey hair at the sides, did not encourage,

9

and the door was closing when Jonathan thought to say, 'Mr Merrick? Charlie Iden sent me to you . . .'

The door swung back to permit another head-to-foot scan but no increase in approval. 'Charlie Iden? Why should he send you? I don't let rooms—'

With a loud dull thump, the barometer immediately behind Merrick fell to the floor, causing him to execute a sudden caper and to yelp. 'Blasted thing!' He let go of the door to stoop to the barometer. 'Second time today. It'll get me next time.'

Seizing his chance, Jonathan propped his clipboard on the doorstep and came to crouch beside Merrick, who was trying to lift the barometer with one hand and keep the other fisted into his spine.

'Heavy, isn't it? No, let me.' Jonathan restored the barometer, a large mahogany affair, to its nail in the wall, marvelling that it hadn't broken—but perhaps it wouldn't any longer work. Then he offered a hand to Reggie Merrick, who was having trouble standing up.

'Bloody back giving me gyp again—don't know why *bodies* couldn't have been better designed. Like balancing on a necklace of badly strung beads. Thanks.' Having regained his feet, Merrick stood looking at Jonathan rather than glaring. Close to he was not less daunting; a man in his mid-sixties, probably; tall, wirily strong, the general impression of pallor owing partly to the silvery hair remaining round the ears. The eyes too were pale, but intense. 'Well, what *do* you want? If you could *keep* the barometer up you'd be some use.' He had a manner of forcing out his words as if they offended him and he spat out 'use' hard enough to make Jonathan want to wipe his chin. He refrained in case it annoyed Merrick further. He was already completely revising his theories about the psychic energy of some teenager causing poltergeist manifestations—this man had enough free-floating psychic energy to bring not just the barometer but the whole house down.

'I certainly wish I could do that.' Jonathan injected as

much warmth and willingness into his voice and face as he could muster, confronted with so much hostility. 'But I wanted to ask you about things like that.'

'Things like what?' On cue, a door at the back of the house slammed violently, the wind of it rushing past them and flattening Jonathan's shirt against his chest before it snatched the front door from Merrick's hand and slammed that too.

'Things like that, Mr Merrick. Your poltergeist.'

'My poltergeist! Who told you about my poltergeist? If it's Charlie, he had no *business* to be talking about my poltergeist.' Reggie Merrick was doing what Jonathan had never been able to visualise: bridling. Jonathan had fancied that only large prima donnas could do this and that it required plenty of flesh and abundant hair to bring off successfully, whereas Merrick was not at all hampered by lack of both. It appeared that poltergeists were private things and best kept behind closed—or slammed—doors.

'Oh no, Mr Merrick. Not Charlie Iden. I read about your poltergeist in a book.'

Jonathan had known this to work before and it worked now. Merrick's bridle metamorphosed into—yes, it could only be called a simper.

'A book! Well now, how remarkable. You read about me in a book?'

'Certainly. And I was wondering, as I'm writing a book myself, if you'd let me ask a few questions.' Jonathan thought it sensible not to say that Merrick had received no personal mention in *Kentish Ghosts*.

'I don't see why not.' He made a pretence of glancing at his watch, clearly a formality. 'I haven't got to go out straight away. Come in.'

Jonathan was in one sense already in, but he collected his clipboard from the doorstep, and followed Reggie down a narrow hallway, white-painted, carpeted in biscuit colour, into a sitting-room of the same discreet pallor, its french windows open upon a regimented back garden.

'Do sit down.' A hand jabbed towards the sofa, that looked, surprisingly, comfortable. Merrick turned to an easy-chair in which lay a crumpled newspaper and a pair of reading-glasses. He folded the newspaper, clicked the glasses shut and incarcerated them in a black spectacle case, and sat down and managed a smile which did not look totally at home. 'So you're writing a book. Is it to be about the village?'

The tone, which so far had been one of comprehensive censure, now contained interest. Jonathan wondered if a book about the village would sound too parochial, or if Merrick would expect to command more space in such a book. He compromised. 'I'm really investigating the supernatural in general. In England, that is. But this village needs a section all on its own, it's so interesting. I'm hoping people will help me by answering questions, and as you've got one of the places *actively* haunted, your contribution will be very valuable.'

There was a thud, as if someone had hit the room's door with a fist. Jonathan jumped but Reggie hardly gave it any attention. He was looking positively affable.

'Whatever I can do. Would you care for a cup of coffee?'

'Well, thank you very much but no, I've just had some.'

'If it was Edie Iden's I'm sure it was *vile.*' One of the French windows swung shut with a metallic clunk, and shifted restlessly as if a wind were blowing it. Merrick stood up and went to open it and jam a brick beneath. Jonathan glanced round the room and found his gaze fixed by a large picture over the fireplace—a storm-racked ship was going down with all hands in a raging sea. Returning, Reggie saw him looking. 'Good, isn't it? You can feel the agony. It was a present from an old friend of mine. Dead, alas. We must all go.' He frowned as fiercely as if he were ready to help a few on their way. 'Pity the best go first. Graham Barnholt and I were at school together; I was talking to him on the telephone not an hour before he died. He was a good man: when he was stronger he spent a lot of time on what I find nowadays is called "the community"—chairman of village committees and so on; an old-fashioned Lord of the Manor. If he *has* left the place to that actor fellow, it'll certainly not be the same; though I'll say for the fellow he was good to Graham, visiting him when he was ill, and so on, which Graham certainly appreciated—had Graham thinking he was some sort of long-lost son. He's hardly likely to live up to what the Manor meant.'

'There's a ghost up there too, I'm told.' Jonathan hoped that his effort to return the talk to his own subject was not too clumsy. 'When did you first become aware of your poltergeist here?'

Merrick stuffed himself more comfortably into the armchair and evinced no hesitation. 'Let me see.' He turned the pale eyes upward and tapped his cheek with a forefinger. 'It was six years ago when I first moved in. I lived with Roy and Phil—my son and grandson, you know—at Manor Walk until Roy died; then Phil and I came here; but we didn't get on. It was not just the music and the mess, although both were *horrific*, but I was not going to have that girl here. The Scatchards are a murderous—' Merrick caught himself back, as if on the brink of an explosion. He paused, snorted and after a brief glance at Jonathan, went on—'But that's history. So I was alone here.'

'But not really alone?' Jonathan prompted, and got back a moment's uncomprehending glare, followed by a bark of laughter.

'Oh yes indeed. Quite. I discovered the thing was living here too. You wouldn't believe it, but the day Phil went, I hadn't set foot in the garden there—' he pointed to the prospect beyond the french windows—'when a stone came at me! Only just missed my *eye.*' He leant forward as if to impress Jonathan that both eyes were

13

still in good working order. 'Of course, at that time I thought it was boys. There are boys in this village who are perfectly appalling.'

'But then you realised it wasn't?'

'Oh yes. Do you know, I've had stones thrown at me *indoors?*'

Jonathan scribbled rapidly on his clipboard. 'Good heavens. Where was this?'

Reggie drew back, eyeing him as if he had said something lunatic. 'I just said. *Indoors.*'

'I meant, which room in the house?'

'In this room, as a matter of fact.'

'The french windows weren't open?'

'For goodness' sake. It was the middle of *winter.*'

'What did you do with the stone? Was it a large one?'

'A pebble. I opened the window and threw it out. Then the mirror broke.'

'Was that with another stone?'

'No, no. It cracked, all by itself. I'd hung it where that picture is.' He pointed to the shipwreck.

'And since then, similar things? Is it just things being thrown, or things moving about of their own accord?'

'If you mean, do things get mislaid without my mislaying them, then yes! I can put a magazine down on this table,' he slapped it, 'go out for a minute, come back and it will be somewhere quite different! *Under* the table, behind a sofa cushion, half-way across the room on the floor! And as for my reading glasses!'

Words here failed Reggie, and he was reduced to snorting.

Jonathan tried to steer him into answering the questions he normally put—was there an alteration in the temperature when the incidents occurred—though this was more usual with apparitions; did anything seem to trigger them; whether any of the flying objects had injured him . . . ?

'One of the magazines came at me like a blasted *bat,*'

he said, but he seemed relatively unscarred by what amounted to a mild persecution.

'Do you know anything about the people who were here before you?'

'I remember that Miss Maxwell died of a heart attack, a bit like my poor friend Graham Barnholt I was telling you about. She was digging the front garden, so at her age it wasn't surprising. The postman fell over her.' He was unconcerned as to the origins of the manifestations and indeed appeared to take the whole business as a challenge, which must be why he had put up with it for so long. He was of a combative nature. Jonathan began to think that without the poltergeist he might be lonely.

One question, however, must be asked where poltergeists were concerned. 'Do children come here?'

Merrick's pale eyes bulged. *'Children?'* Jonathan might as well have inquired about visits from cockroaches. 'What do you think I am—*Father Christmas,* for goodness' sake?'

'No, no. I meant, do you know any teenagers? Your grandson's friends . . .'

'Phil comes from time to time, but I bar his friends.'

I'll bet, thought Jonathan. But the psychic energies of one teenager on occasional visits, even a teenager with what he might have inherited from his grandfather, could hardly be responsible for these happenings. Perhaps this made the manifestation more interesting to readers; it would be a part of the chapter on Biddinghurst and Jonathan would certainly take care to mention Reggie Merrick by name.

To mention teenagers had been a mistake, however. Merrick launched into a minatory outburst on the manners and customs of the young in general and the failings, all but criminal, of the local young in particular; he got back to the Scatchards and in particular to the 'damned gypsy' father of his grandson's girl-friend: Laurie Scatchard came of a tribe of rascals who thought nothing of spilling blood; his daughter was neither more nor less than *loopy* . . . Jonathan scrambled to his feet in the middle of a diatribe on the whole teenage group, including the motorbike antics of one Rafferty, and firmly thanked Merrick for his help and his time.

Merrick was far easier to thank than to stop and Jonathan was busy edging towards the door when, with a heart-stopping crash, the shipwreck picture dropped from the wall, coming to a juddering stop on the mantelshelf, shed its glass, and dislodged a small ornament on to the hearth tiles where it shattered among the splinters.

'My *God!*' Reggie seized his head in his hands and performed a minor war dance. 'You see? Getting stroppy, blasted thing. I just hope the picture itself isn't damaged. It doesn't usually damage things—there are things I'd far sooner see damaged than that. And people, too, let me tell you, not so far from here.'

Jonathan, escaping finally into the sunlight, felt a sense of relief. Whatever the source of the energy causing the manifestations at Reggie Merrick's house, it was looking for trouble. How lucky it was confined to that house!

3

'It looks too olde-worlde to be true.'

Grizel peered doubtfully out of the car window at the cottage over the white picket fence. Humps of flowers, alternately red, white and blue, bordered the crazy-paving path. Purple clematis enwrapped the porch and sent hungry tendrils up as far as the thatched roof itself. This was worn by the cottage at a slumped angle, going downhill over the side building as if a brisk wind might tip it off into the garden. However insecure this looked, the whole set-up, the leaded windows glittering in the sun and crooked, bleached timbering making a patchwork of the white walls, was undeniably picturesque.

'Could be photographed for a calendar on the spot. No old woman with a spinning-wheel in the doorway, though; and no tabby cat sitting fat on the wall.'

'You're just fussy, Daddy.' Charlotte let the car window shut. 'You want the windows made of toffee and those strips on them made of liquorice.'

'Hate liquorice,' said Bone as they got out. He locked the car. 'If it's a cottage made of candy, better watch out for who lets us in. Hansel and Gretel met a witch.'

His wife glanced round the garden, at the sundial and the close-mown grass plot. 'I'm surprised at no gnomes.'

On the way up the path, between twin yew-trees, they did meet what could pass for a witch's cat, a sinuous black creature that raced over the grass, leapt a hump of red flowers, and proceeded to treat Grizel as a long-missing relative safely returned. It came with them to the porch and, purring loudly, tried to knit Bone's legs to Grizel's as they stood waiting for the bell to be answered. A polished section of log fastened to the door announced, in Art Nouveau lettering so curved as to be all but illegible, that the cottage was called 'Sitcom', and Bone was trying to get his women's attention from the cat to point this out, when the door opened.

'Mr and Mrs Bone? *Miss* Bone? How very punctual you are! Oh, don't let Fiddles bother you. My sister's cat, always on the look-out for someone to charm.'

The speaker himself, Bone thought, might have a touch of the same failing. He was not very tall, with light brown hair cut rather short on top and worn rather long at the back; styled more than cut, Bone felt. He was probably in his thirties, with trim features and grey eyes emphasised by black lashes. These eyes creased up now in an engaging smile, which showed small even teeth like a doll's. He shook hands.

'Delighted to meet you. I'm Nigel Wells, as you'll have guessed.' The smile gained extra wattage.

'Oh, yes! "Private Eyeful"—you know, Robert, we were watching on Sunday.'

That accounted for the sense of knowing the face. Bone had wondered for a second if he'd seen him on a 'Wanted' notice, which came of being a policeman. You thought along the lines of your profession; there was nothing about Nigel Wells's face that suggested the criminal, except for a certain impression of falsity that Bone could not pin down. It must be as natural for Nigel to be professionally charming as it was for Bone to be professionally suspicious. A slight nudge from Grizel, who was carrying the affectionate Fiddles, made him realise recognition was due.

'Very well-scripted series,' he offered, a genuine tribute, and saw from a sudden fixity in the smile that Nigel had hoped for something more personal. 'And very skilfully acted.' Nigel's smile recovered brilliance. 'The girl is very funny.'

That was a mistake. 'Yes indeed. Do come in.' Nigel put a stop on any consideration of the skill of his co-star by ushering them into the front room. There was no entrance hall, only a line of wooden pegs on the wall one side and on the other a tall curly hat-rack-cum-umbrella-holder. Bone noticed a flat cap in discreetly checked tweed, another in green oiled silk, and a panama—an actor's hats for all weathers. Nigel had moved into the room and they followed.

'You see I've tried to keep it in period.' A hand was waved, and Grizel made noises of admiration. Whatever period Nigel had decided on, it involved a lot of oak and chintz. The only object probably contemporary with the cottage was an angular settle with a high back, to one side of the huge inglenook; in spite of tapestry cushions piled on its polished seat, it failed to look in the least comfortable; nor did the room suggest that Nigel sat there of an evening, even a winter one in front of a roaring fire, chatting to friends or listening to music. A large oak aumbry, catty-cornered near the window, trailed an incongruous cable to the electric socket and obviously harboured a TV, but still this was not a room to relax in. Charlotte, in pink jeans and navy teeshirt, stood as if marooned, looking round, thoughtfully brushing the end of her fair plait across her mouth.

If the settle and the Windsor chairs weren't there, Bone mused, and with a pair of decent sofas . . . He tried out a scene—his wife correcting books on one sofa, his daughter sprawled on the rug before it, their two cats as far into the inglenook as they could manage without getting cooked . . .

Grizel had put the cat down and was commenting on the ceiling beams. There was a slight pause.

'Have you had the place long?' Always a good idea to see how long someone has stuck it out in a place you want to buy. There was usually a good reason if a place got handed on in a hurry.

'Two years this August actually. My sister used to live here—she's over the road now—and she passed it on to me. She wanted somewhere bigger. And I should be getting somewhere larger, myself.' There was a hint of complacency here.

'The agent did say three bedrooms?' Grizel asked. Bone knew that a lot depended on whether one of the bedrooms measured up to her ideas of a nursery. Like Nigel, like Nigel's sister, the Bone family was looking for somewhere bigger.

'Oh yes. One's a bit small but you can still get two beds in it.'

That might do for Cha, with room for her friend Grue to stay. Cha preferred small rooms—perhaps most teenagers would best like to live in a hole until the difficult years were over.

'Do *you* like old houses?' Nigel asked Charlotte, with an engaging tilt of the head. She came out of a dream, and nodded, smiling. Bone knew Nigel wouldn't get a word out of her, and Grizel knew it too and said, 'The bedrooms?' They were at the foot of the stairs.

'Certainly. Kitchen afterwards!'

Nigel gestured hospitably and Grizel set off. Bone paused to peer up the chimney, calling Charlotte to look, so Nigel did not wait and Cha could take her time up the oak, and slippery, stairs. Bone knew well how much she disliked anyone following her when she was having any trouble with her leg. Bone, going up first, noticed the walls were lined with photographs of Nigel in various roles, smiling, gesticulating, theatrically frowning. How could a man go up and down every day past his own face represented so often?

Upstairs, Grizel exclaimed in pleasure, and Charlotte, who had been imitating one of the photographs, with a rictus for a grin and sticking up her hair with one hand, made her father go ahead across the landing.

One of the bedrooms at least was charming. When Bone caught up with them, neck and neck with the cat, which seemed to be enjoying the tour, Nigel was leaning one hand on the bedpost of a low four-poster canopied in frilled cream linen, Regency style, watching Grizel bend to peer out of the long, low window that gave on to the back garden.

'How lovely! Robert, come and see.'

A beautifully kept lawn sloped down towards a great oak tree, the sun beyond it sending sparkles of light through the leaves. Mercifully there were no beds of brilliant flowers here at the back. Honeysuckle trailed over a trellis and Japanese anemones stood tall, pink and white, beyond. It was a garden a child could play in, could roll down that lawn.

'I can recommend my gardener.' Nigel knew when they were hooked. 'Laurie Scatchard. You have to keep on the right side of him, but he knows his stuff *and* he turns up when he says he will, or at least sends someone to do the job. Or perhaps you like to garden? I haven't time myself and I have to be in London so much.' He switched on the smile, reminding them of the glamorous calls on his time, and led the way to the next bedroom.

20

This overlooked the front, and Bone could see Grizel's suddenly critical eye examine walls and sloping floor. He hadn't married a woman who would allow charm to overwhelm her grasp of the practical.

The kitchen, when they got there, had a curiously mournful air in spite of its red Aga and limed oak panelling, perhaps because of the impression it gave that nothing was ever cooked there except a pizza in the microwave, or coffee. Grizel was examining the equipment, and she asked Nigel about the dishwasher. As he came forward, Cha pulled her father's sleeve.

'Let's get out of here.'

Bone turned to see her frowning. She's tired, he thought, her leg must be playing up. They were coming out of the kitchen, preceded by Fiddles, as assiduous as any keen estate agent, when the door-knocker sounded. Nigel, with an apologetic word, went to answer, leaving the three to wander in the big room and look at the oak again from there.

'What do you think?' Grizel muttered from the side of her mouth while Charlotte let Fiddles show her the inglenook again.

'Well—let's talk over lunch. I'm ravenous. Let's lunch at the pub.'

They moved towards the door, where Nigel was talking to a tall, rather gangling man with carroty hair, an amiable face and a clipboard.

'—I don't know that I can help you at all. I never was aware of them myself.' Nigel looked almost embarrassed. 'And they're gone now. Not hide nor hair of them left.'

'Could your sister tell me anything? I understand she lived here while the manifestations were still going on.'

Bone and Grizel exchanged a glance, which Nigel saw. He laughed, and for an actor it was a poor try. 'Just a story about a haunting that used to be current in the village. You know what these places are. But if there was anything, ever, at any time, it's gone. Totally gone, I assure you.'

'I told you, Robert! One of the best-haunted villages in Kent, the guidebook says.' Grizel turned and addressed herself to Nigel. 'I'm sorry it's gone. There's great cachet about harbouring a ghost. Was it a horrid one, with chains and things?'

Nigel had to rearrange his face, from dismissive to regretful. 'No, not a bit. A harmless old couple and, for all I know, they might still be here. I just haven't heard them at all.'

'Oh, what a pity. Well, thank you so much for showing us round. It's a delightful house!—and we'll let you know as soon as we can—you understand we have other places to see, and decisions to make.' Grizel was doing the wife's job of getting them away tactfully. All Bone had to do was to usher Cha out, past the man with the clipboard who stepped back to let them go. Evidently he wanted to pursue the ghost story further, although Nigel looked unwilling; as they went away past the picturesque flower-borders and the twin yew-trees they heard him directing the man to the house almost opposite, where the sister who had seen the ghostly couple now lived.

'Bidding Arms? Or Crossed Keys which is nearer?'

'I could slay for a sandwich. Crossed Keys it is.'

The Crossed Keys commanded, from its bay-window, a view of Nigel's cottage down the side road across the street, and they regarded it at first in silence, drinking their cider and waiting for ham sandwiches. Cha spoke first, with vehemence.

'He was a *creep*. I'll never watch "Private Eyeful" again. How does that girl Ritz Baker bear to act with him?'

'He's a bit of an ac-tor, but not that bad, surely?'

Cha responded by putting two fingers into her mouth, leaning to the side and making a sick noise. She turned it suddenly into a cough when the waitress arrived with their sandwiches. When they were once more private in their bay-window, she went on, 'I read this story once about vampires on TV, and when everyone was watching they sucked their blood through the screen without anyone knowing. He's as bad as one of them.'

Grizel said, 'I'd not take him for gruesome, only vain,' and Charlotte made a face.

'He didn't touch *you* up in the kitchen, then.'

'Surely he didn't!' Bone remembered, however, the sudden movement Cha had made, and her immediate wish to get out, and he disliked hearing himself being reasonable when instinct prompted him to rush across the road and beat Nigel Wells to a pulp in his own cottage. 'Would he risk your saying something?'

Cha turned her eyes up, which always irritated Bone in its appeal to the gods to witness the idiocy of the Olds. 'He thought I'd like it. He must think girls my age will *stand in line* to get touched up by him if they knew where Mr Lovely Eyeful lived.'

'I'm sorry, if it bothered you. I wonder if he's married. It doesn't sound as if he's gay—' Grizel was examining the cress in her sandwich for seeds—'the dressing table had no women's things on it, only a man's brushes, colognes and stuff.'

Cha made a face at the thought. 'I bet she divorced him. I bet she did. No wonder his sister moved to a different house. There's worse things than just ghosts.'

Bone finished his cider and put the glass down with a decisive thud. 'Leave the man's marital problems alone. What did you think of the cottage?'

Cha once more had the first word. 'If we went there after that creep we'd have to *fumigate* it. I hope he's planning to move a long way off. It'll have to be a really, really big place to get his ego in.'

Nigel, however, was not moving where he planned to go, though certainly farther away.

4

'How do we know this gardener person will be there or that he'll have the keys?' Cha, plodding up the gravel drive, sounded fratchety, and Bone suspected that her leg was hurting. Though it was better, after the car smash which had lost him his first wife and baby son, than anyone at that time had reason to hope it would be, it still, now and then, gave her pain. He should have got those tiresome gates here open and brought the car up to the house, regardless of Cha's claims that she felt fine. Traipsing from room to room and from house to house was much more exhausting than an ordinary quick walk. Cha could do more than she used to, but she still had her off-days. Besides, Bone thought she didn't much want to move. She loved her stepmother's cottage, tiny and cosy, where they could very well have gone on living happily if it were not for the coming baby.

'The estate agent seemed sure this was the gardener's day. And don't worry, we can always come back another time.' Bone, by sounding soothing, was aware he was irritating Cha. She disliked people trying to make her feel better and said it always made her feel worse. Yet he found himself doing it.

'Listen.' Grizel, ahead of them, spoke cheerfully. 'I can hear a mower.'

They stopped the crunch of gravel to hear better: a purr, getting louder, behind the hedge bordering the drive. Grizel's blonde hair glittered in the sun as she bent her head to listen. 'An old-fashioned mower! My grandfather's mower used to sound like that. I thought they were extinct.'

'There must be a survivor. All we have to do is to find the old-fashioned man in charge of the mower and hope he's got the keys. The agent said he had to have them to water the house-plants.'

By this time they had rounded the corner, and came upon the house. They stopped.

It deserved the dignity of a drive, even a short one like this, but its size did not overwhelm as Bone had feared. On the contrary, it looked comfortable, at home against the trees. The Georgian, or early Victorian porch with its slender white columns framed the apple-green door. Long sash-windows reflected the sun, a stone urn on the flagstones spilled pink geraniums and ivy. Grizel exclaimed softly. Cha voiced Bone's thought.

'Can we afford it? It looks pricey.'

'Oddly enough, it's inside the price range I had in mind,' Bone said cautiously. 'The agent told me there were things needing to be done, which brought the price down considerably. If the things-needing-to-be-done cost too much, though . . .'

'Like manky wiring, and a stone sink in the kitchen.'

'Come on. We need the keys to find out.' Grizel set off in determination towards the sound of the mower whose rasping purr was now retreating. An arch in the well-kept privet hedge to the side of the house might be the way to the back, and they followed her through.

The prospect there could have belonged to a larger house altogether. Lawns stretched away to more trees, where a vista gave on yet further grass. A small terrace ran the length of the house, clumps of lavender bordering it where the lawn took over. Unlike the front garden at Nigel Wells's, this didn't go in for flowers and the effect was calming. Bone was not by nature a gardener. He had no wish whatever to let himself in for weekends of toil when he could be sitting and contemplating nothing. There were people, even people he knew and liked, who found their minds got a move on when their bodies were active. He was not one of them. His own father could never sit still in a garden because there was always something to be done. Bone intended to close his eyes to what had to be done, and this looked a splendid garden for that.

'Hoy!' Grizel, as the distant mower turned to begin his march back, waved her arms and did a little dance. Cha, beside Bone, moved abruptly, and he wondered if she were experiencing adolescent embarrassment at the Olds making fools of themselves in public. She had, however, come forward to stare, shading her eyes.

'It's Justin. Daddy, it's Justin.'

Now the mower, still plodding after the machine but briefly signalling with one hand that he had seen them, advanced on his relentless way. Bone saw that it was indeed Justin. The first time he had seen Justin Rafferty, Cha had brought him into the flat at Tunbridge Wells and he had come as a nasty surprise, a warning that boyfriends might arrive in any shape and might, like Justin, wear their hair in bleached tendrils and a jumbo diamanté cross in one ear. Since then Justin had faded out of Cha's life, for which Bone, although he had grown almost to like the lad, could only be relieved. Now, however, he came nearer and nearer until he stopped, and draped an arm over the mower handle as if it were a crutch.

'Hi. You come to buy the place then?' He nodded at Cha. 'Hi. Long time no and so on.'

'It's Justin Rafferty, isn't it?' Grizel had a teacher's excellent memory for faces and names. Bone recollected that she, and he, had last seen Justin at their wedding the previous autumn. The young man hadn't changed much; the bleached hair had been allowed to grow into a fringe on his brow, the tendrils at the back were perhaps longer and whiter, the face still that of an amiable young skeleton. He wore black jeans, faded to a dark grey at the knees but surprisingly unslashed, and a black teeshirt with a tiger's face, in white and full snarl, across his narrow chest. The earrings, silver studs alternating with rings, one diamanté, climbed the rim of his ear to the top, and Bone wondered if he had considered moving on to the nostril or even the nipple. He could prod him to find out. That would make the tiger snarl.

'Have you the keys to the house? The agent said—'

'Not me. They wouldn't trust the keys to *me.*' Justin was clearly aware that his appearance was against him, as though bleached hair and rings up the ears were a disability he'd been born with and he was resigned to the prejudice they aroused. 'You want Laurie for the keys.' He smiled at Cha suddenly, with such blinding charm that Bone was stirred to unease. She was at the age to find the morbid and dangerous deeply appealing, and here was Justin, the skeleton from the Dance of Death, with a mower instead of a scythe. Did the thinness and pallor go with drug abuse? He had seen a boy who could have been Justin's brother lying dead in a squat with a needle still in a vein.

'You coming to the fête tomorrow?' Justin addressed himself to Cha. 'We got a Haunted House. Spooky. You'll like it.'

'I saw a poster in the village. Will it be any good, then?'

Bone remembered having been disparaging about village fêtes. Justin merely grinned at her note of incredulity.

'Our bit will. I'm off now. Getting the ghosts ready.'

'I'd like to see it,' Cha said. 'Depends,' and she glanced at her father. Bone was not prepared to commit himself and, perhaps unkindly, said nothing.

Grizel struck in, 'Where can we find this Laurie, Justin?' Her pleasant voice cancelled the effect of the silence. It was true they didn't have all day. There were two more places to see; though in view of the way Cha looked, in spite of the liveliness she had summoned for Justin, Bone thought this one was the last she was up to.

Trundling the mower towards a garage, Justin pointed behind them. A man came strolling round the far corner

27

of the house, hands in the pockets of a short leather jacket. He waved but did not hurry his pace. This was a man who did as he chose and was not to be fussed if he could avoid it. The face was brown and weathered, deeply lined from nose to mouth, the cheeks hollow; the eyes, unexpectedly light though deep-set under heavy lids, regarded them shrewdly as he sauntered up. Thick black hair curling on his neck gave him the air of a gypsy. His voice when he spoke to Grizel was a caress, his smile of practised beguilement far more overwhelming than Justin's.

'Hallo. You looking for me? I'm open to offers.'

The glance he gave Grizel took in more of her than Bone thought it should. He was not yet used to the way men looked at his wife. His pride at the admiration she attracted did not prevent his wishing to rearrange Laurie's teeth for him; fewer might advantageously impair the charm.

'The offer we're making is for the keys, if you're Laurie.' Bone, to his annoyance, heard himself sounding abrupt and pompous, not a good mixture as he could tell from Laurie's grin. The man had extracted a hand from his jacket pocket to offer round, introducing himself.

'Right first time. Laurie Scatchard at your service. I design gardens—all round this part of Kent—maintain 'em, prune 'em, plant 'em, make ponds, pavilions, parterres, pagodas, really anything you fancy. And yes, I have the keys.'

He produced them out of the leather jacket, with a flourish, and jingled them in front of Bone's face as if he meant to snatch them away should Bone attempt to take them. The keys were readily surrendered, however, to Grizel, and they turned to make for the front of the house. Bone thought Laurie Scatchard was going to come too, but he was delayed by having to pay Justin. Bone ushered Grizel and Cha round the house, took the keys from Grizel, hastily unlocked the apple-green door, hurried them inside and closed the door firmly as he heard the crunch of gravel on the path.

To escape was not so simple. They had scarcely glanced round the hall when the brass knocker rose and fell with reckless insistence. Bone swore under his breath as he turned to open the door; his mood was not improved by seeing Grizel look at Cha and raise her eyebrows. It did not occur to him that this might be a comment on Laurie's hammering rather than on his reaction, and therefore he scowled at Laurie Scatchard cleaning his cowboy boots on the iron scraper by the door.

'Thanks. Thought I'd better water the plants while I'm here. Mrs Bertram'd have my life if any of them died.'

Laurie stepped across the threshold briskly while Bone held the door—feeling like a butler but without the option of saying his mistress was not at home. Laurie turned to Grizel. 'Nice place, isn't it? Mind you, she's not rapt with it. Too big, and she's hardly ever here. The garden's another matter.' He spoke in a soft, intimate tone that Bone supposed he thought sexy—and perhaps it was—and even taking in Cha out of the corner of his eye. 'Got me to redesign the whole thing when she came. Spent thousands. I'm not cheap. And now I've to keep the lawn shaved and titivate the shrubs in case she turns up. Or you arrive.' He gave them all, Bone included, a brilliant smile, and set off down a tiled passage leading, Bone guessed, to the 'small conservatory' mentioned in the agent's blurb. Bone concealed his relief. He was aware of being unreasonable but suddenly the last thing he wanted was to have Laurie Scatchard accompanying them round the house, commenting on it and eyeing up Grizel. Unlucky that this little house-hunting expedition round Biddinghurst had already produced three people he would rather not have met. As a policeman, he really could not afford to get fussy about his acquaintance.

Perhaps Grizel was right about his being overworked . . . At this point she took his hand and swung it.

'Now. Show me the place. What is des. about this res.?'

'Apart from the gardener, that is.' Though Laurie Scatchard had disappeared through a door at the end of the passage, Charlotte spoke in a sepulchral whisper. It lightened Bone's mood that she giggled, and Grizel's look in answer showed that she found the desirable gardener just as amusing. If they did decide to take Mrs Bertram's house, he was definitely against taking the gardener as well. With that and the ghost to which Nigel Wells had been so reluctant to admit that morning, Biddinghurst with all its obvious charms did have some disadvantages. He had naturally no idea that there might be any more sinister ones to be brought to light.

5

The Julian Barnholt Memorial Hall had once been a minor showpiece in Church Field, but having lost its roof in the gale of '87, it was now furnished with leaky corrugated iron, so that its plasterboard walls and its floor had maps of damp-stains. At the moment, too, its space was punctuated with upright posts and battens, some supporting dusty black curtains in the beginnings of a labyrinth. Sprawled on the floor, as if felled in the midst of their exertions, lay the construction team. Only one sat up, her back to the wall, a dark slender girl scowling over a list on a clipboard.

'Fleur: will your father really show tomorrow? If he doesn't, Darren has to do it and we can't spare him.'

The wan, thin girl stirred her head on her boyfriend's

chest without opening her eyes. 'He'll come. He said he would and he will. He came and put up all the frames, didn't he?' She waved a hand at the posts and battens.

'All right. Only checking. It's not everyone who'll sit with their head on a plate, in make-up, half the morning.'

A cheerful, sardonic voice from a supine figure put in, 'It's not a compliment to say you've just the face for a Haunted House. Not everyone's going to take it well.'

'He's cool,' Fleur responded. 'He said as long as he didn't have to have an apple in his mouth.'

The dark girl ticked *Laurie Scatchard* next to *Head on Dish*. 'And you'll get the curtains from Barbary Wells.'

'I'll go up now, Kat, if you want. Phil could come too.'

'Yeah, all right,' the boyfriend said.

'Can't spare Phil. There's the plywood to put up. Justin, you got the tray cut?'

'In the van.' Justin pushed himself up on one arm. Though as thin as the girl Fleur, he was possessed of latent energy; he gave Kat a slow grin, but she did not respond. 'They couldn't get the hang at first—' he spoke without moving his eyes from Kat—'then I said, see two slices of melon with a bite out of each.'

'So long as the bite is big enough for Laurie's thick neck. Darren, you're down for parsley and weeds.'

Darren said, 'Yeah.' He was half asleep, a sturdily built incipient hulk with an incongruous silver nose-stud. 'What about—' it came out as 'worrabar'—'the blood?'

'Nigel's bringing it today.'

Justin, prone in the dust, said, 'Hope he's got all we need.'

'He will have.' Kat got up. 'Right. Break over. We're rehearsing tonight and this has to be *ready*.'

'It'll be ready.' Phil sat up. 'Don't flap, Kat.'

'Cat-flap,' Justin murmured. Kat jabbed a corner of her clipboard into his ribs and he yelped with surprising force. 'Watch it! That's my bruise.'

'So mind your mouth,' Kat said, sugar-sweet. 'Rehearsal tonight with all props and clothes.'

'And then the parties,' a girl on the outskirts said.

'Then the parties.'

There was a short silence.

'Oh yes. Won't miss either of those.' Phil's grin showed a fine set of teeth and made him, suddenly, predatory.

'Kat,' Fleur said, 'Kat . . .'

'Yes. We'll all be there. As planned.'

Charlie Iden had given Jonathan the impression that Barbary Wells was some high-powered glamour chick who condescended to behave like one of the locals. What he had not said was that she was beautiful. Not pretty: beautiful. As Jonathan gazed, he knew how rare this was, but the pointed face, the almond-shaped green eyes above the high cheek-bones, the curve of the mouth, the abundance of glossy dark hair, all contributed to stunning effect. It was not a model's face, stereotyped, all eyes and big mouth, looking good on a six-foot girl. It was a face perfect for the petite creature staring at him and his clipboard.

Jonathan came to his senses just as she began to speak.

'I'm sorry. You must be from the *Kent Messenger*. Nobody rang to confirm a definite appointment but, as it happens, I am free at the moment.' She smiled. It was dizzying.

As she stood back for him to enter, he managed to speak. 'No. No, I'm the one who should be sorry, Miss Wells. I am sorry, I mean. I'm afraid I'm not from any newspaper. Just conducting research. Jonathan Cade. Psychic investigator.'

A fleeting disappointment, perhaps at his not being a reporter, was at once succeeded on that expressive face by curiosity.

'*Psychic* investigator! Why do you want to see me? Do come in.'

She led the way out of the hall—more a large bay-window than a hall. Jonathan had the opportunity to admire her charming figure, in leggings, bronze slippers, and a loose silk cowl-necked tunic, as he followed her into a sitting room on the left. He stumbled into it down a little step she hadn't warned him about, and nearly caught her in the back with his clipboard.

'Oh, I am sorry! I always forget that people can't know about that step. Please forgive me.'

Jonathan would have forgiven her actual severe injury, but he was unable to say so because he was looking down into her face. She moved away, saying, 'Do sit down' and gesturing towards a small Osborne chair upholstered in green velvet. He sat, rather gingerly, while Barbary curled up on a Knole sofa opposite. It, too, was covered in green velvet, and it crossed Jonathan's mind that all this green velvet was there with the purpose of bringing out the colour of her eyes. Perhaps she had also arranged for the white cat which came at once to jump up beside her and stare at him, though only one of its eyes was green, the other being a somewhat dismaying blue.

'Of course I should have known you weren't from the *Kent Messenger.* They'd have sent a photographer too. But how can I help you? What did you want to ask me?'

Jonathan's clipboard slid from his knee and he dived to retrieve it, an action the white cat took as hostile; it hissed and shrank into the circle of Barbary's arm. She kissed the top of its head and laughed. She had a soft little laugh. 'Take no notice of Binkie. He's terrible with men! So jealous!'

Jonathan could not muster a reply to that, but provided with a very believable vision of a cluster of men round Barbary, he took refuge in his clipboard and inquired about the ghostly couple who had, he understood, once haunted the house she had lived in. This time there was no mistaking her disappointment.

'Oh *those*. I'd completely forgotten about them. I thought you wanted to ask about my psyche—you know, how I prepare for my roles and so on, how my mind works. My brother—Nigel Wells, you know—said that I really ought to go on radio being interviewed by that nice Anthony Clare. The psychiatrist.' She put her fingers over her lips and laughed again. 'Of course! Psychologist! That's what I thought you were. Silly me!'

As this was said complacently, Jonathan did not feel called upon to produce more than a laughing murmur in response. Barbary, after kissing the cat again, was ready to be more helpful. She held the cat up on its hind legs, its face under her chin. Jonathan duly thought how alike the faces were.

'It wasn't here, you know, in this house I mean. I was sharing that cottage with my brother still. It was over there . . . Of course, at the time I was quite troubled. Voices, you know, saying things you couldn't quite hear. I did begin to think I might be going mad.' Jonathan was treated to a widening of the lovely green eyes. 'Joan of Arc and all that.'

There was a pause, while Jonathan tried to imagine Barbary in armour and only, shamefully, got as far as taking off the clothes she already had on.

'And they tried to move things—that was enough to drive one mad all by itself.' She let the cat arrange itself on her knee.

'Moved things?' Jonathan collected himself enough to click his ballpoint open and make a note.

'Oh, brushes on my dressing-table. My photographs . . . As if they thought I'd put them in the wrong places.'

'I see. Yes. Did you hear them all over the house?'

She thought for a minute, stroking the cat, her narrow hand gliding between its ears. Its eyes gradually shut, and then flashed open as if to catch Jonathan in some dangerous move. 'I can't actually remember now. Isn't that strange?' The workings of her mind fascinated her. 'I think I didn't hear them much in the kitchen, but then I'm not often *in* the kitchen so it's not surprising. Mostly in my bedroom, I think. And on the stairs. It's very horrid, you know, to come down the stairs with someone whispering behind you.'

Jonathan wrote busily. 'I should think it is! Did you feel they were an unfriendly presence?'

'Well, it is funny you should ask that. I did have the impression that they felt I shouldn't be there, but I never felt they hated me or anything. Lost souls, I thought. I was really sorry for them.'

'I was told that they suddenly became visible when— am I right in thinking she was a medium?—a lady who somehow freed them.'

'Oh yes, indeed, Emily Playfair from Saxhurst. She brought Binkie, didn't she, my darling Binkie-boo? And Tinkerbell and Fiddles, but Fiddles is always running off to see Nigel. I wonder if he'll be running off to the Manor when Nigel—oh!' Again her fingers covered her lips. 'I really must wait for the will to be read before I start talking about *that* . . . ! You haven't met Tinkerbell yet, I think he's in hiding.' Barbary hitched up her cream silk tunic to eliminate a bulge that was nothing to do with her trim figure. Binkie sat up in affront and Barbary, with an absent-minded competence, folded him down again and held him until he had relaxed. Jonathan repeated his question.

'This lady made them appear, then? Did you see them?' The ballpoint was poised eagerly. He had seldom got an eye-witness account of manifestations.

'Well, first we heard the voices and then there was a peculiar noise—'

Absolutely on cue, a violent rapping on the window to Jonathan's left made him jump, Barbary stop, and Binkie burst from her lap and shoot out of the room. Jonathan for a second wondered if Reggie Merrick were not alone in having a poltergeist, then a glance showed him a man outside the window gesticulating quite wildly.

'Oh, it's Henry. Doesn't he look frantic!'

Barbary had brightened. Obviously the more men the merrier, Jonathan thought sourly, retracting the ballpoint with a cross click as she ran out to the hall, pulling down the tunic and fluffing the hair. Just as she had reached the interesting bit, too. Should he leave at once or hang on in the hope of outstaying this Henry and getting back to the 'lost souls'?

Barbary opened a door in the bow-window in the hall, and Henry started at once. 'You will not believe this! It's your brother again. It's a tragedy! He's really done it this time.'

Henry was a sturdily built man who probably saw himself as in the prime of life but to Jonathan was elderly. He might have been handsome when young, but now the hair showed grey streaks in the brown and was in retreat, the skin was beginning to slacken, and chin and stomach displayed signs of laying in provisions for the future. If Barbary had tidied herself for the meeting, Henry seemed to have done the opposite, to have rumpled his hair and pulled his tattersall shirt awry. From the sound of his voice, his lunch had been a liquid one and substantial. He stopped dead on seeing Jonathan.

'I'm interrupting, am I?' Choleric blue eyes were not softened by the business-like air of Jonathan's clipboard. Here was one who saw a rival everywhere.

'He's here to find out about the ghosts,' Barbary said, soothing. 'You remember? The couple who used to whisper in my bedroom—'

Inflammatory words, Jonathan thought, for a man like Henry who plainly had proprietorial feelings about her, but Henry was preoccupied; turning his back on Jonathan, he seized Barbary's hand, a sudden maudlin note in his voice.

'I was going to ask you to come and see her.'

'Who? You didn't say you wanted me to meet anyone.' Barbary obviously didn't care for the sex of this person. 'Who?'

'She was so *like* you! It was because she was so like you. When I saw her standing there, I thought—Barbary with her clothes off!'

Barbary gasped and Jonathan fumbled with the clipboard, wondering if he ought to get up and leave them to it. However, the curiosity which led him to inquire into the supernatural urged him to stay. Henry had folded Barbary's hands between his as if in homage, and a slight parting of the lips and the tenuous indication of a frown showed that the pressure hurt her.

'Oh, she was lovely, lovely! It was going to be such a fine surprise—you couldn't but have loved her! And now smashed into pieces . . .' He stopped and let her pull away her hands and check them for damage; seeing her do this he automatically caught them up again and kissed them, but without paying any real attention. 'It had to be Nigel. Who else would have done such a thing?'

'Sit down, now.' She sat him on the sofa, facing Jonathan, whom he noticed all over again with no increase in pleasure. She crouched before him, distracting his attention entirely from Jonathan, who received a welcome waft of her scent from her closeness.

'Now, Henry! Explain! You're making absolutely no sense at all.'

'And I paid so much for it too! Not that the money matters. It's the statue I mind. So like you! You'd have loved her! And there in pieces . . .' He put his head down with alarming signs of emotion. Barbary patted his hands and looked over her shoulder at Jonathan, inviting his sympathy with a face of such sorrow that he accorded it at once. Her movement, however, brought Henry's head up and his belligerence back. 'Your brother is persecuting me. I know I smashed his windscreen, but what did he expect, the bastard?' It must now have crossed his mind that a sister might find the term offensive and he paused, gripping her hands again. Fumes of wine reached Jonathan along with Barbary's scent. 'I tell you I won't have him sneaking into my garden . . . He thinks he can do as he pleases now he's Lord of the Manor. He thinks he can decide who you see and who you don't!'

'Nigel never—'

'But this is beyond . . .' He let go of her hands and thumped a fist on the sofa arm. 'I tell you I won't stand it! I will not! His bloody-minded spite and damned impertinence! I could *kill* him!'

6

What Barbary might have said in answer to this threat to her brother which, however exaggerated and absurd, had been delivered with alarming energy, was prevented by the door-bell. Henry, alone for a moment with Jonathan as she left them, stared with mounting dislike, his underlip pushed upward.

'You're asking about ghosts? What are you, a reporter? No ghosts *here*, anyway. I don't know why you're pestering Miss Wells. They left when the cats came.' Unexpectedly, he pointed to the windowsill, and Jonathan peered round to see. A cat was crammed under a low shelf at one end of the sill. It seemed to think its cover had been blown, for it squeezed out from under. Tinkerbell, or Fiddles unless there were more cats yet, stood for a moment regarding them both with yellow eyes; this cat, thought Jonathan, might get cuddled under Barbary's chin less often than Binkie was. As to fur, it was a white powder-puff splashed with ginger. After an expressive switch of the tail it tipped itself off the sill and crossed the room, meeting Barbary coming in.

'Tinker, my sweet, where have you *been?*' She bent to caress the cat, which flattened to the floor under her hand and escaped from the room. A girl who had come in behind Barbary, and who now saw there were already visitors, looked as if she longed to follow. Barbary caught her hand and led her forward. 'Now, Fleur! You know Henry, and this is—' she's forgotten me again, thought Jonathan, but after no more than a second she came out with—'Jonathan Cade, who's here about the ghosts. Now, you wait here just a moment and I'll fetch the things.' She bestowed a vague smile all round and vanished after Tinkerbell.

Jonathan and Henry both waited for Fleur to find herself a seat. Driven by the same instinct to hide that had motivated Tinkerbell, she made round the edge of the room for the windowsill and huddled at one end of it, drawing up her sandalled feet until she could hold her ankles and rest her chin on her knees. She was a frail, very pretty girl, not more than seventeen, and had not acquired social graces as yet, for she offered no words and looked at her toes as if they might send her a useful message. Her hair fell blonde and limp, but the lashes concealing her eyes were dark and long. Whoever this Fleur was, she provided as good a foil to Barbary as did the cats, with her orphan-like vulnerability.

It appeared, however, that she was not an orphan.

'When's your father coming to do my pergola?' Henry probably thought he was being genial, but Fleur shrank into herself more, glanced very briefly towards Henry's feet, and muttered indistinctly. Henry went on, 'Got stuff for him to clear up, too. Tell him that statue we put up has been pushed over. In pieces. It's tragic. I'll need help clearing it away.'

Jonathan thought Fleur's mumble in reply contained something about her father being very busy, with no time till after the fête. This ignited Henry.

'*Bloody* fête! Nobody's done a thing in the village for days on account of this wretched fête. Nothing but pester people for stuff for their blasted stalls. There's Mrs Armitage—'

What Mrs Armitage had done was for ever lost as

Barbary returned bearing armfuls of muslin and net and a sheath of tissue-paper balanced on top. This now slid, unwrapping, releasing a pair of long black silky gloves to fall on the carpet. Jonathan picked them up before Henry could, earning himself another scowl, and Fleur unrolled from the windowseat and came to help. It turned out she could speak quite articulately.

'Oh you are kind. What lots of curtains! We can hang some up as well as wear them—and Kat will love the gloves.'

'Aren't you wearing them?'

Fleur shook her head, which let the blonde hair cover one eye. 'Oh, no. Not my style; Kat's going to be a sort of Morticia, you know.'

'Morticia! Should suit my niece down to the ground,' Henry remarked. This reminded Fleur that she was not alone with Barbary, and she drooped into silence again, while Barbary piled the curtains across her arms for her until she stood, obscured under filmy layers, rather like a moth in a web.

'Sure you can manage? I know what, Henry will give you a lift wherever you're taking them, won't you, Henry?'

The smile, the warmth of voice, were not to be resisted, and Henry surged reluctantly from the sofa. Barbary touched his shoulder, rather as if, thought Jonathan, she were telling him what a good boy he was; he escorted the filmy Fleur, opening doors and ushering her out. Barbary hovered round them until they were gone, then came back to Jonathan.

'So sorry! Everyone is in a flap today. The village fête tomorrow, I expect you've heard, and one tries to do one's bit; Nigel and I are opening it, so silly! But it reminds me I've got to look out some books for Mrs Armitage's stall. No one dares not do what *she* wants. But do go on, won't you?' She went to the bookcase between the windows and began to run her finger along

40

the titles on the top shelf. 'Wasn't I telling you about when Emily Playfair came?'

'You heard a peculiar noise.' Jonathan, surprised at her remembering, clicked his pen into working mode and looked hopefully at Barbary's slender back. It was clearly not possible to hold her full attention at any time. She had got rid of the amorous Henry with speed and skill. He should be grateful he was sharing her only with books.

'Oh yes. Miss Playfair had just said "Can I help you?" and there was this strange noise—'

The noise this time, a sharp cry or an indrawn breath, came from Barbary. She was putting the books intended for the fête in a pile on the sill, and she had caught sight of someone in the garden. Jonathan wondered if Henry could have got back so fast, but the name she called, opening the window, was a joyous 'Laurie!'

Jonathan sighed. A man, hands in the pockets of a leather bomber-jacket, was sauntering up towards the window. If the ghostly couple, he thought, never did more than whisper, it was a marvel that Barbary had noticed them at all.

'Laurie! I didn't think you were going to turn up today. Fleur said you were terribly busy.'

'I've trained her to say that to everyone, saves a lot of trouble.' Laurie, leaning in at the window on crossed arms, was at once aware of Jonathan and sent him an extended smile over Barbary's shoulder. He turned to her and dropped his voice to intimacy. 'Company, Ba, or are you being sold something?'

Barbary, Jonathan thought, would prefer to be alone with this man. She held the window-catch with her hand resting on his arm, and stood close. Jonathan got up, therefore, just as she said, 'Jonathan Cade came to find out about the ghosts we had in the other cottage.'

Laurie's eyes had widened at the word 'ghosts' and the long mouth twitched. Jonathan, used to sceptics, recognised one. He said coldly, 'Research. Just research.

Well, thank you for giving me your time, Miss Wells. Perhaps I might be allowed to come one day when you're less—'

It was the newcomer who said, 'You're not going, are you? Barbary, let me in and Mr Brhm and I can talk ghosts for a bit.' He widened the smile directed at Jonathan. 'I get about the village all the time—hear all sorts of things.'

Jonathan hesitated. Never reject information; and check with other local people in case this man thought it funny to feed him moonshine.

Barbary had no hesitation. 'You will stay, Mr Cade?' Henry hadn't been able to resist that three-cornered, cat-like smile, and Jonathan couldn't. He had the impression that she feared Laurie would go away if she didn't do what he said, in spite of his obliging manner. Maybe he was obliging to everyone. Even if Laurie were coming in ostensibly to talk to someone else, Barbary wanted him in. Coming past Jonathan, she made a little gesture of pushing him down in his chair. 'Sit down again, do please. I'll just let Laurie in, and you can chat while I'm making coffee. He really knows the neighbourhood, his family have lived here for ages.'

Jonathan carefully sat on the Osborne again, as Barbary went to open the french windows in the bay next door. Through the window Laurie had just left, Jonathan caught sight of a ginger and white powder-puff legging it across the lawn. Tinkerbell did not mean to put up with any more visitors.

After an intimate silence in the hall, implying an embrace, Laurie strolled in to sit on the sofa. He smiled with great friendliness and settled back against the green velvet, put one booted foot across the other knee and fixed Jonathan with the pale eyes as if he were an interesting specimen of lunatic.

'Tell me about the ghosts. Are you a journalist?'

The usual question; Henry had asked it. Not a lot of people made the study of ghosts a full-time occupation, and certainly Jonathan intended to write about what he had found. It was a question of scale, a book not an article. It made him an author rather than a journalist. As he put this point, Laurie watched him and, although he was not smiling now and seemed perfectly serious in his interest, Jonathan sensed that he was amused.

'. . . so I was hoping for a good deal of useful stuff from Biddinghurst. It has something of a reputation.'

'Not a patch on Pluckley. I think they have thirteen ghosts all told. We've only half as many, if that. Too bad Barbary gave hers the push. Have you tried the Bidding Arms?'

'I'm staying there. On purpose.'

Laurie sat up, as Barbary came in with a tray and put it down on a small gilt table already loaded with magazines. The mugs were blue and white with Japanese designs. Jonathan was given one, with the cranes of longevity flying against an indigo sky, which he rested on his clipboard. Laurie took his from Barbary as she sat beside him, and replied to Jonathan. 'You know the stories, I see. Any luck with the French soldier?'

'What *are* you talking about?' Barbary demanded.

'The French soldier who escaped from Sissinghurst in the eighteenth century when it was a prisoner-of-war camp. You must have heard of him, Barbary.' The voice took on an extra dark-brown tone when he spoke to her. 'This poor monsieur walks up and down in a room at the Bidding Arms, if you get the night right. To and fro.' Laurie shook his head. 'Poor bugger must still be wondering if he's going to get caught.' He gave Jonathan a sudden dazzling grin. 'Doesn't know *you're* waiting to get him.'

But ghosts were not on Barbary's mind, nor to her taste, as Jonathan found to his cost. She turned to Laurie and, by pitching her voice low and looking him in the eyes, managed to cancel Jonathan entirely.

'Have you seen Henry today?'

'Why?' As he looked down at her, the black thick

lashes reminded Jonathan of the girl Fleur—of course, his daughter: *I've trained her to say that.*

'He's raving about a statue that got broken. He says he got it because it was like me. He thinks Nigel broke it.'

Laurie found this very funny. 'Nigel? Not on your nellie. You won't find Nigel waltzing into Henry's garden and busting his statues. He'd be too scared Henry would kill him.' He straightened his face and looked concerned. 'Shame about the statue, though. Must be the one I helped him to put up. I don't think he liked me handling it.' He dumped his mug on the tray and arranged one hand across his chest and the other over his crotch, simpering, 'Nice piece of work it was, and a ringer for you. Much colder, though.' The hand concealing his crotch flashed across to pat Barbary's thigh. 'Henry'll have to make do with the real thing, won't he?'

'Laurie! Don't be so silly.' She glanced at Jonathan, as if to gauge how much could be said in front of him. 'You know Henry doesn't mean anything to me.' She ran her finger up the centre of Laurie's chest, over the white teeshirt that so well emphasised his swarthiness. Her finger stopped when it reached his skin, and rested just below his throat. Jonathan felt a wild desire to block out the scene with his clipboard and announce from behind it, 'Please don't mind *me.*' He supposed that because he was indeed a passing stranger, she felt she could behave as she chose in his presence. Laurie squinted down at the finger and then raised his eyes to meet Barbary's as she breathed, 'Don't forget tonight.'

This, Laurie seemed to seize on as a signal for takeoff. He rose abruptly, leaving Barbary at a loss on the sofa, finger still extended. 'Right, then. That's it. Off to do the Rector's wall; then I've got the battens to finish for the Haunted House. Not your kind,' he nodded to Jonathan. 'Thanks for the coffee, Ba.' He would have got out of the room at a smart pace if he hadn't had to negotiate the gilt table with its ill-balanced tray on the

pile of magazines. As Barbary came to her feet, pro-
testing at his departure, he caught his shin on the edge
of the tray and sent it, with the mugs and the magazines,
to the carpet.

'Sod it! Sorry, Ba—clumsy bugger, me.' He high-
stepped over a small pool of coffee and a rolling mug
on his way to the door. 'Can't stop to help clear up. I'm
late already. Sorry. Sorry. Bye.'

Barbary made the mistake of pausing to look at the
carpet, and in that moment Laurie had reached the door,
looked over his shoulder to see how closely he was pursued, rolled his eyes expressively at Jonathan, and was
gone.

Somehow, although he was alone with her again, Jonathan did not think Barbary was going to be in the mood
for any further questions.

7

Jonathan was totally right about Barbary's mood. As
the front door shut with a final *click,* she gave the mug
by her foot a violent kick which sent it rolling away. She
also swore, and though Jonathan was not such a chauvin-
ist pig as to imagine that swearing should be the prov-
ince of men alone, he was startled by the violence she
injected into the word. Binkie, who had poked his head
cautiously in at the door to scan for aliens, vanished.
Jonathan put his clipboard down and began to try to
mop the coffee with an unfresh handkerchief he found
in his pocket. Barbary came to a crouch beside him with
a handful of tissues she had wrenched from a box. Her
scent, as near as this, was overwhelming. He saw, to his
horror, that she was crying. How could a man treat a

woman so beautiful so offhandedly? He wanted very much to put an arm round her slender shoulders, wipe the tears from those wonderful eyes—but he had seen the kick she gave the coffee-mug.

'I'll get a sponge.' She bunched the stained tissues in one hand and jumped up, averting her face. As she rushed through the hall and opened a door beyond, the knocker sounded a tattoo on the front door. Could it be Laurie, back to apologise? Unlikely; and Barbary clearly thought not, for she called from the kitchen in a strained voice, 'See who that is, will you?'

The knocker fell again, with sharp insistence, just as Jonathan reached the door, and he opened it on a woman still holding the knocker, so that she slightly staggered. Her mouth opened in surprise at sight of him, and he felt as she looked him over that she was cataloguing him in some way. A shout from the kitchen, 'Who is it?' enabled the woman, her eyes still analysing Jonathan's appearance and clothes, to lean sideways a little to shout across his face.

'It's me, dear. *Heather!* I've come for the books!'

Temporarily deafened, Jonathan stepped back before her, because she was certainly going to come in. He was doing his own cataloguing as she stood there in the hall: one of those middle-aged women whose vitality made you grateful not to have been around them when they were younger. She must also have been pretty; her skin, though showing wrinkles round the eyes and mouth, had still a bloom on it. Any grey in the hair had been tinted to a warm brown and the pink and brown summer dress set off hair and complexion rather well, although it had to be in a larger size than most as if her weight were an expression of her abundant energy. She was now looking about her with intense curiosity, as though searching for traces of a recent orgy.

'Where are you, dear? Have you got the books ready?'

Barbary appeared in the kitchen doorway, sponge in

hand. She had clearly made time to cover any damage caused by tears. Jonathan could see nothing but beauty; Heather, taking a step forward, focused avidly.

'Are you all right, dear? Anything wrong?' The look she shot Jonathan made him realise that she perceived him to be the likely cause of any distress she sensed in Barbary. How did women know? How had this Heather person sniffed it out?

Barbary put on a smile and gestured towards him. 'Jonathan Cade. Heather Armitage. Mr Cade is writing a book about ghosts.'

An explanation which might have mystified some people satisfied Heather at once. She gave Jonathan a plump, ringed hand and a beam. 'You're staying at the Bidding Arms! Charlie Iden was telling me all about you.' Something arch in her tone suggested she had heard various disreputable details from Jonathan's past, which Charlie Iden was certainly ignorant of. 'We must have a good chat, some time when I'm not so busy. There isn't much about this village that I don't get to hear about. But it's the fête, you know! If I didn't take things in hand nobody would be ready in time. Now, dear, where are the books?'

Barbary hurried into the sitting room, closely followed by Heather, who cried out at the coffee on the carpet. 'I'd help you to clean up, dear, if only I wasn't in such a rush.' Looking at the two women, Jonathan thought Barbary more than ever a delicate flower.

'Never mind the carpet. There's a box of books behind the sofa, and these as well . . .' She moved to the window and picked up the little pile she had chosen. Heather bustled round the sofa and, as she bent to the box there, Jonathan was reminded irresistibly of comic seaside posters as nothing could be seen of her but her generous rump.

'Oh, I can't pick this up, dear. It's much too heavy,' and indeed her face was flushed as she came upright. Jonathan, unwilling though he was, had no option, and went forward to apply such masculine strength as he had.

Fortunately for his pride, he could heave up the box, and stood waiting with it. 'Oh, *thank* you!' Heather said, and her smile was, to his dismay, decidedly coy. 'Now, I can carry these,' she took Barbary's little burden, 'and you can bring those to my car.'

'It's sweet of you,' Barbary said, raising the green gaze to his and giving him once more the three-cornered smile. She picked up his clipboard and put it on top of the box of books in his arms. 'There! Now you've got everything.'

Jonathan, helpless, realised he was being got rid of as Henry had been; was being shown, literally, the door. He followed Heather Armitage as she trotted down the crazy-paving path to her car. As he stood waiting for her to open the boot, he saw himself reflected in the car window: tall, plain, carroty, and amiable. He was not the man to interest the Barbary Wellses of the world. He was not even the man to cope with Heather Armitage.

This he had proved upon him for the rest of the afternoon. As a man she had found spare, so to speak, Heather fastened on him as porter of her books and in this role he was driven from place to place all over the village and its surroundings. He did manage a protest or two, overridden or ignored by her in a stream-of-consciousness monologue as they went. At one point she suddenly came to a screeching halt, swerving to the kerb, as a stoutish man with a ginger and grey moustache and a dog-collar came out of a gate, waving, and carrying a Marks and Spencer bag that seemed about to explode its burden of paperbacks into the road.

This turned out to be the Rector, whose features reminded Jonathan of someone he had seen recently, he couldn't think whom, and who dealt with Heather in an admirably professional way, congratulating her on her efforts and urging her on to further ones, so getting her back on the road in record time.

'Such a nice man. And he doesn't drink at all!'

Jonathan was pondering the significance of this when they almost literally ran into Reggie Merrick. He had made the mistake of trying to cross the road at the moment when a few of the Rector's books made a break for freedom out of their carrier bag on to the car floor. The avalanche failed to hit the back of Heather's seat but the noise and shock were enough to make her steering go haywire, sending the car straight at Reggie Merrick rather than away from him. Jonathan had been impressed, that morning, with Merrick's energy, as abundant in its own way as Heather's; the next thing for Jonathan to admire was Heather's method of dealing with the situation. As Merrick gibbered on the pavement she drove past, shouting from her open window, 'Don't forget your books! I'm leaving the boot of my car open all night for late contributions!' Turning again to the road, she said, 'Silly man! Jumping about like that. So dangerous.'

By the time he had carried the books into the back of the village hall, where they were to be stored overnight ready for a stall in the field next day, Jonathan was exhausted. He had thought Heather was to aid with this final carrying, but she became involved in an argument with teenagers who did not want anything in the hall, and he brought in the books in quite a few journeys from the car park on his own. He stood for a moment surveying the bustle, while Heather with pursed lips rearranged the carrier bags he had stacked. Laurie was indeed putting up battens for something complicated all across the hall, directed by a forceful dark girl and assisted by a boy and Fleur. Jonathan then realised he ought to have fled as soon as the books were stacked, for Heather turned and invited him, as a reward for his work, to help her with the stall next day. While his life-preserving instinct was still mustering a waterproof excuse, she was distracted by shrieks from the construction team, where something was collapsing and Laurie was shouting at his daughter, and it was with comments on Laurie's uncouthness that she seized Jonathan's arm in a despotic grip and led him off to her car.

She parked the car in the drive beside her house in Manor Walk, and said goodbye 'Until tomorrow', following her farewell with a volley of sneezes. 'Good gracious, have I a cold coming on? This will never do. I must take an aspirin and nip it in the bud. I can't *think* how they'd manage tomorrow without my seeing to things.'

Jonathan crossed the road to the Bidding Arms, and found the Idens in the midst of preparing the big dining room at the back for a dinner party. Charlie Iden, talking as he worked, explained there was to be a celebration for a couple called Hollis, Dave and Midge, of their silver wedding, which was being given by their own and their foster children. By the number of place settings, this was a sizeable crowd. Charlie added, 'See Heather Armitage had you running around for her. You want to watch out for yourself: two husbands worn down, what was left's in the cemetery. She's after the Rector now, though I don't see her getting him while that daughter of his is around—so it could be you!'

Jonathan's grin was properly apprehensive, and Charlie gave a roar of laughter. Jonathan then went to his room to write up his notes for the day. By the time he had finished, he was ready for a drink and dusk was falling. The hum of the bar below, and conflicting pop music from various sources, reminded him that this was Saturday night and Biddinghurst must be getting ready, in its own way, for a bit of excitement.

How much it was going to get he had certainly no way of telling, even when a large stranger accosted him in the bar.

'Aren't you the ghost man? There's a light in the church and no one's there. Thought you ought to know.'

8

Jonathan's immediate thought was: *he's having me on.* The man's appearance was against him, a Neanderthal brow above piggy eyes, sandy stubble on flaccid jowls, the singlet drawn tight over the aggressive belly—was this a man to be reporting ghosts in any serious spirit? Yet there was no twinkle in the small eyes, no sign of hidden amusement. There were none of the signs he knew so well. In a village full of ghosts, people like this man might have got used to them, even take them for granted.

'D'you want to see?' The man gestured with a grimy arm and Jonathan followed the burly shape that made a passage through the bar-room crowd. As in many old country pubs, the way to the door was hazardous; Jonathan bent his head when his guide did, under beams tall men could brain themselves on, and he stumbled down one step and up another before he came out into the cool air of the street and the door shut behind him on the friendly noise and lights and warmth.

Jonathan shivered, either from the air or in anticipation. Was he really on the track of something? His guide had turned to the left and stopped outside the church porch. Jonathan had seen its façade in his journeys up and down Biddinghurst as porter to Heather Armitage. A large hand touched the door.

'There you are. The light's inside, doesn't show from here. Can't be anyone in there 'cos I'm sexton and I locked the place up couple of hours ago and it was clear then.'

51

Jonathan hesitated. 'Have you ever seen this—ghost that's supposed to be here?'

'Nah. I only seen the light twice before. Once last year and once two years before that. Think I'm going in there to see? You must think I'm stupid. I don't know if there's a ghost or not but the light's there and it didn't ought to be, and *I'm* not going in.'

Jonathan took a grip on himself. It was, after all, his job and his opportunity. The sexton obeyed his nod and unlocked the door, which swung open with a soft groan. He stepped into the chill of the church, every sense sharply alert. He thought, *I am afraid. It's true.* He had been in many reputedly haunted places but with a feeling of excitement only. The excitement was there but the darkness and the cold combined with the sexton's reluctance to go in made Jonathan breathe fast. He stepped out from the lobby with its bellropes and fusty smell, into the space of the nave. A single light flickered at the top of the aisle to the right.

He tiptoed along the matting at the back of the pews. A candle was burning beside a kneeling figure at the side altar. All round, the shadows in the vaulted ceiling and on the stone walls shifted to the quiver of the flame like things ready to flow down and seize on him.

Jonathan forced himself to walk past the font, squatting palely to his right, and down the aisle, his footsteps whispering on the encaustic tiles, towards the figure and the candle. The figure . . . The story he had read was of a figure seen in the church. He could not recall if it was said to be, like the horseman at the Manor, a warning of approaching death. Too late if it was—ironic if his book never saw the light because his research had been too adventurous. He became aware that he had been hearing a thudding like a heartbeat, until now only a background of sound but now more insistent. His own heartbeat, not quite in sync, shook him.

He was only a yard or two from the figure. He saw

the hood, the folds of the cloak. It moved, suddenly rose and turned to face him.

Only there was no face.

The hood framed the shape of a face but with no features, pale, blank and horribly with no eyes; yet it thrust towards him as if to see him. The cloak swirled and the candle went out, plunging the church in night. Jonathan, whose heart had seemed to stop at the nothingness under the hood, stood without bearings, terrified to move, terrified at the presence he had seen, terrified that it had come towards him, might touch him. Without eyes, it would find him in the dark.

Nothing happened. Even through the hammering of his heart and that other pulse-beat, he heard a sound, a scuffling, even the faintest creak, as it might be of a hinge. A waft of fresher, grass-smelling air reached him, and a louder pounding of the beat, instantly cut off. Suspicion woke again. He was still trembling, but now anger gave him strength to feel for the tiny torch he usually carried in his pocket, which he had not thought of while the candle gave its light. The thin beam showed nothing where the figure had been, though the smell of candle-snuff hung on the air. The small light, played about the church, reassured him despite the shadows. He strode forward towards the side altar. If someone had been hoaxing him—though how could that un-face be a hoax?—they could not have got far.

His torch found a little side door. He tried the iron ring handle; it would not turn. Ghosts, of course, normally went through doors, not out by them.

Jonathan almost ran, back to the main door. If it was a hoax and the sexton was in on it, would he have completed it by locking the victim in? Jonathan took hold of the handle in fear, but it turned, the door opened.

'You all right then? You look bad—what was it?'

Jonathan left the sexton standing and ran to his left and up a gravel path by the side of the church, hearing a piercing whistle from the street behind him which in-

creased his suspicions. There were a few tombstones in
the grass between the path and the fence, and Jonathan
ran past their crouched presences, the church loomed to
one side and a big house stood beyond the fence. The
extra heartbeat he had heard in the church now resolved
itself into amplified pop music coming from the house.

Here was the little side door; not one in normal use
as the long grass up to its step showed, but the grass
was trampled. Human feet had come from the church.

Sounds beyond the fence caught his ear. He crossed
the mown grass among tombstones and peered over.
Light streamed from windows and doors on to overgrown grass; the insistent drum-beat pounded.

Jonathan played the pencil light to and fro round the
path, the headstones, the grass. Nothing more met his
eyes.

All the same, he found he was still shaking.

He followed the path round to the back of the church.
All was empty. True, anyone could be concealed behind
the gravestones. He stood there a moment. Though
something less raucous had been put on in the house,
he heard the roar from the pub. Above, the east window
of the church was dark, with faint glints of reflection
from village lights. He turned back. There was faint light
out here from the afterglow of sunset, and he pocketed
his torch.

All of a sudden he could hear a curious high keening
or whimpering beyond the fence. His innate curiosity
asserted itself; he once more made his way between
tombstones and peered over the fence. At first he saw
nobody. A small cold breeze had got up and found its
way to his skin. At the same moment he saw a white
figure, from nowhere, a girl with her long pale skirt
brushing the grass she seemed to be floating just above.
Her hands were fastened in her long fair hair and she
turned her head from side to side within the barrier of
her arms and her eerie lamentation continued; there
were words to it: *my baby . . . my baby . . .* She seemed

for a moment to be cradling something in her arms. She drifted towards the house, still desperately moaning, still wrenching her head from side to side, until she was gone in the shadows and her wail was lost.

Jonathan's hands hurt from his grip of the fence. The faceless thing in the church might be a hoax, but the inhuman apparition he had just seen was another matter. He did not know whether its distress were in the present or in the past, or was eternal. He had just discovered how it felt to have one's blood run cold.

9

Heather Armitage woke on the morning of the fête with a groggy sensation that something was wrong. She knew she had gone to bed the night before in the grip of a galloping cold and she checked cautiously for symptoms, looking up at the ceiling—must get that damp patch seen to!—nose clear and throat not rasping or swollen and no headache. The cold remedy had worked! She had been right to take two doses. And of course it was will-power. You must not *give in* to things, no matter what happened. (If John had not *given in* he would still be at her side and not in Biddinghurst churchyard.) So that was not what was wrong. Across the road, the church clock chimed.

She threshed onto her side and, seizing her own little clock on the bedside table, stared at it incredulously. Ten o'clock! The fête was to start at ten o'clock officially, and everyone knew, unofficially, the stalls were ready for business and some of the best things sold, by as early as nine thirty or even before—and here she was still in bed! All the fault of that dreadful remedy! They must put a really powerful sedative in it. There ought to be a warning on the packet and she would write to the makers.

She was floundering out of bed and into the bathroom. No time for her morning bath! She was seeing, as she washed, visions of Dolly Pike on the handicraft stall next to hers, interfering with the girl helping out at the book-stall, and goodness knows how that girl would be managing on her own. Heather spilt talc and could not get her clothes the right way round. No time for breakfast. That would have to be a cup of tea and a bun from the re-freshment stall as soon as she had got going. Perhaps she could find someone sensible to hold the fort. Perhaps the nice man who had helped her yesterday would be wandering about. After all there would be no ghosts for him at the fête!

She smeared shiny green eyeshadow on her lids in the belief that this improved her appearance, she fluffed up her hair and then crushed it with a straw hat trimmed with bright red silk roses that went beautifully with the ones on her dress . . . There was no time for the dia-manté brooch that took so long to pin symmetrically or for the necklace she had been going to look out that morning, but no one was going to say that Heather Arm-itage was falling below her usual high standard.

Buoyed up by this thought, confirmed by a last survey in the looking-glass in the hall, she took her car keys and hurried out, rehearsing what excuse she could give for being so late. Better give none! Never explain, never complain, her father used to say; and he was right, ex-cept perhaps about complaining. You must keep people up to the mark!

Before she reached her car, she saw something which she was certainly going to complain about. Dumped against the hebe bushes bordering her path were several carrier bags, from one of which books had already spilt. Who on earth had been so silly as to do that? She had made it absolutely clear to every single person that, if any one of them had not been able to have their books collected yesterday or had managed to get up a late contribution, they should put their bags or cartons into the boot, which she had purposely left unlocked. Some people do not listen, no matter how often one tells them. Now she would be even more late, getting those bags into the boot—and with no one to help her this time. The thought crossed her mind that perhaps there was no room left in the boot and that was why the bags had been left outside. She flung it open and stared.

She had been right about the boot being already full. A man lay there, on his side, legs drawn up, hands before his chest holding a magazine as if he were reading it. Or was it a dummy? Although it was wearing shirt and jeans, the face was like a clown's, half blue, half green, and the hair, or wig, was shaved up one side. This head lay on one of her beautiful embroidered cushions intended for the handcraft stall.

The children!—she still thought of the village teenagers as children—they had played a trick on her. It must be because she had told them she was too busy to help them with that silly Haunted House of theirs, though she had seen from their little shy smiles when she came up that they wanted to ask her. This was their revenge. It was not a dummy at all, for she half-knew the face under all that; one of the boys was pretending to play dead and watch his chance to jump up and frighten her, like a jack-in-the-box. They'd be expecting her to scream and make a fuss. She would show them! They'd see what she was made of! Valiantly, nerving herself for the shock of the figure unfolding, jumping up, making a noise, Heather leant over and tugged at the fists.

'Come now. This is no time for a joke.'

The fists were cold and stiff. They were not plastic, though, they were flesh but the flesh was dead.

It was not a joke. It was a corpse.

10

Heather Armitage's immediate reaction to holding a dead man by the hand was to let go, screaming. In an instinctive desire to blot it from her sight, she slammed the boot lid down. Then, leaning on it in an access of weakness that threatened to take her legs from under her, she gave her mind to the business of screaming.

Someone would come. Screaming indicated emergency. Heather, exhausted by her efforts, realised where she was leaning, that the object below was looking at her through the metal. She pushed herself upright and staggered on a few paces. No one had come. The empty eyes of the windows of Manor Walk stared across at her. The only observer was the horrible little terrier belonging to Noah Pike, which wandered by and, as always, lifted his leg against her hebe plant. Amazed at the absence of her usual protest, he actually backed away, and gave a bark before he wandered off.

Of course everyone was at the fête. On the breeze came the thump of amplified music from Church Field. The local band had struck up on their wagon bandstand. Heather's screams had stopped. She was moaning now, her brain attempting to make sense of things. Who was there who might not be at the fête? There must be someone to whom she could turn.

Charlie Iden. He would be at the Bidding Arms. People were lunching there during the fête. He would be getting things ready. The inn was her best bet. She made for the road at a fierce trot, the roses bobbing wildly on the brim of her hat. The road was deserted, the thump of the music louder. She put on speed with the night-mare thought that the thing in the boot might force it open and come after her, crouched and gliding—Charlie Iden was wiping down the big window table when he saw her. He said later that he expected to see at least a Rottweiler chasing her, the way she was doing a racing totter across the road. Then for a moment he feared she came with bad news about his wife whom he'd sent to enjoy herself for an hour or so at the fête before she was needed here. Pausing with cloth in hand, he heard the outer door crash open, then a cry as Mrs Armitage tripped down that step, then the inner door was flung back and she stood there, panting, wide-eyed, her straw hat askew.

'A dead man! There's a dead man in my boot!'

Charlie put down the cloth and came forward. He remembered the patient progress of Jonathan Cade, yesterday's helper, and wondered if she'd picked a helper today whose heart wasn't up to it. Charlie was a man who disliked leaving a job he was in the middle of, but it now came to him that this was an emergency. A *dead* man? The nearest doctor was in Saxhurst, but this was Sunday . . .

'Should I phone for an ambulance?'

She grabbed his arm and pulled. 'Come and see. You've got to come and see. He's in the boot of my car.'

Charlie, obeying, thought she had come from the fête, where everyone knew, to their cost, that she was running the bookstall. He could not figure out why she had come up here when there was plenty of help down there. Then he took in that she had come across from Manor Walk, and he saw her car there. He slowed down. In the boot of her car? This was a joke someone was playing on her, and who it was would not be far to seek. Kat Purdey, that crowd of the Hollises, and that Rafferty . . . by now he was curious to see what they had done, for sure as eggs it had scared the daylights out of their victim. He looked round to see them hiding to watch. Heather was babbling of painted faces and cushions and shaved heads. He became more and more convinced that he was going to see something worthwhile and when she sprang the boot lid open he was almost grinning, while she teetered back, hands to mouth.

He saw it wasn't a joke. He also saw what she had missed. He pulled a tissue from his pocket and, stooping, wiped the green- and blue-smeared face.

'Jesus.' He was stunned to a whisper. 'It's *Nigel Wells.*' He turned to the shaking Heather. 'It's Nigel Wells.'

'It can't possibly—'

Footsteps slapped along the pavement and a voice called 'Heather? Heather?'

Even at this moment Heather Armitage was annoyed at Dolly Pike's using her Christian name. Dolly came up to them anxious and smiling. She wore a yellow cotton skirt, an orange teeshirt hoisted in front by her generous figure, and a predominantly purple flowery jacket. Her blonde-grey hair was held up inefficiently by red plastic combs.

Her smile vanished as she saw their faces. 'What is it? I came for Heather. What's happened?'

Charlie reached up for the lid of the boot, but Dolly had sensed the focus of their horror and was looking in. She drew back, staring at Charlie. 'That's Nigel Wells. What's the matter with him? What's he doing—'

'He's dead. Look, Dolly, you run and see can you get Sergeant Jacks. He's supposed to be at the field. But look, don't tell anybody else. We don't want the lot of them pouring up here to gawp, right? I'm taking Mrs Armitage over to the Arms, she needs a sit down, and I'll phone—'

Dolly had instantly set off, her plump face all anxiety. As she pounded past the closed shops a feeling of importance grew in her. Nigel Wells, dead; something the matter with his head, and his face all smeared, and in the boot of a car, Heather's of all people; and *dead*. She had to slow down, she wasn't built for running. And in this heat, though look at that great dark cloud coming up . . . Dead! Bodies in car boots didn't happen every day— Nigel Wells—this'd upset the TV people! And she mustn't tell anybody, Charlie was right. The police car was parked in the line outside the field but John Jacks wasn't in it. He might be anywhere ∴ . . Further along the line of cars someone was unlocking a car door. She had to lean on the nearest car and get her breath back. She felt dizzy. Daft to run like that.

'Are you all right?'

The man had come up to her, a stranger, looking at her in concern. She said, 'Yes. Yes. I've got to find Sergeant Jacks. I'll be all right.'

'Is it a police matter?'

'Well—it is, but—'

He was showing her a little card in a folder. 'Can I help?'

Dolly peered at it. He was certainly Police. She said, 'I have to find Sergeant Jacks. Nigel Wells is dead! It's dreadful—he looks terrible, all blue and green, and he's in the boot of Heather Armitage's car—'

Bone almost missed this bizarre coda to her announcement because a sudden rumble of thunder sounded, ominous as a knell.

Laurie Scatchard, ambling by, his hands in his pockets, grinning, called out to them, 'Somebody up there has it in for us!'

11

Charlie Iden unlocked the boot and let it lift open.

It was certainly Nigel Wells; he looked very different from when Bone had last seen him. The head, roughly shaved one side in swathes, as by clippers or an electric shaver, looked grotesque enough. Eyes and mouth were open. The face was barred with blue and green, smudged, alien.

'Has he been touched?'

'I touched him.' Charlie pointed to a smeared tissue on the floor of the boot by Nigel's knees. 'Thought I knew the face, you see. I dare say I shouldn't have. Did you touch him, Mrs Armitage?'

'Yes. Yes, I did. I took—I took him by the wrist. But he was quite stiff.'

Dolly giggled, and clapped a hand to her mouth, gazing horrified over her fingers; perhaps the literal application of the word 'stiff' in this connection was too much for her.

'I thought it was a trick being played on Mrs Armitage,' said Charlie Iden, 'until I saw him. I called the ambulance, but they wouldn't come, said I was to call the police as he was dead, so I did. Then I came back over here to keep an eye; but will it be all right if I get back home? There's fifty-odd lunches to be got, and opening time coming up.'

'We'll know where to find you,' Bone said. He turned to the women. 'Wouldn't you prefer to wait indoors?'

He saw Mrs Armitage glance towards her house and then doubtfully at Dolly Pike, but he turned back to his own problem, leaving her to work out her social questions. Dolly had no such scruples, and warmly invited Heather to a cup of tea at her place.

Bone had his phone with him, and found out from Base that Inspector Locker and a team were on the way.

It was clear to Bone that Nigel Wells had not come by his present appearance voluntarily. While conceivably for some charade he might have made up in this weird fashion, he would never in the world have consented to the shaved hair.

Somebody, therefore, wanting to humiliate him, must have rendered him unconscious, with drink or drugs or a blow; but a humiliation would be complete only if it involved Nigel's knowing it—waking, perhaps trapped in the car boot—and how had they got him there?—or perhaps shaken awake by an outraged Mrs Armitage.

He looked at what else he could see in the boot without leaning over it: cushions, one under Nigel's head; a pile of paperbacks crushed up behind his feet; a magazine with a nude beside his face. Bone had noticed carrier bags of books under the hebe bushes. They might have been moved from the boot to make room for the body—Dolly Pike had breathlessly explained something about the bookstall and the boot on the way here from the field.

The death of Nigel spoilt the trick being played; once dead, he could not suffer from it. Therefore this death was either accidental, say from a heart attack, or from a miscalculation of a dose used to knock him out. There was enough air in the boot around him, but had he got his face into that cushion beneath him? Mrs Armitage must say how, exactly, he had been lying.

At last a sound of cars. As Inspector Steve Locker advanced into Manor Walk at the head of his little team, Bone gestured towards the car boot; and found that he had still got, under his arm, Cha's waterproof cape which he had gone to his car to fetch. He ought to have given it to Laurie Scatchard along with his message to Cha that he was delayed. Well, she should be all right at the fête, though he must get down there and see her soon; this bad business was officially taken charge of by Steve but it offered Bone a particularly intriguing puzzle, the more so since he had met Nigel the day before.

'You got here fast.'

'Roads were clear.' Steve Locker's comfortable bulk bent towards the rim of the boot. He turned with his mouth pulled down. 'Very odd, isn't it, sir? We'll get on to his doctor in case it's a dicky heart. You don't know about his family, sir? Are they local?'

'There's his sister,' Bone remembered. 'Barbary Wells.'

'You don't say!' Locker put the photographer aside and peered again. 'Nigel Wells! Hardly looks much like he does in "Private Eyeful".'

'There's a definite loss of suavity,' Bone said.

'The Press and TV'll be here like locusts. Shay, let's have those screens up fast. Seems a very nasty little caper, seeing as his appearance was important, really mattering to him, say. Somebody really, really didn't like him.'

They pondered this for a moment while the camera flashed and the band's bass-notes came from the field. The slaty bank of cloud had advanced further. 'What were you doing here, sir? They said a brass band came over on your phone and I wondered.'

'Bringing Cha to the fête. A disreputable acquaintance of hers—you remember Rafferty?—is in one of the sideshows.'

'What's he here for?'

'It seems he lives hereabouts. I'll have to get down there, she's expecting me. Would you arrange for someone to drive her home?'

'Right you are, sir. Who found the deceased?'

'The car's owner. You'll find her in that house round the corner, with a friend. I warned them not to talk to anyone. Then there's Charlie Iden. He put in the first call; landlord at the Bidding Arms. He'll know all the local gen and was concerned in the discovery. He's got fifty people lunching there, not to mention the bar, and I should think the place will fairly hum.'

'Leave it to me, sir.'

'It's your baby, and not a pretty one. I'll get on to the Chief; as it's Nigel Wells he'll have to know. But I want to be kept in on this.'

'Right. We'll get on with the routine. What about the sister? Barbary Wells? Should she be told?'

'She lives here. My God, she'd better be told. I'll deal with that—she was to open the fête, Cha said. I'll get down to the field.'

'Very good, sir. I'd been hoping to get off and play football with the boys this afternoon. Just don't find any more dead bodies.'

'I'll try,' said Bone, and left him.

12

'Message from your dad.'

Cha looked up from the earring she was holding, undecided, on her palm as Laurie Scatchard spoke at her shoulder, cheerfully grinning. She had misgivings at the sight of him. If your father is a policeman, there are people who will dislike you just for that, let alone the others with a genuine reason because he had been the agent of their getting sent down for a crime. She knew better than to try to speak to this comparative stranger, and used one of her subterfuges, a smile and a face of intelligent inquiry.

'Said to tell you he was held up for a bit, but he'd be along.'

'Any hassle?' It was a phrase free of those hazards of speech that she could only negotiate among friends.

'Shouldn't think so. He was holding a mac and a phone. That's pretty,' he nodded at the earring she held. 'Can't stay. I'm late for my job. Haunted House.' He pointed across the field. 'Don't miss it. Next time you see me I'll be dead.'

He wiggled his fingers in what Cha and her father called a micro-wave as she moved away. She nearly bumped into a cheerful rotund clergyman, who fielded her adroitly, saying 'Whoops', steadied her, and was gone before she had to thank him. She saw him veer towards the earring stall, so he must have a wife or daughters.

Not on any account was she going to miss the Haunted House; that was where Justin would be. Whatever she did, though, she must try not to scream or make a fool of herself. When her form had put on a Haunted House at school for the gala, some of the effects had scared her even though she knew how they were done. She must tell herself firmly that, even in this village Grizel said was so haunted, the last place you would find a real ghost was at the village fête.

Jonathan Cade had been looking warily about the crowded field, but to his relief he had not spotted Heather Armitage anywhere. The only stall selling books was being supervised by a rather daffy girl in glasses. A happy thought—Mrs Armitage had felt a cold coming on, so perhaps she was prostrated in bed.

A painful grip on his arm made him think for a moment she wasn't, but he turned to see Reggie Merrick—looking at him with disapproval, though the odds were he didn't know how to look with anything else. 'You won't find anything you want here. It's all trash. Don't bother with it.' He managed a fierce spasm of the facial muscles that could pass for a smile. 'Don't say you've come to look at the Haunted House. I have no intention of trying it; but *you* might be able to give them a few tips.'

He gave a valedictory nod and stalked off. For all his sour remark about trash, he was carrying a brass table-lamp with a flowered shade in brown and amber. Jonathan wondered about the poltergeist. It might be a very expensive guest to entertain.

A muffled scream made quite a few heads turn towards the battered little building that was the village hall. It had a banner nailed over the door: THE HAUNTED HOUSE! and in smaller letters beneath *Do you dare come in?* Jonathan thought that after last night's shocks, a few horrors he knew to be fake might act as an antidote. He made his way past a tombola, a basketware stall, an Instant Portrait Sketch stall where a depressed woman sat for an all-too-accurate study, then a stall which sent an encouraging message of fudge and toffee. The girl who had been at Nigel Wells's cottage with her parents was buying, a slender girl with fair hair plaited expertly up the back of her head. He said a cheerful 'Hallo,' and was disconcerted when she turned a face of apprehension; but then she smiled, and took her bag of goodies without further evincing that she thought him a monster.

There was a short queue at the door of the hall. Cha could hear moans, a jangle of chains, and another sudden shriek, inside. A person of indeterminate gender, with a fright wig, a face painted blue, with black round the mouth and eyes, dressed in a torn, gore-streaked sheet, was taking money, and was telling two girls that they could not go in together. Cha was glad to hear that. She wanted no one making comments and defusing the experience.

While she waited her turn, a car swirled in through the gates past the stewards, who ran after it to the parking line. Cha did not see any more, as her turn had come. She pushed past the curtain. Phosphorescent letters hanging in the dark wavered, and spelt out 'Welcome to the Horrordrome'; a low jeering laugh sounded in her ear. There was music—at least a menacing sound with a low emphatic beat, rather faster than a heartbeat, ominous. Suddenly a gust of cold air hit her face, a hand felt down her arm and took her hand; it wore a thin plastic glove and felt disgusting, but would not let go and led her forward. She was pushed, gently enough, through a wet curtain, the gloved hand relinquishing hers. Here a faint light showed straight in front a tall figure covered in a veil. It threw up the veil and thrust a hideous demon face towards her. She drew back, into someone behind who with the same jeering laugh as before turned her by the shoulders towards the left and said sepulchrally 'Forward!' She could see a huge web stretched across, put out her hands and found the web was painted on a bead curtain. As she parted it and went through, a vast wriggling spider dropped from nowhere and hit her face. Charlotte shrieked. It disappeared.

The ominous drum-beat was louder here. A luminous painted hand pointed to her left; she turned and the hand lifted a curtain to let her through. A chain jangled suddenly by her ear, making her start aside into a veiling net that closed round her. Charlotte's decision not to make a fool of herself was long gone and she screamed again. After various further horrors that undermined her resistance still more, for a long moment she was left in the dark. There was a wolf howl growing in intensity. A curtain slashed open. Beyond it a tall skeleton grinned at her and beckoned.

She came forward into a green-lit space full of veiled figures that moved about. The skeleton had a scythe that hung, swivelling dangerously, over the heads of the drifting, moaning figures. At his side was a tall girl with long black hair on her shoulders, in a long black dress which made her face even more corpse-pale. Her mouth was scarlet, like the glistening wound at the base of her

68

throat, to which she raised black gloved hands with a smile. She beckoned and the Death—who was Justin and yet not Justin—came forward to lead Cha into a dance among the veiled figures, taking hand after hand, towards a banquet table littered with dishes—dishes of raw bones, of horrible fungus-like stuff, a human hand cut off with gory stump and lying in a pool of blackish blood and, as one of the veiled figures reached out and lifted a huge dish-cover from a metal dish, a head, mouth ajar and spotted with greenish mould.

The eyes opened. Charlotte heard herself scream again. All the same she knew who it was—under that mould it was Laurie Scatchard. She remembered his farewell: *the next time you see me I'll be dead.*

The cover was replaced, the Death let go of her and the others, howling, bundled her out under a curtain. It was almost dark and she was alone, but then she saw dimly at the end of a narrow passage to her left, a door with a mundane red sign: EXIT. As she headed for it, she could just make out the green-lit scene she had left, very shadowy through the black stuff of a curtain, with the veiled figures whispering together.

She let herself out, and was on the field at the back of the hall in the light of day. She could hear the cheerful thud and blare of the band starting a tune from 'Oklahoma!' at the far end. She followed a narrow concrete path round the corner and all the crowded field lay before her, sideshows, running children, sauntering people, under a sky clouding over. Putting a lump of toffee in her mouth with a sense of relief, she went towards the nearest stalls.

There was a kill-the-rat stall, a hot-dog stall smelling marvellously of fried onions, a smash-the-plate stall, pony rides, a cake stall, a book stall where she loitered and bought, a junk stall labelled 'Whyte Elefants'—she had got nearly round the whole field when she saw her father. His face was unexpectedly grim as he scanned all about. Cha hailed him and his face changed instantly, lighting up with a smile as he veered towards her.

'I went into the Haunted House,' she said. 'I thought I might have missed you.'

'Was it good?'

'Mega-dread. If you want to see something awful, that's the place to go.'

13

Charlotte knew something had happened, though. Her father was looking across the field to where children were parading in a circle. She could make out rabbits' ears, a couple of pirates, some furry animals, an alien or two, a computer-game figure, wand-waving fairies, some small enough to be led round by stooping mothers. Her father, not entranced by this spectacle, wore his bleak and distant expression.

'What's happened, Daddy?'

He gave her his attention, almost with a start. 'Pet, I'm sorry. Yes, something's happened.' He hesitated. 'Nigel Wells has had an accident—'

'Is he *dead*?' Cha guessed what the hesitation had meant.

'I'm afraid so. I'm going to speak to his sister when she's finished judging the fancy dress. And Steve Locker's going to get someone to drive you home. Grizel is bound to be back from her christening bash quite early; you won't be alone.'

Cha shook her head without speaking, told herself she'd seen Justin which was what she'd come to do, and thought of horrible Nigel Wells suddenly dead.

'I'm sorry, pet,' he said again.

'No problem.' She put on a never-mind face.

A dash of rain wet their heads. Automatically, Bone held out the rain-cape he had been carrying all this time, and she shook it into shape and flung it over her head, emerging to hear him say, 'Will you wait in the car? Here're the keys. Someone will run you home.'

'OK,' she said; and he bent to give her a brief kiss before he set off towards the circling children, and Barbary Wells. Charlotte, doing her best not to feel forlorn, and reminding herself that Barbary Wells had a far better reason for feeling forlorn than she did, clutched the keys, her books and her bag of sweets and headed for the car. Nigel Wells, she thought, only yesterday he was groping me in that kitchen. I hope it wasn't there he was found dead; it's difficult to believe, somehow. A real death, not Justin in make-up. Daddy has to deal with this stuff all the time.

She passed the front door of the hall, still with a queue waiting. A big man in jeans, and a teeshirt that swelled out over a beer belly, was trying to jump the queue and shouting something. As she passed, he solved his problem by lifting the doorkeeper in the ragged gory sheet aside and marching in.

Barbary had been in several minds about what to wear to the fête. Naturally everyone in the village, and the local Press and visitors, would all be looking her over very closely. There would be photographs in the *Kent Courier,* maybe even in *Country Life.* She dismissed from her thoughts that the pictures would include Nigel, that the photographers would be chiefly interested in him just because he had a series on television and she hadn't had anything for months, thanks to Damien Winter turning her down in favour of one of his little popsies; and Nigel wouldn't be slow to upstage her. She looked at the two outfits laid out on her bed, and regretfully she hung up the green silk. Today she needed the warm tones of the peach suit. Pity, because Henry was mad about her in the green. As for Laurie—she was not

71

going to think about Laurie. That was over and thoroughly finished now. He was going to find out that she couldn't be treated in that casual, lordly way. She'd told him, and she would show him. She'd show him, all right.

Whatever you're going to do, look your best doing it.

She took her car to Church Field. Of course it wasn't far to walk, but she had no intention of arriving windblown; and one didn't make an entrance on foot. She put a hand to her hair and leant to peer at herself in the driving mirror as she passed Manor Walk, thus missing the police cars outside Heather's house. She thought of Nigel, and how unaccountable he could be, not answering the phone that morning. Of course he'd have a hangover after the party last night, but it was probable he'd gone down to the fête early, no matter how awful he felt, if only to steal a march on her and do his Lord of the Manor stuff. She would let him know what she thought about that over lunch at the pub, but discreetly because there'd be a good crowd there and all watching them; everyone watched the Wellses, so nearly like royalty in Biddinghurst, and it was part of one's image to put up smilingly with such things as lack of privacy.

Lack of a parking space, however, was another matter. Nobody had kept her a space in the Church Field parking bay. Never mind! Better, more eye-catching, if she drove straight in. Once they saw who it was, they'd let her park anywhere. She knew for a fact there were spaces just inside reserved for disabled visitors. She could have one of those.

This proved easy to do, and almost before she had gracefully swung her legs out of the car, Henry Purdey came charging up to squire her. He must have been waiting. All the same it was due to the position she had here at the fête to co-opt one of the stewards as well; Dave Hollis, who she knew fancied her, came up to protest about the parking, and then saw who it was and became all smiles. Yes, he would do.

'Is Nigel with you?' Dave ducked to see into the car behind her—as if Nigel would ever be second to appear!

'He's not here? He must have the most *crashing* hangover. He's not answering the phone.'

'I'll get somebody to go up to his house and rouse him out, Miss Wells; don't you worry. We have a slight hitch with the public address system, but they'll have it ironed out in ten minutes; can I recommend the Haunted House while you wait? The children have put together some nasty surprises.'

Barbary had in mind that Laurie was helping out at this sideshow. Very well, let's see who gets the nasty surprise.

Graciously she consented. It would also keep her out of sight before she was supposed to open the fête formally—too awful, to be seen hanging about.

Henry was annoyed to be prevented from going in with her, and he still managed to follow sooner than the doorkeeper liked, but the veiled guides inside contrived to slow him down; and in the labyrinth of curtains he never caught a glimpse of Barbary. Once or twice he thought he could distinguish Barbary's little screams, and once or twice they sounded quite genuine, above the sounds provided by invisible throats and by the electronic music and the wolf howls and rattling chains. You had to hand it to them, they'd really made an effect. Even Henry was quite relieved to come out. Oddly, there was no sign of Barbary. Hadn't she waited for him? Had that bastard Hollis whisked her away?

He was staring round angrily when she came out of the exit behind him.

'Barbary! Where did you get to?'

'I got lost. Oh, Henry, it was rather horrid, wasn't it? But I enjoyed it. Where is Dave?'

She was pale, but there was a light in her eyes and as she slipped her arm in his, he thought he had never seen her look more beautiful. It was annoying to have her claimed by Hollis again when they came round to the front.

'They're ready for the fancy-dress judging, Miss Wells.'

Indeed they were. Already a Red Indian had had the feathers of his headdress irretrievably stuck together by an aggressive fairy wielding a lolly instead of a wand. A dinosaur was whining about his loose tail. A squirrel wanted to go home. There was a little dash of rain on the breeze, and if Barbary didn't come and do the judging soon, mayhem would not much longer be contained. Dave Hollis acknowledged the wild signals being made to him by his wife and brought Barbary across the field to the little podium.

Barbary took her place before the microphone, Dave raised his arm to the waiting band, the mothers gave last tweaks and encouragements and, to 'Colonel Bogey', the procession began its circle. Some tall, some short, one nearly spherical and requiring to be led because his spaceman helmet kept tipping forward, the dinosaur delicately holding its tail—and being followed by its father with a camcorder—the cowboy creating his own space by trying to twirl his lasso, they moved slowly round Barbary in a wide ring.

Spectators gathered on the periphery, though there was slight commotion: people had been drifting, some of them even hurrying, out of the field on to Front Street. Barbary wondered if Nigel had got up some distraction; she could not hear, from where she stood, the news about police cars in Manor Walk outside Heather Armitage's. As Heather had not yet arrived, and as Dolly Pike, sent to fetch her, had not returned, speculations spread as if they were established fact: Heather had been arrested for assault; was the victim of an axe-murderer who, lurking, had done for Dolly too. The villagers, most with a more sensible belief that Heather had been burgled—there were all sorts about today—were being sucked out of Church Field by the tide of their curiosity.

The participants in the lawnmower race, due to start as soon as the prizes for fancy-dress had been awarded, had better things to do than listen to rumour. In the rough-mown grass behind the petrol station next to the village hall, they were checking their machines, running engines, tuning up and making ready for Dave Hollis to arrive with his starting flag. One mower failed to respond: it coughed, spluttered and continually died. Every owner knows his machine's idiosyncrasies, knows when and where to give the shake or kick that activates it. In this case the owner was not present and the machine was borrowed. Noah Pike, cursing at the delay and furiously warning everyone not to start without him, set off to find the owner and make him come at once to deal with the recalcitrant thing.

As Bone, with WDS Fredricks, reached Barbary, two things happened at once. The wind brought a heavier and more determined rain; and Noah Pike burst out of the Haunted House, stared about and then made straight for Barbary, scattering a small sailor and a Dalek out of his way. Bone had been waiting until Barbary had announced the winners, so as to cause the least distur-bance. Noah had no such scruples. Dave had signalled to the band, Barbary had cleared her throat and brought the microphone to her lips when Noah reached out and snatched it from her. His hoarse voice echoed round the field in the silence as the band stopped.

'Is there a doctor here? Doctor's wanted in the Haunted House. Hurry! *Emergency!*'

14

Noah thrust the microphone back at Barbary and set off at a clumsy run back to the village hall, watched in sur-prise by the crowd. However, no doctor ran keenly after him, only an eddy of people interested in any emergency, even the fainting of some over-susceptible punter in tribute to the Haunted House effects. Why Noah Pike should make a song and dance about it no one could imagine. Meanwhile the other competitors in the Lawn-mower Derby had prevailed on the steward to start the race without him on the grounds that he had disqualified himself by absence.

Bone, listening to Barbary getting on with her an-nouncement, also speculated about what could have hap-pened to merit the eruption of that large uncouth man with his bellow of 'Emergency!' Someone might have fainted and struck their head, making an accident more serious. An innate comic quality about the man made it hard to believe, but he half turned and told Fredricks to ask Locker on her radio if he'd managed to rustle up a doctor, and to send him down to Church Field in case. After all, Nigel Wells wasn't going to be the better for a doctor now.

'. . . and, once again, congratulations to the winning pair!' While the prizes were being produced for Barbary to present, she turned towards Henry, attentive beside the podium, and asked him if he would be sweet and fetch her umbrella from the car. He was so willing to be sweet that he almost set off without her keys.

The prizes were chocolates and cuddly toys, something for every entrant but the largest for the winners: a fairy in pink satin and a fluff of net, who had the lid off her chocolates in record time, and the dinosaur with the dodgy tail who clasped his cuddly rabbit so tightly under his fanged mask that it seemed the dinosaur was contem-plating dinner. His tail now dropped off, displaying the back of cotton shorts with a check patch on the seat. His father, with the camcorder, nearly cheered; he could now enter the sequence for 'You've Been Framed' and get another prize for that.

Bone, looking round again for Fredricks now that his moment had come, saw her talking to a pleasant-faced woman wearing a steward's badge, who was nodding and pointing to the stewards' tent. He divined that Fredricks was finding a private place and some support for Barbary Wells; she saw him looking and came at once to his side.

Barbary clipped the microphone back on to its stand, and smiled all round, especially at a couple of photographers. Someone—for her there would always be someone—helped her down from the podium. Bone saw a shadow come over her face as he and Fredricks moved forward. They must look ineluctably official, even in plain clothes. He still had to do one of the things he least liked doing.

'Miss Wells: I'm Detective-Superintendent Robert Bone of the Kent police. Can I speak to you for a moment in the stewards' tent?'

What astonishing eyes the woman had! The last time he'd seen such eyes was on Scarlett O'Hara in the old *Gone with the Wind*. He tried to usher her towards the tent, but she would not move. The green eyes in the pointed face were huge and tragic, raised to his.

'It's Nigel, isn't it? Oh, that car! I knew it would happen one day!'

Even while Bone realised her mistake, he saw how dreadfully appropriate the words were; but she could scarcely have visualised that Heather Armitage's car would be the one.

She was clinging to his arm now, tears brimming from those eyes. He could see that Fredricks was wondering whether to put an arm round her. It came to him, wryly, that Miss Wells would always prefer a male arm.

'Come on, Miss Wells. Let the Superintendent talk to you in here.' Fredricks and Bone guided her across the trampled rough grass to the little tent, while people stared; an uproar came from the lawnmower race in competition with the band's 'Surrey with the Fringe on Top'. Fredricks got Barbary to sit in a canvas chair while Bone leant on a table beside a whistle, a jumble of lists and a coffee-cup. Barbary was wiping tears away with her fingers. Bone noticed the silver varnish, the emerald-and-diamond ring.

'He's had an accident, hasn't he? Nigel?'

'I'm afraid he has.'

'Is he—he's going to be all right, isn't he?'

Bone silently shook his head. The words would be worse. Did she understand what he wasn't saying?

'Is he in hospital? Can I see him?'

'Later on, yes.' When they had got that paint off, and hidden the shaved half of his head. 'We'll ask you to give us formal identification.' Surely she would realise what that meant.

'Is he *dead?*' She came to her feet, eyes wide.

'Yes, Miss Wells. I'm sorry.'

'Sir . . .' Bone had been irritably aware that Fredricks had been beckoned to the entrance by a man arriving in a hurry. 'Can I have a word with you, sir?'

He left Barbary with an apology and moved to the entrance, where he had to stand aside for the woman steward with a paper cup of coffee. He bent his head for Fredricks to mutter in his ear.

'Someone's been stabbed to death in the Haunted House.'

The band struck vigorously into 'I Could Have Danced All Night'.

15

Someone had put on the hall's overhead lights so that Bone stepped into a Haunted House stripped of trickery. Bicycle chains clashed as he pressed past them, some curtains had been looped back, a bead curtain rattled, but another noise competed with these sounds—someone, in the depths of the maze of muslin and dark repp, the cords dangling luminous masks, was having hysterics. The sound was not unfamiliar to Bone. As he made his way on, a glove twirling on a string laid its empty fingers on his face.

A man lay on his back between a curtain and a dismantled table, someone kneeling either side of him, surrounded by figures trailing as much muslin and net as Bone had walked through. One, a girl with drippy blonde hair, had flung back her muslin and was shrieking and gasping, while a boy of about seventeen tried to soothe her. As Bone arrived, a tall girl turned, showing a face painted like the queen in 'Snow White'; pallid, with a red mouth and slanting black eyebrows; she delivered a sharp double slap to the girl's face with a black-gloved hand.

One of those kneeling stood up as Bone came near, giving him, against all common sense, a moment's qualm. He saw at once that it was Justin Rafferty, but the naturally bony face had been shadowed with grey, highlighted with white, the eye-sockets blackened and enlarged, the lips black. It made a remarkably convincing skull, the black teeshirt and leggings painted with a white skeleton. It was Death himself standing over the dead man.

The dead man was another and different shock. Justin yielded place to Bone, who knelt to see. The heavy-lidded eyes were almost shut, the swarthy complexion invaded by an ashy tinge under daubs of green make-up, the mouth slack and smeared with red and black paint. It was Laurie Scatchard.

What exactly was going on in Biddinghurst?

Bone looked up towards the young Death standing over him, as if for an answer, but it was the woman kneeling opposite who spoke in a low voice. 'The wound's in his back. I didn't like to—' She glanced round at the onlookers.

Bone said, 'Would you all please stand away. I want

this area empty.' The tall dark girl and Rafferty responded, shepherding the rest away into the labyrinth, although the blonde girl tried to resist. Bone took in that she had a bruised mouth and a black eye, before they drew her out of sight. Another person who remained was standing nearby, a very large man in jeans and teeshirt; it was the one who had seized the microphone to call for a doctor. He did not move.

The woman said, 'I'm Midge Hollis; I'm a nurse.' She was distressed, but still in charge and competent. 'I was feeling his neck and then down his spine for any injury when I came across the blood . . .' She briefly showed him her smeared hand. 'I could feel the entry wound. There was no doing anything, I'm afraid. They'd been trying resuscitation, poor things, but it was hopeless. He was already dead.'

Bone began to say, 'Is there any sign of a weapon?' when looking about, he saw knives everywhere. The floor was a litter of knives, butcher's bones and unpleasant gunge. 'What was going on?'

'He was the head on a plate,' Mrs Hollis said; and then, with a cold draught of air and a trample of feet, Locker arrived, lifting the curtain behind the scene and standing there, some of the team behind him, looking at Laurie's apparently decomposing face, the slaughterhouse debris, and his superintendent.

'Pat Fredricks on the radio said there'd been a stabbing.'

From the front part of the hall a gravelly voice familiar to Bone was raised in plangent remonstrance. Ferdy Foster, the pathologist, had also arrived. Mrs Hollis and Pat Fredricks cleared the hall together, taking the large silent man with them.

Ferdy stood surveying the scene and turned treacle-brown eyes to Bone.

'Two in one morning. You're spoiling me, Robert.' He got down beside the body. 'Been moved, has it?'

'Completely,' Bone said. 'I'm informed that he was

the head on a plate, so I imagine he must have been sitting on that stool and cushion with his head through the hole in the table.'

Ferdy leant to examine Laurie's face, with its green splotches and smeared black and red mouth. 'Doesn't look healthy,' he remarked.

'They tried resuscitation.' Locker was not on Ferdy's wavelength. 'That's lipstick.'

'There's a stab wound in the back,' said Bone. Locker dealt out the plastic gloves and they put them on and turned Scatchard over.

As they laid him down again Ferdy said, 'Either a lot of know-how or a lot of luck. From the angle of the blow I would hazard it went under the ribs upward and pierced the heart; wouldn't need a lot of strength—it would have missed the intercostal muscle.' He surveyed the strewn floor. 'Looking for a knife, are we?'

'Something like that,' said Bone. Laurie Scatchard lay quiet on his back again, ready for the bag and stretcher. Bone, peeling off the plastic gloves, stood up, saw Fredricks coming in with her notebook open, and said, 'What's happened about Barbary Wells, Pat?'

'A friend's taken her home, sir.'

'And what about the people running this show here?'

'We're getting their names and addresses—they're all local. They seem shocked—but there's something odd there. Dolly Pike came down from Manor Walk and told the news about Nigel Wells, and the older ones were looking at each other and at Katharine Purdey. It *was* odd—it looked like collusion. They know something, and so does the Purdey girl, though she didn't look at any of them. We've let her take Fleur Scatchard to her house.'

'Fleur has no mother?'

'The mother left, four years ago.' Fredricks shook her head. 'Alcoholic. According to Mrs Pike. Mrs Hollis has taken the younger children to her house.'

Ferdy Foster broke in, his slow gravelly voice with its curious emphases a contrast to Pat Fredricks's brisk tone.

'I'll be getting back, Robert. Late for luncheon. See you at the p.m. as soon as I can fix it. You'll hear from me.'

Luncheon, thought Bone. He looked at his watch without seeing it. He must ring Grizel, though Charlotte would have told her what was delaying him . . . With a word to Locker he set off, and was nearly at the car park before he remembered that his car would not be there. But it was.

Cha had sat in the back of the car for some time, the keys in her hand, waiting for someone to be sent to drive her home. She spent this time gazing out of the window at people coming and going on the road to the fête. A couple strolled towards it, arms round each other, so absorbed that they almost missed the entrance gate. Families came by, fathers towing toddlers, mothers with pushchairs. Two white-haired grannies marched past, as intent on enjoying themselves as were the grandchildren running ahead. Cha listened rather disconsolately to the oompah of the band. Just her luck to miss the rest of the fun, she thought, and then felt guilty. Nigel Wells, after all, was missing the rest of the fun for life.

Even a Grade-A creep didn't deserve to be dead. It was a shock, really, to think she'd seen him only a day ago and now he was as much history as the Tudors. Perhaps he'd find a new role as a resident Biddinghurst ghost, but perhaps he wouldn't care for the rest of the cast.

After twenty minutes by the car clock had grunted away, she began to wonder what had happened. Her father wouldn't have forgotten her. He'd have given a message to someone and that someone had failed to pass it on. The someone would be in trouble for it, a nice thought in a way. If only she were older and could drive herself! The band was playing 'I Could Have Danced All Night' and Cha kicked her feet against the driver's seat in front. A small boy in a teeshirt that proclaimed him the Terror of the Universe went slowly by, dragging his tongue over a mound of icecream in its cone, and she was visited by an intense longing to be doing the same. Suppose she let the window down and snatched it from his hand? POLICEMAN'S DAUGHTER ROBS CHILD. She stared at his retreating back, which said Megamonster. Sighing, she turned away and saw someone she knew coming from the fête; she let down the window and called out, 'Justin!'

16

Incredibly, instead of merely saying 'Hi!' and walking on, as she had at once feared he would do, Justin veered towards her, opened the door and, as she quickly shifted along, slid in beside her. He wore an anorak, dewed with light rain, the hood half shadowing his face. He smelt of greasepaint. He sat back and she could see the rise and fall of his chest. The luminous bones on his leggings were just thick yellow-green paint, and he had got off most of the make-up, but the eyes he now turned to her were still ringed with Death's black. His lips looked pale with a grey smear of the black lipstick that had made his teeth so white. He was moving his jaw muscles as if undecided. Was he after all going to get out and leave her?

'What are you doing here?'

'Funny, just what I was going to ask you.' Having him so near was disturbing but she hoped she sounded cool. 'Who's doing Death if you've packed it in?'

He was silent for a minute, then put up his hands to push back his hood so that it fell off the bleached hair. With a shock she saw his hands were trembling and a sheen of sweat glistened on his face.

'Laurie's dead.'

'Laurie? Laurie *Scatchard*? What happened? Was

there an accident?' She had a horrible vision of someone lifting the cover and the head coming with it . . .

Justin was looking out of the window. He did not answer at once, and she gazed at his ear and his cheekbone and his hair, and was on the point of venturing to prompt him when he said, almost absent-mindedly, as if he were trying to work something out, 'You could say so. With a knife.' The nightmare vision came to her again, dreadfully. She made some sound, feeling sick, and he turned, as though waking up to realise whom he was talking to. He put a long hand on her knee. The last time he had touched her was with a black glove all painted with white bones.

'Don't worry. *Daddy* will sort it out. He's there now . . . Quite a day's work for him we've provided.'

'Did you see it happen—the accident?'

'Nobody did. Or if they did, nobody said.'

Cha found she was speaking through her fingers. 'It's horrible. Two people dead in one day.'

Justin's eyes came alive in their dark sockets and fixed on her. '*Two?* Who else is dead?'

'Oh, you wouldn't have heard, of course, in the Haunted House. It's Nigel Wells. He was found in the boot of a car, Daddy said.'

Justin snatched his hand from her knee and pressed the heel of it against his forehead.

'Jesus! That's torn it.'

At this point Charlotte saw her father bending to peer in.

Bone was now annoyed by two things: not only had Charlotte not been taken home as he had asked, but this dereliction had permitted a tête-à-tête with Justin Rafferty, never to win Bone's rosette as the World's Most Promising Teenager. Bone had felt quite some relief when Justin moved out of Cha's circle; he had at one time been given a home by Cha's best friend's mother, and left when the son of the house came home needing his room back. Unfortunately this village was where he had moved to.

Cha leant across him and let the window down. Bone, divided in mind between wanting to apologise to her for her long wait, and wanting to haul Justin out by his bleached topknot and boot him away from Cha, found himself, to his own irritation, saying to him, 'Did you leave your address at the hall door?'

Justin looked totally blank, and Charlotte said, 'Isn't it awful, Daddy? About Laurie Scatchard?' giving Bone time to think: he's in shock; this boy was kneeling beside Scatchard when I got there; Laurie was his employer, perhaps he liked him. Of course perhaps he had just killed him, in which case it was very clever to stay at his side, but he's entitled to the benefit of the doubt. In a less aggressive voice he said, 'We need to know where to get hold of you. We need to talk to everyone who was there.'

Then he could turn to his daughter. Her paleness and biting of the lip showed how troubled she was, and he was sure Justin had been telling her all the gory details, exactly what her father did not want her to hear.

'I'm very sorry you've had all this, pet. Steve must have too much on his plate—'

An explosion came from Justin; he was whooping and snorting, his head down on his knees, laughing—crying. Bone was furious with himself for his choice of exactly the wrong words, the dreadfully right words; furious with Justin for this reaction, not so different from the hysteria of Scatchard's poor daughter.

His own daughter put a hand on Justin's back. 'He's really upset, Daddy. I told him about Nigel Wells too.'

Justin abruptly pulled himself out of his fit of hysteria, throwing his head back and wiping the tears off with his thumb, spreading the smear of black. Before Bone could say more, Justin had opened the door and unfolded rapidly into the road. His farewell 'See ya,' was for Charlotte alone. He set off with lanky grace and was lost to sight in a moment among the considerable crowd now streaming, disappointed, curious and talking loudly, out of Church Field and along the road. Some member of the band packing up the drum dropped it on the lorry's floor with a reverberant hollow sound like the voice of doom itself.

17

Half an hour later, as Bone approached the Old Rectory with Locker, he heard the noise of doom again and looked across the street. The lorry stood there and two men were getting the drum, now wrapped in plastic, out of it.

Locker said, 'Shame about their fête. Landlord says it was in aid of their village hall, that's falling down.'

'Did you have trouble rustling up the team?'

Locker grinned. 'Got a few of them away from their Sunday lunches. Shay was mad. He was looking forward to his mother-in-law's Yorkshire pudding, says it's nearer to heaven than anything you'd find in a church.' He studied the face before him, reserved and bleak, more grey in the blond hair than a year ago. 'I'm sorry about a driver for Charlotte not showing up. I put a bomb under Harris for it. Kept saying he didn't realise there was any hurry.' Locker did not pass on the information that PC Harris had finally said he was a cop on a murder inquiry and not a chauffeur for the Super's daughter. Locker had told Harris his fortune; that was not the Super's business.

'Cha didn't mind waiting.' Bone frowned sharply as he recollected the company she'd been keeping on her wait. 'Ferdy was quite happy to take her home. It's on his way and she likes him—apparently he tells her really wicked jokes.'

They walked in silence for a moment, contemplating the really wicked jokes of a Home Office pathologist. Cha had in fact told Bone that they were on the line of the most dangerous thing in the woods being a squirrel with a machine gun, so he was not troubled that they'd give her nightmares. She needed something to lighten her life at this point. It wasn't often that she came so near to the violence that was the material of his profession.

'D'you reckon they're linked, these deaths?'

'God knows. And He's not telling yet.' Bone understood, however, that Locker's question was less about fact than instinct, the sixth sense that distinguishes between a good detective and a policeman. Such an instinct can be at fault, but they had known Bone's uneasiness with the evidence to be justified often enough in the past. 'Here they are, same day in the same village, and as bizarre as any I've met—'

'And you've seen some, sir.'

'But they may be quite separate. Your nose tell you anything, Steve?'

'Lots of bad feeling in the village. You get across someone in a small place like this, they don't forget. And no more does their family forget. Goes on for generations sometimes. I grew up in a place like Biddinghurst.'

Bone took in, without paying much attention, that a TV van had arrived and was setting up on the north side of Manor Walk; and Dolly Pike, alive with importance, was crossing the road towards it. The Chief had already warned him, as if he needed warning, that Nigel Wells's death, accident or not, was hot news. It would be announced shortly. Dolly would appear on the news today, for her moment of fame. Bone hoped the media would not get too much in his hair.

He'd got on to Grizel, returned from her christening, to

explain why Cha was on her way home to Sunday lunch and he wasn't. She had told him that Nigel's current programme, stories based on visits by a scatty tour operator and his voluptuous sidekick to some fairly stately homes—'Private Eyeful'—was scheduled for tonight. Would it be respectfully taken off air, or shown in tribute? Nice to think that was all the dilemma some people had.

Bone turned to Locker. 'What did you get from Mrs Armitage and Dolly Pike?'

'Well, there was one important question, of course. I got the answer I expected.'

'You mean, did Heather Armitage pick up the cushion under Nigel Wells's head and turn it over?'

'Yes. And she didn't.' Locker laughed suddenly. 'Dropped him like a hot cadaver. Explained to me she only wanted to put him out of sight; slammed down the lid of the boot and yelled for help.'

'Understandable. Was that when Dolly Pike turned up?'

'No. Later. She ran across to the Bidding Arms here, for Charlie Iden. And no, he didn't move the cushion either, even though he did wipe Wells's face. Dolly arrived when he'd come over with Mrs A. to see. It was him that recognised Wells.'

'Mrs Armitage didn't?'

'She'd thought at first that it was one of the children playing tricks to plague her.'

'Children? Wells doesn't look like a child.'

'She calls the teenagers children. "They're all children," she told me, "not one of them is eighteen, let alone twenty-one, which is still too young to have any sense." And the ones she means are the ones that did the Haunted House.'

'There's a link?'

'According to Dolly Pike,' Locker got out his notes, 'Nigel Wells was very kind to the teenagers, helped them with their drama group, directed a play for them last Easter, got one of them an audition with someone in London, though it came to nothing. They wanted him to help with their part in the pageant at the fête this afternoon—which has been cancelled—but he'd been too busy filming.'

Bone raised an eyebrow. 'You mean one of them smothered Nigel Wells for not being helpful. What did they stab Laurie Scatchard for? He was being as helpful as anyone could wish. Was he the only adult helping with the Haunted House?'

'Seems to have been no one else but the kids. Pat Fredricks will have got their names.'

They had arrived at the Old Rectory, and turned in together under its tiled porch. 'Make sure she's got Justin Rafferty's.' Bone's asperity made Locker glance at him. 'Found him in the car talking to Charlotte. He was exhibiting shock. I fancy he'd slid out of the village hall before Fredricks could cover the door.'

'You think he's got anything to do with either?'

Bone was silent for a moment, making an effort. He could hear the team in some large place at the back preparing an Incident Room. The Old Rectory was now the village institute, or something like it, and smelt of floor polish, air freshener and, unexpectedly, incense.

'Because Rafferty *looks* capable of anything doesn't mean he *is*. Cha likes him, and her instinct may well be better than mine. Yet I believe the teenagers were responsible for the face paint on Nigel Wells, and for shaving his head; and I believe Mrs Armitage was right in thinking that the fright was intended for her. Do you see her as a favourite with teenagers? How they got him there and why they did it, we'll find out soon enough, but what we need to know now is if anyone looked in the boot before she did.'

'And what about Laurie Scatchard?'

Bone's eyebrow went up again and the corner of his mouth down. 'If you'd heard the Chief on the phone, Steve, you'd know that concerning a television star it's all fingers out; anything else is definitely on the back-burner. A case of first come, first served.'

18

They were upstairs in the former master bedroom of the Old Rectory. Here past rectors of Biddinghurst had looked out over Front Street and the old oaks and sycamores, secure in the knowledge that their wives and servants were running the house; today the Reverend Edmund Purdey lived with his daughter in a small house next door, with a daily woman who came to clean and cook.

This room was already equipped with an old leather-topped desk; now it had a tape recorder and PC Higg in attendance, and a technician in overalls had just come in with a telephone.

Bone and Locker had no need to confer over priority of witnesses. Locker, whose case it was, put a broad finger on the list: the teenagers of Biddinghurst, uniquely qualified. They had organised the Haunted House in which Laurie Scatchard had made his final appearance. They had organised the party where Nigel Wells seemed to have taken his last look at all things lovely.

'Get 'em, Steve. They've already had too much time to confer.'

'You think they're going to lie.'

'They're not fools. They can see it doesn't look pretty to be quite so much on the spot when the corpses come crowding in.'

Locker rubbed his chin. 'Some sort of conspiracy.'

'That's what we'll find out.'

Bone's confidence was not immediately justified.

Higg had produced coffee, and they drank as they looked at DS Fredricks's list. Locker had added Justin

Rafferty's name, but it was the first in alphabetical order that he plumped for.

'Darren Bartholomew. Let's start with him.'

'Wheel him in, Higg.'

The Haunted House personnel had been sitting downstairs in some indeterminate room under the eye of Sergeant Shay. Fredricks had gone to the New Rectory in search of Fleur Scatchard and Kat Purdey, and she arrived now to say that Fleur had been put to bed in Kat's bedroom and would be beyond giving any account of herself for quite some time, the police doctor said. She had brought Kat Purdey along and put her with the others.

Bone listened, as they waited for Darren Bartholomew, to the steady tramp of feet as VDUs were carried in below, and the knock and thud of trestle-tables being set up.

Darren was not particularly tall and he was beginning to look heavily built; he had managed to plateau out on that stage of adolescence when the body behaves like an unfamiliar instrument, such as a supermarket trolley, wilfully out of touch with its user. He slouched in, cautiously, knocked against the chair Higg steered him at, and fell into it rather than sat down. The big desk juddered as his feet hit it.

Locker was never likely to react well to nose-studs and Darren had two, silver, one plain, one star-shaped. Bone thought that a fleshy, shiny nose was not helped by ornament. It was hard to see anything of Darren except this nose, because his hair, dark brown, straight and rather greasy, was parted in the centre, and though quite short at the back, hung in swathes over his ears and face. The make-up they had all worn for the Haunted House he had removed, unless a trace of it accounted for the greenish tinge of his upper lip and jaw. He wore a blue teeshirt, which might or might not match his eyes, and tattered jeans. Locker activated the recorder and named the date, the time, the investigation number and the names of those present, while Darren picked at a loose cuticle on his thumb.

'We have a few questions about what happened last night.'

'Las' *night?*' Clearly he had expected questions about Laurie Scatchard's death. Bone, not for the first time, wished he had a meter that would register the degree of relief—no less revealing than the degree of alarm— evinced by suspects. 'Las' *night? Nothing happened las' night.*'

'You had a party. Here. Downstairs.'

'Yeah, Kat's party.' He flung back the wings of hair, evidently feeling his responsibility had ended. 'Nothing happened.'

'Did Nigel Wells come to the party?'

'Yeah.' He put the side of his thumb to his mouth and chewed the cuticle. So muffled, he said, 'And?'

'Why did he come?'

'Don' know.'

'He was the only adult present, was he?'

'Yeah.' He didn't add 'And?' but they heard it all the same. He had dropped his head forward and the curtains closed.

'Did you invite him?'

'Not me. He jus' came.'

Bone refrained from asking, 'Why did he come?' because he did not expect a useful answer. Locker leant forward, trying to penetrate the hanging curtains with his stare.

'Did you all like Nigel Wells?'

A massive shrug was all they got. Bone could feel Locker's annoyance—the silver studs were quite enough to get up his nose as well as Darren's.

'Please answer out loud. Do you know of anyone who had any particular reason for disliking Nigel Wells?'

'Don' know.'

'Anyone,' Bone cut in, 'who would dislike him enough to kill him?'

'Kill him?' Darren came briefly to life, the curtains flying back and revealing a large, amazed child. 'Nige wasn't *killed.*'

'What do you think happened to him?'

Darren subsided and, partly veiled, looked from one to the other. 'Don' know. I mean, din' he suffocate? Like, choke himself?'

Bone did not reply to this, with purpose; and saw alarm grow in Darren's shadowed eyes. After a pause Bone went on:

'Were you in on this practical joke?'

'Wha' practical joke?'

Locker pushed across a Polaroid of Nigel Wells's decorated face. Darren's own face was conveniently eclipsed as he bent to look. He came up with the right reaction, though.

'Who did that?'

'That's what *we're* asking *you.*' Locker twitched the photo back. 'What did you have to do with that? Taking off half his hair and painting his face?'

Darren had shrunk back defensively. 'Don' know a thing about that. Why would anyone do that?'

'Answers, not questions. Did you see Nigel Wells leave the party?'

'Nah. I'd gone for a leak and when I come back he's gone.' It was an answer and it was swift enough to have been a prepared one.

'What time would that be?'

'Don' know. Don' look at the clock when I'm having a good time. Don' have a watch.' Nose-studs but no watch. Darren's mouth was smug, as if he felt he had countered all the questions, but Bone had another one for him.

'And Laurie Scatchard. Anyone have a grudge against him?'

'Don' know.' Then Darren actually volunteered a theory. 'He used to hit people.' A hand came up and round in a swiping gesture of automatic imitation.

'Who did he hit?' This was a novel idea, the charmer's violent side. 'He hit you?'

'Nah. Gave me the odd shove, like, against the wall.' He offered this as if it suggested grounds for stabbing. Locker grunted impatiently.

'Did you see him hit anyone?'

This needed thinking about, as though Darren had to shift through images of violence until he found the right one. He seemed on the point of speaking and then thought better of it. 'Nah.'

'Were you one of those lifting the dish-cover off Scatchard's head?'

'Yeah, we all did. Turn and about, like.'

'Who was the last person to lift the lid before it was found he was dead?'

'Don' know. I wasn' there.'

'Where were you?'

Oddly enough, the accustomed answer did not come. 'I had to do the stuff with the masks.'

'When you last saw Nigel Wells, how did he look?'

Darren's head turned towards the Polaroid, indicating that he looked at it. 'Just like normal.' After a moment, when Locker was about to speak, he elucidated: 'Just like a stupid wanker.'

Bone's lifted hand prevented Locker from speech. 'Thank you, Darren. That's all for the moment.'

Darren stood up without knocking into the desk, only tipping his chair over. He put it upright and got out of the room, narrowly missing a collision with Higg at the door. Locker picked up the list again and raised a finger to Higg.

'Lucy Hollis,' he said. To Bone he added, 'She's the daughter of Midge Hollis, that's the nurse who went to try to help Scatchard at the Haunted House. She and her husband Dave foster children and a lot of these kids have stayed with them. Charlie Iden says there was a big dinner the foster-children put on for them at the

Bidding Arms for their silver wedding anniversary last night; the local gang came on to this party here.'

WPC Vigo came in. 'Lucy Hollis, sir.'

Lucy Hollis, like most girls, was managing adolescence better than most boys do. Like Darren, however, she was chiefly distinguished by her hair, which gave her a Pre-Raphaelite appearance, raying out from the crown of her head to her shoulders in crimped strands of pale marigold. The face was up to Pre-Raphaelite standard too, with a long thin nose and full, over-defined mouth, but her expression was pleasant rather than soulful. She even managed an uncertain smile. Locker became paternal.

'Just a few questions, Lucy. We're recording . . .' He signed on the tape, and began: 'About the party here last night. Did you see Nigel Wells there?'

'Oh yes, of course. He came about half an hour after it started, I think.'

'And when did he leave?'

Vagueness descended. 'Oh—I'm not sure. I mean I didn't see him go. I mean you sort of look round and notice he's not there. I don't know when.'

Had anyone seen Nigel actually leave that party? Bone had a fantasy of Nigel slipping away behind a curtain, shaving half his head and, after painting his face blue and green, tiptoeing silently off to get into Mrs Armitage's car.

'So you don't know how this happened?' Locker picked up the Polaroid, which Bone suddenly took from him and put face down.

'There was a trick played on Nigel Wells, wasn't there?'

There came a short silence. She looked from Bone to Locker and flushed crimson. 'I—I don't know anything about that. I really don't know.'

'In that case you may find this picture rather a shock.' Bone turned it over and put it before her. She put a hand to her mouth. 'Oh! Horrible! But how did that happen?'

Unless they were brilliant liars, Nigel's grotesque transformation had come as a shock to both Darren and Lucy. Conceivably, of course, they were not in on this particular piece of the action; Lucy's blush at the mention of a trick suggested she might be aware of something planned but the results—especially considering Nigel's death—seemed genuinely to disturb her. She pushed the photograph away with her fingertips as though it might contaminate her.

'Did you like Nigel Wells?'

Was there some sort of hesitation here? But she rallied. 'He was really nice to us all. Sort of helping with the play at Easter and everything. And he was really encouraging. Fleur even thought—' She stopped so suddenly that Bone imagined he heard the squeal of brakes. Locker was interested.

'Fleur Scatchard? What did Fleur think?'

'Oh, nothing . . . I mean, Fleur wants to be an actress.'

Was this the one who had been 'got an audition'? Bone remembered Cha complaining Nigel had groped her during their inspection of his house. Fleur might have seen the glamorous Nigel, with his connections in TV and theatre, as someone whose attentions might be worth tolerating or even perhaps encouraging. His memory of Fleur, in shrieking hysteria over her father's body in the Haunted House, provided no real reason why Nigel should have thought her worth bothering with, but then hysteria itself is disfiguring; she had also acquired a black eye and a bruise; and, for some, youth is all the attraction needed. He hoped for an interview soon with Fleur, though it was, considering the doctor's view, doubtful.

'Was Fleur on good terms with her father?'

'Oh, poor Laurie!' To Locker's discomfort, Lucy's eyes flooded with tears. 'It was so horrible! I can't—do I have to talk about it?'

Bone kept his voice steady but firm. 'I'm sorry, Miss

Hollis. I know this is distressing. We must talk about it if we're to find who did it.'

'But it wasn't any of us! Why would *we* do an awful thing like that?'

Bone ignored the indignation. Teenagers inevitably felt they were being picked on. 'Did you see anyone behave in an unusual way to Laurie Scatchard while you were in the village hall this morning?'

She caught hold of a strand of marigold hair and twisted it as she thought. 'There was Reggie Merrick. He was quite funny. It was my turn to pick up the dish-cover and he sort of poked his head and peered and then he took one of the knives and said something like *I'll have an ear, please.* He hated Laurie.'

Some fingerprints had been lifted from the knife used on Laurie, and they would be compared with Merrick's. Baulked of an ear, he might have gone for a heart.

'Do you know why he hated him?'

Vagueness again. 'Some quarrel, I think in the olden days. I don't know. Reggie Merrick doesn't really like anyone, even Phil who's his grandson.'

'What else did you see that was odd?'

'Well, nothing. I was in the Dance of Death, you know, we were all rattling chains and things, and it was dark, sort of, and we were doing a circle about and round.' She looked suddenly forlorn. There had come a horrible end to their revels. She drooped, a Pre-Raphaelite maiden awaiting rescue and not a knight in sight. Bone was chivalrous.

'Thank you, Miss Hollis. I expect we shall have to ask you more later on, but that's all for the moment.'

She got up, hesitated again, and then said softly, 'I do hope you catch him.'

'Or her,' Locker put in.

'Oh . . . yes, of course.'

As Vigo took Fleur out, Locker turned to Bone with questioning eyebrows. 'She said "him"?'

'It's likely she automatically said *him* as the one with

the knife. Either it's Freudian or—well, look at all the macho young boneheads at home.' He meant at Tunbridge Wells, their base. 'She's likely to be right; or do you fancy a girl for it?'

'Not Lucy Hollis, on present showing. But they're covering up, about something and for somebody.'

Bone tapped the Polaroid. 'They know about this. Young Lucy, I would hazard, hadn't seen the result, but she knew a trick was in prospect. No one's saying yet.'

'Trouble is—' Locker signalled to Higg and indicated the list—'these kids are such habitual liars they don't even know they're doing it. I get to see it with my two— they tell me a spaceman came and broke their toys when I've *seen* them tread on the things. They make themselves believe it just like that!' He clicked his fingers, and Higg, ushering in Phil Merrick, took it as an order to hurry and gave him a push. Phil did not take it well; he frowned as he sat down.

He was an improvement on Darren Bartholomew. A handsome boy, despite a pallor under the slight tan, and in spite of the glower. He had dark eyes and a generous mouth, no earrings or nose ornaments, a clean grey teeshirt and denim waistcoat, and his brown hair was sleekly drawn back and secured by a black thong. The impression he gave, as they put their questions, and got the usual cautious, vague answers, was of a nervous desire to have the interview over. He answered quickly, licked his lips as if he felt a dry mouth, and kept glancing at the Polaroid under Locker's hand.

Bone was endeavouring to iron out his rising exasperation at getting nothing here either, when a rap at the door made Higg open it and look out. He came forward to say, 'Sergeant Shay, sir. Can he have a word?'

Locker had presented the Polaroid to Phil by the time Bone returned from a brief conference outside with Shay, and he was getting the same who-could-have-done-that-it-wasn't-me. Bone, however, was bearing trophies: plastic envelopes containing other, smaller plastic packets, grey and smeared with dusting powder that had rectangular clear patches where Sellotape had lifted prints.

These he arranged in a row on the scuffed leather in front of Phil Merrick, whose mouth had come ajar. Locker was slowly shaking his head. This was what they might have expected. Drugs.

19

'The traces of powder inside these packets are probably cocaine. Samples are being analysed. The packets were found in a bin in the lean-to here outside the kitchen. What do you know about them?'

Phil Merrick had to swallow before he replied.

'Nothing! I don't know a thing about that. I mean, we can't afford stuff like coke.'

Bone did not try *What can you afford, then?* He had just seen the perfect reason why Nigel Wells, creep and groper, should be a welcome guest at a party for those a generation younger. 'But if it was a present?'

'What do you mean, a present? I told you I don't know about this.' Phil made his contribution to the sum total of ignorance. Locker made a sound in his throat like a Rottweiler warming up for action and Bone said quickly:

'Did Nigel Wells give you this?'

' 'Course not. Why would he?' Phil, paler than before, was gabbling, shifting his grip on the sides of his chair as if he could not wait to spring up and dash out. Bone knew the moment.

'Did you help to put Nigel Wells in the boot of Mrs Armitage's car?'

The whites of his eyes showed all round for a second.

He probably had expected more questioning about the drugs. Bone leant forward, forcing Phil to meet his eyes. Phil stammered and Locker moved in.

'When did you put Nigel Wells in the boot?'

'We—I *didn't*. I don't know *shit* about it. I *told* you.' He flung up his hands and leant back. The moment for truth had passed and both Bone and Locker knew it. Bone made a long arm and idly flicked the Polaroid over.

'And Laurie Scatchard? Where were you when he was found to be dead?'

Did the dark eyes show relief? 'I was doing this sort of dance we did. Dance of Death. With Justin.'

'Did you lift the lid on the head at any point?'

'Yeh.' He was anxious to help now. 'I did it before Kat took over. He was alive then—he winked at one of the kids coming through. We didn't show him to the really little kids, he looked so scary.'

So Phil Merrick saw the point of knowing when Laurie was last seen to be alive. Under that make-up, eyes open or shut, he could have been as dead as a dodo for all anyone could have told.

'And did you notice anyone behaving oddly towards Scatchard at any time?'

'Oddly?'

'Did anyone say or do anything to him?'

Phil simply stared. 'What could anyone do?' he offered eventually. 'I mean, he was just a head on a plate.' Clearly he had not heard of Reggie Merrick's bid for an ear.

'Right.' Locker returned to the attack, pointing at the packets in front of Phil. 'Do you think, when you'd had a sniff of this, you didn't *know* what you were doing to Nigel Wells?' He put the Polaroid in line with the packets.

'I tell you I didn't. How many times've I got to say I *didn't*? I don't know *anything* about this.'

'How do you think he got to look like this?'

'*I* don't know. He was fine at the party. He must of met someone after. Why don't you find out about *that?*'

Bone and Locker were silent, each coming to the same conclusion. After a minute during which Phil almost crouched in his chair, mouth open as if he would next be driven to pant like some animal at bay, Locker signed off on the tape. Phil grasped the edge of the desk, nails white with the pressure.

'That's it? I can go?'

'For the moment.' Locker was dismissive. 'We'll be coming back to you.'

Phil disregarded Locker's threat. He sprang up and made for the door with such speed that Bone was re-minded of the old penny-dreadful formula: with one bound he was free. Did he really believe that he had pulled the wool over their eyes? However, people can-not be convicted for behaving in a guilty way or the prisons would be even more full than they are.

'What d'you think, sir?'

'I'm not thinking yet. Let's hear first how much all their stories tally. This stuff,' he nodded at the smeared packets, 'does alter things. Hyped up on that, anyone's capable of feeling invulnerable. Might conceivably not believe they'd done what they had. Would seem to be a brilliant thing to do at the time.'

Locker sighed. 'Katharine Purdey's next, sir, the Rec-tor's daughter. Pat brought her in after they'd got Fleur Scatchard settled in next door at the Rector's. It seems she clung to Miss Purdey . . . There's no one at Fleur's own home now.'

Bone made a rueful grimace. There were times when his job seemed more comfortless than ever. 'Katharine Purdey, then. Let's see if the Rector's daughter can tell the truth.'

It was plain when WPC Vigo ushered her in that Kat Purdey was an entirely different kettle of fish. She had style. Bone had met her in the Morticia gear, hair flow-ing, deep red lipstick, long black gloves, somewhat as the queen in 'Snow White' might look if she ran a nightclub. Locker's eyes widened. No gloves, no long black dress, but a form-fitting scoop-necked black teeshirt that showed off a slender figure, black shorts brief enough to be underwear though made of leather, and laced Victorian ankle-boots that would have looked right under frilled petticoats but were now at the end of long bare legs. The hair still flowed, a background to huge silver hoop earrings. The low scoop of the teeshirt was filled in with silver strands of necklace and a black ribbon that dangled a heavy silver Celtic cross. If this were the Rector's daughter, what did the Rector think of her?

'Do sit down, Miss Purdey. How is Miss Scatchard?' The formal address was one of Bone's strategies.

'She's a mess. As you'd expect.' She met their eyes, composed and straight on her chair. The face, for all the curves of youth, was severe. They, not she, might be under interrogation.

'Miss Purdey: what can you tell us about the party here last night?'

'What do you want to know about it? It was for the lot that stayed on from the Hollis dinner at the pub. They're all my friends.'

'Including Nigel Wells?'

She lifted slender shoulders, making the earrings swing. 'Including Nigel.'

'He came to the party bringing cocaine.' Bone's flat statement produced no violent reaction. She nodded.

'He probably did. He was a cokehead.'

'You were aware he took drugs.'

She rolled her eyes slightly. 'Who doesn't?'

'There's a few of the population still left who don't.' Bone could see she was impatient of any implied criticism. She could look around and see a world her own age, living it up on Ecstasy at raves, for whom taking drugs was no more remarkable than it had been, as a child, to eat sweets. People like Nigel would not be seen as freaks. What did surprise him was that, unlike the others, she seemed to have decided on honesty. 'Were you taking any drugs last night?'

'Me? If I did, do you think I would tell you?' The look she gave them both was sharply contemptuous.

'Now look here, young lady—'

'Miss Purdey.' Bone sympathised with Locker, but that line would never succeed with the girl before them. 'We really want to know about Nigel Wells. Did you see him leave the party last night?'

'No.' There was no vagueness here.

'And this.' Bone felt that Kat Purdey needed no protecting from the ghastly face in the Polaroid. 'Who did this?'

She picked up the photo, made a face of brief disgust, and then examined it. 'He looks revolting.'

'Partly because he is dead.' Bone spoke with clarity, hoping to get through to her. 'We need to find out how he died.'

She leant across to put the photo face down before him. 'I thought it was supposed to be obvious. He ran out of air.'

'That's how we all die in the end, Miss Purdey, but not all of us because someone stuffs us in the boot of a car.'

'But could it be me?' She raised long, slender arms a little and let them fall with a clash of silver bracelets. 'Even dinky old Nigel must have weighed a ton.'

Bone shifted location fast. 'And Laurie Scatchard. He didn't need picking up. He couldn't even fall. Who was near him before his death was discovered?'

The impatient roll of the eyes again. 'Who was near him! Everyone was near him. People were going past all the time. It was a sideshow at the fair, for heaven's sake.'

'Who were the last people through?' Bone was having to remind himself it was vital not to let the girl needle him, particularly as he sensed Locker's burgeoning annoyance.

'Barbary Wells; my uncle Henry; Reggie Merrick . . .

I can't possibly remember. I know Barbary came before my uncle because he kept trying to catch her up; he was so afraid she would be ever so fwightened. Barbary's a lot tougher than he'd like to think.'

'Did you see anyone do, or hear anyone say, anything unusual to Scatchard?'

'It was me lifting the cover when Barbary went through.' Kat smiled, and it gave her face an animation that made it almost beautiful. 'It really was a laugh. She twisted his nose till he yelled.'

'Twisted his nose? Why?'

'Ask her. Cheating on her? Or made a pass she didn't want—a *lot* less likely. Laurie was a tom cat; not like Nigel, who only fancied *himself* for all his roving hands. I told Nigel if he laid a finger on me I'd chop it off.'

Bone didn't doubt she would have. Kat Purdey struck him as a formidable young woman; it might be her strength that made the girl Fleur cling to her, rather than any quality of sympathy. More interesting was the news of a possible involvement of Barbary Wells with Scatchard. If she showed such hostility, she might possibly have seen her chance to plant in him one of the knives so invitingly lying about.

'Do you know of anyone with a grudge against Scatchard?'

'Reggie Merrick.' The answer came promptly. 'Family thing. Been festering for ever. There's so little to do in a village, believe me, people are grateful for a feud or two to take their minds off the crap on the telly.' Kat wrinkled her nose. 'I mean this sort of thing that's just happened. Gruesome and horrible. The village will live on it for the next hundred years. It's full of trash, this place.'

The door opened, Fredricks put her head in and spoke to Vigo, who came towards Bone. He rose, anticipating her message, and went out to Fredricks on the landing.

'We've just cleared the end room next to the Incident Room, sir; this was underneath the long window curtain.'

She held out two plastic packets. Bone turned to the

window to see their contents better. Inside the plastic was a jumble of stuff like a mouse's nest, the shade familiar.

'Looks like Nigel Wells's missing hairstyle,' he said, wondering how, in his fantasy about Nigel shaving his own hair, he had thought about a curtain. 'Of course, for all we know, some moggy moulted a clump in terror at the noise they were making. Have that sent to Dr Foster for matching. I'll keep this one for now. How is the Incident Room coming on?'

'It's set up, sir.'

'Fine. And well done, Pat. This was precisely what we needed. Oh—any luck with Fleur Scatchard?'

'Mrs Hollis has been to see her and says there's no chance of her coming out of sedation for quite a while.'

Bone palmed the packet of hair and went back into the room. Locker reported his return to the tape, and Bone sat on the edge of the desk. 'Miss Purdey, when did you last see Nigel Wells?'

'Couldn't say for sure. I think he left when we turned the music down and he found we were all paired off and nobody with a yen to be groped in a corner. But actually I think he was off to see someone.'

'I suppose,' Bone said, 'that you meant to clear up here today after the fête.'

She turned her dark eyes to him coolly, but the Celtic cross started up a sudden pulsing gleam. 'Well, yes.'

'You would have swept up this, I expect.'

She looked at the hair. She picked up the packet and put her head on one side to peer at it.

'I expect we would if we'd come across it. Why? Is it supposed to be important?'

'I think you know very well what it is.'

'I haven't the least idea.'

Locker turned the Polaroid over and passed it to her.

'Oh. *Ah.* You mean it's Nigel's hair?' She looked once more and pushed both exhibits back across the desk. 'It does look like it. But I don't know anything about it.'

She put her own hair back behind her shoulders. 'I don't know anything about it at all.'

'How do you account for its being here?'

'I've no idea. I just don't know.'

So, for the next quarter-hour, to their cool, or heated, or reasoning, or sarcastic, or incredulous questions, she returned the same answer. They were up against an unfathomable ignorance in the Rector's daughter.

20

Heather Armitage had rarely spent a more exciting day. After discovering a body in her car in the morning, and finding it was no less a celebrity than Nigel Wells, and then being interviewed by a nice, big, polite policeman who obviously understood the importance of all that she could contribute, she had the thrill of being in front of cameras for the television reporters and knowing that her face and words would be beamed to millions that very day. How lucky it was she'd had her hair done for the fête! She had been delightfully conscious of the small crowd listening as she talked, and people stopping even in Front Street yards away, to stare. Indeed her coffee mornings would be crowded in future with those curious souls who would like to know more detail than she was able to give in the short time the cameras were on her. Such a pity they didn't take better advantage of her! These television people were in such a hurry; they cut her off when she started to tell them her theories about who could have put the poor man in the boot, and about the books for her stall.

After that, it was hard to calm down, and to know what to do next. She was banishing from her mind the actual moment of horror when she had taken hold of the dead wrist. *Happy* memories kept one young . . . It was very hard not to feel cheated at never having got to the fête, and after all her hard work for the bookstall too. She had not been there when she could have been of real use. Those poor children in the Haunted House! Who could have committed such a crime when there were children about? When first she heard the news of Laurie Scatchard's death from Dolly Pike—and *what* a gossip that woman was, to be sure—her first thought had been that another practical joke had gone wrong. They might have been pretending, in that silly way young people have, to do something dreadful, playing with knives. Dolly kept saying his head was on a plate, but the poor thing couldn't have got it right.

If only the children had let her organise it, as she had been perfectly willing to do! There would have been no chance of any dreadful accident. Dolly said the Haunted House had been awful, truly scary, and that wasn't right for children. Real knives were far too dangerous. Dolly insisted the police were treating it as murder, but she was exactly the sort of woman who always tried to make herself important by dramatising things. Lucky, indeed, that it hadn't been Dolly in her place that morning— she'd have gone to pieces and been quite incapable of doing the sensible thing and going for help.

Help, now, was what she was going to bring. The moment she heard about Laurie Scatchard her first thought had been for poor motherless Fleur. So shy and fey, poor thing, keeping quite the wrong company with that louche Merrick boy, and sadly in need of a woman's guidance. Dolly had come round to tell her, breathlessly, shedding a pink plastic comb into Heather's copper bowl of dried blooms, that Fleur had been put to bed at the Rector's house. Just like that good man to take her in, but how could she be looked after when there was only the daily woman who spent half her time at Barbary Wells's house, besides another motherless child, poor

Kathy? Heather would have received Fleur into her own house if she had known in time. However, the Rector would be back at any moment now from taking morning service at Saxhurst, whose turn it was this week, and it would be such a good idea to trot over and find out how Fleur was and what she could do to help; and at the same time she could tell the Rector everything that had happened that momentous morning. He had been going to make a brief visit to the fête before leaving for Saxhurst, which he must have done well before any of the events that had so disrupted the village. Poor man, to have left his village in the morning peacefully beginning the fête that was to provide a fund for the new church hall, and to return to a place seething with reporters and police, and with two of his parishioners dead, conspicuously and horribly dead! He would need all the support she could give.

Heather was lucky. She arrived at the house just after the Rector arrived from Saxhurst and while his daughter was still talking to the police next door. She had been right in supposing that the Rector had heard nothing of the monstrosities taking place. He was surprised to find Mrs Hollis coming down from his daughter's bedroom to answer his call that he was back; and then when the doorbell rang to find Mrs Armitage bursting with news on the doorstep . . .

The Reverend Edmund Purdey was an easy-going and good-natured man, and sometimes no match for Heather Armitage. She was in a black dress with a white pleated collar and a white pleated frill that zigzagged down over her bust, and he could tell from her expression that she was anxious to impart unpleasant news. He would have preferred to hear unpleasant news from lips that relished it less, but choice in the matter was not left to him. Midge Hollis came down, saying something about Fleur but completely annulled by Heather who, as Edmund Purdey knew, never heard anyone when she was talking. He understood from Midge's urgent mime that someone upstairs must not be disturbed, so he led the way out of the narrow hall into the sitting-room; if it was his daughter who was not to be disturbed he was the last person on earth to venture to do it. Heather then poured out her story, affirmed by Midge—who had her moment of glory, solo, as she described how she had found the wound in Laurie's back, which Heather quite wanted to hear—both women standing before him ignoring his invitation to sit down and thereby forcing him to stand.

'You say these were accidents? How could—'

'He was suffocated, poor man! If only I had gone out sooner, but you see I had taken—'

'But Scatchard? A knife in his back?'

'The children must have been playing about with the knives, so dangerous to have them and so irresponsible . . .' Heather recalled that it was Kathy whom she seemed to be criticising, and paused.

'The police,' said Midge Hollis, seeing a rare chance for a climax, 'are treating it as murder.'

At the horrid little word there was a silence. The Rector took off his glasses and rubbed his eyes, as if to help him to see the situation more clearly. 'Appalling. I cannot believe it possible anyone could do such a thing. Here, too.' He turned to Midge, managing to ignore Heather's attempt at override. 'Poor Fleur. Who is looking after her?'

'The doctor's seen her. She's resting upstairs. Mr Purdey, I'm sorry, but I have to get back to give my brood their Sunday lunch. I'm glad you're back as I don't like to leave Fleur alone in the house. I've been waiting for Kat to come back from talking to the police.' She was heading for the door.

'Talking to the police!'

'Don't worry, Rector.' Mrs Armitage lowered herself into the sofa and patted the cushion beside her. 'I'm here now. I'll look after everything.'

Midge Hollis, catching a certain look on the Rector's face, wished she could either have stayed or manoeuvred

Heather into coming with her, but there were Dave and the children waiting for their Sunday lunch and Lucy trying to cope. The Rector insisted on seeing her to the front door, and Midge felt he would have liked to shut Heather indoors and dash into the street. He peered across the road. 'I suppose those are police vehicles; when I drove up I somehow took them for part of the fête.'

'Police and TV,' Midge said cheerfully, and left him.

'I'll just pop up and see if that poor child is all right.' Heather's ruffles were being borne with determination up the stairs. As her feet thudded upward, the Rector, while feeling she would add nothing to the comfort or serenity of the unhappy Fleur, could not find the words to discourage her. He was immensely glad, therefore, to hear a key in the lock behind him and know that his daughter was there. One look at her face told him she was in no mood to tolerate him, let alone put up with Heather Armitage, and a cunning hope woke in him.

'My dear, Mrs Armitage has just been telling me about the dreadful—'

'Is that her banging about upstairs? I saw Midge going home.'

'Mrs Armitage has of—'

'Christ! Can't that old cow keep out of anything?' She was up the stairs at a pantherine pace before he had a chance to say more. He wondered how she had got on with the police; her expression had told him it could not have been an enjoyable occasion for either party. He stood, irresolute, in the hall, hearing voices hissing like vipers on the landing, and was not surprised to see Heather come blundering down, flushed and discomposed. She managed a nervous smile when she saw him.

'I'm afraid I can't do anything for the poor child at the moment—she really shouldn't be disturbed—I'm sure the doctor was right, it seems he was very firm—I'm sure Kathy will look after her very well . . .'

Kat, descending after her, might have been carrying

not only whips but scorpions. Heather Armitage, as if conscious of their blows, pressed past the Rector to the door, almost choking him with the scent of lavender water.

'Goodbye, Rector. Goodbye, dear. You know where I am if you want me.'

As the door closed behind her, Kat said, 'That'll be the day.'

21

If Heather Armitage had found the day exciting, Jonathan Cade had found it a let-down. He was a single-minded man and he had come to Biddinghurst to collect material for a book on ghosts, and now all of a sudden the whole village was far too interested in the recently dead to spare the time or concentration to discuss ancient spirits. Of course he was not so callous as to feel indifferent to the fate of the two men, each of whom he had met only the day before their frightful ending. Perhaps what was foremost in his mind was whether such deaths might provoke a certain restlessness in the other world: a desire, who knows? to return to the scene. However, he had not intended to hang around waiting for new ghosts to materialise and he was beginning to feel frustrated. He knew now that someone, and he would dearly like to know who, had hoaxed him with the faceless creature in the church, for he had seen the 'faceless' mask being worn in the Haunted House, but the strange floating girl, crying for a baby in the garden afterwards, haunted him still. He could find no mention of her in *Kentish Ghosts* but he was positive he had experienced something genuine. It was the passion, the anguish, that lingered, an emotion that would survive death. He must find out more about who had lived in the Old Rectory.

While Jonathan contemplated finding out more about past inhabitants, Bone and Locker, together with the team, were trying to find out more about the present. Apart from Chrissie Hollis, whom Fredricks was going to interview at home now that her mother could be present—Mrs Hollis's mention of Sunday lunch had been spoken of in the Incident Room to fetch a universal envious groan—there was only one teenager left to see.

'Get Justin Rafferty, will you, Higg?'

Bone hardly expected anything in the way of revelation or even of interest from the young man—could he be called that at scarcely eighteen?—who lounged in to disassemble his limbs in the chair opposite. Bone had last seen him sitting beside Charlotte in the car, and had taken the dark shadows round his eyes to be the remains of make-up. It was now plain that even with the make-up perfunctorily wiped away, the natural dark hollows left were hardly an improvement. Bone thought at once of the packets retrieved from the bins. He didn't need Forensic to tell him what they had contained, and here on the far side of the table was a creature who looked as if drugs were his daily bread. What hope of getting truth from him when the others had failed to crack? Bone felt that 'undue pressure' would be the only means of obtaining sense from this tedious band.

'Now, Rafferty,' Locker was attempting geniality which was, Bone knew, usually the prelude to cutting up rough before long. 'We'd like to know whether you had a hand in the practical joke played on Nigel Wells last night.'

Justin glanced down at his own hands, as if they might tell him if they had been involved. Then he looked indifferently at the Polaroid as Locker pushed it across.

'Nah.' He peered more closely. 'Don't he look a prat?'

Bone registered that not one of the teenagers had shown even a smidgen of liking for Nigel; if they had played a trick on him it was not an affectionate one. Surprising that he was asked to their party if they held him in such contempt. Cocaine was not unfortunately so hard to get that they were forced to put up with Nigel to get some; though if it were a free gift they might. And if it were, why did Nigel want to ingratiate himself with this lot? The reason when found was likely, Bone thought, to be a sordid one, but was it to be found in this maze of stone walls?

Justin, like the others, had not seen Nigel leave the party. He had no idea why anyone should have provided him with a new hairstyle and war paint. He had nothing to do with putting him in the boot of Mrs Armitage's car. As for the drugs, he simply shook his head.

'Don't do drugs. Mugs' game. Don't know who could have binned these.'

'Miss Purdey,' Locker consulted his notes, 'said Nigel Wells was "a cokehead". Would you agree?'

'Could be. Showbiz blokes are, right?'

'Did he ever give you drugs?'

'Told you. I don't do them.'

'Did you see him offer any?'

The glass-grey eyes shifted towards Bone. 'Nah.'

He was equally positive as to not knowing of any grudge or ill-will towards Nigel. ' 'Cept if you're talking about the village, there's Henry Purdey. He hated him. Really hated him. Went for him with a hammer once.' His face almost woke to emotion. 'Wish I'd seen. Epic. Our Nige didn't love Henry to death either.'

'Went for him with a hammer?' Locker's voice livened up a little and Justin grinned and stretched his legs under the desk so that Locker had to draw his back.

'That's the stuff, eh? Henry's got the bad luck of living on the corner of the lane, right where Nigel has to turn off if he's coming from the motorway. So our Nige used to belt back from London in his high-powered motor late at night, early morning, coked to the eyebrows.' Justin's grin widened. 'He'd cut the corner over Henry's grass, time after time, sounding the horn. You get the picture. Ruts all over. I should know, Henry got me to dig 'em out and patch the turf up; till the next time.'

'What's this about the hammer?'

'Henry found the car parked on this grass one night. Nige had crashed on these big stones Henry'd got Laurie—me that means—to put all round the verge there when Nige was working in London. Laurie said they oughta be painted white and Henry said yeah yeah later. So Nige's flash motor hit them and was into Henry's fence and the grass ploughed up and Henry comes out in his py-jams and takes a hammer to the windscreen.' Justin's thin fingers combed back his bleached locks. 'Shame Nige had staggered home by then.'

Promising gossip. Bone spoke out. 'And Laurie Scatchard. You were there when he was stabbed.'

Justin was not taken unawares. 'Suppose we all were. Don't know when it happened, do we?'

'Did Scatchard hit you?'

'Someone been talking? It's a joke. He hit *anyone* if he happened to lose his rag.'

'Was he a good employer?'

'He paid right. He mostly did what he said he would.'

'Did he get on with people?'

Once more the skeletal grin. 'And off, with most of them. Laurie was our local Casanova.'

'Who in particular,' Locker asked, 'was he carrying on with?'

'Oh—he was smart, covering his tracks. A milkman has to leave his float outside, right? But no one goes in a garden peeking about for a lawnmower that gives the game away.'

Bone, contemplating the smooth planes of the young face before him, the bizarre elegance of it under the bleached crest, the lines of humour round the mouth, wondered if Justin too availed himself of this anonymity of gardeners. He saw, suddenly, the village like a map, threads laid across it in all directions invisibly connecting and binding people; and as with a spider's web, a touch on any thread sent a shiver through the whole. As their questions started a vibration, whom were they warning?

'And where might this lawnmower be seen?' Locker took up the idea, but Justin shook his head.

'Anyone he could pull, he'd pull.' A swift grin. 'I'm not planning on being up for defamation, right?'

'Did you notice anyone say or do anything unusual to Scatchard in the Haunted House this morning?' Bone supposed that Justin, who it appeared had been leading the Dance of Death, was unlikely to see anything else that went on.

'Yeh well, when I took Henry up to the feast and the cover got lifted, he was really chuffed, seeing Laurie all over mould and everything.' Justin curled a forefinger and tapped the side of it on his underlip. 'Yeh. He said "First the seven veils and now John the Baptist. Couldn't be more pleased if I was salami." He must've meant *Laurie* was salami, but there's no Health Inspector would have passed *him* on a plate.'

Bone had sufficient memory of Bible stories to suppose Henry referred to Salome and her request for the Baptist's head on a plate. Justin's mistake made the report seem true; but, more importantly, Justin's testimony made Henry Purdey a very promising candidate as remover of both Laurie and Nigel. That he should suddenly have got rid of both men within twenty-four hours was surprising, but there was no knowing what had been the detonating factor—the word or action or look even, that provoked murder; and one such deed could go to the murderer's head. Serial killers showed that.

Certainly they had uncovered enough festering under the surface in Biddinghurst. It came to him how the village had appeared yesterday when he was house-hunting. The sunny picture was unbelievably remote, like something in another life.

Justin had yielded one or two interesting remarks which they could pursue; and possibly which he hoped they would pursue, leaving him alone. He had not implicated himself in any way.

When he was gone, Locker took out the tape and frowned at it. Bone was conscious, suddenly, of feeling very tired, even depressed. It would be wonderful to be at home, full of an excellent Sunday lunch, chatting to Grizel, listening to his CDs. A happy marriage is the support every hard-working professional needs, to function at his best, so what if you didn't manage to get home to one? He had seen enough police marriages founder on this to hope that Grizel was taking his absence philosophically.

'So what do we have, sir? Right lot of little monkeys: saw nothing, did nothing, know nothing.'

'Fair's fair, Steve. One or two of them did hear something. Scatchard seems to have collected more enemies than Wells, which is a surprise.' Suddenly Bone remembered his own feelings about the man and his easy charm yesterday. 'Count it up: Barbary Wells pulls his nose, Merrick asks for an ear, Henry Purdey—'

'Henry Purdey took a hammer to Wells's car. We'd better see him pronto.'

Bone flung up a hand. 'Hold on, Steve. Send for him, yes, but let's have some good hot coffee and some sandwiches from the pub.' As Locker brightened, he said, 'Let's have a word with Henry when we've had something to eat . . . I'm not ready to face another Purdey on an empty stomach.'

22

Dolly Pike was on the local lunchtime news, and so was Heather Armitage, watched avidly by everyone in Biddinghurst including themselves. Noah Pike was sprawled in a close-fitting armchair in front of the TV set which in summer he treated like a fireside, close to it as if for warmth but in fact so that he could control its vagaries by a swift nudge with his stocking foot. He made a disparaging remark about his wife's hair. Dolly, her mouth open as she followed her amazing image on the screen, ignored him, for to please Noah, as she often said, she'd have to go round with a paper bag over her head, and *then* how would he get his dinner cooked?

Her image said, in a voice higher, surely, than her real one—'ever such a charming man, and kind to everyone'; Noah's snort blew the potato crisp out of his fingers and on to his stomach.

'God, you can curtsey, woman, can't you?' He soared into falsetto, 'Ever such a charming man! That bleeding wanker *charming!*'

'Women *find* nice manners charming.'

The camera had left Dolly on the last syllable of her tribute and swung to take in Heather, hurrying up for her moment of glory. Dolly had noticed at the time that Heather, whom she had conducted home and had left lying on her bed feebly accepting cups of tea after her ordeal, which had included a long interview with the police, had bravely triumphed over these tribulations, changed her dress and done her hair again. Dolly felt it was fair that Heather, who had suffered the shock of

117

finding Nigel, should have all the kudos from relating the discovery.

'I knew he was dead straight away. I went at once to get help.'

As no witnesses had seen Heather slam down the boot lid and lean on it in order to scream better, no voice could contradict this adjustment of the facts. Heather had been about to add her belief that Nigel had died during some practical joke, designed to alarm her alone, which would have given her a special significance as the innocent cause of his death. Alas, the camera abandoned her even more abruptly than it had Dolly, cutting to Bone caught on his way to the Old Rectory and the Incident Room.

'Look at Daddy pulling down the blinds,' was Cha's comment to Grizel, as they saw Bone's face of alert inquiry become expressionless. 'Bet he wishes he'd been wearing a suit. You don't wear suits to fêtes.'

Bone, saying nothing very politely, had been aware that the Chief would be watching this, and he was aware, too, of the media's area of interest. However gory the details of Laurie Scatchard's stabbing, what they really wanted was action on Nigel Wells. People were never going to be as interested in a man who landscaped gardens for a living as in one who beamed into millions of homes doing a sort of Stately-homes-on-wheels, and who had been applauded in many a long-playing sitcom.

'Was it a joke that went wrong?' Mammoth woolly caterpillars dangled rigidly round Bone's head and he looked at one severely.

'It's too early in our investigations to tell. Certainly the public will be kept informed.' Looking curiously frivolous in the pink shirt donned that morning for the fête, he was escorted the few steps to the Old Rectory by a crowd of vocal TV and Pressmen.

'Is it true Nigel Wells had been disfigured?'

Bone, with the useful barrier of Locker and Shay, reached the Old Rectory and went inside. The media were afforded a little consolation by the discovery that there did exist pictures they could use: a camcorder owner, taking pictures of his son in the fancy-dress procession, had been co-opted by the local reporter covering Barbary Wells's speech; he, seeing the camcorder riding on the man's shoulder just when word of police activity in Manor Walk had filtered down to Church Field, had with promises cajoled him into pelting up to Manor Walk and getting pictures of the police tapes and screens. The father of the dinosaur, for it was he, had taken his chance and reaped his reward—a glimpse, when Ferdy Foster had finished for the moment, of the wrapped form of Nigel Wells, now making a brief, last television appearance he could not have planned.

Those concerned with the Haunted House that morning felt the tragedy there was being played down. The media knew that the one death commanded a ready-made audience, whereas the death of a man who pushed lawnmowers for a living did not. The dinosaur's father had trotted down to the village hall in the wake of police summoned there, and had secured shots of dismayed teenagers and children in ghoulish make-up and wind-blown muslin, giving their names to a policewoman; this did not appear on the news.

The sudden realisation that Barbary Wells also lived at Biddinghurst had sent the whole covey of the media up to her cottage. Even when Henry Purdey—who had taken her home and was, literally and metaphorically, holding her hand—opened the door on one reporter and pushed him into a rosemary bush, they were not put off. A shot of a weeping sister! They set up camp in the lane, and when rain came on, sheltered in their vans and cars. After some bargaining, two of them went to the Crossed Keys for provisions, while the battery of lenses remained aimed at the house, hopeful against likelihood that Barbary would kindly show herself at a window in a state of collapse.

Justin Rafferty and Phil Merrick deserted the caravan

where they lived in the Hollises' orchard to come into the house to watch the news, and Midge was unable to prevent the younger children from watching too. The twelve-year-old Chrissie was loudly indignant at the poor coverage given to the Haunted House.

Reggie Merrick's poltergeist interfered with reception, and caused him to damage his toe kicking the TV.

23

It had been a long session and a confusing one. They were striking when the iron was no longer hot and were having to keep the various lines of inquiry clear: there was the party, held here at the Old Rectory, where Nigel Wells had apparently last been seen. Then there was the Haunted House death. The Chief wanted priority given to Nigel Wells but, as Bone pointed out, no one could yet say for certain that the two were not connected. The only link so far was that both men were last seen by the teenagers of Biddinghurst, and that these teenagers were suffering from infectious amnesia.

Higg had brought sandwiches: ham, no mustard, for Bone, double of beef with mustard and salad for Locker. Bone thought Locker took the salad because he believed it to be slimming, but he did not say so. There was a picnic thermos of coffee made by Shay, one of his talents.

'What do we have from these juveniles?'

Locker brooded, chewing, reading over his notes. 'More on the Haunted House than on the party. We have some ideas on Scatchard's popularity.'

'Let's see.' Bone tilted his chair back, looked at the dingy ceiling with its blobs of Blu-tack and shreds of paper-chain, and closed his eyes, reciting, 'From Barbary Wells, "Dished up on a plate, now's my chance!" '

'And twists his nose!' Locker chuckled. 'Doesn't seem to square with Charlie Iden's gossip about him and Miss Wells having a thing going.'

'On the other hand, perhaps it does. It's not a thing you'd do to someone you didn't know well. What about Dolly Pike's report . . .' Bone reached for Locker's notebook, leafed back and found the page. 'Sorry about the butter; here—Midge Hollis told her she'd seen Barbary Wells's car in front of Scatchard's house and then there'd been shouting, late last night. We'll have to check that with Mrs Hollis. We have it from Darren Bartholomew that Scatchard lost his rag if things didn't go the way he wanted. He slammed Darren against a wall when he got annoyed with him, and though I don't see him trying that on Miss Wells, there may have been some high-powered wrath passing between them.'

'Sir, Miss Wells is a fragile lady. Quite small.'

'Is there any rule about fragile, quite small ladies not being almighty spitfires?'

'No.' Locker had got a piece of lettuce linking him to his sandwich, and had to deal with that. It impeded a fuller answer.

'But it was the daughter, Fleur, who was sporting a black eye when we arrived at the Haunted House. Could the row have been with her?'

'She told Pat Fredricks she got it walking into one of those battens in the dark. God knows anyone could have walked into anything in that maze.'

'Scatchard didn't. He just sat there and it came to him.' Bone got up and carried his coffee-cup to the window and stared down into the neglected shrubbery. The morning's showers had deepened into heavier rain, and the leaves shook and gleamed. 'There's still the outstandingly curious fact that in both cases the one adult who seems to have been helping them is the one who gets zapped. I'd like to know a lot more about what

Nigel Wells did for this bunch. The drugs at the party, now. We're going to have to put pressure on.'

'You too think he was their mainman? I still like it, sir. His showbiz connections, his going up to London all the time; he'd have every chance of a better supply than they could easily get locally. But if he was, and if it was a freebie, why kill him?'

Bone shrugged, listening to the soothing hurry of the rain washing the garden. 'We don't know that it was one of them who smothered him. Indeed, why even play the nasty trick on him if he was supplying them? They just might—let's give our credulity a little exercise—be telling the truth and know nothing about either. Not one of them let on that they thought his death anything but an accident. They can't say they heard it on the news. They say he left here before the party ended. We let them believe they've got away with that, until we talk to them all again. You know, Steve, I'm quite looking forward to their next story.'

24

The trouble with wanting to talk to Henry Purdey was that he could not be found. He was not in his house and no one had seen him. The reporters camped in Apple Lane had never heard of him; the man still smelling strongly of rosemary had not asked his aggressor for his name. Locker sent for Noah Pike to be getting on with.

Noah was not best pleased with this encroachment on valuable drinking time. He stumbled into the room with a glare and, invited to sit down, dragged the chair gratingly back from the table and gave himself room for his belly. There was an expansive slovenliness about him that was nothing to do with his singlet and jeans, which were clean; what grew on his face and neck might pass for designer stubble on another man. He looked on sourly as Locker started the tape and announced the formula; he punctuated the mention of his own name with a belch. He was evidently a man proud of being what he was, and with less reason than most.

'Mr Pike, we are investigating the death of Nigel Wells and want—'

'Nigel Wells! What you want to know about him for? What you doing about Laurie Scatchard? Of course he wasn't one of your poncy TV types—' Noah put a hand behind his neck and gave a vast writhe—'so you're not bothered about him, right? Finding out who stabbed one of my best mates won't get your face in the news, right?'

Bone, one of whose main desires was to keep his face off the news, preserved his usual lack of expression. Locker, an edge on his voice, said, 'The more we can gather about things in general, the faster we'll get to Mr Scatchard. When did you last see Nigel Wells?'

For some reason, this slightly threw Noah Pike. Perhaps it was the simplicity of the question, but it might be the need to conceal something. Bluster had been his style, now he gave the matter serious thought. 'Let's see.' It was his turn to regard the dabs of Blu-tack and crêpe paper on the ceiling, giving Bone and Locker a privileged view of the greying carpet on his chins. He scoured this with one hand and the rasp of it seemed to inspire him. 'That's it. Musta been lunchtime yesterday. Seen him in his motor going up the London road.'

'Can you be more exact about the time?'

'I told you. Lunchtime. I was off up to the Crossed Keys for a jar. Twelve-ish.'

Bone was thinking: we—Grizel, Cha and I—saw Wells just before lunch ourselves. We went to the Crossed Keys but not in the main bar, and it was easy enough to miss even a man of Noah's size if you weren't looking.

If Nigel were to supply drugs at the teenagers' party

that night, he well might go up to London to get a supply. Surprising that, in this village, no one in the door-to-door inquiries so far had uttered a single word about Nigel's connection with the village youth being at all odd. In any village there were those ready, and very willing, to put the worst construction on the most innocent of actions. Still, early days. There might be a cluster of inhabitants who'd dish the dirt on Nigel Wells. Noah, for one, hadn't thought the world of him.

'Twelve-ish.' Locker made a note, keeping the details in front of him even though they were on tape. 'And you didn't see him after that?'

'Told you.' Noah folded his arms on the useful ledge provided by his stomach and looked quite benevolently resigned to this lapse of memory on the part of Plod.

'He went to a party here last night. You didn't see him then?'

'Do you mind? Kids' parties?' He gave a sniff and, suddenly, his eyes smiled. 'See me at a kids' party?'

'Have you any idea why Nigel Wells was asked to it?' Bone's question came quite casually and the small eyes turned towards him, still with a twinkle.

'Nigel Wells sucked up to anyone who sucked up to him. He made a profession of fancying himself. He was on TV and they wanted a piece of that.'

'You mean they hoped he'd get them acting work on TV?'

Noah shrugged seismically. 'Acting! There was their play at Easter. Dolly dragged me there. Boring enough to freeze your bum off. That Fleur drooping about thinking she was Garbo. Pathetic.'

'Nigel Wells directed the play. Were they pleased with that? Grateful?'

'Whyn't you ask them?'

'And you didn't see Wells after the party?'

'Je-sus!' The eyes turned up. 'How often do I have to say? Can I go now?' He rose, pushing at the desk so that it jarred. The tape registered the noise with an obedient whirr.

'Wait a minute, Mr Pike.' Bone motioned him to his chair. 'Were you one of those going to contribute to Mrs Armitage's book stall?'

'Me? She wouldn't ask me. I don't read.'

'Mrs Armitage says,' Locker tapped his notes, 'that you were going to provide some books, but you forgot.'

'She'd be thinking of Dolly. Dolly reads.' Noah grinned and a gold tooth caught the light. 'But I think our Heather wouldn't want Dolly's books on her stall.' The large hands sketched further bulges on the ones his chest already had. 'Bodice-rippers. Know what I mean?'

Bone, genially enough, nodded. Locker consulted his notes again. 'Your wife says you told her you would take the books to Mrs Armitage's car.'

Noah's eyes opened fully. 'I might of said that. Not that I remember. Can say a thing and not do it. I mean, the women ask you things all the time and you forget.'

'She says the carrier bag with the books was not in the hall this morning. Bags of books were under the bushes by Mrs Armitage's car. Whoever put Wells in the boot had clearly taken them out to make room.' Locker paused deliberately, and studied Noah's face which was showing sudden loss of confidence. 'Your wife has identified one of these carrier bags as being full of her books. If you didn't take them to the car, and she didn't, who did?'

A sixty-four-thousand-dollar question, and Noah seemed short of any answer.

25

'**W**hat books was it?'

Noah had elected to become truculent. This had very
likely carried him in success through quite a few situa-
tions in his life till now, given his weight and the air of
possessing some muscle left under the fat.

'These.' He might not have expected Locker's move.
Diving sideways under the table he had produced some
magazines, 'books' only by appellation, which he fanned
out on the table in front of Noah Pike like a hand of
cards: a girl who would have needed a Zimmer-frame
to support her bosom had she ever attempted walking,
displayed her disability on the top cover in the touching
confidence it would earn her a good living if not a respectable one. On the next a blonde bore a similar burden, with fortitude although her sulky pout argued that
it irked her. Noah frowned at both.

'Well, what about it? You trying to say they're mine?
Got my name in, have they?'

'Your wife says they're yours.'

A fleeting surprise vanished. Bone saw that Noah had
thought his wife didn't know. Locker put the magazines
tidily in a pile, eclipsing the pout. 'She says she knows
where you keep them. She says she recognises them.
They were found in the carrier bag with her books, the
Catherine Cooksons and the Barbara Cartlands.'

'Where was this carrier bag then? In the boot along
of Nigel Wells? Must of been a big boot.'

Locker was silent and Bone, from long practice, knew
his turn had come.

'Just when did you put this—' he extracted the blonde

126

pout and showed it to Noah—'in the boot with Wells?'
He paused while Noah gathered himself up to bluster.
'It must have seemed a good joke at the time. Heather
Armitage finds Nigel Wells looking at a porn mag in the
boot of her car? Pity you couldn't have watched her
find him.'

He was right. The belly heaved and the gold tooth
gleamed; Noah exploded in a series of snorts. 'And him
half blue and half green and shaved like a bloody Mohi-
can! She'd have got her knickers in a twist she'd not
have got sorted till Tuesday.' He fell silent suddenly.
Perhaps he recalled that Heather had indeed got such
a shock, with the added provocation that the man she
discovered in such a state was a corpse.

Noah might also have realised that he had blown his
pretence.

'When did you go to the car?' Locker, leaning forward, matched the angle of Noah leaning back. 'What
time was it when you put the magazines in the boot?'

'It was a joke! We was going to just leave the books
in the car and hope old Heather'd get an eyeful—or
maybe lay them out on her precious stall without catching a dekko first—I mean, finding *him* was a bonus! We
thought, that was great! They'd done a proper job on
him, poncy little git.'

'You mean, he was dead.'

Noah was contemptuous. 'I'm not stupid! If he'd been
dead we wouldn't just have left him there, would we? I
told you, it was a joke, we could see that. Whoever did
it, they didn't *kill* him—what's the point, killing him before anyone could see him? Wish I could have seen him
trying to give away prizes at the fête in that get-up.'

Bone had already formed the opinion that Noah,
though he might be brutish, was not a fool. The elaborate cruel joke certainly lost its purpose if its only audience was to be the police and the pathologist. Bone was
also visited by the thought of Ferdy Foster, called from
carving the Sunday joint, using his skills on Nigel Wells.

'So if Wells wasn't dead, what was he doing? Did he thank you nicely for the books?' Locker countered contempt with sarcasm, to some effect.

Noah pointed a stubby finger at him. 'Don't you get funny with me, copper. And don't you make out I had anything to do with his death, either. Snoring the way he was; turned out to be only a matter of time before he chucked and choked on it.'

'You saw him there drunk? Lying in the boot drunk?'

'Pissed as a newt. He'd had a skinful somewhere. But no, if you ask me, he didn't crawl in Heather A.'s boot to die. He'd have to've been proper pissed before they could of done that hair job on him. Like us, they must've thought it was the max to dump him in Heather's car—she'd pestered the whole place for contributions to her stall.'

Bone cut in before Noah could launch into his laugh at this. Gallows humour was often a professional necessity, a safety valve to those whose business it was to deal with death, but he felt distaste now. It might be the callousness of the murderer himself they were hearing; but he had a question.

'*Us*, Mr Pike? *We*? Who was with you?'

The grin was gone. Instead came something that looked like genuine grief, not really at home on those lax features.

'Laurie. Laurie Scatchard, me old mate, that's who. And why the hell aren't you asking who done *him* in, I'd like to know? Here's a nasty little bugger chokes on his own vomit, and you're on about him and a lot of bloody books and all the time there's a decent bloke stabbed to death and you're not taking a blind bit of notice. Save me from the bleeding police!'

Bone, regarding Noah bleakly as he thanked and dismissed him, wondered if this salvation were possible. Noah might be saved; but if they wanted corroboration of his story, it was undeniable that they would have to apply to the morgue.

26

'Sir.'

It was PC Higg, who had now been allotted the task of going through the books dumped in the bushes near Heather Armitage's car. The porn magazines that had been tucked into the boot beside Nigel had already yielded their reward in forcing Noah's admission about Nigel being alive but drunk somewhere towards midnight. What more had Higg to offer?

He had a copy of *The Nine Tailors* with the flyleaf neatly inscribed 'Reginald Merrick' which had been as neatly crossed out.

'There's a dozen or so of these, sir, in one bag; same name in each, crossed out. Two more bags of porn mags mixed with historical bodice-rippers, sir, but no name; and a bag with only this as bookmark in *The Infamous Army*.' He held out an envelope, creased and folded. As Bone smoothed it out, the name and address were perfectly clear. Bone smiled and held it out to Locker.

'Looks as if Henry Purdey took his books along to the boot. One has to admire Heather Armitage ... Higg: Henry Purdey has got to be found. We want him here. Is his car in his garage, for instance? Tell Action that he's to be found.'

'Sir.' Higg went out.

'So we want to know what Henry Purdey saw on his late journey to Manor Walk that night.'

'What do you reckon, sir? Clear as mud, beautiful mud. Pike can be lying; for all we know so far, he too had a grudge against Wells—'

129

'If he had he wasn't disguising it. *Poncy little git* isn't a customary term of endearment.'

'So finding him in the car was perhaps an opportunity.'

'With Scatchard's co-operation?'

'Like I say, if he's lying at all there could be that much more. No evidence of any books of Scatchard's? Why was he helping Pike to deliver his porn?'

'In on the joke. They seem to have been drinking mates.'

'We can get that confirmed.'

Bone took a turn towards the window again, massaging the back of his neck with one hand. The rain had dwindled now to an undecided drizzle, and the grey light was strengthening as cloud thinned, as if reminding itself that this was after all a summer's day and it wasn't yet over. Bone thought wistfully of Grizel getting dinner that evening, something he was unlikely to be back for, and sitting down with Cha to enjoy it, perhaps watching 'Last of the Summer Wine'. They wouldn't be watching 'Private Eyeful': Higg said there'd been an announcement on television that there was a change of programme. If Nigel Wells had died in his bed or even a hospital bed, they'd have been putting on an extra showing, or one of the B-films he'd made his name in. As Bone reflected on the importance of dying in the right place and in the right manner, there was a knock and Higg made his reappearance, out of breath and rather wet.

'He's gone, sir. Henry Purdey's gone up to London. He drove Miss Wells there.'

Locker said two words loudly which had Bone's hearty concurrence.

'When did this happen?'

'About ten minutes ago, so far as I can tell. There was still no one at Henry Purdey's house and I met some TV blokes coming away from Barbary Wells's place further up and they told me. There's a legman from the *News* who recognised Purdey as they went by. Apparently he's a journalist of sorts. They were seen driving away in her car.'

There was a short silence weighty with feeling.

'Find Miss Wells's London address, Higg. Is Pat Fredricks there?' Bone made a summoning gesture and Higg went out; they heard him on the stairs calling, 'Sergeant Fredricks! Wheel yourself in.'

Fredricks appeared, in a loose teeshirt and a grey linen skirt. Bone fleetingly registered that although she had become even plainer since he first met her as a WPC, her face had also become more open and animated.

'You told Miss Wells we'd want to speak to her.'

'Yes, sir. I asked her to be in readiness.'

Bone had expected as much. 'I'll want you to come to London. Have you managed to get lunch?'

'Charlie Iden sent pies and sandwiches, sir.'

'See if you can get a London address for Henry Purdey; and we'll want Miss Wells's address and number too. Alert a driver and be ready to go right after the Wells post-mortem. But first we want to see Reginald Merrick—tell Higg, please. Right, Steve? Let's have a look at the obvious enemies now.'

Higg came to say that Mr Merrick, duly summoned, was unable to come, having tripped on the stairs and, he thought, cracked a rib only half an hour ago.

'What does the doctor say? Or couldn't he get hold of one?'

'I don't know, sir. He's done it before, he said—cracked a rib. So he knows he's done it again.' Higg hesitated. 'He's not half in a mood. Snapped my head off. Shall I send a car?'

Bone, who had had two ribs broken for him once when he was on the beat many years ago, was not surprised at the bad mood. He said, 'Send the car Fredricks ordered, when it's ready, to collect us from Merrick's; for the p.m. first at Tunbridge Wells, and then to go to London. Steve, let's visit this crocodile in human form.'

Bone looked at the blown-up map of the village that Shay had pinned to the wall. 'Where is he?'

'Here, sir; just past Church Field down the street.'

'One thing about this place, we're within walking distance of everywhere. Unless it's raining.' Bone gave one of his infrequent smiles. Higg, who was nervous about his failure to get hold of Henry Purdey, brightened. The Super was not keen on your making mistakes, but he did not seem to think Higg had made one, and Higg was hoping he'd get taken along when Barbary Wells was interviewed.

Bone remembered Merrick's neatly written name in the books, neatly crossed out, when he and Locker, with DC Berryman bearing the tape recorder, trod the path up to the front door. Two rows of flowers, each a ruler's length from the next, lined the route, their symmetry destroyed by the casual hand of the rain which had flattened them every which way.

Bone had expected Merrick would take his time to answer the door, but he had not expected the vigour with which it was jerked open, or the consequent loud yelp delivered in the visitors' faces. Merrick looked as disagreeable as Higg had reported, and his temper had had time to marinate. His mouth was set with the corners downward.

'I suppose you're the *police*. You'd better come in.' He stood back, a grimace prefacing a groan, and nodded down the hallway. 'First on your right.'

'I'm sorry to hear about your fall, Mr Merrick,' Bone said as he led the way.

'Bloody thing left a shoe on the stairs. Of course I fell.'

Bone supposed he spoke of a dog. He might be one of those people reluctant to admit responsibility for even the simplest accident.

Merrick supervised the placing of the recorder and everyone's seating, and finally settled himself on the arm of a chair, as it evidently pained him to sit back. His face was a little drawn, and Bone did not suspect him of faking the pain; he held himself in just the attitude in which Bone had tried to forestall agony.

Yes, certainly he had taken books to the boot of Mrs Armitage's car. He had been out when she called collecting, 'but she left one of her infernal little notes; *and* she stopped her car after nearly running me down and shrieked at me as well. An impossible woman. I took some books to avoid being bothered again. There was nothing in the boot when I went, apart from some quite *hideous* embroidered cushions.'

'And did you see or hear anything unusual?'

'I saw absolutely nobody. As for hearing! *Hearing!* Do you mean the atrocious racket those young idiots call music? The stuff they were playing at their party here? It's a wonder the walls are still *standing*. You could hear that all over the street. I don't suppose anyone got any sleep at all. It went on until midnight. When I rang up the Rector he told me he had made them promise to stop it at midnight and I suppose I must say for them that they did.'

The said young idiots had already mentioned this when interviewed. Keeping their promise had, however, not earned them good marks from Reggie Merrick.

'Did you know Mr Wells?'

'Of course I *knew* him! You couldn't *escape* him round here. Go to the pub and he'd be smirking there, walk down the *street* and he'd be showing off in that swank car. You couldn't even turn on the television without the risk of seeing him in some advertisement or in that show. I'm not in the least surprised that someone thought they'd had enough of him.'

Bone felt Locker freeze. Why did Merrick suppose Wells's death was not an accident? Neither he nor Locker drew attention to the remark. 'So he had his enemies, then.'

Reggie produced a sound like a dog choking on a bone. 'Not everyone loved Mr Nigel Darling Wells, let me tell you. Even the teenagers only tolerated him for what they could get out of him.'

'Which was . . . ?'

Bone knew that Locker too had drugs in mind, but Reggie merely referred to the Easter play which, surprisingly, like Noah, he had attended. 'My grandson Phil had a part. Ghastly rubbish but he did it well.' Something, a distant cousin to a smile, illuminated Reggie's face for a second, and Bone had to accept the idea that this disagreeable man might have such an attribute as family pride, even affection.

'Any particular enemy?'

The answer came immediately with no racking of brains. 'Henry Purdey. Henry loathed him. Wells would come back drunk at all hours from London and drive that swank car over the grass outside Henry's place. Great grooves in the grass. Then Henry—' Merrick stopped for a moment to shift his arm and put a hand to his side. His sharp blue regard swept the three of them as if he savoured the information he was holding. None of the faces before him betrayed that they had heard this before. 'Henry put up a row of big stones along the verge at the corner one day when Wells was up in town. He said he was going to have them painted white.'

Merrick threw back his head and barked, nearly losing his balance on the chair arm and instantly grimacing and holding his side. 'Damn thing! Then back comes Wells, cuts the corner as usual, hits a stone and ends up through Henry's fence. Not such a smart move.'

As they considered this, the radiator behind Bone suddenly broke out in loud staccato clankings, as if attacked by gnomes with hammers; and Merrick, once more forgetting his broken rib, sprang to his feet, emitted a brief howl, and stood still.

'*Bloody* heating's come on again. Second time this week.'

'Don't you have it turned off in this weather?'

'Of *course* I turned it off! It turns itself on.'

Locker's large hand began to tap the notebook before him; Bone did not need him to say aloud: How much can we trust a man one sandwich short of a picnic?

'Smashed his windscreen too.' Reggie Merrick returned from switching off his heating, and his voice suggested a philosophical enjoyment. 'Took a hammer to it. *What* a kerfuffle that was.'

'I take it Mr Wells was not in the car at the time?'

'No,' Reggie conceded. 'He'd got out and gone home. But I'm sure Henry wished he was.'

Justin Rafferty's story was confirmed, it seemed. More and more it looked like time to go to London and talk to Henry Purdey.

27

'**H**e didn't sound pleased.' Locker shifted in the car seat. 'He said he'd gone to bed.'

Bone swung up his wrist to stare at his watch. 'To bed? Nine-thirty's a tad early for a journalist. Did he say who with? Or merely put it down to shock?'

Locker grunted. Two pie-and-sandwich meals a day never agreed with him. 'Claims to be all stressed out. He'd expected to be with Miss Wells, but she has a woman friend with her, who wouldn't let me speak to her either until I came the heavy . . .' Bone smiled as Locker went on. 'Then Miss Wells did come to the phone, all fainty and brave—'

'The woman's just lost her brother, Steve.'

'I know, I know. But there's something—'

'Something false? You think she's putting it on?'

Locker gazed out of the window, where a sign told them they were entering Sutton and exhorted them to drive carefully, as if the lives in these thirties houses in the tree-lined avenues were more important than lives elsewhere. Did the back of the notice say: 'You are leaving Sutton, now drive as carelessly as you like'? Locker said, 'I saw her once in some film on the telly. Terrific looker; she was being some sweet heroine or other and you somehow couldn't believe in her.'

'Could be just bad acting. We've seen enough villains to know you don't have to be honest to sound sincere. Remember Colly Adams—he could really make you believe him innocent of murder if you found him with an axe in someone's head.'

'He'd be trying to get it out without hurting them! I know. Anyway, bad actress or no, she's consented to see us tonight. Doctor says she shouldn't, but she'll do it for us.'

The words BIG DEAL lit in Bone's imagination. Locker, turning over his pockets for sweets, added, 'And for her brother's sake, she said. It seems I had timed the call well; the friend had just made a call and put the phone down; they're keeping it on the answering machine because of the Press, who've got the place staked out—asking for an interview with the team of her choice. They want something juicy from the grieving sister for the late-late news and the Monday papers.'

'You think she's overplaying it? What if she'd popped along to Heather's car and stopped him getting more screen-time?'

Locker's search of his pockets for the peppermints that usually lived there turned up two, in crumpled paper wrapping. He offered one to Bone, who shook his head. 'She'd have to know about the joke, then. Course, she might have been behind it all from the start.'

Bone thought it typical of Locker that he should give a fanciful thing his serious attention. He was not a man to dismiss the unlikely; often enough they had worked on cases where the unlikely turned out to be reasonable compared with the facts. Bone was aware that Locker's prejudice against Barbary Wells was infectious, and he recalled his own brief interview with her, when he had broken the news of her brother's death. He wondered if he had seen any real shock or expression of grief—and he had seen, in his job, plenty of both. She had in fact seemed to be *acting* shock and bereavement; then perhaps everything became filtered through the mannerisms she had acquired to express emotions; it was as if she had reached for a drawer marked 'Reception of Terrible News'. How did you know when a woman like that was telling the truth?

'Well, Henry Purdey first. If he's got out of bed to answer the phone, it's the least we can do. Let's hope he's not carrying a hammer.'

If Henry Purdey had got out of bed once, it would appear he had got back again. Bone and Locker stood on the cobbles of the mews lane and rang the bell, and stood long enough to attract the attention of a cat which had been sleeping on top of some flowers in a tub at the end of the mews. It came to inspect them. Henry's attention was harder to attract, but after Locker's heavy-duty fist had hammered on the door, a sash window above was flung up and a truculent voice called, 'Hang on, hang on! Don't be so bloody impatient!'

A thudding and a curse beyond the door heralded a stocky man in a silk dressing-gown, whose scrutiny turned to a scowl directed at Bone's ankles, where he suddenly aimed a kick. 'Bloody cat! Pees on the doorstep. Come in *quick.*' They followed the silk dressing-gown, red diamonds on navy blue, up a steep narrow flight of stairs obviously designed for someone to break their neck falling down; Henry could certainly not have hustled to open the door. At the top Locker had a little difficulty with his shoulders in the narrow turn to the sitting room. Bone glanced into a bedroom as they passed. The bed was still made up, almost without a crease.

Henry turned and gestured at a small ginger sofa. It

might have been chosen, some years ago, to match his hair, now thinning in pepper-and-salt. He had gone straight to a drinks table in the corner, splashed a jumbo helping of gin into a tumbler and said over his shoulder, 'Don't suppose there's a future in offering you a drink if you're on duty. You *are* police, I suppose?'

Bone produced again the card that had been ignored on account of the cat. 'We have a few questions about what happened today.'

'Good lord.' Henry, bearing his glass, came to stand by the hearth and find a resting place for his elbow between a Victorian brass candlestick and a prim-faced china dog. 'Why not ask someone that might know? I'm as baffled as any policeman.' He gave them a grin not intended to ingratiate, and waited. He had the coarse skin of a drinker; he was in his late fifties but, despite the hair, and the bulge behind the knotted cord of his dressing-gown, there was a burly readiness about him. They knew he could wield a hammer, but it didn't need much strength to kill an unconscious man or, for that matter, to drive a knife into the back of a man perched on a footstool with his head trapped in a hole and held there by a tin tray. It only took malice. How much of that Henry Purdey possessed had still to be found out.

'At what time last night did you take a bag of books to Mrs Armitage's car?'

Henry lowered a measure of gin before he answered, but Bone had seen the moment of discomposure.

'Oh, I took a bag of books to old Heather's car, did I?'

'You left an envelope bookmark in one of them.'

The simplicity of this had little appeal for Henry. 'Envelope? That supposed to prove anything? If I find a bus ticket or an envelope in a library book I use it as a bookmark and leave it there. Saves trouble.'

'You could save us some, Mr Purdey, if you'd tell us when you left the books.'

Henry shrugged, and tipped some more gin down his throat with a practised movement. It may have given him the necessary fortitude to tell the truth. 'Oh, I can't be sure. Some time after eleven it'd be, because the pub had shut. I got home and found the damn books in the hall. Fell over them, as a matter of fact. Realised I'd have no peace if Hag Heather found out I'd forgotten my contribution—the power of a stupid woman! So I staggered out with them *pronto.*'

'Did you see anyone on your way?'

Henry thought about it, smoothing the rim of his glass against his underlip. 'Not many people around. Biddinghurst keeps early hours even on a Saturday night. Apart from our young, that is. Filthy noise blasting from the Old Rectory where they were having a rave-up. You'll have heard about that, I imagine.'

'Yes, sir.' Locker could sound repressive, and more so for sitting on a sofa too small for him. Bone had chosen to lean on the arm of it, preferring not to be below the level of the man he was talking to. 'What did you find in the car boot?'

'Books, of course. Carrier bags of books. Were you expecting I'd say "Nigel Wells"? If I'd seen him there I'd have told you at once.' Henry paused and tapped the glass against his lower teeth. His regard was both casual and sly. 'Is it true his face was painted and his hair all shaved off? He must have looked a treat.'

'Where did you hear that?'

'Common talk. Barbary's cleaner, I believe.' His face now showed definite satisfaction.

'Were you on good terms with Nigel Wells, Mr Purdey?'

Henry made time over this by going to freshen his drink. Pouring, he achieved the casual, 'Oh, I don't think I was the only one who didn't like old Nigel.'

'I understand you attacked his car—'

'Then you'll know why.' Henry did not seem disposed to elaborate on that. 'Bit of a creep in general, he was. Up to no good with the children.'

The sofa arm shifted under Bone as Locker leant forward, although Locker's tone was also casual. 'In what way, Mr Purdey?'

'Offering them stuff. You know, drugs. Though when I take a look at some of those kids I have to hope they came to be like that *with* a little help from illegal substances. It would account for it, I mean. But every kid seems to take something these days, even if it's only pot.'

Bone as usual thought with dread of Cha. Would the common sense he so admired in her be proof against peer pressure, against the particular appeal the wretched Justin seemed to hold for her . . . For some natures it took only one lapse to make an addict; as he had heard, it was in one's genes. While he himself hardly bothered with alcohol and had been too cautious to experiment with drugs, perhaps his obsession with his job counted as addiction. Cha might not be safe at all.

Locker was talking. 'Have any of the young people involved—' he could sound numbingly pompous when he chose—'mentioned anything about drugs and Mr Wells to you?'

Henry ferried back a refreshed glass and sat down, this time in an armchair covered in deckchair canvas, its stripes wrenched out of line by the assaults of Henry's bottom. Bone put down 'Going to bed early' as a euphemism for drinking oneself into a state where it would little matter if one went to bed or not.

'Drugs and Nigel? Not a dickybird. It's only an impression I got. Nigel often looked stoned—God knows he drove as if he was. It's logical to think the kids had a strong ulterior motive in putting up with him. Kat, my niece—and I quote her gracious words—said he was the biggest lump of shit she'd met outside a farmyard.'

Bone watched Henry drink, trying to trace any family resemblance in the florid face to the contained, pale one of Kat Purdey. Perhaps it was a certain belligerence.

Locker had shifted gear. 'And Mr Scatchard. Did he get on well with them?'

Henry looked up sharply. 'How should I know? Fleur

could get her dear papa to do that jape in the Haunted House because he was so bloody good-natured; he was also bloody bad-tempered. He made any balls-up in your garden and you'd better pretend it was your fault. I've seen him send that Rafferty boy flying to the ground for doing something Laurie didn't fancy to a bush. *My* bush, mind you.'

'Am I to take it you didn't like Mr Scatchard any better than you liked Mr Wells?' Bone knew how and when to sound disparaging, and he saw Henry's mouth purse up in irritation.

'If you're suggesting I did either of them in because I didn't take to them you can just as well go and arrest half Biddinghurst. All I can tell you is that when I went round the Haunted House, Scatchard was alive.'

'How could you be sure of that?'

'Because he winked at me.'

Locker made a note. 'Who was after you, sir? Did you happen to see?'

'No idea. The kids made people go through separately. I was busy looking for Miss Wells.'

'And did you find her?' Bone cut in, sensing something.

'Oh, she'd got lost on the way out. She was before me, you see. I'd expected to find her waiting outside, but she only saw the way out when I'd opened the door. Easy to lose yourself in that maze. All the curtains.'

Bone was silent. Henry had sounded almost defensive, as if he too suddenly wondered what Barbary might have been doing in those interesting moments before Laurie Scatchard was found to have got his chips on a plate.

28

'So. Do you fancy Henry Purdey for either, Steve?'

Locker had been steadily making his way through a tube of Rolos he had bought at a newsagent's before they got into the car, and toffee muffled his reply. 'Might be the type for a knife, but I don't see him killing an unconscious man.'

'Struck you as too decent, did he? In that case would he knife a man in the back who couldn't move?'

Locker popped another toffee in his mouth and grunted. 'Whoever did it wasn't having any worry about the victim fighting back. Could be a woman, even a kid.'

'Well, we're awash with those, and possibly stoned out of whatever minds they've got.'

Locker crushed the empty wrapping in a large fist and pocketed it. 'We're going to have to see them all again, sir. Lying through their young teeth, the lot of them.'

'You don't think Henry Purdey's lying.'

'Do you, sir? His type generally shows it.'

Bone, not sure how Locker classed Henry Purdey as to type, still knew what he meant. Their work would be a doddle if they could always tell when someone was lying; but with some people it was easier. Barbary Wells, for instance, might very likely seem to be lying when she wasn't.

Summer twilight was creeping into the streets now, and lights were coming on, bright and intrusive. Bone recognised the Albert Bridge, so they could not be far from Barbary Wells's flat. They were in Chelsea. Locker leant sideways to look at a passing youth with green hair, a silver nose-ring attached by a chain to his lower

142

lip, and a black teeshirt cut out in a heart shape on a concave white chest. Bone knew that he and Locker had been reminded of the same person when Locker growled, 'That Rafferty could well know a thing or two he's not thought we should hear. Painting up Nigel Wells would be just his style . . . Might even think it was an improvement.'

Their driver was pulling up before a small Georgian house, shabby-elegant, a decayed aristocrat. They got out. Beside the door they found a vertical row of bells, showing how far the house had descended since it was first built to accommodate one family and the servants necessary to look after it. Now, Bone thought as he surveyed the elegant façade, those who once might have afforded the whole house and the servants, were grateful to pay far more to live in the servants' quarters, attic or basement. Wells, for the name printed by the bell gave away no more, occupied the first floor. Locker rang the bell.

Their car took up a disproportionate space in the narrow street, and Bone could see no sign of the expected Press siege—unless a couple of men lounging in the porch of the dingy church on the corner across the way were lying in wait. Nevertheless he thought it unwise of Barbary to insist, by means of the entryphone, that the police should stand out in the street and show their cards. She should be able to recognise Bone from their interview, and for another thing she would need binoculars to read their cards, and for a third, it attracted the attention of the loungers at the church door, who erupted and arrived panting on the doorstep just as Bone, Locker and Fredricks were buzzed in, giving Locker the satisfaction of ignoring their shouted questions and shutting the door in their faces. Of course Barbary may have had just this in mind as a tease for the Press.

Barbary's friend received them at the head of the stairs. She was tall, imposing, with soigné grey hair; Bone

143

was reminded instantly of Dorothy in 'The Golden Girls'. She even wore clothes of the same fashion, a charcoal silk tunic and ivory trousers. Perhaps she consciously modelled herself on Dorothy, for the likeness was taken further by a penetrating scan from dark eyes and an acerbic admonition that Barbary should not be tired or upset; the admonition was in an American voice.

'You are . . .'

'Dr Beth Dillon. Doctor of Psychiatry, University of Minnesota. An old family friend. She's been in a very stressed state and is not coping well with the bereavement experience. She does not need harassment.' She said it the American way with the stress on the second syllable. 'She really needs to be allowed to go through this nightmare in her own time.' She indicated the room door severely. 'You'll find her lying down. Please keep the interview as brief as you can.'

A slight motion of Locker's eyebrows, as Dr Dillon put a hand to the doorknob, told Bone that he felt a mental health check by a psychiatrist to be exactly what they all needed.

If this woman was a family friend, how much could *she* tell them about Nigel?

Barbary Wells lay on a *chaise-longue* at the foot of a repro Victorian brass bed, which had tall rods supporting a net canopy and head curtains, reminding Bone instantly of the draperies in the Haunted House. Pink-shaded lights either side of the bed cast a soft warm glow on the drapery and left Barbary herself in protective shadow. Late evening light from the windows was still enough to reveal that, crushed by grief or no, she had managed to eliminate any trace of tears she might have shed, and wore a skilful minimum of make-up. If the bed looked Victorian, Barbary came from a thirties movie, in a cream satin peignoir, piped in pink, over matching pyjamas. On her feet were pink satin mules. This was grief in style. Bone wondered what she would think if she knew what a bad impression it made.

'Oh, Superintendent Bone! I do hope you aren't going to ask me too many questions. I really don't think I can help you one bit. All I want to do is forget.'

Just what the doctor ordered, Bone thought. He said, 'We shan't keep you long,' reserving the reply that what she wanted to forget was exactly what they needed to know. He himself did not intend to stay standing; Barbary, in an effort either at one-upmanship or to keep the interview short, had not invited them to sit. He took a small gilt chair from under the window, saw Locker glance at its twin and then sit on the sturdy dressing-table stool. It was Fredricks who took the other gilt chair, near the door.

'Now, Miss Wells. What can you tell us about your brother's drug habit?'

It was the shock he had hoped. She even sat up, the satin dressing-gown falling open. '*Drug* habit! Nigel! What on earth do you mean?'

Bone was quite ready to tell her Ferdy Foster's words about the condition of Nigel's nasal passages, but he merely said, 'We know he took drugs, Miss Wells. Can you tell us how long he had been doing it?'

She lay back, as if realising that theatrical ignorance would get her nowhere if the police had the facts. She rearranged the peignoir and laid a delicate hand on it to hold it together. 'It's true.' The voice was a rueful whisper. 'He did have a problem. But he'd got over it— he was so brave. He went for treatment and tackled it like a hero. It wasn't easy—the strains of our kind of life . . .' She paused and looked at them doubtfully, the marvellous sea-green eyes under thick, raying lashes. 'Why are you asking me? It can't have to do with— what happened.'

'It might have, Miss Wells. Were you aware he gave drugs to some of the village teenagers?'

'Oh no, he wouldn't do that.' She was quite confident. 'Nigel would never, ever, do anything that could damage anyone. He was so *kind!* The kindest man.' She pressed a pink tissue to her mouth and said, indistinctly, 'You don't know how kind.'

'Suppose you tell me,' Bone suggested. 'You see, we need a full picture of his character. He was kind to the teenagers?'

'I can't tell you how kind. I've sworn not to tell. I can simply say it was unbelievably kind. And of course he gave his time to help them with their little play. And then there was old Graham Barnholt. Nigel never failed to go and see him, and spent hours talking to him and finding books for him.' The tissue was applied beneath her eyes. 'It's so sad about the Manor. He was looking forward enormously to living there. He never thought of Graham leaving it to him, but he did. Graham knew what Nigel had done for him! He recognised kindness, no matter what disagreeable, jealous people said.'

Neither Bone nor Locker showed that this was news to them. It was not a reaction from them that made Barbary suddenly sit up and hit the cream brocade headrest with her small fist.

'How could they do that to him? Those beastly, beastly children! You can say what you like, they killed him! They were responsible, they put him in there. How could they! He'd been so good to them! Is it true they'd made him up? How could they be so beastly?'

At last Bone believed in her reaction. That she still looked distractingly lovely did not take away from the genuine note in her voice. Of course it fetched Dr Beth at once from the next room; giving Bone a brief glare, she went to Barbary and sat beside her, an arm round her in silent support.

'Oh, it's stupid to be so angry. But I hope you punish them. They're foul, ungrateful, cruel, heartless . . .' Her voice failed her. She choked, and burst into tears. Bone looked at Locker, and raised an eyebrow. They both stood up. Barbary, shaking with sobs, crammed pink tissues to her eyes and put her face in her friend's shoulder.

Dr Dillon, oddly enough, did not reprove them but concentrated on Barbary's grief. As they went out, Fredricks mutely gestured: should she stay? Bone shook his head and she followed them out into the sea-green sitting room. Locker regarded his notes.

'I was beginning to think she wasn't feeling it,' he said.

'It can take time.'

'Interesting that she broke out because she was angry.'

The telephone light pulsed and the answering machine clicked on.

'So Nigel had recently been left the Manor. We have to find out about this immense and secret kindness he did for the teenagers.'

Locker said, 'What makes me think he was not just a saintly generous bloke but a creep?'

'A dead creep,' said Bone. 'Most of Biddinghurst seems to agree with you.'

The door opened and Dr Dillon came out.

'She needed to do that,' she remarked, but her voice acquired a sardonic tone as she went on, 'though it would have been better had it arrived naturally and not under your interrogation.'

'This particular question was about Nigel's kindness,' Bone said blandly. 'Would you say he was kind?'

'Very kind,' Dr Dillon replied, 'if it didn't cost him.'

Given the psychiatrist's perhaps naturally jaundiced view of human nature, the remark chimed well with the picture of Nigel already forming in Bone's mind. He said, 'Have you an instance of it?'

'You think I'm just talking,' she said without rancour. 'Barbary asked him one time to give me a ride to the clinic, but he said it would make him too late for rehearsal—until he realised he could pick up some shirts he'd ordered from near where I work. I could cite several incidents like that.'

'What about his drug habit?'

She shrugged. 'He went on a cure. A friend of his in

Biddinghurst paid for it, and give Nigel his due, he went through with it. I don't think he had the grit to stay clean, but I have not seen enough of him since then to be sure. Barbary doesn't do drugs, but I'd swear the kid Fleur took a fix when she was here.'

'How long ago would that be?'

'Earlier this year. March maybe. She was sick, and she was drooping round the place like a wet Sunday until a little visit to the bathroom brought her out sparking on all cylinders. But I was leaving right then and maybe she was just pleased to see me go. I was of the opinion that she had a fixation on Barbary, but admittedly I'm judging on a very brief impression. I understand she wants to be an actress; strictly a non-starter, I'd say; not the personality of a stage prop.'

The answering machine clicked once more.

'I'd better catch some of those,' Dr Dillon said. 'They're mostly reporters. She should change her number again.'

'We must have another word with Miss Wells.' Bone saw resistance stiffen Dr Dillon's whole body, and went on, 'It's not in our interest to upset her, you know.'

'I *don't* know. You and I are both perfectly aware how fruitful for our very disparate intentions it can be to upset a subject.'

Bone slightly raised his hand and let it drop, in acquiescence. 'But not today.'

She gave him another severe look and moved towards the bedroom door. 'I'll see.'

Fredricks's shoulder bag suddenly began to cheep, as if it held a frustrated chick. She took out the bleeper and silenced it. 'Shall I go to the car, sir?'

'No. Call from here when this line's clear.'

The answering machine clicked off, and she switched it over and made the call. As she was listening to the message, Dr Dillon returned. Fredricks rang off, pulled out her notebook and wrote, and showed Bone the page.

'There's this news from Forensic . . .' It was what they had expected. Bone read in silence, and went on to the next item. 'I.R. message: Henry Purdey rang them to say he remembers seeing Rafferty and Phil Merrick in his brother the Rector's car, eleven-thirty or so last night.'

Bone thought: Nigel Wells's hearse?

29

Somewhere, a bird was woken and remarked on the lateness of the hour. Bone tripped on a tussock and said something suitable in reply. In spite of their torchlight playing over the long grass ahead of them, Locker and he were making heavy weather of the approach. Rotten burglars we'd be . . . Bone could smell honeysuckle; there had been a cluster silhouetted over Dave Hollis's head when he opened the back door to them, an anxious Midge in a dressing-gown behind him. Locker had asked the whereabouts of Justin and Phil, had answered the Hollises' worried inquiries with reassurance, declined Dave's immediate offer to come with them to the caravan, and thanked Dave for telling them the way. Few people care to be woken up after midnight, specially by the police and specially if the call was not for them but for someone for whom they are very much concerned.

The moon did little but alleviate the dark from behind cloud. There was a faint track through the long grass; it was wet from yesterday's rain, soaking Bone's trouser-ends and ankles. This, and having had no proper meal that day, and knowing that Grizel would have been in bed for hours, as he wanted to be, was not, he hoped, going to prevent him from conducting an impartial questioning of Phil Merrick and Justin Rafferty, however strong his desire to bang their heads together for wasting his time earlier on, in the afternoon a lifetime ago.

The dark hulk of the caravan showed up among the gnarled shapes of old apple-trees and their thick foliage, shipwrecked in the long grass. Locker's torch picked out a name painted in curly letters on its dingy side: *The Mary Celeste*. Ah yes, the ship discovered afloat on a calm sea, a meal half-eaten on the cabin table, everything in its place, no one on board. High time this dodgy pair gave up their mysteries. Bone found himself approving of the ferocity of Locker's thumping on the door, which rocked the caravan slightly and brought muffled noises from within. Bone would have liked to assume Kojak's air of intimidating nonchalance, to unwrap a lolly, stick it in his face and genially suggest, *Wake up and let's have the truth, baby. Come clean.*

Clean they were not. Phil Merrick battled with the door—it was warped, and he swore at it and at the visitors before he finally got it open, when it swung wide suddenly, sending him backwards into Justin. Both were in underpants and frowsy teeshirts, Phil's with a ragged tear over the navel, Justin's a washed-out black, greasy and frayed. Grizel would have rejected either garment as a duster for fear of contaminating the furniture.

Phil, spotlit by the torches, the orderly sharpness of Merrick features obscured by swathes of hair released from the ponytail, blinked as if he had not slept for a week.

'What the blazing *hell!*' Phil was Reggie's grandson in more than features. He looked both louche and dangerous, hanging on to the door, Justin's skull face appearing over his shoulder. 'What do you *want?* It's the bloody middle of the *night.*'

'We want the truth, young man, this time.' Locker had stepped up on to the block before their door, and now pressed onward. Phil drew back before his bulk, while Justin disappeared into the shadows. 'Where's the light in this place?'

One of them switched on a light bulb that dangled from the end of a flex looping and trailing like intestines over various hooks and nails under the roof. Bone followed Locker into an atmosphere almost thick enough to repel physically as well as aesthetically—unwashed male, frying, stale food and the odour of cannabis. Facing Bone was a small fibreglass sink crowded with a disorder of used plates and mugs and dirty cutlery, the plates not so much stacked as unevenly balanced, with the effect that one more plate could bring disaster. To the left was a cooker, holding the overflow of pans from the sink but dominated by a frying-pan where a solitary sausage reared up from a sea of grease. Bone in his youth had lived a bachelor existence in shared digs and it had taught him to be fastidious; these two could vie for Slob of the Year. Pity Charlotte could not see how Justin chose to live— but such was the irony of life that she would very likely see it as romantic chaos.

Thoughts are fast. In this moment, Phil Merrick had recovered so far as to say, 'What's the big idea? You grilled us once today already.'

Justin had retired to his bunk and sat in the welter of duvet, which, incredibly, had Snoopy designs all over it, and simply stared at them as if the scene were part of a dream he was still having. Locker sat on the bunk too, making even the wafer-thin Justin move up to sit on the pillow with his arms around his knees. Bone chose to stand, in the only spare bit of room, forcing Phil too to sit on his bunk.

Locker opened fire, and Bone held his.

'A witness tells us that he saw you both late last night in the Rector's car, near Mrs Armitage's drive where her car was parked and Nigel Wells was found. What were you doing there?'

Bone saw the swift glance Phil shot at Justin, and suspected that, though Phil might be the mouth, Justin was the one who decided what was to be said. Justin did not look back.

Phil said, 'We were getting more drink—juice and stuff. We'd run out and Midge, Mrs Hollis, always has pints in the kitchen for the kids. You can ask her. We borrowed the Rector's car because Kat knew where the keys were. She said he wouldn't mind. And Just's got a licence.'

'We couldn't ask the Rector because he'd taken a sleeper so's not to hear our racket.' Justin seemed amused by this, and put his chin on his knees. For some reason this made Bone's temper slip; the boy looked so much at ease. He spoke.

'We have now received confirmation that Nigel Wells was murdered. He was smothered by someone holding a cushion over his face.'

30

Bone might just as well have produced a gun.

Phil's mouth fell open. The whites of his eyes gleaming through the tangles of hair made him look suddenly manic. Justin sprang up, all but knocking his head on the low roof, his feet thudding to the floor. Locker moved instinctively to the ready as Justin leant towards Bone, snarling, 'We didn't. We bloody didn't. All we did was put the sod in the boot. I put the cushion under his head myself. There was masses of air.'

'No use masses of air when there's a cushion cutting it off.' Bone, Justin's face close to his in the crowded space, had for once no disadvantage of height because in here, Justin had to bend his head. The black smears still left of Death's paint made him haggard and frail. Sweat had broken out on the forehead under the bleached crest.

'You bloody can't fit us up for it. We put him in there alive and we bloody *left* him alive!' Phil was on his feet now, to give Bone an ill-considered push. Bone got his wrists and forced him back down onto his bunk, Justin's lunge to his aid being thwarted by Locker's seizing his shirt from behind and sitting him, off-balance, abruptly down again. The caravan rocked and one of the dishes in the sink left the Leaning Tower in a plunge for freedom and shattered on the floor.

'No one's fitting you up, you silly berk.' Locker held his grip. 'Start at the beginning and give us the lot. You'll need to say it again in a formal statement but let's have it. Let's hear it in your own words: did this start at the party in the Old Rectory?'

After a long pause, which Bone allowed to become oppressive, Justin said, 'Right.'

'Whose idea was it?'

A pause.

'I reckon it was everybody's,' Phil said.

'We started thinking what we'd like to do and it sort of . . .' Justin's hands described a blossoming or a slow explosion.

'What was your reason?' Bone asked.

Phil and Justin mutely consulted. Justin said, 'We wanted to make him look like the fake he was. But we didn't kill him. No *way*. We didn't want to kill him! I mean we wanted to put him through it, get home to him. We thought he wouldn't sue because it'd broadcast it nationwide.'

Phil said, 'We thought she'd open the boot right on the fairground. Everyone seeing him, like.'

'We didn't kill him because what's the point?—I even put the fucking cushion under his head.'

'Yeah, he did,' Phil said. 'I mean, we wanted him to be all right for the morning.'

'How did you render him unconscious?'

There was a short silence. Justin said, shrugging, 'Like a Mickey Finn. Little cocktail. One of the Rector's sleepers in his drinks. Look, if we wanted him dead we could've done it with sleepers. We wanted—like—a bit of humiliation. The great Nigel Wells fished out of a car boot with only half his hair and his face a mess. Like it would have been epic. We kept listening out all morning for a mega lift-off. Then I thought it could've happened and everyone got discreet and hustled him out of sight.'

'You didn't think of repercussions.' Bone was about to repeat this more simply, but 'repercussions' was a word Justin knew.

'He wouldn't have sued.' His voice was confident.

Locker answered scornfully. 'You're telling us that a man in his position would let you get away with—'

'Yeh. He had to.'

'Why?' Bone saw there must be some hold the group had on Nigel. He thought of Cha's report of being 'touched up' at the cottage. There was a silence. Phil was gripping the edge of the mattress. 'Did he make sexual advances to any of you?'

Phil's dynamic surge from his seat was foiled by two hands—a large preventive one using minimum force and a skeletal violent one. He fell back on his bed. He had uttered 'The bast—' when the wind left him.

'Cool it, Phil. Sorry, Super.'

Well you might be, thought Bone. Phil was about to be useful, and you shut him up. 'So he did make sexual advances,' he said drily. 'Who to?'

Justin grimaced, an odd convulsion of a face where every muscle showed. 'All of us. I mean he was gross. God's gift to us kiddies, that was Nige.'

'And did he get anywhere? Sleep with any of your crowd?'

'Basically he was just a groper. You'd get him on "interfering". We had a theory he was a dead-dick.'

'How much?' Locker demanded.

'Impotent. Anyway he was thirty-six.'

Bone, acknowledging that his few years more than

that placed him in decrepitude with this mob, said only, 'You resented his groping?'

'We could handle it. No big deal.'

Phil stirred, glowering through his hair. 'He was a voyeur.'

'Was he now? What makes you say that?'

'Well, I mean—nothing; just he never *did* it.'

'Did he provide you with drugs?'

Justin's eyes widened in their dark hollows. 'Supply? He brought some along to the party.'

There was an unfinished note about the sentence and Bone and Locker, the experts, waited. Justin regarded the mangy strip of carpet for a moment, massaging his knee. 'He offered Chrissie Hollis some. He was telling her it was fun and everybody was doing it. They were in the little room next to the garden, you know?'

Bone identified this as the one where the hair had been found, now being fitted up as an office.

'Kat and Darren heard and went in there, and he put the stuff away, Kat said. I don't *know* what she said to Nigel—' Justin anticipated the question—'but Darren took Chrissie home. Back here,' and he gestured towards the house.

'How old is Chrissie?'

'She's twelve,' Phil said.

'That was the reason,' Justin added, leaning back on his elbows, 'why we shaved the bugger's head and did up his face. We put him in the Rector's car and I drove to Manor Walk and we got him into the old cow's car; and put him in the recovery position if you want to know, though curled up a bit, like. And a pillow under his head. Then we went back to the party.'

'When did the party end?'

'Dunno. We had to cool the music at midnight, we had it low down, and the lights, and went on partying.'

Bone briefly marvelled at the young, partying, with drugs and drink, obediently turning the music down at midnight. It argued a strong mind, and a dominant hand on the volume control, somewhere among them, and the face before his mind's eye was that of Kat Purdey.

'Didn't it occur to you that it was an extreme thing to do to someone of Nigel Wells's standing?'

'Standing?' Justin said derisively. 'Is he Ken Branagh or something? A lousy sitcom-series—he's a shit.'

'Chrissie, you know, she's like our sister.' Phil's intervention made Justin regard him watchfully. 'I mean, that was enough.'

Something was still being masked by this wretched pair but he had a strong sense that pressure would not easily force it out of them. Although, on the surface, Phil was the more vulnerable, now that he sat up and pushed his fingers through his hair, a strong and obstinate face emerged.

And after the day Bone had spent, he had no energy left for pressure; no, nor for subtlety either. These boys had slept already. They were fresh enough despite their earlier dazed looks, to resist his probing. They had the stamina of youth, whereas he had fleetingly envied them even their frowsy bunks. Bone was a great believer in sleeping on problems, letting the chaos in the brain take form, present some creative image of significance. He got up abruptly, attended by the gaze of both boys.

'Enough for tonight. We'll talk again tomorrow.'

Better to leave them with a threat, wondering what more questions he could put. They were not to know that so was he.

31

Monday mornings lack widespread popularity. Bone woke up, as he always did, just before seven and swung his feet to the floor to give himself no chance of falling asleep again. So far from clearing his mind, sleep had churned up the images of the day before, mixing and blurring them. In his dreams he had kept seeing a green face. It might have been the imitated mould on Laurie Scatchard's or the paint on Nigel Wells's but the hair above had been white or bleached—Justin Rafferty's crest. The thing had haunted his night, floating through dreams, appearing and slowly dissolving like the Cheshire cat and, like the cat, wearing a grin that mocked him. Bone sat for a minute, while the tea-maker did its stuff on the bedside table and he stared at the carpet's pattern as if it might suggest a pattern for this case.

Grizel sat up, stretching, tousled. She punched the pillows into a back-rest and he passed her one of the cups of tea.

'Do I expect you back at any definite time, Robert?'

'When you see me, I think; and then don't strain your credulity.'

Grizel put her half-empty cup on her bedside table and kissed his neck. 'Cha and I will be going to see those houses round Saxhurst today. We'll let you know if there are any worth your seeing as well.'

How well she knows me already, Bone thought as he headed for the shower, to the sound of Cha's radio playing pop music next door. She won't ask me questions about the case until I start talking about it.

If I started talking now it would be gibberish. And

very shortly that's all I'll have to offer the Chief when he rings. He'll be under pressure from the media to come up with something about Nigel Wells who, despite Justin's opinion, is yet the darling of television audiences. He won't be a darling for long, once it gets out about the drugs and—and what? Bone knew there was more, something shadier than touching up, that the teenagers were in a conspiracy to hide, and that must be ferreted out.

He had a score of things to do that morning, urgent paperwork, a disciplinary matter, Inspector Garron's health, a complaint about discrimination. All that must be dealt with before he was free to join Locker at Biddinghurst. Locker would be in the Incident Room, reading the collated results of yesterday's house-to-house and hearing the tapes of the interviews. Ferdy's assistant would have had the full report of the post-mortem on both the victims delivered. Forensic might even have the results, identifying the detritus Ferdy had scraped off the inside of Nigel's nose and throat as particles from the cushion stuffed under his head which they believed had also been stuffed over his face. Bone suppressed the memory that, under the brilliant lights reflected off the white tiles, Nigel Wells, with bits of his anatomy showing, had looked vulnerable as well as grotesque. A pity it wasn't possible to force Phil and Justin to witness a p.m.; it might loosen their tongues as well as their bowels.

An hour and a half later, Bone's talk with George Garron was interrupted by the Chief's phone call, and his opinion on how the case was being conducted. The results of the p.m. had been 'unfortunate, very unfortunate'. Rather more so, Bone thought, for Nigel Wells, but he could appreciate what the Chief was saying. If only Nigel Wells had had the decency to choke on his own vomit instead of being suffocated by another hand, the police would not be obliged to spend their valuable time hunting for his murderer under the censorious public eye. As for Laurie Scatchard, who had conspicuously not stabbed himself in the back, he was definitely a sideshow; though the Chief was pleased to make a jocular reference to having Bone's head on a plate if nothing useful about Nigel Wells came through soon.

It was a relief to get to Biddinghurst and arrive at the Old Rectory in the fresh sunlight. He found Locker with a concertina of print-out in his hands, in the small room, now made into their office, where Nigel Wells's hair had been found.

'Morning, Steve. I hope you're carrying a full confession there; it looks like the jumbo economy size, confessing to both: Cushion Killer Takes Up Knife.'

Locker grunted, and folded the print-out to present part of it before Bone. Clearly he too had not spent a refreshing night. 'Something here you might be interested in: the village has been dishing the dirt. Some of the stuff goes back to World War Two. People don't forget, round here.'

'But are they remembering what we want to know?'

Bone sat down, laid the paper before him and looked where Locker's blunt finger pointed.

'Reggie Merrick. He doesn't like people and not a lot of people are keen on him. Shay's impression is that folk are cagey about Scatchard and Wells, but willing to spill the beans on Merrick.'

Interesting indeed, if you bore in mind that Reggie Merrick had put in a request for Laurie Scatchard's ear, picking up a knife in what might not have been jest. If in jest, the story here showed what a bitter jest it must have been.

'Can you follow it, sir? I've got someone doing a résumé on these interviews and I thought of getting Shay to draw out a family tree to see if it would be clearer. This story mostly comes from the older people, but it hangs together.'

Hanging, in fact, was the point. Some time during the war, in the forties, Reggie Merrick's older brother Jack, home on leave, had got Rose Scatchard, Laurie's father's sister, pregnant. Not a disaster, perhaps, even in those days. An unmarried girl having a baby, in a small village full of disapproving eyes, would have had a hard time but, as Mrs Hemsted told Shay, there was a war on, people looked for her to marry Jack in the end, or to marry anyway. What made a disaster of it was that Jack Merrick, returning from the wars to be presented with a brand-new baby, refused to believe it was his.

'You'll see, sir, several people thought him in the wrong. Rose Scatchard was a good girl, never had eyes for anyone but Jack. General opinion was against him. You see here: "All very well for a young man still wanting to play the field, but he'd got the child", and Thomas Henshaw says: "He just didn't want to be lumbered. He knew it was his all right".'

'So what did she do? "Went mad"? What do they mean?'

'Unhinged. Killed her baby, sir.'

'Good God.' Bone turned up the next page, with a twinge of feeling for this long-ago desperate girl. 'Sent for trial. Found guilty. Hanged at Maidstone Jail in '46 . . . Poor girl. That would certainly account for Laurie Scatchard disliking Reggie Merrick, if you think of him holding his aunt's death as a family grievance. You'd think they could have pleaded "unsound mind" and got her off.'

'Unlucky in the judge, most likely.'

'But why the other way round? Why does Reggie take a knife to Laurie?'

'Read on, sir. It's what happened in '47 that counts.' Locker moved the sheet. 'Jack Merrick went off to seek his fortune in London; it's said people here turned against him. But he didn't find his fortune and he came back to stay with his father and his brother Reggie, they had a junk shop with second-hand furniture and so on.' Locker was warming up. 'Then—' he made a fist of one large hand—'he finds Tom Scatchard hasn't forgotten about his sister Rose. Very likely been brooding on it, waiting till Jack Merrick comes back—'

' "Like a spider in his web," to quote Mrs Ollenshaw.' Bone read. ' "He picked his time and he picked his fight. Jack was never up to his weight and Tom was a killer with his fists." '

'And that's what he did, sir,' concluded Locker triumphantly. 'Killed him. Knocked him down in a pub brawl. Jack hits his head on the fender of the fire in the snug, fractures his skull and dies that night.'

'Didn't they hold that it was accident? Was Tom Scatchard held responsible for the fender?' Mentally, Bone saw a younger Reggie as his brother, with his precise, disagreeable features, reeling before an onslaught by Laurie Scatchard transposed to his father Tom.

Locker was shaking his head. 'Everyone Shay spoke to that remembered it, they said Tom Scatchard meant to do for Jack one way or another. Here's Bert Thirlwell: "If Jack had not struck his head on that fender, Tom would have packed him off to his grave soon enough." '

'And this Tom Scatchard is dead.'

'Yes, sir. Died not so long ago at Saxhurst, where he went to live after Jack Merrick died. Laurie grew up there but he used to come here to see his grandparents and he moved here eventually and the word is Reggie Merrick's been on the boil ever since.'

'The sins of the father coming home to roost, so to speak. Not a pretty story.' Bone got up, oppressed suddenly by the smallness of the room, feeling the hatred in the story almost rising like a poisonous gas from the print-out on the table. He went to the long window and stood, hands in pockets, looking out at the overgrown garden of the Old Rectory, at a lawn that seemed never to have been allowed Laurie Scatchard's attentions, at hedges like tangled hair. People's minds could get choked, could overgrow with thoughts run wild that should have been pulled up years ago.

'And that's not all, sir. There's something Pat Fredricks heard. She was over at the Hollises' to see if she could talk to Chrissie yet.'

'Hang on a minute, Steve. Anything from Chrissie? Did Nigel offer her drugs?'

'Not a sausage from Chrissie. She's going to have a tooth out today in Tunbridge Wells; Midge Hollis is taking her and they don't look to be back till late. The poor kid's in pain, holding her face and crying, not able to talk.'

'Poor kid.' Bone, a coward at the dentist, sympathised. 'Hope to heaven she'll be up to it soon. We need a clue to what it is those boys are sitting on and she may provide it. So—what else was it you've got?'

Locker folded to another page of print-out. 'As to where Barbary was the night her brother got smothered.'

'Don't tell me. Taking books to Heather Armitage's car, along with half Biddinghurst.'

'No, for a wonder. But not so far off. Pat couldn't get Chrissie to say a word, but Midge came across: she was fetching back a couple of the foster-children from the party here on Saturday night—they were younger than the rest, and Darren had just brought Chrissie home as we know—and she noticed a car parked in Scatchard's driveway.'

Bone glanced at the map pinned up.

'She's all but sure it was Barbary Wells's car. She said it was hard to tell in that light because it's an odd sort of violet-blue with a silver sheen that Barbary goes around saying is like a butterfly's wing—'

'I can imagine. And was the butterfly inside?'

'So Mrs Hollis thinks. And if it was her car, it isn't likely anyone else was sitting there.'

Bone took a paperclip from a little tray in front of him and bent it out of shape. 'Barbary Wells waiting for Laurie, we must presume. Where was he?'

'According to Noah Pike, drinking with him at the Crossed Keys before they went to collect Noah's porn and Dolly's bodice-rippers to dump in the Armitage boot. But the interesting thing, sir,' Locker sat down opposite Bone and eased the knot of his tie, 'the interesting thing is, this fits in with what Dolly Pike told me, on Sunday morning when you had gone down to the fête for Miss Wells.'

Bone looked up from his mutilated paperclip, which now had one arm raised signalling for help. 'She heard a row next door, right? People shouting and making a noise.'

'That's it. If Barbary Wells was waiting for Scatchard, it wasn't to give him a kiss. Put together with the way she behaved to him in the Haunted House, she could be a suspect there, all right?'

Bone had almost straightened the paperclip, and now he made a random archipelago of holes in the print-out with the end of it. 'Though I don't fancy Butterfly Wells for that job, you never can tell. Stinging butterflies wouldn't be the oddest thing we've ever seen.' He skewered the paper to the table with the paperclip, which crumpled in the process. 'We're spoilt for choice, then? Lovers' tiff or family feud. And nothing more on the egregious Nigel, the charmer they love to hate.'

There had been pictures of him on the front page of every paper at the newsagent's, even *The Times,* smiling his false smile, small even teeth in a wide mouth, the eyes not friendly, the smile he had given Bone, Grizel and Cha an unbelievable two days ago. Thousands of people at breakfast all over the country must have studied that smile, trying to imagine the styled hair above it half-shaved, the face daubed blue and green. It wasn't the way he would have liked to be remembered. The teenagers, if they had been disappointed of his being discovered at the fête, had got an audience wider than they could have dreamt.

'I've got the team working on his papers now. They're checking his address book, letters, the usual.'

Bone nodded. This kind of patient, boring work most often came up with the clue that unravelled the whole mystery. Intuition might play a big part for him in deciding what line to pursue, but every case relied on the steady teamwork of the Incident Room. A man like Nigel, taking drugs, moving in the world of showbiz, might collect enemies as unconsciously as a dog collects burrs; the odds were long on any one of them popping down to Biddinghurst and pressing a cushion to his lips in farewell. Nevertheless, something might surface—perhaps something which would indicate just what it was the teenagers were so stubbornly united to conceal. Bone threw down the wounded paperclip.

'Right. So we pull in Reggie Merrick—'

'Cracked ribs notwithstanding.'

'Cracked ribs notwithstanding, and he can tell us a bit more what he did in the Haunted House. Miss Butterfly Wells, too, can come back from London if we ask *pretty-please*—'

The telephone rang briskly and Bone extended a hand as Locker picked it up.

'Forensic here. Thought you'd like to know. We've got prints off that knife you gave us. Not easy, they're smudged but they match up with—hang on, yes, sorry—Reginald Merrick.'

'Thank you very much.' Bone put down the phone and raised his eyebrows at Locker. 'Looks as if the family carries the day, Steve. Touching, isn't it?'

32

Fleur Scatchard could not be said to have passed a restless night. She had been too heavily sedated to toss and turn. However, when Kat brought her some breakfast on a tray on Monday morning, Fleur looked as if she had not slept for a week. Dark hollows round her eyes melded with the yellow and livid purple of the left one, and her long blonde hair lay in wisps and strands on the pillow; pillow, hair and face were pallid together. In the Rector's study were two prints, one of the *Lady of Shalott* lying in the boat that was to carry her to her death, the other Millais's *Ophelia* floating in the brook where she drowned. Kat had looked at them for so long that she no longer saw them, but both came to mind as she looked at Fleur.

She put the tray down. 'Coffee and cornflakes,' she said. 'Have a stab at it.'

Oh God, she thought, here am I talking about shoes to a man with one foot.

Fleur had started to sit up, but now flung herself back with a moan that irritated Kat. Sitting on the edge of the bed she took up the bowl of cornflakes, proffering it curtly. 'Go on. Have some. You've got to live.'

'No. No . . .' It was not clear whether Fleur refused cornflakes or the need to live, but she turned her head away and tears slid down her bruises. Kat regarded her thoughtfully and ate a spoonful of cereal.

'The police want to see you *at* the earliest. One of them's been bothering Daddy at the door.'

Fleur sat bolt upright, her blue eyes wide between the

wet lashes. 'Police! I can't talk to them. Kat, I can't. What can I say?'

'Say you can't remember anything. They'll like that.' Kat crunched the cornflakes and took more. 'You don't have to worry about the police. They can't prove a thing.' She pushed the bowl at Fleur, who took it automatically. 'Simply babble at them. They can't get cross with you. You have a right to act weird.'

Fleur was eating now, with application, as if she had forgotten what the process was like. A ray of sunlight crossed the room, falling like a spotlight on an Aubrey Beardsley print—a young man, naked to the hips, against a distant dark forest, raised a hand in farewell, grave and beautiful. The words *Ave atque Vale* were written in the space above his lifted arm, and Fleur had once had it explained to her by Kat. The young man, in a poem in Latin, was at a graveside greeting and saying goodbye to his brother, drowned far from home. Luckily Fleur did not see what the sun picked out, for she had cried bitterly at the story the first time round, without the association of present personal grief.

'Kat, would you do something for me?' Fleur put down the empty bowl and started on the slightly blackened toast. The Rector was used to whatever his daughter provided in the way of cooking, beyond the meals produced by the visiting woman who kept them from starvation; and Fleur too was in no mood to criticise. She had just discovered the effects of having eaten nothing since Saturday's party. Kat regarded her indulgently.

'What d'you want? Shall I do a striptease for the fuzz and take their minds off you? These flowers are from Phil, by the way.' She indicated a bunch of rather blowsy roses, white and yellow, thrust into a jug and already dropping petals on the bedside table. 'Out of Midge's front garden, I'd say, when Dave wasn't looking.'

Fleur stopped eating. 'Have they been at him? About Nigel?'

Kat laughed, shaking her hair back. 'They've been

grilling us all like Welsh Rabbits. Don't worry. I've told you, no one can prove anything. All they know is that Phil and Justin put him in the boot. Phil said so when he brought those. Have some more toast.'

'No. Thanks, I mean. I must get ready. I've got things to do. Will you—could you—get some of my things from the house. I *can't* go back there.'

'Shouldn't think they'd let you. They've more or less sealed it off. They're going through all your father's things.'

'Father's things? But why?'

'It's what they do.' Kat's tone was tolerant. 'Looking for who owed him money and so on. Or a grudge like Phil's grandpa.'

Fleur looked distraught. 'How will I get my things?'

'I'll have to pretend to be nice—the Rector's nice daughter. I'll get in. What do you want?'

'Oh,' Fleur pulled at the crumpled white teeshirt she was wearing. 'A dress. Something clean. And—do you think they'll watch you all the time if they let you in?'

Kat shrugged, and twitched the leather pelmet she wore for a skirt a little higher. 'Only the parts I select for them to watch. What's the idea?'

Fleur hesitated. 'Well, I need money. There's some in a purse in the drawer under my bed—you know.'

'With all your old cuddly toys. Yes.'

'The police won't have taken it, will they?'

'We'll find out, won't we?' Kat got up, suddenly brisk, and smiled at Fleur. 'The bathroom's free and Daddy's off helping old Mrs Masterman to conk out peacefully, so you've got a clear run. Horrible Heather won't call, because Daddy's out, Phil said he'd leave you to rest, and if the police come just don't answer the door. Super-woman's off to give it a twirl.'

After Kat had slammed the front door, Fleur got out of bed and stood, testing herself for steadiness in a world that had a tendency to slip sideways. She had something to do that day which was going to take all her determination.

Half an hour later, she was peering between the bedroom curtains, anxiously, at the street, when she saw Kat crossing the road towards the house. In a minute Kat was with her, tossing the holdall on to the bed, offering the purse.

'There. I was an age because I had to get pig permission for every move I made; but even they couldn't see why you shouldn't be allowed clean clothes, so I got my way. The young pig who was supposed to keep an eye on all I did kept an eye devotedly on my rear while I was scrabbling in the drawer under your bed and so he totally missed my taking your purse under a teeshirt.' She watched Fleur open the bag and count the notes inside. 'I don't know if they'd have let me have it anyway. You planning a bribe for the Super?'

'I can't tell you what I'm going to do.' Fleur looked almost manic as she clutched the purse to her chest. 'The police might ask you and find out somehow—'

'And do you think I'd tell? Thumbscrews went out of fashion a few years back, hadn't you heard?'

Fleur ignored this. She was at the window again, peering into the street.

'My God! There's police everywhere.'

'Their Incident Room's next door. Where we had the party.'

Fleur was at the mirror now, sweeping back the fine blonde hair to examine her eye and cheek. 'Oh no. It shows like anything. Everyone would know who I was. What am I going to do?'

'You don't want people knowing who you are? Easy. A cover-up job. People do it every day.' Kat went to her dressing-table, bare of frills or flounces but adorned with cats given by friends—an inappropriately twee kitten garlanded with flowers; a little china cat on its back holding a red ball in raised paws, which her father had brought from Limoges; a sleek minimalist sleeping cat in wood. She wrestled a drawer open. 'There you are. I put the stage make-up here after Easter. Stuff here would cover anything, we ought to offer it to the pigs to cover up their Fraud Squad operations. Want me to put it on for you?'

But Fleur thought she could cope, so Kat left her to dress and make up on her own. When she returned, Fleur was wearing a coral dress that threw a rosy light into her face, improving its normal pallor. The black eye had disappeared under a careful layer of Max Factor, and Fleur had added a touch of coral blusher and a generous amount of mascara and eyeshadow. Kat regarded her with approval.

'Great! And now the final touch.' She brought out, from behind her back, something which Fleur at first thought was a small woolly dog. 'I got this from the wigs-and-costumes box in the attic. They'll see just one of Daddy's parishioners fresh from a weep on the Rector's kind shoulder.'

Fleur giggled and, turning to the glass again, she bundled up her fair tresses. She fitted the wig on, manoeuvred it down to her ears and tucked in stray hair. The brown curls transformed her, from a sprite to a faun.

'Perfect. You look a bit like Madge Prescott. She's always round here bending Daddy's ear. She's got a violent boyfriend, a drinking problem and a new baby.'

'No! No! I can't! I can't!'

Damn. Damn, thought Kat. She's off.

Fleur had torn off the wig and dashed it down. She bent to seize the hem of the dress and pull it off. She sat down suddenly on the bed, tears threatening the make-up.

Kat was beside her at once, cursing herself for once more saying the wrong thing, putting an arm round her.

'You'll be all right. I can give you something that will make you feel much better. Left over from the party.' She produced a wad of tissue from her pocket and shook out two pills into Fleur's eagerly extended palm. 'If you're still dopey after all that stuff the doctor zonked you out with, you need these to get your head together.'

Fleur needed no encouragement. There was still water in the glass by the bed and she washed the pills down. As she was swallowing, a loud knock on the front door made her nearly choke.

'Oh God! Suppose it's the police?'

'If it is, you can cope. Get back into bed, and when they come, act loopy. Just babble.'

So it was that Bone, attended by Locker and Fredricks, mounted the Rectory stairs at Kat's heels, and found the bereaved Fleur in what seemed no better state than when he had last seen her. Kat left them to it, but Fleur, though not now in hysterics, was making no more sense. Any attempt to ask her what had occurred on Sunday morning produced pure incoherence.

The sunlight had moved from one Beardsley print to another: a pilgrim caught in a thicket of briars stretched longing hands towards a distant mountain. Bone glanced at it as they listened to Fleur's ramblings. She seemed to be quoting from some play. He looked at the picture again as they went out and thought it expressed their frustration better than words.

'You didn't stay long.' Kat Purdey came out of a downstairs room, cool and self-assured as usual, in a green teeshirt and a black leather skirt that was, in Locker's eyes, literally no advance on the shorts she had worn yesterday.

Although she was not smiling, Bone had the impression that she was amused. He said, 'The police surgeon thought she would be recovered sufficiently to talk to us today. Do you know if she's been taking any more sedatives?' He didn't add 'or anything else', as Kat was unlikely to tell him had Fleur been sniffing, gulping or snorting whatever had put her so effectively out of action.

Kat opened the front door for them, raising her eyebrows. 'Could be. I don't keep her under surveillance.

She's got a lot to forget. You can't expect her to spring back.'

Dismissed, they stood in the Rectory porch for a minute, Locker grumbling under his breath. Fredricks, coiling more securely the cable of the recorder they hadn't been able to use, remarked, 'She's beginning to get over it, I'd say, sir. Did you notice how much make-up she had on?'

33

The night porter at Ballester Mansions was not surprised to be asked for Damien Winter's flat, so late, by the goofy-looking blonde. He thought she was under the weather and definitely under age. That was Winter's style. People like Winter could get away with bloody anything. If he himself were to lay a finger on one of those appetising schoolgirls who passed his own door at home on their way to the comprehensive up the road, he'd be in the chokey before you could say 'Gotcha'. This stoned-looking little tramp was going to land in a luxurious bed with Damien Winter and the only person liable to disturb them was the manservant with the morning tea; or morning champagne maybe. The porter shut her into the lift and pressed the penthouse button, and his sigh echoed the lift's noise. He went back to his pools coupon; if he were to win a million or two, if Lady Luck showed him her face instead of her arse he could be like Damien Winter, at this moment, probably welcoming that spaced-out kid. Money opened all legs.

The manservant whom the porter had visualised bringing in the morning champagne was ready to arrive with the evening's supply when he heard the lift stop. He too was not surprised to see the blonde, nor did he look at her too closely; so many of them passed literally through Mr Winter's hands that any variety was indistinguishable. They didn't even need to be blonde as long as they were cradle-fresh. Powys was beyond approving or disapproving. His function was to provide perfect service and be very well paid. He reserved his standards for that. Arranging olives and crisps in Chinese rice-bowls on the silver tray, he carried it through to the sitting room where Mr Winter was already pouring drinks. The girl was gazing round admiringly, as well she might.

The room was huge, the ceiling domed and palest blue like a spring sky. At night it was made to glow mysteriously by soft up-lighting concealed in the columns that seemed to support the dome; now on this summer evening it was dappled with gold discs reflected from the surface of the swimming pool. Outside on the marble terrace, and set about with palms in huge terracotta pots, the pool still caught the gleam from the setting sun. When Mr Winter had ushered the girl in to dinner, already prepared in the room beyond, Powys would press the switches that lit the palms in dramatic silhouette and made the pool glitter under the night sky. Mr Winter liked to impress. Powys supposed it likely he would be hearing splashes and shrieks from the pool before the night was over. A fine night, all that lovely—and warm—water, the roof open to the stars: what more natural than to take off one's clothes and have a swim? Not that the girls who came here needed much persuading to do anything. Mr Winter had not only money. He had power of a different sort. If he chose, he could put this girl on silver screens all over the country—all over the world.

Powys put the last touches to the elegant little supper he had laid out, hearing the laughter next door. The last blonde hadn't known what cutlery to use for what, and this one looked as naïve, but with Mr Winter they need only know how to use one thing. Powys had no idea just how famous Mr Winter was about to make this particular girl.

At almost the same moment that Powys put his finger on the light switches to illuminate the pool, where only the stars in the night sky above glinted, someone was breaking a side window of Nigel Wells's house in Biddinghurst. The noise of the glass breaking had been timed in the middle of an outburst of barking from a pair of German shepherd dogs that lived at the end of the lane. As they barked at anything, significant or not, or just to keep each other company, no one could think that for once they had something to bark about. Most likely they were too absorbed in their own enthusiasm to hear the small crack, and the glass fell indoors. A hand in a thick glove raised the handle and pulled the window ajar enough for the bar on the sill to be flipped from its peg. A body crouched on the sill and climbed in. As the owner of the cottage was occupying a slot in a Tunbridge Wells mortuary, there was no clutter of dishes on the draining-board inside to make a noise or impede.

A pencil torch showed the way across the red-tiled floor, but the hand holding it jerked violently and switched it off when suddenly, dreadfully, a sound broke the house's silence. The front door was opening.

The intruder, crouching at once behind the kitchen table, waited for lights to be switched on. There were quiet footsteps, but no light—except that the half-open kitchen door showed, after a moment, the light of another torch—a brasher beam than the pencil torch's furtive ray. The intruder had only to follow it, which he did so quietly that the woman with the torch had no idea that she was not alone—that someone was so close that if she had stopped and flashed the torch about she would have seen him. She was too absorbed in her quest, and by the time she had reached the place she wanted, so had he: behind the thick, lined curtains drawn back at the living-room window.

Her torch had not hesitated on its path across the floor. Hers was not an uninstructed search. The armchair in the corner by the dresser had to be pulled forward and she gasped a little over that. Then she set to work properly. He breathed in the musty smell of the curtains as he watched. This was perfect, exactly what he needed.

After that, the only problem was to be out of the room, out of the house, before her. Luckily she was making enough noise pushing back the armchair to cover the shadow of sound he made crossing to the kitchen. He trusted to her being too anxious to get away herself to be alert to his scuffling as he slid out of the kitchen window.

The front door opened again and she stepped out, with no torchlight to guide her or give her away. Nevertheless she was being watched, by different eyes.

Jonathan Cade had not despaired; once the village settled down a bit from its morbid excitement over the drama of involvement in two murders and seeing itself on television, he hoped to get more of the material he needed for his book. He had not even begun, for example, to make proper inquiries about the horseman alleged to gallop along the coast road that passed north of the village. People had heard this on moonlit nights when walking their dogs. The dogs cowered or ran when he passed, and afterwards refused to go along the road. Jonathan hoped this would prove a particularly interesting manifestation. He had read of similar hearings on other roads round here, that led from Canterbury to the coast, for the knights who murdered Thomas à Becket at the cathedral altar had parted after the deed and fled, making for France. What more likely than that riding, with such a powerful emotion of guilt, remorse and horror, should drive them still, beyond death, along roads they had ridden with the saint's blood on their souls?

It would make such a good section of his chapter on the ghosts of Kent.

Charlie Iden said that only last month Mr Birkett had

had trouble with his terrier along that road when they heard a rider in the near distance. No rider had turned up, but the terrier had gone through the foot of a hedge with a speed that Mr Birkett at the time put down to rabbits and led Mrs Birkett, when the terrier arrived trembling and whimpering on the doorstep soon afterwards, to believe that her husband had met with a frightful accident. By rotten chance, the Birketts were on their annual visit to their daughter in Provence. It was annoying that the terrier, which had of course been left here in the care of a neighbour, had probably seen a lot more than had Mr Birkett but couldn't help.

Yet Jonathan was here to collect information, if he could, from the invisible horse's mouth, you might say. He was making for the coast road, and after midnight, because Charlie Iden had heard that while Mr Birkett generally went out earlier, on this particular night the Birketts had sat up watching a film and the terrier had been taken out to get his leak well after midnight. The time might be crucial. Research had assured Jonathan that although some of these intruders from the past were not fussy about requiring darkness or any particular ambience in which to operate, some of them appeared to work to a species of timetable not discernible from this side of the Styx. Although this was far from the time of year at which the saint had been martyred, Jonathan thought it was at least worth a try.

Everything smelt fresh and alive. It was cool after dark and Jonathan had put on a bodywarmer, stored his torch, notebook and battery recorder in its convenient pockets, and set off up the village street towards the coast road. He was aware of an excitement tinged with reluctance. Impossible to forget the shock of that thing with no face in the church, fake or not, and that drifting, moaning girl in the garden. In coming to Biddinghurst perhaps he had woken the psychic in himself, something which, although his interest in ghosts dated back to

childhood, he had never yet found. It was more disturbing than he had imagined.

The street was empty. Only a few lights glowed in
upper windows here and there where perhaps some people were still getting to bed or sitting up reading or discussing the events that had made Biddinghurst, for a day
at least, nationally famous. As Jonathan walked past the
antique shop with brass tea-kettles and a quilt in the
window, a small face, pale in the gloom, advanced to a
windowpane and gave him a start, but another look
showed it to be the shop moggy minding the store. He
tapped the glass with a finger but it glanced at him and
away, not interested. He walked on, thinking of Barbary
Wells because of her cats. Poor woman! How devastated
she must be by what had become of her brother. She
could hardly lack for comforters, of course, that choleric
Henry Purdey one of them, though the gypsy charmer
Laurie Scatchard was permanently off the list. What
awful things had been happening . . . Yet here he was, on
the prowl for an echo of awful things that had happened
perhaps six hundred years ago.

By this time he had reached the part of the village
that had only an occasional house, with lanes leading off
to a cottage or two. Down one of these, he recollected—
yes, this one here—Barbary lived, almost opposite to her
brother's cottage, but Charlie Iden said she had gone to
London. He glanced down the lane and saw a light, a
faint shifting light, behind the windows of one small
house. It was the one belonging to the dead man.

To his credit Jonathan did not hesitate. He ran down
the lane, on the close-mown grass verge for quiet. Natural or supernatural, he was going to find out who—or
what—it was. He had established in his mind instantly
that the police would not be the source of a light like
that. He thought of burglars—most probable that someone was exploiting the unoccupied state of the place.
Didn't professional thieves read newspaper funeral no-
tices and visit houses when everyone would be at the

graveyard? There were murderers abroad in Biddinghurst, why not thieves?

It did not, luckily, occur to him that there might be both.

To his disappointment, when he ran across the cottage lawn, the light had vanished. He stood irresolute in the clouded moonlight, steadying his breathing. The light might not be of this physical world. Lights that came and went, like will-o'-the-wisp, had always been regarded as omens.

As he debated, moving forward into the inky shadow of a yew-tree near the gravel path, the question of the supernatural was settled for him. The front door was eased open, and a woman glanced about from the protection of the porch before stepping out. She softly shut the door and had hardly taken two paces, and Jonathan was about to accost her, when the light thud of running feet made him turn his head. Someone came round the side of the house, fast, on a collision course with the woman.

It happened too quickly. She fell beside a yew-tree by the path; the runner stooped over her for a second and Jonathan expected an apology and an offer of help. Instead, the runner was instantly off again, leaving the woman gasping and sprawling.

Jonathan reached her side just as she managed to struggle to her hands and knees. There was a heady smell of scent. He took her arm.

She gave a moan and looked up at him, crouched in fear. The moon came swimming out of the cloud and obliged with a theatrical spotlight, nothing new to her. It was Barbary Wells.

34

Tuesday morning began one of those late August days on which there is a faint, exciting hint of autumn long before its time. The summer is showing its fatigue. Trees droop heavy worn foliage with one or two traitorous gleams of yellow, or even red, where leaves are considering their rest. The air too has that unmistakable tinge, not yet of bonfires but of the first cool breath. Bone leant out of the window of the flat in Tunbridge Wells and sniffed the breeze.

Another night's sleep had offered no illumination of the problem before him. There was Reggie Merrick in the cells waiting to be questioned again this morning, but Bone had little expectation of getting any further than last night when all the bile of Reggie against the Scatchards had burst out as though he had been waiting for this moment in the bleak interview room to put literally on record the way in which his family had been treated, pouring out pent-up rage as if to put his grievances officially before them, regardless of all their efforts to get him to the point.

To Bone's mind, the Scatchards' grievance was far worse than that of the Merricks, but Reggie saw it otherwise. Reggie's brother had had an affair with Rose Scatchard and then rejected the child as not his. Very possibly he had consoled himself with others while he was away, making it easy for him to suppose she would have done the same; Reggie might believe Jack was justified, and so hardly responsible for Rose going what he described as 'totally doolally' when Jack refused to father her baby.

'Is it sane to murder your baby?' Reggie had demanded, glaring from Locker to Bone. It was clear he thought his brother sensible to have refused to have any more to do with such a woman. Woman! Bone recalled that Rose had been hardly twenty-one when she was hanged at Maidstone. As he'd said to Locker when they came out of the interview room, the question was not whether Reggie had killed Laurie, but why Laurie hadn't killed Reggie.

Locker couldn't understand why Reggie was so wholly convinced that Tom Scatchard had set out to kill Jack Merrick. He might well have wanted to, holding him responsible for Rose's awful death, but how could he have knocked the man down in such a way that he would be sure to split his skull on a steel fender? Reggie, however, had obstinately insisted that it was an intentional act; and the village had agreed, during house-to-house inquiries, in stating that Tom Scatchard had bitter malice in his heart towards his sister's destroyer.

Strangely and pathetically, Reggie Merrick seemed to have no idea that this airing of his resentment gave weight to the possibility that he had stabbed Laurie Scatchard. Confronted with the evidence from Forensic over his fingerprints on the knife, he had not been at all concerned. Naturally his prints were on the knife. Hadn't he seized it at the sight of Laurie handed it to him, as it were, on a plate, in order to make his remark about wanting an ear?

Bone was inclined to accept this, though he did not say so. However, when Reggie demanded scornfully how he could have taken the knife away with him to stick it into Laurie's back, Bone thought it would have been quite possible. Whoever was lifting the dish-cover on Laurie's head—Reggie declared he could not remember, and not one of them—except Kat Purdey as Morticia and Justin Rafferty as Death—was recognisable under muslin veils—was likely to have kept track of the knives, of which plenty lay on the table. Besides, confusion had been deliberately created. The players passed and re-passed, hanging curtains obscured much of what was going on, such light as there was had been fitful, the music with its urgent heartbeat created a sense of distraction as Bone had found when the tape was replayed to him, and at the time when Reggie might have abstracted the knife, the strongest light had come from a torch beamed by the cover-lifter on Laurie's mould-encrusted features.

Reggie had not been shaken by any of their suggestions as to what he might have done. He remained his disagreeable self. Once he had expressed his indignation at being brought in at all—even though it had been done discreetly in an unmarked police car—and at having to spend the night in a cell, suffering as he was from broken ribs; and once he had vented his rage at his brother's death at Tom Scatchard's hands, he was content to sit and stare at them, denying with sarcastic incredulity that he could have murdered Laurie. Yes, he detested him but, as he elegantly put it, he'd as soon have stabbed a turd.

To Bone it had the ring of innocence. Locker was not convinced. They might get more out of him this morning after a night in the cells, but when the thirty-six hours they were allowed to hold him were up, they must charge him or let him go. Locker was for charging him on the evidence of the fingerprints alone, while Bone pointed out that they were smudged as if the knife-handle had been wrapped in a fold of curtain before the blade was thrust into Laurie Scatchard. It might be simple coincidence that the murderer had picked up the knife Reggie had left his prints on. Locker countered with: if the murderer wasn't Reggie, how had he or she avoided putting their own prints on it? Or was it one of the teenagers who had seen him pick up the knife? In any case, the same thing applied. In the darkness and noise and movement, how could anyone spot which it had been? Bone felt they would be very lucky indeed to find out.

In the midst of these gloomy thoughts, two things happened. Grizel called up the stairs that breakfast was ready, and the phone rang. He shouted that he was on his way and picked up the bedside phone.

It was the Chief. How far had Bone got with the Nigel Wells case? Bone suppressed the desire to make funny noises on the phone and pretend they'd got a crossed line. Instead he spoke serenely of 'fresh developments' and of his hopes of 'getting back' to the Chief with 'further information' very soon. By the irritable tone of the Chief's voice, he hadn't had breakfast yet either, and Bone suspected that someone had already been on to *him* demanding results this morning. There is always a whole hierarchy of pressure to be applied.

'And have you seen the papers this morning, Robert? Winter's dead.'

'Winter?' Bone inquired, thinking: I know autumn's coming but is winter cancelled?

'Damien Winter. The director. Drowned in his pool last night, apparently. The Press are trumpeting the connection with Wells.'

'The connection with Wells?' Bone was aware of sounding stupid.

'Aren't you awake yet, Robert? Damien Winter directed that series Wells was in *and* the last TV film he made. The media are behaving as if sudden death was catching.'

'But if Winter fell in his pool, Wells's death was no accident. That's an established fact.'

'Pity then that you can't establish who did it.'

'Are London satisfied Winter's death was in fact an accident?'

'I'm in touch with London over the matter; I'll suggest they ferret about a bit. After all, we found our accident wasn't one, didn't we?' The Chief, thus assuming a responsibility for all the section's painstaking work, said goodbye, cheerful at the prospect of spoiling someone else's morning.

Bone put down the phone and stood a moment looking at the unmade bed, not seeing it. There could only be a link if Winter's death were no accident and, even then, only by a long stretch of the imagination. True, elastic imagination was sometimes just what was needed.

'I poured your tea, Robert. It'll get cold.'

Time to stimulate the brain. Bone ran downstairs into an aroma of toast and Grizel's coffee and the sound of Cha's radio—a bouncy tune with handclaps like applause. Perhaps this was the day on which something useful turned up. After the Chief's reminder that the world, his wife and dog were all a-quiver to hear if Nigel Wells's killer had been caught, he'd better get straight to the Incident Room and hear reports at first-hand there. Locker must interview Merrick on his own and come on to Biddinghurst, preferably with a full confession. Merrick at least should have spent not too bad a night, the police surgeon having examined his ribs and given him painkillers and ordered a supplementary pillow; but it was too much to hope that his temper would show an improvement.

Bone had not expected amazing developments when he got to Biddinghurst, so he was not disappointed. He was told that Fredricks had already gone to the Hollises' to see if she could interview Chrissie while her mother was there getting the children's breakfast. For some reason, Bone had a picture of illimitable little Hollises and foster children, and he hoped Fredricks could fight her way through this to get an interview. Who knew what she might come up with? Children of twelve have not always acquired the defence mechanisms so perfected in adolescents. With a little luck, Chrissie might not even be sure what she ought to be lying about.

'And there's a Mr Cade asking to see you, sir. He won't talk to us lot.'

Shay was trying to be amused at this rejection, but it

had got to him. Bone smiled involuntarily, amused still more to see Shay brighten in response. 'So will you see him, sir? He's a sort of ghostbuster—or not so much a buster, more a collector, from what I make out. Weird either way.'

Bone consulted the notes. He was right in remembering Cade as a patron of the Haunted House; professional interest, no doubt, but he had been unable to give Fredricks any information of use. Wouldn't it be nice if he'd come to say he'd forgotten to tell Fredricks that he'd picked up the knife Reggie Merrick had brandished and had stuck it, wrapped in curtain, into Laurie's back? Perhaps, to collect spirits, he simply separated them from bodies.

He was shown in. Bone saw a tall, rather gangling man with the light red hair that got called 'Carrots' at school, whom he had seen briefly at Nigel Wells's door on Saturday. Invited to sit down opposite Bone, he did so, cleared his throat, said, 'Well,' and then cleared his throat again. Bone maintained an encouraging silence and finally Cade managed to begin.

'You see, I'm afraid I'm here against someone's wishes.' He hesitated. 'It's because—you see I saw something last night which I think was dangerous but the person affected doesn't think it was. She didn't want me to report it.'

Bone raised his eyebrows. 'At the moment, Mr Cade, anything that seems dangerous in this district needs reporting. You have to remember we have a murderer at large.'

At this alarming reminder, Cade's face cleared. 'Then I'm right. That's what I told Miss Wells but she insisted—'

'Miss Barbary Wells.' Locker had tried all the day before to get hold of her. There had been no answer from the Chelsea flat; when they finally got in touch with Dr Beth Dillon at her Wimpole Street clinic, they got no joy from her but a little grief instead: Dr Beth was firm, even trenchant, in her denial of any knowledge of Barbary's whereabouts—yes, she had gone to the clinic and no, she was no longer there—but also, in Dr Beth's opinion, privacy was the paramount need if Barbary were to recover from the blow Fate had dealt her.

'Miss Wells knows nothing material to your inquiry and I cannot agree your policy of harassment.' Dr Beth closed the connection before Locker could say that he did not want the relevance of Miss Wells's knowledge decided for him, thanks.

Now the elusive Miss Wells was in Biddinghurst?

'I was walking up at that end of the village, you see, late at night—'

'What time of night?'

'Oh, towards midnight, it must have been, because I wanted to be on the coast road by midnight.' Cade paused, shifted his glasses and his feet and explained. 'I'm writing a book on ghosts and there are stories of a horseman on the coast road . . .' He studied Bone's expression, saw nothing there to imply that looking for ghosts on roads was not a perfectly normal activity for a sane man, and he went on more firmly. 'I was passing the end of the lane where Mr Wells had his cottage, and I glanced that way and there was a light in one of the windows, a sort of flickering light, I mean. I went to see what it was.'

Bone's mind had leapt ahead of him. Barbary Wells, at midnight in her brother's cottage: what was she up to? A flickering light? A torch. Why not turn the lights on? Now Cade was fidgeting. He had come to what she had not wanted him to report.

'Well, when I got there the light had gone. I was sure I'd seen it and I was standing dithering in the garden when she, Miss Wells I mean, though I didn't know it was, came out of the front door and then suddenly this person came running round the side of the house and bumped into her and she fell. I thought he'd stop and help but he just bent over her a second and then ran on. I was coming to help her and I thought it was funny the way he behaved, and anyway a jogger wouldn't be in the garden. Then after I'd helped her up she got down again on all fours and looked about with the torch.'

'What was she looking for?'

'She was so upset! I got down to help and I asked her what we were looking for and she said it was a contact lens and she'd found it. But . . .' He hesitated again. Bone made an encouraging, interrogative noise and he swallowed and went on. 'I'm sure she said, "Oh God, he's taken them", when she first began to look, and when she came out of the house she'd had the torch in one hand though it wasn't switched on, and when she shut the door I'm pretty sure she had to put this packet under her arm to have a hand free. A folder or packet about this size.' He indicated with both hands an oblong shape of about ten by six, and thick. 'She said it wasn't at all odd, someone running past like that, just an acci-dent. I saw her to her door of course, and she insisted I shouldn't tell anyone about it. She said there was trouble enough without fuss over something that didn't matter. But suppose she's in danger? Her brother was murdered.'

'This runner. Man or woman? Did you see the face?'

Cade held his glasses up on the bridge of his nose while he thought. 'Too tall, I'd say, for a woman. I didn't see his face. But you know?' He gave a quick apologetic smile. 'I got two feelings at the same time. That he was old and young, I mean. I couldn't think why until I'd worked it out on the way back. He ran like a young man, very light and fast, but his hair was white. I suppose it was the moonlight.'

Bone considered this, quickening with a definite ela-tion. He leant forward and pressed the button on the intercom.

35

Pat Fredricks had to lean on the bell before any Hollis came to answer the door. The moment it was opened, by a seven-year-old with a piece of toast in his mouth like a dog with a bone, she could hear why. Breakfast was a convivially noisy occasion here.

After she had picked her way over and past the bikes in the narrow passage, and been welcomed by Midge Hollis into the kitchen at the back, she was offered a cup of tea in a voice necessarily raised above the yells of two small boys contesting possession of a jumbo packet of cornflakes. Chrissie was not present. Midge, a small lively woman in jeans, teeshirt and a butcher's apron, poured the tea from a large yellow pot and shouted at the boys to be quiet.

The quiet she was asking for broke out very suddenly when the cornflake packet, violently jerked from one pair of hands, erupted in the other, spewing its contents over both boys, the table and the floor. Midge seized the moment of shock.

'Now you can both go without. Quick, upstairs and make your beds. I'll clear this up. You'll only make more mess. Off with you now!'

As they trailed, disconsolate and crackling, from the room, Midge turned to the boy who had opened the door and was now spreading butter on another round of toast. 'Alan, go and get Chrissie. Tell her not to bother washing, just come down right away.'

Alan lodged his toast in his mouth, without protest or comment, and crackled out on his errand. Midge began brushing up the cornflakes on the blue checked cloth

186

into a heap, while Fredricks drank her tea from a mug with a frog on the side and a small chip on the edge. From the window she could see the orchard-like garden with long grass and the apple-trees and the caravan beached half-way down, everything shining in the morning sun.

'What the boys did—you know—with Nigel Wells at the party. Dave and I went and talked to them after your people left last night. We were so anxious . . .' Midge stood with her hands flat either side of the cornflake pile on the table, and spoke fast in an undertone. 'It *was* cruel. It was inexcusable. But they meant it for a joke. I mean, if somebody else hadn't found him and put the cushion—I've known those boys for most of their lives. Their part in this *was* just a cruel joke.'

Fredricks had no time to make more than a noncommittal sound before Chrissie appeared in the doorway, a pale child in a red towelling dressing-gown, who yawned, stopped and held her jaw. Mousy hair straggled unbrushed over her shoulders. She put her hand down, showing one hamster cheek. Midge moved to put an arm round her shoulders, while Chrissie eyed the room in disgust, remarking, 'Beasts. They're making a mess upstairs now. Duvets and pillows all over the place. I don't want breakfast.'

'Sit down and don't be silly. I'll make you some bread and milk, nice and warm.'

Chrissie kicked cornflakes aside as she came to the table. She sat down facing Fredricks, who reflected that Midge might have a lot on her hands but the children she was bringing up seemed to do as they were told. Chrissie even attempted a polite, lopsided smile.

'Hi. Have you found out who killed them yet?'

'Not yet. I expect we shall quite soon,' Fredricks replied cheerfully, untruthfully. 'Do you think you'll be able to help us today by answering a few questions?'

Chrissie nodded, and put a hand to her cheek as if to make sure it would behave. ' 'Fraid I can't talk very well.

I'll come out on the tape like Donald Duck. It's gone down but it's still all sore.'

'Oh, it's just a few questions first, and then we might record.'

Chrissie was silent for a moment and Fredricks wondered if she were disappointed. She had evidently heard that the others got recorded. It might lend some importance to the interview. It wasn't that, however.

'Does Mummy have to be here?'

Midge, busy at the stove behind her heating milk, turned with a look of surprise, but held her tongue.

'Yes. People your age have to have someone like a parent present when they're interviewed. It's to make sure we don't bully you.'

Chrissie half smiled, but pressed on. 'Does it have to be Mummy?'

Midge stopped pouring the milk over the bread, and returned Fredricks's glance with astonishment. She finished pouring and put the bowl before Chrissie, and rested her hand on her daughter's shoulder, saying, 'Love, is it something you don't want me to hear?'

Chrissie nodded. Her mother, looking down at the top of her unbrushed head, moved her hand to draw Chrissie's hair back over her shoulder and then to smooth it from her ear. 'If it's something nasty—' her eyes consulted Fredricks with something like anguish—'would it be good to get it out, like a tooth, say. It might feel better afterwards.'

'Is it to do with Nigel Wells?' Fredricks kept her voice casual but her pulse-rate had risen. This might be something very useful to the Super. She sprang the button on her Biro and waited. Beyond the open windows a blackbird started scolding; a cat must be in the long grass. Chrissie looked down at the bread and milk, fiddling with the spoon.

'I'm glad he's dead. He was disgusting.'

Midge gallantly continued smoothing the swathe of hair. 'Was he, love? Tell this lady why.'

The blackbird's scolding had become frantic. Chrissie looked out towards it and whispered, clogged by her swollen mouth. 'He took pictures of me with my clothes off. He said it was just for fun but it wasn't fun.'

Midge put her hands to her face. 'But why, why did you let him?'

Chrissie shrugged and began to push the bread about. 'He'd said he'd get those tickets. You know, the ones to Archangel's concert Dad took me to London for. No one could get them and they cost a bomb.'

'I thought he gave them out of pure good nature! He was always giving things to you kids.'

'Yes, well.' Chrissie got to work on the bread and milk, spooning it in cautiously on the good side. Midge came to sit by her, heavily, as if she had been hit physically by what she had heard. She started to ask something and then, heroically, closed her mouth and looked at Fredricks.

'Did he do anything else but take pictures?'

'No. Yeugh.'

'Do you know where the pictures are that he took?'

There was a prompt, pleased answer. 'Yes. Justin's got them. He came to tell me in the middle of the night. He said it was all right and I wasn't to worry. Before he went out to the caravan.'

Instinctively, Fredricks looked out of the window. No sound from the blackbird, no sign of the cat, but someone moving out there in the long grass under the apple-trees beyond the caravan, and a slow curl of smoke rising.

Dropping Biro and pad, she jumped up just as the radio in her bag bleeped. She nearly overturned her chair to reach the back door, and she was answering the bleep with a code call as she ran down the garden making for the smoke.

The grass was soaking Justin's feet, and the blackbird was making a fuss. The incinerator, a wire-mesh basket with the charred twigs of Dave's last bonfire in it, stood on a patch of scorched earth that weeds were trying to colonise, well clear of the apple-trees. Justin thrust newspaper into the basket, catching his knuckle on the wire and cursing, and put the packet on top. It seemed an age before the newspaper caught; of course it was damp—most things from near the caravan sink were. He crouched and blew at it. The edges blackened, thin red fingers running along and then going out, while a little tower of smoke idly built itself upwards. A flame licked. He heard the kitchen door open and turned his head. The policewoman from the Old Rectory was haring over the grass towards him.

He panicked.

Fredricks, crying out to him to stop, was met with a flat-hander in the chest which sent her sprawling. He was striking another match when she scrambled up and, wasting no effort in tangling with him, reached for the packet she could see in the incinerator. By this time smoke was looping into the air and the plastic beginning to curl. Justin dropped the match almost on her foot and grabbed her arm, trying to twist her away from the fire.

Phil Merrick, yawning in the caravan doorway, tried to make sense of the wrestling match beyond the apple-trees and the sight of two policemen on a fast course towards it.

'You did the right thing, Mr Cade, in coming to us, and we're very grateful.' Bone, shaking hands with Jonathan as he dismissed him, let none of his surging impatience show. Fredricks would bring in Justin, of that he was sure, but at this moment he needed, far more, to see Barbary Wells. Shay and Vigo had been sent off with firm instructions to return with her regardless of any wiles, pleas or excuses of ill-health, and Shay had promised to summon an ambulance to transport her if he had to. Until she came, Bone was in a silent fret to find out exactly what it was she had gone to look for in

Nigel's cottage, although he had something of an idea what it might be. He was angry that she had so easily got in; true, they had thought she was in London, but who was supposed to be keeping an eye on Nigel's cottage? He gave orders for it now to be searched thoroughly from roof to ground. The superficial search on Sunday was clearly inadequate; at the time they had asked for the drugs squad with a sniffer dog to come, and they were due this afternoon. Bone pictured fleetingly the chintz and oak interior so proudly displayed by Nigel only a couple of days ago. Plenty of hiding places among those beams, behind the bricks of the inglenook, for what it was he had to hide.

Jonathan Cade, on his way to the door, paused to glance at the garden. 'This must be the garden I was looking into on Saturday night.'

'Really?'

'Of course, you can't ever be sure about psychic manifestations. You can be deceived by people or you can deceive yourself, particularly if you want to see something and have an idea what it is, but I certainly didn't expect to see this girl—' he gestured out of the window—'sort of floating about in the grass and moaning. And twisting her arms about. I thought at one moment she was holding something in her arms and then she gripped her shoulders. It was pitiful.'

'Really?' said Bone again. 'Where were you at the time?' He did not picture Cade at the teenagers' party.

'Next door. In the churchyard actually. I looked over the fence . . .' Cade was embarrassed. He pushed his spectacles firmly into place. 'I had reason to think someone had been playing a hoax on me and I wanted to see where they could have gone to; then I heard that moaning . . .'

'I understood there was loud music here that night.'

'I think they must have been changing a tape or something. It was quite quiet when . . .'

Locker appeared at the door.

'You'll have to excuse me, Mr Cade.' Bone raised an eyebrow at Locker, who conveyed by one massive shrug that Reggie Merrick had not after all obliged them by confessing to both murders. At the same moment, the phone rang. Reaching for it, Bone said to Jonathan Cade, 'You're staying in Biddinghurst?'

'At the Bidding Arms.' As Bone nodded, Cade vanished into the dark corridor as successfully as any phantom. Scarcely had he gone before Fredricks appeared and crossed the room to put a scorched packet down on the table. Its charred wrapper gave way and, instead of the packets of powder Bone had expected, a swathe of photographs spread out over the blotter. Also spread out, wearing an expression of dazed meekness and nothing else at all, was the girl in the top photograph. It was Fleur.

36

'I'm sorry, sir. I couldn't get her to say more. I blew it.' Fredricks, who normally looked like a pleasant horse, now looked like an overdriven one. She was nursing one hand in the other and Bone saw that it was red and swollen.

'What's happened there?' He got scorched packet and sore hand together and pointed to the small washbasin in the corner. 'Hold it under the cold tap till it hurts. Till it hurts more than it does now.' He gave her one of his rare smiles, but Fredricks was too distressed to respond.

'Chrissie is furious with me. She just kept crying and hitting me, saying now people would see the pictures.'

Not a pretty profession, Bone reflected. Fredricks,

who had set out to help, knew that Chrissie felt betrayed by her. Justin Rafferty had been the unlikely knight riding to the rescue.

Bone pointed sternly to the washbasin and Fredricks finally obeyed him. He said, over the noise of the running water, 'These photographs give us another and more sinister light on the dumping of Nigel Wells in that car boot. Suppose he had to be dead before these photographs could be retrieved from his cottage. You got Rafferty all right?'

'Yes, sir. He's downstairs. Do you want him now?'

'No, later.' Bone was glancing at the photographs as Locker's blunt fingers pushed them out across the table. None of Justin, which he had half expected—he could imagine anything of Nigel now; yet here were some boys, who didn't look more than seven or eight and bore an air of defiance as if they were aware of doing what was naughty but were not sure why. Another girl, on the verge of puberty, looked actively annoyed at her pose. He said to Fredricks, 'Recognise any of these?'

She had wrapped her hand in wet tissues and came over. 'That's Chrissie, sir. I don't know this one. Or this. I think this is Lucy Hollis with Fleur Scatchard, isn't it?'

This one was as much a collision of hair, dripping fair and marigold ripples, as an entwining of bodies. Bone was reminded of the Beardsley prints on Kat Purdey's bedroom wall, the pure lines of long limbs, in contrast here with the impure attitudes. Fredricks had picked out the photographs of the two small boys.

'Oh *no*. These are the two I saw at the Hollises' this morning. Tim and Kevin, I think they're called. I'm not sure if they're the Hollises' own or fostered. No wonder those pictures were under the carpet—Rafferty saw Miss Wells get them out.'

'Steve, we'd better have both the Hollises in. For all we know this has been happening with their cooperation.' It was not a nice thought but it must be considered.

'Pat, go and get that hand properly seen to.'

She managed an uncertain smile and turned to go, but then, remembering something, turned back. 'Rafferty, sir. He's got some bad bruises. He's only in jeans and it looks as if he's been in a fight.'

'Ah. Thank you, Pat. Now . . .' He pointed at her hand. In a fight. Rafferty might have been, not in a fight, but beaten up. This would be nothing new to him, for Bone had seen his record. His father had regularly laid into him both with fists and with a buckled belt until young Justin collected the nerve and the muscle to turn on his parent and reverse the procedure. Rafferty senior had landed up in hospital, decidedly damaged, and Justin had landed up in care. His mother had refused to have anything to do with him, and readily gave permission for fostering. Justin had therefore come here to Biddinghurst and the Hollises, a few years ago. It was here that he had returned after a year of taking any work he could get and living in the house of Nicola Grant, a social worker and mother of Cha's best friend.

Had he come for revenge? Might there have been pictures of a younger Justin? But then Nigel would not have been the one to beat him up; the last few days had informed them of someone who would. Hadn't Justin been working for Laurie Scatchard?

'Thinking what I think, Steve?'

Locker had no time to reply. A buzz on the intercom heralded Shay's voice, announcing with some triumph the safe arrival of Barbary Wells. Bone did not hesitate. He needed to know more about those photographs before he talked to Rafferty and the Hollises. It seemed that a good person to tell about them was the one who had dashed back from London, for all her touching demonstration of physical and emotional frailty—of how incapable she was of handling further stress—had dashed back to steal them in the night.

'Bring Miss Wells in.'

Locker gathered the photographs and restored them

194

to the singed packet. 'She's got some explaining to do. D'you reckon she'll be up to it?'

Bone laid a folder over the packet. 'Dr Beth Dillon would be on to us for ha-*rass*ment no doubt. Crushing the life from a wilting flower. Tell you what, Steve. I fancy a bit of harassing would do us the world of good just now. Have a bucket of water ready in case the flower turns all fainty.'

Barbary Wells seemed aware she was facing unsympathetic eyes when she was ushered into Bone's office, but she had evidently decided to play it for bravery, the sweet little woman persecuted and misunderstood.

She had settled for wearing a black dress, perhaps to remind them she was mourning a brother, perhaps too because it made her appear vulnerable and dignified, a touching combination. No doubt to avoid notice from reporters on the way to the Incident Room, she was wearing dark glasses, which she now took off, and a headscarf which was unknotted to release the shining hair. Bone wondered, as she offered him a tremulous smile as she sat down and took a little time over crossing shapely legs in black tights under a very short black skirt, how much being so beautiful had destroyed her chances of being a reasonable person. She must have become entirely used to having her own way, since childhood, used to being spoilt and doted over, so confident in her power of manipulating people—or at least men— that it could be hard to pierce through to any real woman living behind that wonderful façade. There might not be any real woman at all. So far, in his dealings with her, Bone had only once seen a sign of genuine feeling. Perhaps he was misled by preconceived notions about actors, or by the fact that she was herself under suspicion.

'Miss Wells, we had asked you to let us know of your whereabouts. When I saw you on Sunday evening you gave us to understand you were staying in London, to recover a little from what had happened here.' He was careful to avoid saying 'your brother's death', as that might precipitate tears and give her the chance to load the interview with pathos. Yet, from the wide, reproachful look of those wonderful green eyes, she took his words as a lecture.

'I really, truly, had no choice but to come back. I had a duty to Nigel.'

She had taken an interesting line here. Even Locker stopped fidgeting with the file Bone had carefully placed over the packet of photographs.

'In what way?'

She opened her eyes so that the painted lashes touched the underneath of her eyebrows.

'You can't run away from grief, Superintendent. Nigel and I *lived* here. Nigel had only just become Lord of the Manor. I think I may say,' she dipped the lashes modestly, 'that the village have come to look to us. To set an example.'

Locker's mind may have been on the photographs; he produced something dangerously like a snort.

'Why were you at your brother's cottage last night, Miss Wells?'

He was treated to the eyes again, and a little merry laugh. 'Oh! Mr Cade's been talking! He promised he wouldn't but he was so anxious. The whole thing was an accident. I'd been to Nigel's to—well, I suppose to say goodbye to him there. Privately. I lived there once myself, you know. It was full of memories.'

She sighed, and both men thought of what else was there, which she had apparently taken.

'Mr Cade tells us that someone knocked you down when you had left the cottage, and took something from you.'

'Oh, certainly someone did bump into me. But they didn't take anything. Mr Cade got it wrong.'

'Miss Wells,' Locker, anticipating from an incipient movement of Bone's, produced the packet and pushed it towards her . . . 'I think you had better revise your story. *This* is what you went to your brother's cottage to collect.'

The singed packet lay before her. She stared at it as if it were marked with the fires of Hell, and spoke in a whisper.

'Where did you get that?'

It was a mistake. She knew that at once. Complete innocence is best not spoilt by the slightest knowledge. Her hands made little sideways movements.

'Justin Rafferty, who took them from you, was intercepted before he could destroy them. What can you tell us about them, Miss Wells?'

She looked from Bone to Locker, needing a cue line more promising than this one rather sharply offered. Bone found he had a vague echo in his head—was it the words of the Red Queen to Alice?—about the efficacy of a little kindness and putting the hair in curlers. Barbary's hair needed no help, but it might be the time for a softer tone.

'This is very distressing for you. I'm sorry but it must be done. Did Nigel tell you about these photographs? Did he show any of them to you?'

Locker shook some from the packet and fingered them out before her. 'These, for instance? Do you recognise them?' It was Fleur and Lucy playing mermaids. Barbary shut her eyes quickly. When she opened them after a few seconds, nothing had altered, nothing had gone away, the two men and the uniformed girl by the door were still there, and there were answers expected.

Barbary breathed deeply and began.

'I knew he took them. It was harmless. Not what you're thinking at all.'

'What am I thinking, Miss Wells?'

'Nigel loved beautiful things. Artists paint nudes, you know. It was artistic. Nigel couldn't paint so he took pictures.'

'Beautiful things?' Bone turned up the one of Chrissie angrily displaying herself. 'Does this qualify?'

She pushed it away with a silver fingernail, making a little *moue* of repugnance. 'Oh, well. Picasso, you know. Lucien Freud. They painted *extraordinary* pictures.'

Bone thought it was time they stopped trying to view Nigel as a misunderstood genius. Egon Schiele too might make a focus of parts of the body from which people usually averted their eyes, but he didn't hide his drawings under carpets.

'What were you going to do with them?'

'Burn them.' This at last was a definite statement. 'I knew where Nigel kept them. I knew just how they might appear to people who didn't know him. And of course I was doing it for the children too.'

This was nauseating. Bone's professional mask held, but he could not stomach Barbary's claim to protect the children her brother had exploited. She was more likely to be protecting her own image from contamination. The papers were running rave obituaries on Nigel's subtleties as an actor, his concern for the global heritage, his kindness to the young. If the nature of this kindness emerged, they would be still happier to dwell on it, with relish, colouring the name of Wells, poisoning her future with casting directors and producers. The image of Damien Winter, whose death had made the headlines that morning, floated before his mind's eye, and if it floated face-down in a pool, still it had the connotation that Winter had worked with Nigel and, casually, he asked, 'Did Nigel show these photos to other people? Did he sell them?'

'Sell them? Oh no! Nigel would never do anything so disgusting.'

If the photographs, according to her, were purely artistic, it was to be wondered how the sale of them was disgusting. He pointed at one.

'Fleur Scatchard. She stayed with you in London.'

'Yes, in early spring. April, was it? A sweet girl . . . she was auditioning, you know. But looks aren't enough, these days.'

198

Bone awarded her full marks for letting them know that she herself had more than looks. It was also a useful reminder that she, as a capable actress, could deceive.

'Was she on drugs?' It was Dr Beth Dillon who thought Fleur's mood and energy had improved after a visit to the bathroom. Barbary was shaking her head, the pretty brown hair with gold highlights doing its stuff.

'I'd have known, I'm sure. She's so confused, that girl, you might think she was on something, but she's been like that ever since I've known her. So dependent on kindness.'

Kindness! Bone was beginning to be sickened by the word. Along with the photographs it was too much. He could quite sense the pleasure it must have been to shave the man's head and stripe his face with blue and green. He experienced a surge of sympathy for Phil Merrick, and Justin—for whom it might even have been fun to give this demure beauty, so appealing in black, a good shove on to the garden path. He thought he would try a mental shove.

'You were seen on Saturday night sitting in your car outside Laurie Scatchard's house; and then later there was the sound of a violent quarrel indoors. What was the quarrel about, Miss Wells?'

The switch of subject took her by surprise and, for one moment, her expressive face showed indecision: whether to deny the quarrel altogether . . . She had been seen in her car . . . Had she been seen going into the house? Then she gave her merry laugh. 'Oh, I was really quite cross! Laurie was coming to dinner with me and—would you believe it?—he completely forgot! I let him have it, I can tell you.' She swept her lashes at them and Bone almost expected to feel a breeze. 'No woman cares for being stood up, you know. He made all sorts of excuses—poor Laurie!' She quite obviously recollected at this point that she was talking of the dead. 'I wish now I had been nicer to him. It's so terrible, you know, simply realising one isn't going to see him again.'

'What sort of excuses did he make?'

'Oh, he said he was busy with Noah Pike, of all people, playing a practical joke on Jonathan Cade. Did you know Mr Cade is writing a book about ghosts? He came to see me about some we had at Nigel's place when I was there. Laurie said he was so wrapped up in this joke that everything else went out of his head.' She made a brief but sweeping gesture to express the flight of Laurie's memory. The movement had an unreality about it, as if it had been evolved for the stage. What play had she used it in? She added, 'Can you imagine?'

Bone could imagine. Though she smiled now, she must have been very angry. How could she accept that a man's attention, once she had responded to it, should not be exclusively focused on her? A mere practical joke, the companionship of the gross Noah Pike, as superior attractions for her company, must rate as a mortal insult. So had it proved mortal for Laurie Scatchard?

'You were still angry with him next day. Angry enough to pull his nose.'

This provoked a laugh that could only be described as silvery. 'Oh, that was fun! I felt so much better! Seeing him on that plate covered in mould was funny anyway, but he was completely at my mercy! And I made the most of it.'

Locker shifted and coughed. It had to be asked.

'Miss Wells, did you, on the morning of Sunday the twenty-first of August, take a knife from the table and stab Laurie Scatchard?'

Shock. Horror. Tears. Yet still this element of theatre, so that Bone wondered if she thought: had she wasted all that acting on them, that they believed she could be guilty?

37

The coffee was welcome. Bone savoured the bitter warmth. He could hardly believe it was only eleven—it felt like the end of a long, hard day. His shoulders ached. A brandy might have been more restoring than coffee . . . He ate a digestive biscuit in silence while Locker was finishing his second, brow furrowed in thought. They both started to speak at the same time and Bone laughed.

'Bet you're going to say what I am, Steve. Destination, nowhere. Speed, doing a ton. Reggie Merrick had nothing to offer but complaints; we have to let him and his cracked ribs go tomorrow if we've nothing but smudged prints on a knife anyone could have used. Justin and his bruises . . .'

'Do *you* believe his story? Scatchard going for him because he ran into that statue with the motor-mower?'

'Considering what we've heard of Scatchard duffing up all and sundry on impulse, I can't see why not. If Henry Purdey, owner of the statue, had known, I dare say he'd have added a swipe or two on top, and it appears Scatchard was decent enough not to tell him.'

'Purdey thinks it was Wells knocked the thing down.'

Bone drained the last of his coffee and considered asking for more. 'Popular to blame Nigel. We'd no joy in getting young Justin to admit he detested him enough for murder.'

'That boy has nerve. He's got time, opportunity, motive, for smothering that slimy bastard. Just sits there with his white hair and his bruises and his earrings . . .'

'Opportunity, motive, no proof, Steve. That's what's

making you get poetic over him. He can sit there until *our* hair turns white if we can't get a witness or Forensic to show our lad used a cushion in anger.'

Locker sighed. 'He could have done Scatchard too. Weaving about in the dark, nobody sure where anybody was, take it for granted he's there; or he could pretend to get a leak, pick the knife up as he passed—he was wearing those gloves with skeleton bones painted on.'

'Not the only gloves around, Steve. Kat Purdey had them, up to her elbows as Morticia. A couple of the ghost kids had white nylon or plastic ones. Any of them could have done it. But all their statements are consistent.'

Locker pressed the intercom and asked for more coffee. Then he went on, 'Kat Purdey wasn't in Nigel's photo gallery. We can leave her out for that and I doubt if Laurie Scatchard forced his attentions on her. Can't see that young woman agreeing to anything that didn't take her fancy.'

'Here we are at Nigel again; we're nowhere on Scatchard.' Bone was examining three packets of photographs now. The vestiges of dusting powder stuck to some. The team had turned over Nigel's cottage thoroughly, with the help of the Drugs Squad and the sniffer dog. The latter had been disappointed, though it had nosed into every inglenook and cranny in the place, but the team had found Nigel's photo cache under the carpet; Barbary had been less thorough than she should. Further, under the floorboards, were two extra packets now on Bone's table. No fresh faces—if that was the right term—certainly no fresh lines to pursue. The only unknown had been identified by an appalled Midge Hollis as another foster-child now back at his home.

Bone accepted the fresh instalment of coffee gratefully. He said, looking at the photographs, 'My only wonder is that he doesn't seem to have gone in for video.'

'Glad he didn't,' Locker said. 'Perhaps he couldn't get the kids to do it. A pose is one thing, but . . .' He shook his head. 'We do have something interesting on the info from Wells's bank, here.' One hand spread out statements faxed from London, as he drank. 'The team's come up with this. There are no regular payments, except from the TV company, but there's something funny in March where he paid out this on the twelfth.' Locker pointed to a sum highlighted by one of the team in lurid pink. 'Wells's cheque stubs are no use, he didn't fill in the payee half the time; but the bank says that it was paid to the Pauling Clinic.'

'We've checked out the clinic?'

'Yes, sir. They mostly do gynaecological stuff. Terminations.'

They looked at one another. Bone said, 'So Nigel Wells was more than just the voyeur they say he was. The soup is getting thicker, Steve.'

38

The Incident Room held a steady hum of sound, a constant flicker on the VDU screens, a voice on the telephone, the small rattle of a keyboard as the team worked. One or two heads were raised, or turned, as Bone and Locker came in, but most were too absorbed in what they were doing. Pity the Chief couldn't see, Bone thought, he got a buzz from watching concentration. The fluorescent strips overhead gave a spectral glare in contrast to the sunlight beyond the open french windows.

Bone came to stand where Higg led him, to look over WPC Wilkinson's head. She paused to let him read the figures on the screen, her fingers on the keys. What we need now, Bone thought, reading her correlation of bank statements, cheque stubs and information from bank files—what we need is a key that will flash up some useful names, such as who the murderers are; or murderer if we're going for the economical solution.

He straightened up. 'Thanks, Shona . . . I don't know about you, Steve, but I'm going to stretch my legs out there.'

He needed to stretch his brain. This information about the clinic was, at the moment, more a confusion than a clue. He walked out into the garden with a sense of relief. The day had consented to make up for the rain and cool breezes of the weekend and was behaving as summer should, banishing the hint of autumn he had smelt in the morning. The sun struck hot on his head as he strolled in the grass, Locker after him, and a pigeon cooed energetically not far off.

Locker batted away a cruising bee. 'You think one of the girls here was having his child, sir? Lucy Hollis, Fleur Scatchard?'

'Ye-es. His sister paraded how kind he was to them. Of course it may be someone he worked with in TV or some other village ex-maiden, but I don't imagine any teenager in this village, even in these enlightened times, caring to be a single unmarried mother.' He halted, brushed twigs and rosettes of lichen off a half-broken seat encircling one of the ilex-trees, and sat down. 'But not, I think, Lucy Hollis. The clinic's in London. Who was staying with Barbary Wells in March, when Nigel paid the clinic?'

'So she was.' Locker, not bothering to sweep the bench, sat down heavily and another slat cracked. 'Fleur Scatchard. D'you think it was her?'

Bone looked over the trampled grass towards the house, and imagined night, Saturday night last, and moonlight, the loud heartbeat of the drums silent for a minute, and Jonathan Cade looking over the fence from the church side, seeing a girl with floating fair hair, wandering over the grass, rocking her arms as if she held something he could not see; the baby she had not had . . . Poor Fleur.

'I think it very likely. If so, I wonder how many of her friends were in on the secret.'

'And if they knew, how much it was behind the trick they played on Wells. Isn't Phil Merrick Fleur's boyfriend?' Another slat gave way and Locker got up quickly. 'Bloody bench! You'd think they'd get someone to keep up the garden, wouldn't you?'

'Someone like Laurie Scatchard? I don't suppose the WVS, or whoever uses this place, could afford him.' Bone paused, watching Locker's search for a safe place to sit. 'Ah. Steve: if Laurie got to know what his daughter was up to with the lovely Nigel?'

Locker straightened his back and stared thoughtfully. 'And he went to the car with Noah Pike and the porn mags. He could have come back later and put the cushion over his face. Perfect opportunity.'

'After a row with Barbary got him in the mood.'

'Or before? Could he have missed his date with the sister because he was busy smothering the brother?' The pigeon cooed breathily, soothingly. From somewhere came the delicious smell of new-cut grass.

Bone sighed and stretched his legs out before him. 'Do you ever get the feeling we can't think like normal people any more?'

'Because we don't deal with normal people. What's normal about a bunch of druggy teenagers and a man who takes porn pictures of them? What's normal about a man getting stabbed in the back?'

A ladybird had landed on Bone's thumb-knuckle, and proceeded to walk, with wings not fully sheathed, across the back of his hand, negotiating the fair hairs with determination and tickling him considerably. 'Normal, Steve! You're right. Getting stabbed these days is normal. Used to be thought medieval; now hardly a day passes without someone putting a knife in someone, in a fight outside a pub, or some old lady on her way to church. What is insane is that it's done sometimes almost out of curiosity: what's it *like* to stab someone?'

The ladybird made up its mind, unsheathed its wings properly and took off, most likely to lunch from the layers of greenfly Bone had seen on the straggling, un-pruned roses round the french windows.

'If you're looking to Nature, Steve, to show us what's normal, then it's normal to kill. In fact it's normal to eat your dinner while it's still kicking your teeth.'

Locker had picked up a small apple from the grass and was examining it for wildlife. 'You're talking about killing for food, sir. That's natural. Animals don't kill for revenge, so far as I know.'

Bone watched Locker biting into the apple with relish. 'I wouldn't be sure. Ask David Attenborough. But is this revenge? A lot must depend on when, and if, Scatch-ard got to hear about Nigel and Fleur. It happened in March—at least the abortion seems to have done, we're still talking hypothesis—so why didn't he kill before? A man of impulse, who duffed up all and sundry on the spot, why should he bide his time?'

Bone stopped suddenly, and Locker stopped before the next bite and regarded him. 'Who knew about Fleur, had given her a bed in London, and had a row with Scatchard on Saturday night?'

'If Scatchard did for Wells, then we're only left with: who did for Scatchard?'

'I'd dearly like to see the Chief's face if I tell him Wells's murderer is in the morgue.' Bone got up and dusted the seat of his trousers. 'Well. We'd better or-ganise some sweet nothings for the TV crews in the street.'

'There was one in the churchyard,' Locker nodded towards the fence, 'trying for shots in at the windows. Higg says the Rector made them leave, so he must be quite an impressive sort of chap.' Bone's vagrant fancy supplied a vision of a club-wielding cleric.

He said briskly, 'After the TV bit I think we'll have

to force the reluctant Fleur to make a little sense for us. She's the one who can tell us whether her father knew what we think happened, and when he found out. Don't forget that black eye.'

'What you bet—' Locker spun the apple core into a spread of lilac, startling a pigeon out—'she's taken something else by now and can't make sense enough to spread on a biscuit.'

Bone's laugh cut off as the pigeon let fall a tribute on his shoulder. He pulled out a tissue and tried to scrape it off. 'The cameras'll love the super with shit all over him. Save the reporters the trouble.'

Locker assisted in cleaning off a bit Bone couldn't see. 'Don't forget, sir, birdshit's supposed to be lucky. Fleur Scatchard may be ready to open up.'

39

Bone was not the only soul in Biddinghurst conscious that the presence of TV cameras necessitated a decent appearance. Heather Armitage had had her moment of glory on Sunday, but it was a good twelve minutes short of Andy Warhol's predicted quarter-hour of fame. She was, however, optimistic and thought she might well make up time still.

There had been a van in the lane outside Nigel Wells's cottage, taking pictures of the outside; but apparently, though they had planned taking pictures of the inside, they couldn't get in yet. The police were still busy there. Just what they were doing they would not say, but Mrs Parker, who 'did' for Barbary Wells almost opposite, said she had seen a German shepherd dog on a harness unloaded from an unmarked van in the drive and taken inside. That seemed to tally with the rumour that the cottage had been broken into during the night, though surely they didn't expect intruders to be still on the premises? Perhaps they hoped to track whoever it was through the village. Another rumour flying around said that Justin Rafferty had been arrested for Nigel Wells's murder. Dolly Pike had been in the street when he was brought out of the Old Rectory and put in a car, a police car, and driven away. Dolly hadn't actually seen handcuffs, but they'd pushed his head down when he got into the car, the way you see them doing on TV, so of course the handcuffs must be there.

Heather said that if she'd been there watching Justin Rafferty removed from Biddinghurst, she'd have clapped. She might have cheered. How like the ungrateful young, to turn against the very people who made such efforts to help them. Suppose he was the murderer—and she wouldn't be in the least surprised—then it was to be hoped the judge would make absolutely sure about giving that man a proper life sentence that wouldn't let him out while he still had the strength to strangle defenceless women.

What more likely, too, than that he had stabbed his employer, that Scatchard man, who was no loss to the community either. Great gypsy with a habit of making eyes at every woman he met! At least, nearly every woman. Heather was glad to be able to say he had never made eyes at *her*.

The arrest and removal of Justin Rafferty had disconcerted that faction who voted for Reggie Merrick as murderer, probably of both victims; their opponents believed there to be a serial killer in the village bosom. Reggie was leading candidate because there were so few people he had not quarrelled with. The older inhabitants, with vivid memories of the feud between the Scatchards and the Merricks; of such terrible things as the hanging of Rose Scatchard, scarcely twenty-one, for murdering her own baby, and the resultant death of Jack

Merrick at her brother's hand—the fatal part played by
the club fender being ignored: these older people felt
that such deeds were bound to result in things just as
terrible later. Reggie had simply waited forty years, that
was all, for a Haunted House to turn up, with groans
and shrieks laid on, darkness to shroud his deed, knives
ready to his hand, and Laurie Scatchard himself a far
from moving target.

Dolly Pike's wide advertising of Rafferty's arrest, however, caused a kaleidoscopic realignment of village opinion. Many older villagers at once identified a teenager as
a likely source of violence, many of the younger instantly
crediting that a man in his sixties would carry a grudge
deep enough to make him kill, especially this man, who
had never in his life been shy of demonstrating other,
minor grudges.

Almost universal was pity for Fleur Scatchard. Her
mother had been an alcoholic, her father, for all his abili-
ties, was an acknowledged scamp, and she herself always
thought of as a helpless creature, 'a bit of a drip', risible
in her ambition to be an actress, courting trouble in the
bad company she kept with types like Rafferty and Phil
Merrick. Now she was herself a victim, her collapse was
viewed with great sympathy.

Heather had been several times across to the New
Rectory with little gifts such as a Thermos of her best
broth, whose efficacy had been testified to by both her
late husbands when they were ill, but which was received
with a sniff by the Rector's daily woman who cooked.
She had taken a bunch of flowers, and this had led to a
tiff with the daily woman, who had implied that these
were taken from the tributes to Nigel Wells which had
been laid in Heather's drive where her car had stood—
Heather resolutely ignored the sightseers who congre-
gated in Manor Walk; she had given her account to the
television and newspaper reporters, and was not going
to repeat it to any silly sensation-seeker. She had taken
some of her biscuits, and a herb pillow, made with her

own hands, intended to ensure restful sleep. She had hoped to avoid the Rector's daughter, whose manners were so inappropriately disobliging, but the girl had twice barred her way on her mission of mercy, and Heather had been forced to abandon biscuits and pillow to her hands.

Once, though, she had bumped into the Rector on his way out and had managed to redirect him into his sitting room, where she had an uplifting little talk with him about his parishioners' need for comfort in these dreadful times they were living through. She was pleased to think, later as she put on her flowered silk two-piece for the Parochial Helpers' meeting in the afternoon, that she had given him one or two really helpful ideas. He had said several times that he was very grateful, before rushing off to put them, she hoped, into practice.

The Parochial Helpers' meeting had to be in the Rectory itself this week, the police having taken over the usual venue. Heather looked forward to being able to pop upstairs and give the poor child Fleur some words of gentle encouragement. Kathy Purdey was quite unlikely to be about; word had spread among the Parochial Helpers that she had referred to their meetings as 'a lot of old cats in the snuggery', and that she would make a point of being out when they came. The Sleeping Beauty would not be guarded by her thorns.

The coffee-cups were all laid out on the table in the sitting room when Heather arrived and, unusually and to her annoyance, everyone was already there, gossiping in excited undertones while the Rector could be heard clinking about in the back, opening biscuit tins while he waited for the kettle to boil.

Heather plumped her handbag down on the sofa, where Dolly Pike and Mary Markham had been sitting before they got up to peer out of the window and keep the others informed about the movements of a TV van progressing slowly down the street. She shot a quelling glance all round. Tittle-tattle made such a bad atmosphere in which to start a meeting. Then she went out to the kitchen to help the Rector, ignoring someone's call that he had refused any help. She was in time to put back the biscuits she had made for Fleur into their tin, playfully tut-tutting at the Rector for thinking of using them for the meeting, and opening a packet of wholemeal biscuits instead. Her mind had not quite come to grips with the thought but when, in the coming autumn, Kathy went to sixth-form college in Canterbury, she anticipated the chance to help the Rector a great deal more than was possible at the moment.

The meeting went well. Heather could congratulate herself, and silently did, on keeping things moving and to the point. Mary Markham had an irritating tendency to ramble and to interrupt when Heather was explaining what ought to be done, but it was a simple necessity to ignore such bad manners, raise one's voice a little and carry straight on. The Rector never liked these meetings, he was fretful and ill at ease, and this time he fidgeted a good deal. He might well be on edge, with media people trying to interview him, as Dolly had mentioned. How wrong it was to harry a man under whose roof nothing dreadful had happened, when a woman in whose front garden the very worst had been discovered was paid no attention at all.

The Rector's roof was about to earn its own reputation.

Heather had managed to marshal the Parochial Helpers into the hall after the meeting, forestalling the lingering dawdle of some of the wretched women who would attempt to bother the Rector. She herself meant to be the last. After a little chat with the Rector, she would nip upstairs and see Fleur.

Fleur was going to save her the trouble.

Heather was manoeuvring Dolly's ample hips towards the doorway, blocked by Mrs Markham who was bidding an affected farewell to the Rector, and Miss Hartingdon on the step beyond, when a noise from behind made three of them turn and all of them rigidly gaze.

Fleur was coming down the stairs towards them, holding out raggedly slashed wrists from which blood dripped and fell soundlessly on the carpet. She broke out shrieking, 'I can't! I can't do it!'

Nevertheless she seemed to have had a good try.

40

The ambulance on its way back from Adlingsden was directed to Biddinghurst and arrived, siren blaring, within minutes, bringing village traffic to a halt and citizens and visitors from shops, pubs and café on to the pavements in hope of fresh disaster. It drew up outside the New Rectory, where a small woman with grey hair and spectacles was gesticulating by the gate. Two paramedics got out the stretcher and ran up the Rectory steps, hampered by the small woman now in the doorway.

Another obstacle was cluttering up the hall, and for a moment they had to be prevented from treating this as their casualty. Heather Armitage had not been proof against the sight of Fleur's blood repatterning the Rector's stair-carpet, and had passed out, bringing down the hall table, the telephone that stood on it, and the Rector's hat, which had landed chastely on her bosom. There she lay, a beached floral whale, as the Rector and Dolly broke out of their horrified trance a second later and made their way, round and over Heather respectively, to Fleur who had sunk weeping on the lower stairs, mingling her tears with her blood.

The Rector took her wrists and held them over her

head, while Dolly ran to the kitchen and found and soaked some tea-towels. They happened to be the Rector's souvenirs from Sissinghurst and Cragside, but he wrapped them about Fleur's wrists. Mrs Markham picked up the telephone from the floor and rang the emergency services.

The paramedics, therefore, arrived at the scene to find a stout, anxious, pretty woman in pink and orange holding up one arm of their patient, while a man in a clerical collar held up the other, like referees in a boxing match proclaiming the winner. Fleur, crying, bleeding, shaking her head at the Rector's reassurances, looked to them very like a loser.

They checked her injuries. The damage was not too severe but would need stitches. The loss of blood called for treatment—one of them checked on the copious trail leading from upstairs to estimate the blood loss while the other applied dressings; he also checked the recumbent woman for damage and found none. They lifted the girl on to the stretcher and past the recumbent figure, whom a little grey-haired woman was restoring to consciousness by pouring the contents of a small watering can over her head. Mary Markham had suffered much from Heather Armitage; this was her chance to repay with Christian kindness and she was not going to miss it.

Dolly, leaving a message for Noah with Miss Hartingdon, got into the ambulance. Bone arrived at the house as the paramedics were leaving it. Locker, behind him as they watched Fleur being slid into the berth on her stretcher, eyes closed and looking convincingly dead, muttered, 'I don't believe it.' Bone, as sometimes happened when things were going badly, was seized by the desire to laugh. It was callous. Though Fleur was not dead she might be seriously ill. Yet she was, he suspected, the sort of frail creature who would come crawling out of a crater when an earthquake had swallowed all else. This wild impulse to laughter had in the past kept him from getting into serious rows with his late wife Petra and, it was to be hoped, if any arrived with Grizel it might stand him in good stead there too. The moment of controlling the laughter, of distancing himself, made him able to keep perspective.

'Pat, find out about this, will you? And where she's going.'

As Fredricks went forward, producing her card, a small crowd which had collected on the pavement, and those craning from windows, watched and discussed. The Serial Killer theory was gaining ground, and an elderly man by the Rectory gate, who had parked his shopping trolley to drink in the scene, remarked lugubriously, 'First the father, now the daughter.'

All speculation was cut short by the sudden descent of the TV crew, grey lollipops and huge woolly caterpillars extended, camcorders shouldered. 'What's the latest development, Super?' 'Another death?'

'You saw she was not dead. You'll have to inquire at the hospital.'

'Is this connected with Nigel Wells's death?' 'Who is the girl?' 'Is Nigel Wells's killer found?'

Bone suppressed a strong wish to point to the elderly man with the trolley, crammed into the Rectory railings by the reporters but clinging to his point of vantage, and to declare, 'There he is! It is he! The Cushion Killer!' Instead, he assumed his usual Press face of intelligent concern and said, 'I can give you no more information at this moment, but of course the public will be kept informed of the progress of our investigation.' It was the formula.

'Is a serial killer involved?' 'Is the man arrested being charged?'

This was better. Where there's more than one question you can shrug them all aside if you keep the look of someone doing their duty in adverse circumstances. Bone evaded the caterpillars and, followed by Locker, escaped back to the Old Rectory and the buzz and clatter and voices of the Incident Room. Fredricks was close on their heels, with news of what exactly had happened to Fleur, and Higg came forward with an air of importance.

'Something else interesting, sir, turned up on the bank statements.'

It was Shona Wilkinson once more, who had the answer on her screen. The bank had come through now with names from the cheques credited to Nigel Wells, and one was a name in the news. Damien Winter had paid the sum of £355 into the Wells account on 20 April of this year. This was not very surprising as Nigel had worked for him; but the sums for work were paid by the TV company, and what had attracted Shona's attention had been the exact correspondence of the amount of Winter's personal cheque with the sum paid out in March by Nigel Wells to the Pauling Clinic. Suddenly, a new perspective opened.

'Nicely spotted, Shona. Well, Steve? If Fleur's child was Winter's, could Nigel have been the agent in the case? Fixing the termination up for him, saving him the hassle and keeping his name out of it. Getting his sister to bring her up to town and do a cover-up here talking about auditions. And had he showed those photos of Fleur and others to Winter to start him going? Was he a bloody procurer as well? Check whether Fleur went up to London for an "audition" '—he made the inverted commas with his forefingers in the air—'some time before March; perhaps with Barbary. We mustn't forget how kind she and Nigel were to that bunch.'

Locker was growling like some bear with dyspepsia. 'Not just a creep, a pimp as well.'

'That is going to go down beautifully with the media. If it's fact. Makes a tastier dish than the squeaky-clean Nigel, favourite of millions, that they're serving up now. Though if they're on to the sniffer dog working Wells's cottage, they'll be changing the menu already.'

'What do you reckon is our move now?' Locker, in the growing heat of the Incident Room, had taken off his jacket and loosened his tie. August was having a last fling.

'You mean, until we can speak to Fleur. You'll be thinking of putting someone by her bedside, Steve. We want to make sure she doesn't try more silly tricks.' Aware of being less than charitable, he added, 'Poor child,' and turned to the Action Allocator. 'I'm not asking if we have anyone to spare, Mike.'

'You're right, sir; I'll see what the station itself can do—Fredricks says the girl's been taken to Tunbridge Wells. If they've no one there, it has to be Wilkinson, Vigo or Fredricks from here.'

'Let's hope not . . . I need to know as soon as Fleur can be talked to. Meanwhile, let's talk to whoever it is in London who can tell us any more about Winter. Drowning in your own swimming pool isn't the most intelligent move in the world.' As he went across to the office he was using, Bone toyed with headlines: CUSHION KILLER STRIKES UNDERWATER. PILLOW IN POOL.

Locker followed him. Bone on the intercom was asking to be put in touch with the London police over Damien Winter's death.

He sat down behind the table and pulled his tie off.

'Let's launch into speculation, Steve. We've got Fleur in London in March, which is when Nigel pays the Pauling Clinic. We have Fleur here in August crying in the garden and cradling imaginary babies, having left a party at which Nigel is a guest. A humiliating trick is played on Nigel at this party, said to be on account of his behaviour with a camera; or at first said to be because he offered Chrissie Hollis dope. The stories so far.'

'We need to know who else in the party knew about this termination.'

'Definitely. Then we find Damien Winter paying Nigel the same amount as the clinic fee, so he may be concerned—but let's stick to Biddinghurst for a bit. Say that Barbary Wells knew about this hypothetical termination. Barbary has a shouting match with Fleur's father on Saturday night and Fleur has a black eye on Sunday. Suppose Laurie beat his daughter because of some word from Barbary. Remember he's stood Barbary up, she's a woman scorned and will say all she can to hurt him. Fleur, duffed up because of Nigel, goes past the car where he's lying on her way to take refuge with Kat Purdey. All her misfortunes stem from the man in the car.'

Locker's slow, thoughtful nod answered. 'As things stand, it's likely. She wouldn't have had to get her fingers on the car except on the lock, which Heather A. and Charlie Iden handled in the morning.'

'Whose prints are on the car's surface?'

Locker got out his notebook. 'Armitage, Pike, Henry Purdey, Dolly Pike, Charlie Iden, Reggie Merrick, Rafferty.'

'Not Phil Merrick. He helped put Wells in there.'

'No. Only Rafferty must have touched the car. No sign of Scatchard's prints. Must have been Pike that opened it when they were going to put the porn books in.'

'But if Scatchard had that info from Barbary about Nigel and his daughter he might well have gone back and made sure Nigel never woke up; yet no prints.'

'If he went to smother him, he'd take care there weren't prints. What about Scatchard's stabbing, sir? Are we speculating about that too?'

'It gets more hypothetical still. He'd hit Fleur, Phil Merrick and Rafferty lately . . . We've got the young girl, who on all counts at present is floating way above her trolley. Her eye hurts, she may still be under the influence of whatever they were taking at that party; there's a disturbing soundtrack; there are knives and she's seen her father threatened with one. She has possibly, we're saying, smothered Nigel Wells. It's easy, nobody knows she did it; we don't know what her father said or did to her before she ran to Kat Purdey, but it could have sent her over the edge. She *could* have done it.'

'It's a scenario, sir.'

Bone made a face. 'But she's very much a case of "diminished responsibility"—'

'I reckon you could say that of most murderers. I know what you mean, sir, but it's not our job whether she gets off or gets sent down, is it?'

'You're becoming fractious, Steve. Time we had lunch. I suggest the Bidding Arms and see if we can get inspiration along with a hot pie. I've a feeling still that the village holds the answers.'

'What we need,' said Locker, getting up with the ease always so surprising in one of his build, 'is a visit to the Middle Ages. Give me a chance to roast these kids over a slow fire and we'd get all the answers we need.'

Bone, knotting his tie, laughed. 'More! We could pick out only the answers we liked. A thing that interests me, reading about the law in those days, is the way that witches, even before anyone tortured them, were eager to boast of their powers although they knew it could get them burnt. One witch swore he'd conjured up a storm that nearly killed James the First's queen on her way from Denmark to marry him.'

'*He?*'

'Now you're just being sexist, Steve. Witches could be men. The Devil's always run an equal opportunities scheme.' Bone got his jacket on, ready for any stray TV camera. 'But I suspect you could put it down to something these kids know all about: I suspect those witches were on to magic mushrooms, or some such, that induced hallucinations of flying.'

Locker wagged his head. 'So whoever smothered Wells and/or stabbed Scatchard could be swanning about wondering if they did or just fancied they did. Makes our job really simple.'

The Bidding Arms was, as usual, full at lunchtime. Media interest in the village was marginally less, thanks to a juicier multiple murder in North London which was yielding bodies in satisfying profusion, but the August

tourists had put Biddinghurst into their itinerary on their
way to see Canterbury or Chilham with its flying hawks.
They were getting very good value going to Church Field
to stare at the dilapidated hall that still hid the remains
of the Haunted House, and hearing enterprising village
children describe what the performance there had been
like, for fifty pence a go. Then they made their pilgrim-
age to Heather Armitage's front drive.

Charlie Iden, even dealing with the welcome crush at
the bar, had eyes for his clientele beyond, and served
Bone and Locker over the shoulder of an apoplectic man
in green and purple cycling shorts, burdened with an
enormous camera in the centre of his chest. Bone was
relieved and grateful Charlie did not address him or
Locker by rank, as he wanted his lunch in peace. Charlie
even emerged from behind the bar to move a dawdling
pair from a secluded wall table into the garden. The bar-
room was noisy, even though it lacked a jukebox or
games-machines, but one could, after a minute or so, cut
out the noise. Contributing to it was the sound on TV,
turned sufficiently high for the voice of the one o'clock
news reader to be heard occasionally over the buzz of
talk. Bone's eye was drawn to the screen, where he recognised from the morning papers the face of Damien
Winter. The announcer was saying that the police were
treating the death as accidental but wanted to get in
touch with a girl who had visited Winter's apartment the
night before and who was probably the last person to
see him alive.

There followed a brief interview with the porter at
Winter's block of flats. He had something to say about
the mysterious girl who could be of help to the police
and whose presence gave a scent of scandal. 'Long
blonde hair with a silk scarf tied round—' the porter's
pale soft hand moved across his forehead—'purple with
little silver discs on it, and a long skirt and a sort of
loose top.'

'Sounds the image of Fleur Scatchard.' A voice spoke

near to Bone, who turned to see Noah Pike's face dipping into a tankard. He emerged, wiped his mouth and said, 'Poor kid's always got up in granny clothes, like they were left over from the seventies. Laurie got her a scarf like that, don't remember the colour but I've seen her in it . . .'

'Looked like a gypsy out selling clothes pegs.' An older voice came from beyond Noah. 'Useta come through here every year round Derby Day.' Noah paid no attention, having captured Bone's interest.

'And how much longer are you going to take before we hear something useful on the news about *our* sodding murders? Funny how slow the fuzz can be once people are watching to see they don't fit anyone up, right? Someone sticks a knife in my mate on Sunday and here you are Tuesday putting back the pints in the bar and no handcuffs on anyone yet. I heard you all right on TV with your "keeping the public informed of our progress"—' Noah made a grotesque face of refinement and aped Bone's voice, giving it an accent Bone had never aspired to but which evidently represented the superior aloofness which had irritated Noah. 'Progress I *don't* think. You couldn't fit up Reg Merrick, I saw his horrible old mush going down the street not half an hour ago. He was moaning about a broken rib and how he never had a lawyer, you'll be hearing from him all right. And young Rafferty, you nab him on account of he wears an earring but you can't make anything stick. He's back. Who's it going to be next?'

'You volunteering?' Bone asked, and Noah, with a falsely hearty laugh, drew away.

'Volunteering? Ha ha—that's good. That's a good one.'

Bone, however, had almost thanked him for information given just before. A wild idea, though no wilder than many that had turned out to be the truth: if, *if* Fleur had, as he'd suggested to Locker, killed both Nigel, the cause of her shame, and her father who seemed to have punished her for it, then might she, helped on her way by drugs which could give her that energy and confidence she seemed normally to lack—might she have gone to London to get Winter herself? But who could suppose that a girl seen the day before lying in bed in Biddinghurst rectory, unable to be questioned, could be the blonde who had been in Winter's flat at the time of his death?

Fredricks had remarked on Fleur's thick make-up which concealed her black eye. All dressed up with somewhere to go?

The attempted suicide today—might it be the final death she had contemplated?

41

'I'm sorry, sir. I finally got on to the doctor in charge of Fleur's case, and he was categorical that she couldn't be interviewed yet. I gather she's once more under sedation, as she'd been struggling and trying to get her bandages off.'

Fredricks, facing him across the table in the office, looked apologetic and strained, both unusual with her. Bone knew how distressed she had been by Chrissie's accusations over the photographs. Her burnt hand was bound to be hurting as well. He said, 'Pat, for you a cup of coffee and a rest. That's an order.'

Fredricks closed her mouth on a protest and went away.

Locker, his face gloomy, predicted that Fleur Scatchard was going to be under sedation permanently.

'Sedated or no, Steve, I wonder if she's ever going to be much use. Suppose we interview her, what's the odds on her making any sense? Perhaps the termination unhinged her. We have to try, though. I'm going to go back to base, ring the Chief, get abreast with at least some of my paperwork, and then go home, see my wife, change my shirt . . . You get a bit of time off yourself. Give me a call when you and Pat can meet me at the hospital.'

There was no need to involve the London police yet. Bone thought it premature to air any more theories about Fleur to professionally cynical ears until he had a great deal more substance to prevent his sounding as doolally as she seemed to be. He was looking forward to refreshing himself with the eminently sane conversation of Grizel, and he hoped fervently that he would catch her at home; nor had he glimpsed Cha for more than a moment since that Sunday, when the village fête had turned out such a disaster. He worried about the trauma for her of coming so close to murder, and he hoped that she and Grizel had talked it out together.

Wife and daughter proved to be at home, when at last he got there. They were discussing not murder but houses they had viewed that day, and vying with each other in turning them down. They were putting dinner together in the kitchen, and Bone leant on the doorjamb, resting his eyes on them.

'Daddy, you never saw anything so *grim*, the Old Dark House itself, empty and echoey. And one of the bedrooms had such a slope on it you nearly took a header through the window at the other end, and another one had just a telephone sitting on the floor in the middle of the room—'

'It looked like a malevolent toad,' Grizel said.

'—I was terrified it would ring, suddenly, and I'd have to answer it—'

'You could have picked it up and done some heavy breathing.' Bone took in how grown-up Charlotte was looking. Now that holidays were here, she was out of the elephant-grey jersey it was the school fashion to wear pouched over wrists and hips—even throughout summer, as the school frocks were so detested; and she had the look almost of a stranger, a young woman in pink and green patterned leggings, Roman sandals and a huge white teeshirt with a seal's head staring out wistfully from the middle of her chest. She had recently taken to earrings that reached her shoulders, in various geometric shapes that reminded Bone of the diagrams in Maths he could never work out the meaning of—never get the hang of, he thought now, watching the swing of the pair she was wearing.

Grizel looked at him and said, 'Are you hungry, Robert? Dinner won't be for another hour.'

He came in and bent to kiss her head, smelling the delicious scent of her hair, something between sandalwood and new pencils. 'I'm ravenous but I'm filthy. It's been a hot day and the Old Rectory is the sort of house that's never clean. I dare say it's subtly disintegrating, like my brain. And the case is the sort where, if we get a lead, it points straight to the funny farm. I'll shower and I'll change and I'll eat. First I'll be the eternal debtor of anyone who'll organise me a pint of tea. Then I'll get down to the paperwork I've still got. And later I've to go to the hospital to see Fleur Scatchard—'

Cha had wandered through to the sitting room. Bone had to raise his voice over the TV as she played the channels.

'—who had a bash at doing herself in.'

'Poor child! After what happened to her father . . .'

Grizel's face was alive with sympathy and then, seeing Bone's expression, she paused. 'But what is it?'

'Some dodgy things have been coming to light. Skeletons in cupboards.'

Sudden bursts of music changed to quacking cartoon voices. Bone, on his way through, caught the breathy tones extolling a shampoo and saw on the screen the slow-motion tossing of quantities of glossy hair. As he went to dump the briefcase of work in his study, the matter-of-fact tones of a newscaster came on, but he was not listening. His study, contrived by Grizel from a species of large cupboard, was still a novelty.

Cha squealed, 'Look, Daddy! Look, it's the earring I didn't buy at the fête.'

He emerged briefly and saw the earring that filled the screen, its leaves enfolding an animal or creature with a blue stone in its mouth. The next second it was gone, the announcer began, 'Now: Sport—' and Charlotte zapped him.

'They've found an earring in that director's flat. You know, the one that drowned, it was in the papers this morning. They want to talk to the person it belongs to. Why should they want to, if he drowned?'

'Accidental death, always investigated. Are you sure it was the one you didn't buy?'

'Positive. I liked the look of the animal, and the way it was holding the ball. First go off, I thought it was a foetus. There was a woman selling them, she had lots of plaits and a sort of crooked face. She had this stall, just a little one selling jewellery, next to the book stall.'

'Right.' Bone returned to his study, shut the door sharply and reached for the phone, pushing aside the briefcase and the work that once more he had not time to start.

42

The smell of hospital did its usual trick of lowering Bone's spirits, which had not been sanguine in the first place. Going to interview a girl who had already suffered quite a bit in her short life, and who had demonstrated that she would prefer to be out of it, constituted a form of persecution, and did not appeal to him. However, it was his job, and preventing crazy adolescents from trashing the people who bothered them had to count as priority.

Their guide, a brisk, competent nurse, strode along a pace ahead of him, as though every minute counted and they were wasting time better spent saving lives. Her shoes squealed on the over-polished lino as if in protest, and her expression, as she indicated the room off the main ward, suggested that Fleur's life was not one she'd have troubled over.

'You won't get much sense from her. Not in the real world. That type will do anything to be noticed.' She turned, hand on the doorknob. 'It's called a cry for help, but if you ask me they don't want to be helped, simply to get attention. We've had to use restraints, we're too short-staffed to keep an eye on those who don't want to get well. Doctor says not more than twenty minutes.' With a sniff, she was off down the corridor to tend worthier patients.

Bone had heard that some nurses were unsympathetic towards attempted suicide, but here was an object-lesson in pre-judging. Yet if the nurse had known the reason for Fleur's misery, would she have been more tolerant? It is hard to understand a nature different from one's own. Bone hoped to find a clue, himself, to the maze of Fleur Scatchard's thoughts.

It was lucky the nurse had warned them about the restraints. Fleur's bandaged arms were rebandaged skilfully to the bedframe. She sat propped up on pillows, her blonde hair in a waterfall on her shoulders, staring at them as they approached as though the three of them were some recurring nightmare. Last time they had seen her, Fredricks had remarked on Fleur's heavy make-up, covering the black eye. A cursory face-wash, as if delivered by the ruthless nurse, left traces of mascara smudged by tears that darkened the hollows under her eyes, the brownish-ochre hues blending with the bruise round one of them. Under the restricting bands could be seen a tunic of some chiffon material, tie-dyed in pink and purple and with little beads sewn in a scatter. The man in the Bidding Arms had talked of gypsy clothes, and the London police had reported the description from Winter's manservant of the girl who had come to supper. From the sound of it she had worn something very similar.

'What do you want?' The eyes were huge, the pupils tiny. How much was she still under the effects of sedation? She looked at them as a prisoner bound to the rack might look at approaching torturers; but there was no use in beating about the bush. The sooner this was over, the kinder to her. Bone nodded to Locker, who issued the caution and asked her if she wanted a lawyer to be present; he began to explain how she could obtain one; she looked, at that moment, as if she'd be better off with a teddy bear.

'I don't want a lawyer,' she interrupted. 'Why are you here?'

Bone sat on the one chair provided by the bed. Locker, whose weight had he sat on the bed might have capsized Fleur, remained standing, while Fredricks put the tape recorder on the table that spanned the bed and gave date, time and names. Fleur watched as if visited by aliens doing incomprehensible things.

'Miss Scatchard—Fleur—we have to ask you some questions about the death of Damien Winter.'

Unexpectedly, she nodded, as if nothing could be more natural.

'I killed him. Drowned him.' She spoke with satisfaction, looking past them at the wall as though she could see a film of what she had done flickering there. Bone glanced at Locker, who raised his eyebrows. Wasn't this a bit too easy?

'When did you do this?'

'Last night.' She returned her gaze to him as if surprised he should ask. 'I pushed him in the pool.'

Bone did not point out that those pushed into pools

usually swam. The limit of twenty minutes nagged at him. 'How did you get to see him?' He had thought it strange that Winter should want to tangle with an obvious hysteric like Fleur more than once; men like him generally preferred fresh meat.

'I rang him up. I've got his number. It's ex-directory.' She turned her head restlessly and wriggled her fingers that emerged palely from the bandaging. 'I wish you'd undo this.'

'Why did you kill Winter?'

Bone hadn't been ready for the shriek she gave, so near his face, and he flinched. Tears began to pour down her cheeks, streaking them with black.

'He took my baby away! He and Nigel took my baby away!' She hiccuped, pathetically, and added, almost in defiance, 'I killed Nigel too.'

'How did you do that?'

'I put the cushion over his face.' She was matter-of-fact. Bone could hear the noises of the hospital, the trundle of a trolley not far off, the sound of nurses' voices, cheerful and confident, a murmur of talk from the ward. Was he also hearing the truth?

'I did it in the way you smother babies. I wish someone had smothered *me* when I was born.' The tears, no longer flowing, shone on her face like snail's traces.

'Who was the baby's father?' It had to be asked. They had been assuming it was Winter, but with the outside possibility of Nigel or even Phil Merrick, said to be in love with her. Would she know? She sat upright, straining at the bandages.

'Ask my father! He knows! Barbary told him.'

Bone carefully did not look at Locker, who had stirred. He made his reminder gentle. 'Your father's dead, Fleur.' After a moment he said, 'Do you know who killed him?'

The black-badged eyes squeezed shut. 'Everyone dies because of me. Everyone . . .' Her eyes opened tragically on Bone. 'I killed poor Mr Barnholt too, you know.'

Mr Barnholt? Who on earth was he? She was well into the realms of fantasy now. Bone kept his voice low and soothing, aware of the keen attention of Locker and Fredricks. 'How did you do that, Fleur?'

She wriggled her fingers again, sitting back, and looked seriously at Bone. 'I dressed up as a ghost. Nigel said it would be a joke. But Mr Barnholt had a heart attack and *I did it.*'

Her voice had risen plangently and this brought a brisk squeal of footsteps and the starched authority of the nurse. If she had saved any lives since she brought the police to Fleur, it had not softened her mood. She stood there, and Bone was in fact grateful that they had to leave. Before he spoke to Fleur any further, he wanted to consult the London police on the Winter case. They would want to send someone to be in on the next interview; and Bone considered too that, no matter what Fleur said about it, she needed a legal representative. As it was, he could imagine that if the case ever came to court, counsel for the defence would wax dramatic over police treatment of a frail-witted girl, recently orphaned (was her mother still living?) and driven to despair by the catastrophes that had overturned her life.

Bone had also the distinct idea that, if questioned any more, Fleur would start to claim responsibility for any in Biddinghurst recently carted off to the graveyard. As an Angel of Death Fleur was poor casting, to say the least, but perhaps she was the more unnerving for that reason.

43

Rumour in a place as small as Biddinghurst has no obstacles to its spread.

Those who had barely spoken to each other in years, now gave way to the seductive urge to communicate. Sermons by the Rector, or working together for a worthwhile cause, were not half as unifying in their effect as were the various horrors of the last few days. Biddinghurst had seen itself on television, had been on the lips of the nation, had got tourists coming specifically here instead of driving straight through to formerly more rewarding villages. This was not for being the best-kept village in Kent as Heather Armitage had always longed, but for hosting two grotesque murders within twelve hours and, in particular, being responsible for depriving the nation of a very popular TV star. The village experienced a sense of communal injury and a general very strong suspicion that the police were as usual dragging their feet. True, people had been taken away for questioning. There was an agreeable ferment of speculation when Reggie Merrick (no surprise, that) and then Justin Rafferty were removed from the scene, and a natural disappointment when they were released.

When the police had gone to the Hollis house in the morning, and with obvious urgency, reporters who had almost given up the local inhabitants as a source of copy felt invigorated. Scare stories about negligent foster-parents had been news lately, and perhaps something could be cooked up to tie in with the murders, enough for a para in the Evenings and very likely a whole article in the Local. The Hollis parents had gone with the policewoman over to the Old Rectory and been kept there half an hour, and the wife was tearful when they emerged. Unfortunately they would not speak, but luck was in for one reporter in the shape of two Hollis foster-children slipping out to buy icecreams.

The two boys had viewed the removal of Justin, by three policepersons invading their orchard, as more than a liberty. They had been told by Midge to talk to no-body—indeed, not to leave the back garden—but the pleasant woman who offered them money for sweets was already familiar, having been around since Sunday. Awareness that they were disobeying Midge made them now and then rub the fronts of their shoes on the backs of their legs, but they were ready to talk. They were flattered that their opinions were sought as much as any of the adults'. Chrissie, they said, hadn't stopped crying since the policewoman went away. The police had taken Justin because he wanted to burn some photos and Chrissie was mad at them for stopping him because the photos were naughty ones Nigel had taken of her and other people and now everyone would see them. They were naughty because Chrissie and the others were bare.

The reporter was quite dizzy with her luck. A scoop, and she had only parted with two fifty-pence pieces! Nigel Wells, the dead darling, taking filthy pictures! She was in such a hurry to get to the nearest phone that she nearly fell over a large benevolent dog tied up outside the newsagent's, and he barked so loudly that she at-tracted attention all round. Embarrassing; but her story would soon be attracting attention all over the country. Nothing more newsworthy than the overthrow of a hero, and the overthrow of a dead hero is poignantly enjoy-able; and she had scooped the lot.

As a direct consequence of that phone call, Heather Armitage bought an evening paper.

On her way to post her letters—friends in the north would be anxious for her first-hand account of these stir-ring events—she saw people in the street with newspa-

pers outspread, exclaiming and comparing, and she had
no intention of asking to have something shown to her
when she could read it herself and claim to have known
all along. The newsagent was shaking his head and tut-
ting as he parted with copies of his doubled order of the
paper to the queue jamming his tiny shop; and as his
behaviour could hardly indicate an objection to the sales
he was making, the paper itself must be the cause of his
moral outrage.

'Outrage' was not an exaggeration. Heather glanced
at the headlines as she edged her way out of the shop,
so as to be forearmed for gossipers in the street. She
stood, mouth open, motionless in the doorway as she
read, blocking the way. After the Excuse *Me*'s finally
penetrated her consciousness, she stepped down on to
the pavement and had actually to lean against a wall,
despite an awareness that it was certainly not clean.

Biddinghurst had been betrayed.

Nigel Wells, of whom they had been so proud, who
had been their claim to distinction, was a monster.
Under his cloak of charm, his kindness to the young
people of the place, he had been corrupting them to his
sinister purposes. A snake had sidled its way into the
village's collective bosom. Heather gave hers a comprehensive shake, with a tremble of flowery frills, to expel
any lingering infection. Pornographic pictures, indeed!
Not gifted with imagination, she was not able to visualise
such pictures, but she was thoroughly horrified. How
dreadful for the children! How dreadful, too, for poor
Barbary now that her brother was exposed in this way.
There was of course one consoling feature of the situation: Nigel was dead.

What could *she* do? This was a crisis. Quite a few
people would need the comfort of her presence! And
how lucky that she had not posted her letters, which
would all have to be rewritten! She reviewed her priori-
ties. The Rector, of course, would need her backing in
this crisis, but Miss Hartingdon had said he was in Tun-

bridge Wells seeing Fleur. Swiftly blocking all thoughts of Fleur and the dreadful scene at the Rectory, Heather ranged in mind for who else was in need. She must devote a little time, later, to Midge Hollis, who would be so terribly shocked by what had been going on among children entrusted to her care. Although in Heather's opinion, which she had never grudged imparting, Midge was too indulgent by far, she would now be in a chastened mood, glad of Heather's comfort and open to her experienced advice.

No! The one who needed her most was Barbary. How lucky that Mrs Parker, who had the key to Barbary's cottage, had been cleaning there this morning and had found she'd returned from London but was 'lying low', pretending not to be at home because of the Press. Poor girl, how much more reason she had now for lying low! How she must be longing for a friendly face!

It was even possible, thought Heather as she set off up the street, that shut up in that cottage Barbary did not know of the latest, dreadful development in her personal tragedy. Heather was too artless to suspect Barbary of any knowledge of her brother's disgusting activities; she felt a curious stimulation at the idea of being the one to break the news to her. She would take the newspaper, as Barbary would be bound not to believe at first. Heather saw herself stemming tears, patting hands, making coffee in that nice little kitchen . . . what a pity she couldn't take the opportunity of leaving by the front door, target of any cameras waiting for Barbary! But of course it was out of the question. She intended to avoid alerting the Press by approaching Barbary's by the field way behind the cottage. There was that dreadful stile at the head of the path, but one must suffer for friends! Once down the path, she might be lucky enough to find Barbary in her secluded garden on such a lovely warm evening.

Whether she was lucky or not in the end she would not have been able to decide. Certainly she caught her

tights on the stile, but the tall gate in the back fence
was not bolted and Heather went in. Part of the lawn
had been mown—the smell of cut grass lay sweet and
fresh on the air—and as she came round the azalea bed
she found the mower lying on its side. Could Barbary
have been making a brave attempt to mow the grass
herself? Laurie Scatchard had always looked after Barbary's garden and sent the wretched Rafferty boy to do
the mowing. Surely, even though the police had let him
go, most unwisely in her opinion, he wouldn't have the
nerve to turn up and expect to get on with the job as
usual?

Suppose the police had merely failed to find enough
evidence to put Rafferty properly in prison—suppose
after all he was the murderer, and had come, under
cover of his innocent garden work, to find Barbary and
kill her? If he had killed Nigel, why not think the unof-
fending sister involved in what was going on? Agitated,
Heather trotted at a brisk pace up the lawn, past the
tiny pool on the terrace, the lounger beside it, to the
french windows. They were ajar! Rafferty could be inside, now, attacking Barbary.

She tiptoed, instinctively, on the tiles of the bay recess.
She had no plan of action. Indeed, if she came suddenly
on a scene of carnage she would more than probably
faint, as she had at sight of Fleur's wrists, and fall unconscious, defenceless, at the feet of the murderer!

Curiosity has its own courage. She pressed on, fists
clenched—the newspaper in one of them—elbows tight
at her sides as if ready to defend herself. A sound from
the sitting room to the right froze her where she stood.
The sound was succeeded by another, and yet another—
odd, urgent sounds—if Heather had not patiently
thought of England rather than about her husbands in
the past, she might have recognised it at once.

Thinking therefore of expiring breaths, she craned her
neck around the sitting-room door and, although the
window curtains were drawn because of the Press, she

could see what she had feared, Justin Rafferty struggling to overcome Barbary Wells.

After a few seconds, Heather grasped that Barbary was not a victim but a collaborator in this struggle. Something as private as murder was taking place here, before her eyes, and she must, she must get away without being seen.

Heather's exit down the lawn and out of the gate was made at a speed that would have done credit to any woman of her build pursued by an axe-murderer, and she bundled down the field path, with a scarlet face, panting as loudly as the pair she had left behind.

44

Edmund Purdey, the Rector, was glad to reach home. Even with the evidence of the police presence next door, it was good to be in the pleasant surroundings, under garden trees. His worries came with him, but they seemed less burdensome here.

The child Fleur! As good as orphaned, for her mother, traced by the social services that morning, had wanted nothing to do with her. Never very strong in body or in head, and now in a distressed and wandering state . . . her claim that she had killed Graham Barnholt, probably stated also to the police, made nonsense of all her other confessions, for Graham had died alone at the Manor, collapsed against his own front door. Poor Mrs Parker had told over and over of her shock, pushing the door open, finding what was holding it shut.

Was Fleur suffering from the effects of drugs? Was it merely the sedatives causing hallucination? That Nigel Wells had been purveying drugs to the children was unbelievable; the Rector looked up into the heights of the beech-tree beside the house and pondered on wickedness.

He was putting the key into his front door when a strange noise like a dilapidated steam-engine made him turn. Then he wished he had not. Heather Armitage, every part of her in motion, was tottering down the street and gasping as she came.

She saw him, lifted a hand, tried to speak, and pushed open the front gate. The Rector, inwardly saying *Be strong and of a good courage*, went to help her in. He led her to the sitting room and brought her a glass of water, although she was so anxious to speak that if she could have got up from the sofa to follow him she would have gasped out her news in front of Mrs Parker, making the evening casserole at the kitchen table. She took the glass and sipped. Her wide eyes and turned-down mouth had told him already that the news was not the heartening kind. 'I simply can't credit it, Rector! I had to believe my eyes, but I would never have thought it possible— never! I thought he was attacking her. I thought he was killing her. That boy is capable of anything.'

The Rector's apprehension played him a series of faces of village rapscallions. 'Who, Mrs Armitage? Please say what has so upset you.'

'Barbary Wells. I thought that dreadful Rafferty was attacking her! But he was—she was—she didn't *mind!* And I went there thinking she would be in need of comfort.' Her hand shook a splodge of water on to her bosom, and she held out the glass to him while with the other hand she brushed the water off over the sofa and her newspaper. 'Why didn't they keep that boy in prison?'

Why indeed? thought the Rector. He was thinking of his brother Henry and his attachment to Barbary.

'Mrs Armitage—'

'Her brother isn't even buried yet!' This aggravation

of culpability struck Mrs Armitage so forcibly that the Rector was afraid Mrs Parker would hear in the kitchen.

'Mrs Armitage. It's very sad—very sad. I agree. People's feelings aren't always under their control, you know.' He did not think Heather Armitage was quite up to understanding the different forms that a need for comfort might take. 'What is important is not to judge people, don't you think? In particular people from a different background from our own.'

'The Stage!' She spoke as if he had suddenly cast an explanatory light on the event which had so appalled her. She could not clarify exactly why she had come to the Rector. On a deep level, perhaps, because she needed to appal someone else, and the Rector, as proper upholder of the moral order, was the obvious choice—and the right one, for he had made it comprehensible.

The Rector had not intended to denigrate the Stage; to him 'a different background' did not, as Heather took it, denote an inferior and disreputable one; nor was he appalled. He found Barbary's behaviour pitiable more than blameworthy.

'Dear Mrs Armitage, you've had a very unpleasant experience . . .' He would not inquire how she had come by it, but Kat's expression came to mind: *Always poking her nose in. One day she'll get it covered in dirt* . . . 'You must do your very best to forget all about it.'

'Oh, I don't see that I ever can! Barbary and the Rafferty boy! Your poor brother!'

A new apprehension seized the Rector. He called on the cunning of the serpent. 'I want you to do something very difficult,' for he could see her hastening it to break it gently to Henry. She assumed devoted enthusiasm and he went on: 'Not to speak about this to anyone. I know I can count on you for this.' Deep disappointment filled every curve of her face. 'Now you must go home and rest.'

His matter-of-fact tone made her struggle from the sofa and stand up. 'Yes, Rector. Yes, I shall.'

'Make yourself a good cup of tea, and rest.'

He ushered her to the door and into the hall. Kat was on the last stair but one, coming down, a hand on the banister, and he had the odd impression she had been standing there. He wished she could sometimes bring herself to look agreeable.

He opened the front door. 'Things have been so hard for all of us,' he said. 'So much that is unpleasant, so suddenly. But time passes. Courage, Mrs Armitage.'

With a wan smile, a brave nod, she hurried out, and he shut the door. He looked up at Kat, still on the stair, and expected a scornful remark, such as Dad's 'tabbies' always evoked.

She was silent and he wondered if she was learning some charity at last.

45

While the Rector was being presented with evidence of Barbary's moral obliquity, Bone was trying to find out more about that of Fleur. His colloquies with the London police had been at first chilly, but he had persevered, leading to an admission on their part that they were increasingly regarding Damien Winter's death as suspicious. Contributing to this was the failure of the missing girl to come forward, and this argued something to hide: it might only be that the fact she was out at all, let alone her going to Winter's flat, had been kept from her parents, if she was as young as the porter and the manservant believed; but it might mean knowledge of his death. The post-mortem had revealed a bash on Winter's temple, which had caused his unconsciousness and consequent drowning. Some worm might have finally turned and the injury have arrived with extraneous help rather than simply as a result of a drunken collision with the terrazzo prior to sliding into the pool. Drink and drugs had been taken, certainly, enough to slow down reaction if he had been attacked. Bone tried to imagine Fleur, high on something, high on her slowly festering rage against the man who had 'taken away' her baby, seizing Winter's head with its coiffeured iron-grey locks and slamming the distinguished profile on the pavement.

There remained the question of how she could have got to London. That was Locker's pigeon at the moment.

Bone was not yet able to help London over the earring. Shay and Fredricks had got the list of stallholders on Church Field from Dave Hollis, the organiser. The woman, a Celia Madison, who ran the jewellery stall, had been located. She lived in a tiny cottage-workshop in Saxhurst, made the jewellery herself and travelled, especially in summer, to fêtes and craft fairs all over the south-east, selling her work. She recognised the fax of the earring at once, when Fredricks showed it. There was no TV in the cottage and she lived a reclusive life— no one had told her of it. It was one of her best designs and not cheap. All designs were original. Copying bored her and she made each pair of earrings, each piece of jewellery, subtly different as a rule, though she was not sure she had bothered with everything she had brought to Biddinghurst on Sunday as she had been in a hurry to finish enough to show.

But though she knew the earring for hers, she had no idea who had bought the pair, or even if it was the only pair of its kind. She had sold them on Sunday at Biddinghurst for sure, that wasn't a problem. Her jewellery had attracted a lot of interest and had sold well, until the frightful stabbing in the Haunted House, when most of the local people had gone home and the few visitors were soon discouraged by the atmosphere, the silence and the police presence. Sales took a sharp dip. She remembered several people before that who had spent a little time turning the pieces over; one of them had looked so like a gypsy that she thought he might buy one for himself. Bone thought of Laurie's swarthy, amused face. He had spoken to Cha at the jewellery stall, saying he was late for the Haunted House; Bone remembered, at this, the caustic comment of one of his aunts: *you'd be late for your own death.* He had left Cha there. Bone knew her reluctance to risk conversation with someone she didn't know. At times like that, her speech reverted to some of the incoherence she had struggled with after the car smash. Cha seemed to be another person the stallholder clearly recollected handling those earrings: 'A blonde girl, long hair, couldn't make up her mind. Think she had a bit of a limp.'

Bone smiled wryly. How misleading evidence could be. Now if Laurie had lamed Fleur with a kick to the shin as well as blacking her eye . . .

Thinking this, he had been crumpling and bending the edge of a folder before him on the table. Suddenly he flattened it under his hand and sat up. Fleur, of course, could not have bought the earrings herself. She was fully occupied being a ghost in the hall. In any case, a black eye was going to be noticed by Celia Madison. Laurie, now, could have wanted to placate the daughter he had damaged the night before, and bought the earrings before Cha had arrived.

Laurie's easy charm and roving eye had irritated Bone when they first met. Now he was annoying him all over again by being incapable of answering vital questions: was Fleur living entirely in a parallel universe or was there truth in some of her assertions? Now that the death of Winter seemed linked to that of Nigel, a single murderer looked likely. Fleur was the only person so far visible with a motive for both. She had also claimed to be responsible for her father's death, but there had been no time to question her in detail about it. The idea of her accepting the earrings and taking a knife to the giver was not pretty, but murder never presented an appealing face.

Necessary, too, to remember that more than fifty per cent of crime they had to deal with these days was drug-related. If Fleur had been within shouting distance of her right mind, none of this might have happened.

He must have more proof. A confession got in hospital from a girl whose father had recently been murdered—whether or not by or because of her—and who was in the hospital because she had just tried to commit suicide, would never make a case, and as for standing up in court . . .

The London lot had not swooned with gratitude when he told them what he'd got, but they were sending Inspector Lamb tomorrow to discuss the case and have a dekko at Fleur, who might even be out of hospital by then. It could be Lamb's treat for the day. Bone yawned, and stretched. The sunlight still shone, bright on the upper floors of the building opposite, sending a glow into his room. He was in shirtsleeves for the heat.

He had dropped in at the station on the way back from hospital. He had seen several people on administrative matters. He had rung the Incident Room for news about the earring and anything else they might have turned up. He had read and initialled various memos, signed yesterday's letters, and now he was looking forward to going home again in time—and he checked his watch—for a nice dinner cooked by Grizel and Cha. There had been a delicious aroma earlier on in the kitchen, reminiscent of one of his favourite stews, a treat: lamb with plum jam. He had been amazed, when Grizel first made it for them, to see her take a great dollop of jam and mix it into the casserole; now it made his mouth water just to think of it. True, there was the paperwork waiting for him afterwards, but first things first. He found he was smiling in anticipation as he got up from his chair. The phone rang.

It was London again. Forensic had just come up with something. The blonde hairs found in Winter's flat—notably on the mattress by the pool—that supported the accounts of the manservant and the porter, were dyed, and Oriental in origin. Also, they had not been attached to anyone's head for some time, as they lacked roots and had only the kink of a knot. Forensic were saying that if Winter's killer was the blonde, she was wearing a wig.

So that Fleur was unlikely to be the killer unless she had pretended to be the blonde she already was.

46

Henry Purdey was deep in problems. He had failed, despite phone calls and efforts at the front door, to get hold of Barbary at her London flat. Dr Beth Dillon, for whom he had an ardent dislike, was no use at all. She merely parroted that Barbary needed absolute rest and could see no one until she had come to terms with her brother's murder. She was not, Dr Beth said more than once, to be harassed, a word that made Henry's hackles almost literally rise as, on hearing it, he had violently pushed his hand through his thinning gingery hair until it stood upright. Anyone would think he was the police. He jammed the handset down so hard that he almost cracked the plastic. Then he shoved his hands into his pockets and stood glaring into the street, wondering what to do.

He had come up to town doing Barbary a favour by transporting her in his car, and he had hoped for favours in return. He was not being callous, he told himself. Barbary must in time realise she was better off without that damned creep of a brother with his gruesome charm and his drugs. Drink was the only drug Henry bothered with, and he poured himself one now and turned once more to stare into the street.

The other problem was that it was Tuesday, quite late on Tuesday at that, and his copy was due in first thing on Thursday. It wouldn't do to be late again after the growls from the editor last time, with talk of getting fresh blood, for all the world as if he were Dracula. Henry was justly proud of his talent for sarcastic humour, and knew that his column under the heading 'The Old Buffer' had a reputation among his colleagues. It would have surprised him unpleasantly had he known that this *nom de plume* was thought to be a perfect description of him; he thought of it as an affectionate joke. The Old Buffer was half-way through a denunciation, in his usual style, of wheel-clamping, and the article promised to be one of his best; only, unfortunately, he had left it at Biddinghurst.

By the time his glass was empty he had made his decision. He would run down to Kent, do some work on the article, spend the night at the cottage and perhaps come back to town tomorrow to see if he could get through to Barbary on the phone. The poor girl must be suffering horribly with only the ghastly Beth Dillon to confide in. Henry rattled his keys in his pocket and frowned down at the street. If he had his way he would sweep Barbary off to some gorgeous place—the Seychelles, perhaps—and help her to forget in a sensible way, without American doctors. His frown turned to a smile: Barbary in a bikini.

An hour and twenty minutes later he was in Biddinghurst, turning the corner round the turf in front of his cottage, turf still bearing the scars where Nigel had driven ruts through it and Justin had patched it.

He was reminded, with irritation, that Laurie was no longer available to carry out the ambitious garden schemes he had in mind. If he had any theory about who had stabbed Laurie—so inconsiderately for those whose gardens he serviced—it was that Reggie Merrick had. The bile so evident in his nature had chosen that moment to overflow. If not Reggie, then the most likely runner-up was the delinquent-looking Rafferty boy, and Henry determined to warn Barbary about him when she came back to Biddinghurst, in case she still thought to employ him.

That is, if she had not already come back . . . As he shut the garage door he paused and turned to listen, squinting into the evening sun. He thought music was coming from over the way, at the back of Barbary's cottage. He had not been surprised at the absence of reporters and cameras when he arrived, since they had cottoned on to her not being there. When he carried her off on Sunday night she had slipped out the back way from the garden gate behind the house, down the fields to join him on the London road where he waited with the car.

But if Barbary had come back, wouldn't they all be here again?

What actually brought Henry to Barbary's front gate, needing to find the source of the music, was Justin's transistor playing at the far end of the garden, where he was sprawled outside the toolshed, smoking a cigarette in calm contemplation of the half-mown lawn and out of sight of the house. Henry, tapping hopefully on the front door, was rewarded by seeing the closed curtain on the window by the porch quiver, and then, the greater reward, the door opening on Barbary herself.

Henry found he had forgotten how lovely she was, even in the space of a couple of days. In the dim light of the hall, glowing in her apricot silk negligée, her hair tumbled over her shoulders, she disrupted his heart. Never had he seen her so sleepily sexy, so very desirable. She held the door for him to come in, and stepped back, the negligée falling open on one slender leg, and his pulse shook his body.

'I didn't expect you, Henry. I thought you were in London.' Her voice was husky. She had to cough.

He hardly knew what he was replying. 'I thought *you* were in London. Why didn't you tell me you were coming back?'

'Oh, Henry! Don't you start.' To his dismay, the wonderful green eyes filled with tears. 'Everyone's got it in for me . . . the police . . .' She put the apricot sleeve to her eye to catch a tear, a gesture so forlorn, so unaffected that it touched him deeply. He put an arm round her shoulders.

'Don't let the bastards worry you. They have no business to ask you anything. Did they make you come down here?'

She led the way—how frail her shoulders felt—towards the sitting room, where the drawn curtains diffused the low sunlight into a mysterious golden radiance. The sofa was strewn with crumpled cushions. He must have disturbed her in an effort to rest.

She slipped from his encircling arm and sat, tucking her bare feet under her, in a corner of the sofa, and he sat as close to her as he could get.

'*Did* the police make you come down here?'

She shook her head, pulling apricot silk over the legs he would have preferred left as they were.

'I came because of Nigel.'

'Nigel!' He did not speak his mind, which was: you don't have to bother about him now he's dead; but perhaps it was in his tone and she glanced at him quickly.

'You don't understand. I've had a terrible time. Nigel . . .' it was time for tears again. He moved to take her in his arms. She let him do so, and lay against him as if exhausted.

'Tell me everything, my darling. I'll try to understand.'

It was a moment before she replied, and he was about to encourage her again when she said softly, 'I'm so ashamed.'

'Ashamed? What could you possibly—?'

'Have you seen the papers?'

'The evening papers? No, I came straight from London. What's wrong?'

She looked up at him under wet lashes with a pathetic shadow of mascara smudged underneath. 'Nigel did dreadful things and now everyone knows. He took pictures—nasty pictures—of the children here. There were people he knew, interested in stuff like that . . .' Her voice lost itself in a sob. She mastered it and went on, '*You* know I had nothing to do with any of it.'

Henry tightened his arm round her shoulders. Just what he would expect of Nigel, slimy bastard. How like him to know people like that. Well, Henry knew people like that, but it took Nigel to make profit out of his obscenities. And this was to have been Biddinghurst's new Lord of the Manor, if it was true about Barnholt's will. That wouldn't be known till it came to probate; and, now Nigel was dead, would Barbary inherit? From what he could remember of an article he'd written, if Nigel had died intestate his sister would come into only a share of his property. Either way, the media would enjoy speculating.

Barbary whimpered at his grip, and he relaxed it. 'How absurd to think you'd have anything to do with that. How you must have suffered . . .' Just to imagine that slimeball of a brother contaminating Barbary from beyond the grave! Well, from his slab at the morgue anyway. It briefly pleased Henry to think of that. 'You mustn't make yourself so unhappy.' He kissed the top of her head, warm and scented under the silken hair. How she stirred him!

'Henry.' She raised the heart-shaped face with its gleam of tears. 'You're the only one I can trust. I'll never be able to show my face in this place again. The reporters—' she gave a little sob and bit her lip like a child but, unlike a child, she did not make her nose red when she cried. She still had this sleepy, sensual air he had been aware of when she opened the door to him. He drew closer and pressed his mouth on hers, tenderly at first and then, unable to help it, passionately. She made no protest, as she had in the past when he became intense; she melted against him.

The noise of a lawnmower, suddenly starting up in the garden outside, brought Henry not so much to his senses as out of them for a moment. 'Damn Rafferty boy, is it?'

She shrugged. 'I expect so. He was in the garden earlier on.'

Henry sat up. 'You ought not to let him come any more.'

Barbary had her eyes half shut from the kiss still, and that delicious cat-smile which had enticed him first. 'But he's very good, you know. Now Laurie's dead, I think he'll take over.'

The lawnmower came almost up to the windows in a crescendo of noise, making Henry bristle. As if it were of the same mind, a cat pushed out from behind the curtain, and dropped to the floor. Without glancing at them it went out, switching its tail. At least the curtains were drawn, affording them privacy and saving Henry from seeing Rafferty's insolent face, but the mood was broken.

'That boy could be dangerous. Do remember they haven't caught the killer yet.'

Barbary had sat up, and was straightening her negligée. Henry saw that, thanks to that wretched youth and that machine, his chance was gone, a misfortune all the more poignant because, as she adjusted the apricot silk, he caught a glimpse of a naked Barbary glowing ivory in the dimness of the room. He was overwhelmed.

'Darling Barbary—why don't you marry me? Come away from this place. We could live in London if you want to, or get a little house somewhere else. I can work anywhere.' He slid down rather awkwardly on his knees before her, trying to hold up his head so that she could not see the thin patch. He caught her hand and lifted it to his lips. 'Say you will. I'll give you anything you want.'

It may have been this promise, or it may have been that Barbary was vulnerable to an offer of respectability when her reputation needed all the support she could muster, but Henry Purdey left the cottage an engaged man, sufficiently triumphant and exhilarated to be able to spare a genial nod to Justin Rafferty wheeling the mower round to the small patch of grass in the front. Barbary had persuaded him the boy was harmless, the police had let him go after questioning him. She had also persuaded Henry that she was exhausted, unable to celebrate that night as he wanted. She must have, she said, time to recover. He had embraced her tenderly before she let him out at the door, telling himself there would be other and more auspicious times. No need, he assured her, to have one single worry about her future. He would be her protector.

As he hurried off, eager to give his glad news to his brother at the Rectory, he had no idea in what grave need of protection Barbary was.

47

The day, instead of cooling down, seemed to be concentrating its heat. As if in reparation for the chill breezes and sudden showers on Sunday and into Monday, now on Tuesday evening after a day of sun, there was no breath of wind, yet a stifling hot air as if someone had let a celestial oven door open. People who had worn shorts all day now sat before their television sets with doors and windows wide to catch the breeze that didn't come. Children ran screaming through the sprinklers on the lawns, and pestered their parents for icecream money. Refrigerators were raided for ice-cold beer and drinks, and the regulars at the Bidding Arms, Noah Pike included, sweated stoically as they drank theirs warm in the bar. Those who had cooked hot suppers wished that they hadn't, while even those with cold suppers picked at their salads and wondered at their lack of appetite.

Locker had not lost his. Bone fancied that the end of the world would find Locker hastily taking a mouthful before the Last Trump could finish sounding. Nevertheless both Locker and Bone had been obliged to call their respective wives and say they would be late home. Cherry Locker had been a policeman's wife for a long time and was matter-of-fact. Steve's dinner would keep as it was Saxhurst ham; she would put the chips on when he came back, whenever that might be. Grizel, who had had much less time to adapt to the routine of having no routine, was more sympathetic and promised 'something nice' for a late dinner.

She and Cha reported having seen a pretty cottage on the outskirts of Benenden, complete with Tudor woodworm, which the owner thought would still be available for viewing at Bone's leisure, whenever that might be. Cha came on the line to remind her father that he was to go on keeping his fingers crossed for her GCSE results, expected tomorrow. Bone, agreeing to do so in spirit, smiled as he rang off: crossed fingers were surely of hypothetical use at any stage, but superstition does not depend upon logic; nor was logic, at the moment, doing him any favours.

'What we have to keep in mind, Steve, is that whoever did Winter in must have been here on Sunday and bought that earring if this,' he consulted the paper in front of him, 'Celia Madison is telling the truth when she claims it was a limited edition of about three pairs and she sold all of them at the fête on Sunday. So, if it wasn't Fleur . . .'

'It could be anyone who came to the fête, and they needn't even belong in Biddinghurst.'

'You think of the loveliest things. You're saying we can throw it wide open all over again.' Bone suited an action to the metaphor by pushing the casement window as far as it would go before drawing it back and putting it on the bar latch. The heavy air brought with it the smell of box from an untrimmed hedge, almost over-whelmed by the weeds. Bone fleetingly wondered why no doughty Church lady of the brass-polishing and altar-vase brigade had taken on a garden that parish meetings must look out on. Perhaps communal responsibility meant that no one cared. It wouldn't be the first time he had found that.

Locker joined him at the window, undoing his shirt at the neck while Bone leant out in the hope of a breeze.

'No, I meant perhaps none of the murders are con-nected after all. Such a thing as coincidence.'

Bone shook his head. 'But too much to think that this business of Fleur and Winter is connected by accident. The connection may be out of sight for the moment but I'm sure it's there.'

'The hospital says she can come out tomorrow. I sup-pose she'll be at the Rectory again. I'll check. Hospitals haven't a lot of time for suicides, as we gathered. D'you think we'll get anything from watching her—see who comes to visit and so on?'

Bone had no time to give an opinion, as the phone rang and Locker went to answer it. Bone, still sniffing box-hedge and regarding the long evening shadows on the rough grass, heard him say, 'Right, let's have those names again,' in a tone that made him turn round. Locker, writing in the scratch-pad, was putting the phone down.

'The earring, sir. It seems Celia Madison went to the Ladies' in the village at some time on Sunday morning and left her assistant in charge, a girl who's been away in Hythe until this evening. That was her on the phone: she distinctly remembers Barbary Wells buying a pair, though she can't call to mind which because she was so excited at it being Barbary Wells that she didn't take in much else. And while she—name of June Foley—was keeping the stall, a clergyman bought a pair and so did the man who was running the fête and escorting Miss Wells round.'

'Dave Hollis? And I suppose the clergyman is the Rector. Some questions, then.'

Down at the Bidding Arms, Jonathan Cade was asking some too. It was his nature to be dogged and, all through the events that had devastated and bewildered the village, he had stuck obstinately to his original purpose. If a book on British ghosts was to get written, and his presence here paying money at the inn was to be justified by its sales, he needed more material. He planned a section of 'Most Haunted Villages' and had pinned high hopes on work in Biddinghurst. It was true that pattern haunting, one of his particular interests, where the sequence of events is always the same—monks processing at regular times for prayers, say—did not happen here, but the ghostly messenger who brings a warning, usually a true one, of approaching death, was perfectly exemplified by the horseman at Bidding Manor who had, Nigel told people, been heard by Graham Barnholt before he dropped dead. Such an insubstantial being could kill merely by its visit.

Charlie Iden, with his illimitable fund of information about the village, had told him that the late and now very unlamented Nigel was said to have inherited the Manor under Graham Barnholt's will. If that was so, why hadn't the horseman done his stuff for Nigel? It was a bitter thought that, on the Saturday night wasted on the horrible hoax of the faceless man in the church— he'd like to be able to confront Noah Pike and get the truth from him as to who had worn that mask!—the horseman had perhaps come and gone, and he, Jonathan, might have chanced to be up near the Manor and heard him. It was too frustrating to bear thinking about. Had Nigel himself even been down at the Manor that night and heard the horseman of doom? Did it come immediately before death, as it had for Graham Barnholt, or could it give fair warning? It would be distinctly unfair if supernatural warnings were laid on when no one was there to receive them. And then, for all he knew, the ghost was a snob and arrived only to Barn-holts about to die, not to upstarts like Nigel Wells.

Jonathan had not yet seen the other horseman of Bid-dinghurst, the murderer of Thomas à Becket, the one reputed to flee down the coast road beyond the village. If he had only not stopped on Monday night because of the light in Nigel's cottage, he might have got lucky then. It was not too late tonight, the moon was almost the same, and he meant to go on there after pursuing an-other inquiry tonight.

The jogger of last night must be a little eccentric to pursue his run across a garden, or to be jogging at all at that hour, and not stop when he did bump into some-one; but it was natural enough to cut across the garden of a house known to be empty, and he had not, as Jona-than had at first thought, stolen something from Barbary. He had bent over her to see if she was all right and then, like any jogger, not wanted to break his rhythm further. So she had assured Jonathan; but all the same she had been agitated, even frightened, and he had de-termined to go to the police all the same.

If she had been agitated, he was excited. The light moving in the cottage had turned out to be only Bar-bary's torch, but the thought of it reminded him that he never had heard the whole story of the ghosts that whis-pered after her down the stairs. He was very short on first-hand narrative in the book. Too often did stories about hauntings turn out to be legends passed down the generations, with no recent sighting, no *I saw it, I heard it,* such as Barbary could provide. So it was that his pro-fessional curiosity got the better of his tact. Later on, he was shocked at himself. He should never have asked her, so recently bereaved, so upset by this last event, what-ever she bravely pretended. Yet he *had* asked her, on impulse, as he was escorting her home from Nigel's cottage, and she had agreed at once. She would see him, she would tell him all about the whisperers, at eight-thirty tonight, Tuesday. He had wondered if she would think better of it, but no message had come putting him off; after all, she did know he could be reached at the Bidding Arms. Charlie Iden could be trusted to deliver a message, no matter how busy he was with the welcome windfall of visitors in the bar.

Charlie could be relied on for other help too. When Jonathan let slip that he was interviewing Barbary that evening, and perhaps 'let slip' was a euphemism for boasting, Charlie Iden advised him, first, not to tell any-one at all that Barbary was back at her house in case the Press got wind of it. Reporters were here already trying to find and talk to the children who'd been Nigel's victims—'taking porn pictures of our kids', Charlie put it. He seemed to be sympathetic with Barbary's position and said if Jonathan wanted to avoid leading reporters to her, he should approach the cottage by a back way, a circuitous field path the secret of which, surprisingly, no one in the village had yet sold to the media; the inhabitants of the cottage further down Apple Lane, overlooking Nigel's garden, had, it was known, sold bacon butties on the spot to reporters on the siege on Sunday at a fiver a time, and access to their toilet for a pound less. When the police had put cones up and banned all vehicles except those of residents, these en-trepreneurs had let TV vans park in their driveway at ten pounds an hour. The landlord at the Crossed Keys, the nearest pub, had doubled all prices . . .

Jonathan was disturbed to hear about Nigel's mis-deeds. It made the meeting with Barbary more embar-rassing. He could hardly condole with her about it, and he decided to avoid the subject of her brother altogether, recognising the usual ploy of the British when faced with others' bereavement.

Another awkwardness was whether she intended, con-sidering he was invited for eight-thirty, to offer him

something to eat. Here again he decided to do nothing.
If he arrived with a bottle of wine it would look as
though he presumed a meal. He was therefore armed
only with his little tape recorder in one pocket of the
loose linen jacket, and his notebook in the other, as he
negotiated the back way. Because he thought he must
conceal what looked like the equipment of a reporter
heading for a story, he wore a jacket, but the heat was
surprising. It rose from the ground and seemed to be
pressed down by the deep sky. The few people in the
street were in teeshirt, shorts, the thinnest of cotton
frocks, the boys and some of the men stripped to the
waist. It was supper-time. Even the reporters were catching up on gossip and refreshment in the pubs. Jonathan
ducked down the small cobbled passage between two
houses, on down a weed-grown path between their gardens, and out on the path that led round the fields to
Barbary's garden gate. She had not told him to come
that way; now he worried about it—would it give her
a shock?

What he did not anticipate, as he sweated through the
fields in his jacket, was that she had entirely forgotten
he was coming. The only person he met on the path was
one who seemed familiar with it, a tall lanky lad he had
seen round the village and whom he identified now as
the Death in the Haunted House. Death, this evening,
was smoking a cigarette and looking well pleased with
himself, as if he had come from some small tidy massa-
cre. The bleached hair was tucked back behind an ear
trimmed with studs and rings, which gave the skull face
a certain bizarre elegance. He waved a hand at Jonathan
as he passed, unsmiling, all in black, and Jonathan was
visited by the thought that, were he superstitious instead
of being interested in the supernatural, he might feel
himself hailed as the next victim.

He opened the high gate in the fence and went diffi-
dently in, glancing towards the house. Something was
happening, on the little terrace outside the french win-

dows, slightly obscured from here by bushes, that his eyes failed to interpret properly.

Two people were bending over the small ornamental pool at the terrace edge, though 'bending' was not quite it, one of them was prone on the flagstones and seemed to be drinking the water like an animal. The other, a girl with quantities of straight black hair, kneeling, seemed to be holding her head. The gate swung shut with a loud clack and the kneeling girl looked round quickly. It was Morticia, the ghoul with the gloves.

'Help me! She's slipped! I can't get her up.'

To his horror, as he arrived running, he saw that the one with her head half in the water was Barbary. He grasped her by the shoulders and swung her out of the pool. She lay on his arm, with closed eyes and dripping hair, and she was not heavy, but he supposed Morticia hadn't the strength to manoeuvre her out of the water.

'Did she faint?'

The girl's eyes were huge, the pupils tiny in the full evening sun. She stooped now over Barbary, combing the wet strands from her face carefully as though it was important for her to look good, half-drowned or not. 'I think so. She put her drink down and just fell forward.'

There was an empty glass beside the lounger. He took that much in but returned to Barbary. Was she breathing? Panic got him. He should have checked on that. He laid her down and tilted her head back, put his ear to her lips, watched her chest. There was nothing. He did what he had seen on television. He pinched those delicate nostrils shut and lowered his mouth on to the parted lips. If he had imagined kissing her when first they met, in his hopeful fantasy there had been some response from her. He breathed, paused, breathed. Didn't you check for a pulse? Was there a pulse? Shouldn't you put fists to the breastbone and shove? He did not feel Morticia would know; but she had put a finger behind Barbary's ear. He glanced to see if the chest was heaving and saw that Barbary had on only a silk negligée and nothing else, as it had parted on exquisite legs as far as her waist. He quickly reached to pull it together.

Morticia said, 'I think there's a pulse. Should I call an ambulance? Is she going to be all right?'

'I think she's breathing . . .' There was a soft motion of her breasts. 'Perhaps you'd better. To be on the safe side.' The sheer beauty of Barbary, and her near-nakedness, distracted him. 'She's not dead, thank God, but she hasn't come round yet. Shouldn't we get a doctor instead? I mean, to wake up in hospital . . . Do you know who her doctor is?'

'I think it's Dr Mingardi. Dad has him too. From Sax-hurst. His number should be in her book. I'll see if I can get him.' Thank God she's efficient, thought Jonathan, watching the faint movement of Barbary's silken bosom. Suppose she'd been one of those girls who shriek and fantigue, how would I have coped?

He could hear her voice on the phone just inside the french windows, and a bird in the trees down the garden sounding the alarm call. There must be a cat about.

At this moment something touched his leg between sock and trouser and he started. The thing materialised into a cat, Binkie if he remembered rightly, who now with outstretched nose whiskered his mistress's face. Morticia had arranged Barbary on her side with one knee drawn up. Binkie seemed to be inquiring what his mistress did there, on the flags of the terrace so far from his supper. Jonathan put out a hand to keep the cat from bothering Barbary, even though she was incapable of being disturbed.

In this, she proved him wrong. As Binkie's whiskers connected lightly with her nose, Barbary twitched it and half opened her eyes. Binkie backed before her confused gaze, lowered his white rump to the flagstones and stared at her. Barbary stirred her head to look at Jona-than just as the Morticia girl came out from the house and exclaimed, 'Oh, Barbary! Thank goodness you're better. Dr Mingardi's coming, so you'll soon be quite all right.'

She knelt beside Barbary and raised her, supporting her head, letting the wet hair soak her black teeshirt with no thought for herself. Jonathan found her matter-of-fact competence reassuring, as he stood there under the regard of Barbary's green eyes. He felt awkward but could not leave before the doctor came. It would be putting too much on the girl.

'Kat, what happened?'

Why on earth should Barbary inquire of Binkie? Then he realised she must mean the girl. Hadn't the dreadful Heather Armitage, during her confidential commentaries on the day he had been hijacked as her book porter, spoken of the Rector's daughter Kathy?—"I never call her Kat, it sounds so spiteful."

'You must have fainted. You slid forward off the lounger and nearly fell in the pool. *He,*' Kat made up by emphasis for not knowing his name, 'came along just at the right moment and got you out. Sir Lancelot.'

The faintest of smiles visited Barbary's pale face. With returning life came the charm that was natural to her. Strands of wet hair framed her face, dark lashes framed her eyes—she looked like some convalescent mermaid, save that her slender legs were evident.

'It's Jonathan, isn't it? Thank you.' She shut her eyes again, as if exhausted by the effort. Her speech slurred a little. 'I feel so sleepy . . . can't think why.'

'It's shock,' Jonathan volunteered. He was feeling it himself. Just inside the french windows, by the tele-phone, stood an array of drinks; the Hennessy was what he needed.

'Do you think you could get Barbary on to the sofa in there? I'll find a towel for her hair.'

Kat was in charge of the situation still, picking up the glass Barbary had put on the ground before she col-lapsed, and the one she herself had used. She came into the sitting room shortly after Jonathan had laid Barbary on the sofa, her languid arm was still sliding from his neck. Kat had two towels, one to spread on the cushion and the other to fold round Barbary's head so that she looked suddenly biblical. Then she drew back the curtains on the last of the evening light, as if to encourage a healthy wakefulness. In this she failed, as Barbary's eyes closed against the light immediately. Kat went round the room straightening magazines and the strew of cushions, disturbing—momentarily—a cat asleep through all disturbances. Jonathan sat on the edge of the chair he had been allotted when he first called on Barbary, and waited, feeling useless and experiencing a certain relief when the front doorbell rang.

Kat brought Dr Mingardi into the room. Small, dark, and with an air of being on his way to a more important case elsewhere, he cast a rapid glance at Jonathan as if nailing him as responsible for the patient's condition, and advanced on Barbary with a series of clucking noises such as might be used to encourage a hen to lay.

'I hear you've been a bad girl this evening. A little faint, are we?'

Barbary did not reject the sympathetic plural, but murmured assent as Dr Mingardi, certainly less faint than he had claimed, set about checking her for damage. Jonathan wondered if he should leave, and how to do it without drawing more attention or seeming like a deserter. Dr Mingardi now ignored him and opened Barbary's gown to listen to her heart as casually as if her state of undress and Jonathan's presence implied a degree of familiarity between them which excused it. He produced the soothing cluck again.

'Nothing to worry about! You've had plenty to trouble you recently. Plenty. Let's just get at this arm and take your blood pressure, shall we? That's it . . . No problem there. I'll give you something to calm those active nerves of yours, and you must take life easily for several days.' He was packing his bag as quickly as if he had a plane to catch. 'I'll call again towards the end of the week.' He stood up and raised an admonitory finger. 'Now, no rushing about, but no moping!' With this comprehensive programme, he turned to go. Jonathan received another glance. In the hall Dr Mingardi was making a fuss of a friendly black cat while saying something to Kat about a 'fugue from reality'. Jonathan, left alone with Barbary who had shut her eyes again, thought that few people had better cause to flee from a reality that included a murdered brother who turned out to be a pornographer of sorts, and life in a village whose children he had tried to corrupt.

48

Bone was chasing an earring.

Conducting inquiries in a village stuffed with reporters swarming back in pursuit of scandal as well as horror—the cherry on the cake—was never going to be easy, but luck for once was on his side. Those who had arrived thirsting for a story about teenagers abused by the murder victim had been driven by the heavy heat of the evening to slake a more mundane thirst in the tree-sheltered gardens of the Bidding Arms and the Crossed Keys. They were drowning frustration too, as most of them had been sent packing by Dave Hollis after further attempts to lure out his small son and a foster-child for an interview. Lucy Hollis had shaken her head at them and kept her mouth shut. Dave had certainly opened his mouth, but with nothing printable. The *Saturday Fun* reporter did plan to fax in a series of asterisks as Dave's opinion of the man who had betrayed his trust. A photographer had got an excellent shot of Midge Hollis shaking her fist at him, and quoted her as saying, 'I hope he rots in hell.'

Nigel Wells's reputation was enjoying a nosedive.

No one, therefore, caught a glimpse of Bone and Locker as they crossed Front Street from the Old Rectory to the Hollises' house. Only two little girls sat on the traffic railing outside an antique shop, licking ice-cream cornets very slowly, comparing progress and studying the noble lines of a Victorian rocking-horse in the shop window. Bone and Locker scarcely interrupted their view.

Bone was suffering from frustration: the theory that Fleur, driven off her never-very-stable trolley, was responsible for killing her father, Nigel and Winter, had never appealed to him even when it had seemed to fit so neatly. Instinct had rejected it, but he wished, now that instinct had been substantiated with fact, that instinct would provide a better candidate. This curious link of an earring, making a connection between Winter's death and Fleur, could equally, as Locker pointed out, apply to anyone who had been at the fête.

Nor was Fleur the only under-age girl exploited by Damien Winter. The London police said as much. Nigel might have introduced others from Biddinghurst, such as Lucy Hollis, as well. If Dave Hollis had bought the earrings for his daughter she might, revenge being in the air, have gone to wreak some. Bone remembered those shots of Lucy in Pre-Raphaelite dishevelled locks and nothing else, which seemed the sort of thing that turned Winter on.

But provided by Nature with such luxuriant marigold tresses, why would she have worn a wig?

Locker, lost in his own thoughts, which included a wry speculation as to why his super was bothering personally with a piddling little bit of the inquiry like this, also had the photo in his mind.

'At least it wasn't little Chrissie,' he growled, as he put out his hand to the doorbell.

Dave Hollis answered the door; Bone had thought at

the fête what a friendly face he had, the lines on it formed by past smiles. He was frowning now.

'I've nothing more to add. Why can't you leave us in peace? This place is getting to be a hell on earth.' A small boy trotted down the narrow hallway and took up a position under Dave's elbow to stare. Bone, looking down into the large blue eyes studying him, and recognising the face from those photographs, was conscious once more of a vivid sympathy for the unknown person who had pressed Heather Armitage's best embroidered cushion so firmly over the face of Nigel Wells. It was one of the ironies of his existence that he must bring to justice, at times, murderers more congenial than their victims.

'I'm sorry, Mr Hollis. Another line of inquiry has emerged. We have to ask a few more questions, if we may.'

His politeness appeared to mollify Dave, who stepped back and, brushing the child's hair with his arm, became aware of him. He added, with sudden fierceness, 'No more talking to the kids, though. They've had enough.'

Bone had not intended to trouble the children and, for that reason, had left Fredricks behind. He knew, though she had not said so, that she was unwilling to face Chrissie's passionate reproaches again. He followed Dave in, saying, 'I don't think there's any need for that.'

The small boy said, 'I don't mind questions,' and Dave, cupping a hand round the back of his head, propelled him towards the stairs, saying 'Find your mother.' The child said 'OK!' without demur, and trotted off as Dave went into the small sitting room where two sofas, strewn with toys and pummelled cushions, faced each other as if in challenge. A very old Kermit, his green faded to yellow, sat in the evening sun on the windowsill brightly regarding the view.

Dave was saying, 'An *earring?*'

'You bought a pair of earrings at Celia Madison's stall on Sunday. Did they look like these?' Locker produced the fax, and Bone went on, 'And do you still have both of them?'

Dave examined the fax, still surprised. 'That's the ones. Or very like them. She had quite a selection, you know. I thought Midge—my wife—would fancy them. We had an anniversary, Saturday, bit of an occasion, and an extra present doesn't come amiss.' His smile clouded as he looked at Bone and Locker again. 'What's this to do with Nigel Wells, then?' He said the name as though it disgusted him; Bone remembered Shay saying that Dave Hollis had become quite violent on seeing the photographs, furious at the treachery of a man he had taken at face value as genuinely fond of the children.

'I'm afraid we can't say any more at present, Mr Hollis. Could you ask your wife . . .'

Dave went out into the hall and bellowed 'Midge!' Somewhere upstairs a door opened on a sound of splashing and laughter. 'Those earrings I got you on Sunday. Have you still got them? The police want to know.'

'Hang on a tick!'

After a short pause, during which Locker gloomily regarded Kermit, Midge Hollis called from the stairhead, 'I thought for a minute Lucy had borrowed them—she'll take anything that fits. But they're still here. Kevin's bringing them down.'

That left Barbary and the Rector.

It was not Jonathan's day for communication. His purpose in going to Barbary's had been thwarted, even forgotten, in the drama of events, and he knew no more of the whispering ghosts than before. He meant, however, to do something useful while also passing on some of the drama. Kat Purdey, whom he had left in charge of the still somnolent Barbary, had let fall that her purpose in coming there had been to offer felicitations on Barbary's engagement to her Uncle Henry, who had just joyfully been telling the Rector his news. Jonathan, remembering Henry's scowling resentment of his presence when they first met at her cottage, could imagine how happy he must be at having secured his prize—and pictured his concern if he heard he had nearly lost it face down in an ornamental pool. Jonathan decided it would be kind to tell him this news, as he would certainly want to go to her. He did not intend to tell Henry how he had resuscitated Barbary. As far as the kiss-of-life went, Henry might be grateful for the life but balk at the kiss.

Although it was stickily hot, Jonathan hurried. Grasshoppers scattered before him like spray as he went through the field. He took off and carried his jacket. Emerging on Front Street he saw someone he knew, the Superintendent, on the pavement outside the Rectory, that large, economy-sized Inspector beside him. They were bidding farewell to two men in a red sports car Jonathan had seen here before. It was Henry at the wheel and his brother beside him. The engine revved and Jonathan tried to speed into a run, waving. Henry saw someone he did not recognise saluting him in the distance, and he waved back before he swung the car into a turn and sped off in the opposite direction. The Rector, short of a car because Forensic still had his for examination, had called on his brother's good nature to ferry him to an ailing parishioner some miles away. Henry, harbouring perhaps one celebratory drink too many, had a firm belief that God would look out for him while he had the Rector on board. His speed out of the village therefore drew a cry of protest from his brother. It also drew a cry of irritation from Jonathan, who had reached the Rectory gate and Bone.

'Something urgent, Mr Cade?' Bone's curiosity woke. 'Did you want the Rector? I understand he won't be back straight away.'

The Rector had in fact just been putting Fleur in the clear. On Monday night, when Winter drowned, the Rector, getting up during the night to go to the bathroom, had seen a light in Fleur's room, feared she was awake and brooding, and looked in. The light was on, certainly, but Fleur was fast asleep and he remembered his daughter had mentioned giving her one of his sleeping pills. 'Excellent they are, too. They have no side-effects, no drowsiness next day. No nodding off in the pulpit.'

So they must look further for Damien Winter's killer. The Rector had examined the picture of the earring, and thought it was rather like the ones he had bought for Kat—'She's fond of the unusual.' Henry had laughed and muttered an affectionate, 'I'll say.' During all this, he had been jingling his keys in his pocket, rising and falling on his toes as if anxious to go. He had gone, and here was Jonathan Cade the ghost-hunter explaining his need to see him.

'Barbary Wells? What happened?'

'Apparently she just collapsed. She fell forward into the pool on her terrace. I turned up just as Kat Purdey was trying to save her from drowning. To tell you the truth, when I gave her mouth-to-mouth I really had a strong reason to think she'd been drinking, and after all that's happened you can't blame her. And I expect she was celebrating too.'

49

In the car Locker said, 'It makes sense all right.'

Bone was abstracted. He seemed to be regarding the back of Fredricks's head, before him, with absorption.

'It would affect her name, I mean, Nigel being in all this unsavoury business. She can't have been innocent about some of it, though—she knew about Fleur, I suppose, bringing her to stay in London like that.' Locker thought Bone was about to speak, but he said nothing, so he went on, 'All part of Nigel's *kindness*. It's possible she didn't know Winter was the father or that Nigel had pimped for him. I suppose it was all for her vanity—her reputation and her vanity.'

After a pause, Locker took up, thinking aloud. 'She came down here specially to get the photos from Nigel's house in case we discovered them—which we ought to have done. She hired the car and came straight from London. Of course she'd need the wig at Winter's—anyone would recognise her, the doorkeeper would. But even with a wig and make-up Winter would have recognised her; she's very pretty but she's not seventeen any more, however tiny and kittenish. Winter would have to be stoned out of his mind before she got there; and I suppose the doorkeeper didn't actually turn a spotlight on her. She could *act* young. What did she have against Winter?'

Fredricks said, 'I heard he didn't cast her for a series.'

'Again it's her vanity. It all fits together. Winter rejects her, Scatchard forgets her, Nigel fouls up her image. When she gets engaged, it's to the Rector's brother. It couldn't be more respectable as a cover-up.'

He was used to the Super's silences, though this time he thought that Bone barely heard him. He went on considering Barbary Wells, that too-perfect fragile prettiness and his sense that she acted a perpetual role. The car swung into Apple Lane, past Henry's house, past Nigel's, to stop outside Barbary's opposite.

Bone sprang out before Fredricks could come to open the door; he was through the gate before Locker caught up with him. Locker, not given to fantasy, had the sudden idea they must put their skates on to stop Barbary from doing a Sleeping Beauty on them and sliding off into a world where they couldn't reach her. Fleur was enough, for ever zonked out. Lucky that Kat Purdey, that competent young madam, was apparently there.

Lucky indeed. Bone had now attacked the door, slamming with the knocker and leaning his thumb on the bell more like a hooligan than a police superintendent. No one came. No one appeared at the window to see who it was.

'Come on. The back may be open.'

Round the back, past laurel and rosemary, was a terrace, with the pool they had heard about, a lounger, chair and open french windows. Bone went straight in, Locker and Fredricks at his heels, and called out, 'Hallo?'

A moment later, glancing into the sitting room where a white cat sprawled on the sofa, and seeing Fredricks emerge from the kitchen shaking her head, he started up the stairs two at a time. Kat appeared on the upper landing; for the first time they saw her startled, even frightened.

'God, I thought you were the TV people.' Her usually pale face was flushed. 'All that row outside. I was afraid Barbary would be disturbed.'

'Where is she?'

'She's having a bath. She's very tired and wants to go straight to bed.'

Bone reached the top of the stairs and, startling Locker, pushed Kat aside and turned the handle of the door behind her. Clouds of steam issued, enveloping him as he vanished from view. Locker followed into the fog.

Barbary lay in the bath, in a green-tiled alcove, her face flushed even more than Kat's, her eyes closed; she had slipped so that the water was up to her mouth. Bone took hold of her under the shoulders to pull her up. The angle was awkward because of the alcove wall, she was as slippery as a piece of soap and nearly escaped from his grip. Locker pulled out the bath plug and together they got her out and laid her on the fluffy white mat beside the bath. Pat Fredricks put the thick green bath-sheet over her while Bone felt for a pulse and checked that she was breathing. Then, swathing her in the big towel, he lifted her and asked Kat, wide-eyed in the doorway, 'Where's the bedroom?'

Kat led the way. Bone carried Barbary along the landing to a room whose ceiling was tented in silvery grey silk, ribbed like a gleaming cobweb, with walls of palest rose and a carpet to match. The bed on whose pillows he propped her was a four-poster with barley-sugar columns of mahogany and a grey silk tester. If Barbary cared about her image, this bedroom did not let her down.

'Is she all right? What happened?' Kat was the other side of the bed, swift, concerned, bending over Barbary, her dark hair flowing to mingle with Barbary's, wet on the pillow. 'She's been so dopey this evening. Has she taken something, do you think?'

'I think it very likely,' Bone said, and what else he might have said was interrupted by more loud knocking at the door. 'See who that is, Pat. If it's the Press, tell them we don't want any. Then I think we'd better have a doctor.'

A wish no sooner made than granted. Fredricks's voice could be heard in the hall, and then another, flat, sardonic, American, came closer up the stairs, so that Bone was ready for the sight as Dr Beth Dillon came striding into the room, in purple tunic and lilac trousers, unflustered by Fredricks's efforts to impede her.

'Just what goes on? Have you made the poor girl sick? I knew she shouldn't come here on her own.'

The American term for 'ill' made Bone wonder if Barbary ought to have had emetics. He was given no time to disclaim responsibility; Beth Dillon was feeling Barbary's pulse, pulling up her eyelids, bending down to put an ear close to her face.

'She fell asleep in the bath.' Kat offered the facts. 'I'd only left her a minute and she seemed to be fine. She must have taken something, I think. A sleeper.'

'H'm. Better establish exactly what.' Beth's dark eyes regarded Bone. 'How do you come into this? No, forget that till later.' She turned to the bedside table, with its lace cloth over grey silk, on which, beside the lamp with its matching shade, stood a phalanx of bottles, hand-cream jar and pillboxes. Beth opened them all, sniffing some. 'Nothing but herbal stuff here. If she took any of these she's all right.' To Bone she added, 'I *am* medically qualified, though it's some time since I practised.' She glanced round and, dismissing Kat as a possible errand boy, sent Fredricks to search the bathroom shelves and cupboard. 'Taking a tub was the last thing to do if she'd had a sleeper.'

Bone was aware it might have been the last thing Barbary had ever done.

Fredricks returned, saying there were only toiletries in the bathroom. She had brought a small towel from the rail.

'Who's a clever girl?' Beth actually gave Fredricks a smile, which took the sarcasm out of the comment; and turned to Kat who was in fact spreading Barbary's wet hair out from her head. 'Give it to Iras or Charmian or whoever—will you dry Barbary's hair for her?'

Kat's expression was never one of amiability, but she took the towel and got on with it. Fredricks said, 'Could Miss Wells do with some coffee?'

'She'd be better sleeping this off; but I could sure do with some.'

Fredricks silently sought permission from Bone, who nodded, and she went downstairs. He said, 'Are you sure Miss Wells shouldn't be in hospital?' He was taking off his wet jacket.

'I wouldn't think lavage is necessary. I'm here to monitor her condition and she's not deeply unconscious.'

Suddenly, from nowhere, a black cat leapt on the bed and stood on Barbary's stomach. Pleased to discover somebody supine, it set to kneading with dedication.

'Get that damn cat out of here,' Beth said, sweeping at it backhand. Kat, who was gently swathing Barbary's head in the towel, stopped and made a lunge to field the cat, who sprang past her and fled under the bed. Kat disappeared from view as she went after it.

Locker, undoing wet shirt-cuffs, muttered something about the bathroom and went and shut himself in there. Fredricks called from the stairs 'Sir?', and Bone went out on the landing. She was holding her phone. 'Sir, the IR says London called you. I've got the number. Do you want to call from up there or down here?' Bone descended the stairs and she turned and preceded him, saying 'There's an Aga in the kitchen, sir, you could dry your coat.'

The kitchen, like Nigel's, had not the air of a room much used. Its blue and primrose had unscratched, pristine surfaces. A carved spice-rack held full jars of spices, their labels meticulously aligned. The blue Aga's warmth made the room too hot despite open windows and door.

Fredricks put the call through, and Bone, taking the phone from her, heard Inspector Lamb.

'We've got the p.m. results on Winter, sir.'

'Fire away.'

'Cause of death—well, it amounts to drowning, sir. Severe blow on the temple corresponding to the smear on the pool's edge. Skin broken. Then there's alcohol in the bloodstream, but the amount is unreliable because of the hours since death, and the immersion. Then there's also traces of a sedative and the state of the stomach membrane suggests it contained antihistamine. He's added a list of sleeping tablets marketed over the counter which contain this; Still-nite, Sweet-sleep, Sereenox, Drowsine. The manservant says Winter never used sleepers—said a good meal and a nice hot girl was all he ever needed. It seems this girl in the wig was just too hot. Have you had any luck with the earring, sir?'

'We've got a lead,' Bone said. 'Thanks, very much indeed. We'll let you know.' He broke the connection.

From habit, he had been looking round.

'New-washed glasses. Did you wash them, Pat?'

'No, sir. They were there when I came in.'

Bone swung a chair towards the Aga, to hang his jacket on the back of it. A well-worn black denim bomber-jacket, lying across the seat, began a slide to the floor. He rescued it. A small card fell to the floor and he stooped for it and then stood still, and put the phone down on the table.

'Pat. You saw that?'

'Yes, sir.' She stood with the coffee-pot in one hand as the kettle began to make its seething hum. She and Bone looked at the bubble card of Sereenox. 'It fell out of the pocket.'

He looked round. The kitchen had all amenities. He pulled a tissue from the roll on the wall, and a plastic bag from the container beside it, and he was packaging the bubble card when feet came drumming down the stairs and a black shape streaked into the kitchen closely followed by Kat.

Bone draped the tea-cloth over his package and stood, like Fredricks, rigid while Kat flung herself down and caught the cat. She got to her feet, glowering over the cat's head and, without explanation, left the room, went to the french windows in the hall and dropped the cat into the garden. She shut the windows, turned on her heel and went upstairs.

There was a thud from the sitting room. The cat appeared in the hall and immediately legged it up the stairs past her. They heard a furious yell of 'Shi-it!' as Kat pursued it.

Bone caught Fredricks's eye. Neither of them smiled, but somehow shared the moment. Then he picked up the tea-cloth and hung it over the rail of the Aga.

His eye took in something else on the chair, half under the denim jacket. Morticia's long black gloves lay there, escaping from a sheet of crumpled tissue paper. They had elegant satin-covered buttons on the ruched wrist. Fredricks, making the coffee, watched him as he packaged these too in a plastic bag. 'You're witness, Pat. Now, can we label these?' He pulled out a drawer under the smooth primrose worktop, and found cutlery. Another drawer had more tea-cloths.

Fredricks also rummaged, to more purpose. She produced a wax pencil, for use on freezer bags, and she labelled the packages with date and where found. Bone and she initialled them. Through the plastic, a bit of print on the back of the bubble card showed plainly: Sereenox. Do not take with alcohol. Read leaflet in . . . Sereenox. Do not . . .

Several of the bubbles had been punctured.

'She used these, sir?' Fredricks was putting the coffee on a tray, with sugar and a jug of cream. Bone had a brief private bet that Dr Beth took neither. 'But the gloves, sir?'

'They might just have a message for us.' More than that he would not say. If the bomber-jacket belonged to Barbary, a garment faded, torn, which he doubted she would have consented to be seen dead in, the gloves might be an irrelevance; but in Bone's mind a terribly convincing scenario was continuing to put itself together.

Fredricks had got cups on the tray and was carrying it upstairs when they had another visitor.

Henry Purdey had delivered his brother to the farmhouse of the ailing parishioner in record time, and had been assured that the old woman's son would convey the Rector home after he had had a chat with her. Both the brothers had felt splendidly relieved at this, and Henry had sped back to Biddinghurst with a song on his lips and the wind in what remained of his hair. He dropped in on the Bidding Arms for a celebratory pint or two, and there met Jonathan Cade who, drawing him aside, lost no time in telling him about Barbary's collapse.

Henry, frantic but mindful of the reporters thronging the place, dived out by the side door and, subduing his haste on Front Street, slid down the little passageway that led between houses to the field path.

Anxiety and speed had combined to turn his face a mottled scarlet at odds with the tousled ginger-grey hair as he burst in at the french windows and stared, panting heavily, at the steadily retreating trim back of Fredricks on the stairs. If he had ever noticed Fredricks's impassive horse face in the background during Bone's visit to him in London, he had certainly no idea what the back of her looked like.

'Who the hell are you?' He meant to bellow, but as he had not the breath, it emerged as a croak. 'Where's Barbary?'

Beth Dillon came out on the landing to relieve Fredricks of the tray and, looking down over the banister rail, she said, 'I guess we had to have you sooner or later. She's far too pooped to see *you* right now—if you'll excuse my medical language.' Carrying the tray into Barbary's bedroom she said over her shoulder, 'Call back tomorrow and I'll let you know if you can see her.'

Bone, watching from the kitchen, wondered if Henry would add to the good doctor's workload by having a stroke. Instead, after a long moment standing there gaping, his face turning visibly darker, rage gave him strength. He put one meaty hand on the newel and, with a wrench that made it creak, charged upstairs. Bone, interested to see him assert to Beth Dillon the rights of a fiancé above those of an interfering friend, and having also reasons of his own, followed.

When Henry burst into the bedroom on Fredricks's heels, his eyes were only for the woman on the bed, wrapped in a bath-sheet, her head turbaned in a towel, her bare shoulders and moonstone pendant giving her the air of an odalisque. Beth Dillon, pouring coffee at the bedside table, straightened up and bestowed on Henry a dark glare.

'I thought I told you to stay out. This is no—'

'Barbary. Darling. Are you all right?'

Striding eagerly forward to the bed, Henry tripped on the black-clad rump of his niece, reaching for Fiddles under the bed. Both Purdeys shot forward and Henry crash-landed on top of Barbary. Beth's coffee went all over the lace cloth. Henry tried to prise his face out of

Barbary's bosom by leverage, his hands beside her ribs. Under the bed a violent hiss and Kat's yell showed that results had not been good there either.

'Henry . . .'

To astonishment all round, this came from Barbary. With Henry's brusque descent, her eyes had jolted open; now sense and speech had come back to her. Beth reached for her wrist and began to ask how she felt, and Henry, overcome at recognition from the adored object, beat Beth to the hand and mumbled kisses on it.

'Where is Kat?' Barbary, however feeble her voice, seemed to remember who had last been with her. She turned her head as, on cue, Kat scrambled to her feet beside Henry. So might Lady Macbeth have looked when asking for the daggers, such was the fury on the pale face—streaked with blood from an angry scratch when Fiddles had defended himself from the intrusion of a human cannonball. This face, thrust towards Henry, made him recoil.

'Why can't you keep away from that slag?'

She followed this by a two-handed shove full in her uncle's chest, which sent him sprawling to the floor. She stood over him with hands now clenched at her sides. 'She's poison like her brother. Why can't you see that? Do you really want to get yourself tied to a creature who's just been humped by the gardener an hour ago? She's as much of a sleazebag as her bastard brother! Wake up to it!'

During this tirade Henry's mouth wasn't the only one that stayed open. Fredricks stood, mouth ajar, at Locker's side; Beth stood speechless, her hand stretched still towards Barbary's wrist. Kat, in charge, long legs astride, was at last letting go. Bone noticed Barbary shrink deeper into her pillows when Kat pointed at her, the lovely eyes terrified. 'She's shit, I tell you, better off dead—'

Henry was getting up.

'—polluting this world. And you want to marry—'

'Hey now, steady *on!*' Henry was more inclined to mollify his niece than argue with her, and for this no blame could attach to him. She could have stood in for an avenging Fury at this moment. It was Beth Dillon who had the courage to intervene.

'Now you listen, young lady. You're to leave this room. You've said enough—'

'I haven't said the half of what's gone on. If you all knew!' She cast an all-embracing, contemptuous glare round. And if *you* knew, thought Bone, what Fredricks has got in her bag.

Time to try his luck. But, before he could step forward, it was a voice from the bed that halted all action, and Barbary's turn to point, frailly.

'She . . . she tried to kill me.' She struggled up on the pillows, hastily supported by Beth. 'In the water. I kept slipping. I thought I was going to drown . . . and there was such hammering on the door and the bell ringing I thought it was in my head . . . and Kat came in and I wanted her to help me but she didn't. She stood there. And she leant over and I thought she would pull out the bath plug.' Her voice was strengthening. 'She took hold of my ankles. She was starting to pull at them. Then there was some noise. You—' her eyes turned towards Bone—'you must have come in. She swore and went out. I don't remember, except I think you were lifting me. Henry . . .'

She began to cry, the tears rolling down under the lashes without sob or sniffle, while Beth automatically patted her shoulder and Henry continued to stare at his scornful niece as if she had turned into a cobra.

Action was needed and Bone took it. He stepped forward and began the usual formula of cautioning, without affecting in the least Kat's pose or expression. There was silence when he had finished.

Under the bed, Fiddles sneezed.

50

It was towards midnight that Bone got home, so weary that the stairs to the first-floor flat appeared to stretch before him like the climb to Machu Picchu. As he shut the front door, music, melancholy yet soothing, drifted down from above. He thought he recognised *The Swan of Tuonela*. That meant Grizel was still up, and he was energised to climb at speed.

She was lying on the sofa, book open in her hand, head turned to gaze out at the night sky. Evidently Sibelius had masked the sound of Bone's arrival for, seeing him, she cast the book on the cushions and sprang up to meet him. They stood a long moment, her head on his shoulder, arms wrapped round each other, while Bone felt his tensions dissolve in her warmth. Finally she stepped back, holding him by the arms, and looked at him.

'My dear, you're worn out. Come in the kitchen and I'll get you something to eat. Cha's still at Grue's watching a video, but she should be back at any time. I've got cold soup,' she linked her hand in Bone's and towed him after her, 'cold lamb with plum, and cold apple-pie. How does that tickle your fancy?'

'I'm laughing already,' Bone parked himself on the kitchen settle, formerly fairly uncomfortable and therefore once stacked with newspapers and magazines but now upholstered by Grizel in a Morris pattern of cream daisies on cinnamon, and comfortable. He watched his wife go briskly about the business of putting supper on the table. As she put two bowls down and began to ladle smooth, thick, light-green soup, he said severely, 'You

274

haven't eaten yet. You haven't forgotten you're eating for someone else, I hope?'

'Someone else is your son, please remember. I'm convinced about that, whatever you may say.'

Grizel sprinkled shredded mint from the chopping board on to the soup, raised her eyes and gave him a sharp look. 'And what's wrong with seconds? I'm a cook who likes her own work.' She sat down at his left and picked up a spoon. 'You look as if you've been supping with the devil; I take it you've not found out who did it yet.'

Bone took his first mouthful of soup, delicate, cold, fresh, and it came to him suddenly how hungry he was. 'No. Trouble is, I think we *have* found who did it. Possibly all three men—Wells, Scatchard and Winter—were murdered by the same person.' He tore his roll open to butter it, while Grizel stopped to stare at him.

'Winter? So the earring Cha saw *was* a clue. But who on earth? Not Fleur Scatchard, I hope, poor girl.'

'She thinks she's to blame for it all but no, it's not her. Is there more of this soup?'

'Plenty, but you must leave room for the lamb, not to mention the apple-pie.' She leant to take his soup bowl. 'But I think I'll not give you anything till you tell.' She stopped suddenly and the soup bowls clattered in her hands. 'It's not Barbary Wells! She couldn't have murdered her own brother!'

'She could, I expect, and I don't know that I'd have blamed her if she had. No, it's the daughter of, I suppose, Biddinghurst's most respected citizen. The Rector.'

Grizel had put the bowls in the sink. She turned, eyes wide. 'Kat Purdey! I taught her when she was ten, at Wimbury Park before I went to Haddon House. Are you sure?'

Bone sighed. 'Sure enough. It isn't as yet a case that'll stand up, and so far we're holding her only on attempted murder. I've a feeling Forensic will produce what more we need.' He took a plate from Grizel, of delectable cold stew. He had been too tired to see her properly; now he pleased his eyes: blonde short hair, blonde tussore shirt, cream trousers; her quick movements . . . 'At the moment all we have, and it might not convince a jury if a sharp defence counsel's on the job, is Barbary's evidence that Kat tried to drown her in her bath.'

Grizel, turning with the blue bowl of rice salad, suspended all action. 'Tried to drown Barbary too? You're making me into some kind of Greek chorus here, Robert. You ought to start back at the beginning and tell me why she's done all this. I look at the fierce child of ten that I knew and I can't make sense of it. I suppose she was one of those of whom Nigel Wells took his revolting pictures.'

'Has that been in the news already? Yes, I suppose it has.' Bone fended off an infiltration by Ziggy, Cha's cat, beside him on the settle, extending a long grey glove to tap his wrist, the message being that lamb was always acceptable. He thought of Barbary's cats. He could not imagine Beth Dillon feeding them; more likely brushing them aside.

'It was on the local news on radio and in the evening paper. You can see the headlines later—"ORDER OF THE BOOT"—"PRIVATE EYEFUL—STAR'S PORN SECRETS." Cha says she knew he was a creep even before he tried to grope her.' Grizel sat down and offered a sliver of her lamb to The Bruce, her own cat; Ziggy hastily leapt down to remind The Bruce that this was his territory still. When the family stayed at Grizel's cottage The Bruce had supremacy, and Bone wondered how things would be settled in the new house, when it was found. Grizel said, 'Even at ten years old, Kat wasn't a child you could take liberties with.'

'That may be why we haven't seen anything of her among the dodgy pictures. Lucy and Chrissie Hollis, some of the Hollis foster-children—you remember I told you about the Hollises—'

'They'll have social workers coming out of the woodwork, those poor Hollises. Will they take the children away?'

Bone spoke through salad, 'I hope not. I'd put in my word for the Hollises. Decent souls, I'd say, and as much taken in by that treacherous garbage Nigel as anyone else in the place. The children seem to have kept their parents, and everyone else concerned, well in the dark; more successfully than many criminals manage to do.'

'No news to me. I'm a teacher.' Grizel glanced at her watch. 'I'm surprised Cha isn't home yet; but it *is* holidays.'

She fixed Bone once more with her gaze and he wondered at the difference among green eyes. Barbary's, he decided, had no humour in them. A life that centred on herself—the eyes were beautiful, but had none of the energy that sparkled in Grizel's.

'Robert: you have to make a better show than this. I've a mind to hold back the apple-pie, *with* cream, unless you make sense. If Kat Purdey did not smother Nigel Wells for taking dodgy pictures of her, why did she? And why on earth stab that poor man in the Haunted House? What had *he* done to her?'

Bone held up one hand, riveting the hopeful attention of Ziggy and The Bruce. 'Learn the rules of interrogation, woman. Ask too many questions at once and you'll get the answers to none. You won't believe the only answer we've got, anyway. I'm not sure I do.'

'Try me, Robert.'

'It seems she was killing to protect.'

'Protect! Whom had she got to protect?'

'Fleur Scatchard for one. She'd taken her under her wing. A girl with an alcoholic mother who doesn't want to know about her, even when she'd had a go at cutting her wrists; and a father with loads of charm and a roving eye. He beat Fleur up and I suspect did worse. Kat was her champion.'

'Ah. I see that. She was like that at Wimbury, standing up for the inarticulate and oppressed; very strong on justice. We had a wee problem with some parents, I seem to remember. They objected to her punching a playground bully in the stomach.'

'The girl hasn't changed, then.' He leant across to grasp Grizel's wrist as she drew the apple-pie towards her. 'I married the right woman. I get home a wreck, thinking I made a fool of myself; and you make me feel I've come into harbour. Keep it up, Kinloch.'

This reference to her middle name, which her husband professed to see as sibylline, indicating her power to deal with problems, Grizel received with composure. 'You'd do well to let go my wrist unless you want a slice of hand instead of pie.' Then, as she cut the pie, she went on, 'How did she kill Nigel Wells? The news just said he was smothered. How do they know that?'

'Medical evidence of asphyxiation; but at the party they'd played that humiliating trick on him and there was paint all over his face. That paint was on the *under-side* of the cushion his head was resting on. Half the village left their prints on that car, putting in books for Heather Armitage's stall—and I wonder what she's done with them all?—but Kat left no mark. She must have come after everyone else, very likely in the early hours of Sunday morning, wearing those gloves she'd borrowed for the Haunted House act, and I should imagine she held the cushion on Nigel's face with as little compunction as if she'd stepped on an earwig.'

'Save the Whale and Kill the Bastard? I suppose I joke because it is dreadful. Lucky it doesn't take away your appetite: more cream,' she pushed the blue jug across to him. 'Then there was the news story about drugs. What about them?'

'Nigel used to be, probably still was, an addict. Ferdy said at the p.m. there wasn't much left of the membrane of one nostril, it had been snowing so hard. Cocaine may be the social drug but it's a wrecker. And he knew where to get anything the teenagers were interested in experimenting with, and he brought it to the party for free.

Perhaps a sweetener in return for their posing for his feelthy pictures. They evidently didn't think it a fair deal.'

'Robert, it's not Christian to say so, but that girl deserves a medal. You must have felt sick over the pictures. But what made her suddenly turn into an avenger, if they'd already punished him with their nasty joke?'

Bone grimaced. 'Fleur. It seems when she got home Fleur's father laid into her, and she fled to Kat. Or so the Rector said, for we're getting nothing from Kat herself and Fleur has a minder now in the form of a psychiatric social worker. Laurie Scatchard in the Haunted House was a sitting duck. Whatever he said or did to Fleur on Saturday night signed his death warrant. Kat must have seen she'd never get a better chance: almost total darkness with lights at random, screams supplied for free, knives a-gogo, not to mention the bonus of people with grudges against him going through.'

Grizel offered more pie, which he accepted with alacrity. 'You know, Robert, I'm having second thoughts about the medal. Scatchard seemed a bit of a rascal when we met him on Saturday, but not in the same class with Nigel Wells. To think of Kat sticking a knife in him is not pretty.'

'A lot of what I have to think isn't pretty. When it's a fact, and not a thought, it's uglier still.'

'I had not considered that I'd be sorry for the landscape of your mind.' Grizel offered, in token of her sympathy, a warm thin hand for him to hold. 'But you've not said yet how this ties in with that man Damien Winter and his drowning and—' She stopped and put a finger to her lips. 'I am not to ask more than one question at a time, sir.'

'Picture once more the avenging angel. Enter another villain with a bill to pay, this time for violating Fleur.'

'Fleur and Kat aren't an item, are they?'

'Fleur's in love, I understand, with Phil Merrick—a Romeo-and-Juliet affair disapproved of by his grandfather; though his grandfather already has an Olympic bronze in disapproval. No, I think Kat's protection is purely altruistic . . . Winter was a customer for Nigel's porn pics; the London fuzz discovered a lot more, from various sources, in his flat. He most likely fancied Fleur and ordered a takeaway, so to speak. Fleur, with ambitions to be an actress, goes up to town escorted by kind Barbary for an audition. Winter, just as kind, gives her one and a baby into the bargain, though I don't suppose he meant to do that.'

'Then it's very incompetent of him.'

Bone shrugged. 'I can only suppose he overestimated her sophistication, thought it was up to her, that she knew what the score was and would be on the pill. I'm inclined to think that for Fleur it all came as a nasty shock that she wasn't prepared for in any way. Not every teenager these days is leading an active sex life.' He paused, aware that Grizel knew he worried about Cha. In that second, he was galvanised to look at his watch. 'Where the devil is she? It's half-past twelve! How was she proposing to come home?'

'Grue said her father would give Cha a lift back as soon as he came in. He's out with Grue's mother somewhere and I suppose they haven't got in yet. She's a sensible girl, thank goodness; not like the ones we're discussing. What happened to poor Fleur? I take it she didn't have the baby?'

'Kind Barbary ferried her up to town for the termination. Kind Barbary's kind brother arranged it all and paid for it. It was the fact that he got reimbursed by Winter to the exact amount that put us on to it—'

'Couldn't she have had the child?'

'In that village? But I should think the abortion was even more traumatic—it sounds so tidy, get it all removed; but she still grieves. It seems she'd planned to run away, though she was vague about any destination; she was ready, made-up and with clothes and money, and even a wig for disguise, on the Tuesday evening; but she told Pat Fredricks, "I fell asleep instead," and I think Kat Purdey's pet Sereenox was probably responsible, while Kat went up to London to terminate Winter. I have a theory that Kat only heard some of Fleur's woes on Saturday night or over the weekend when Fleur stayed with her.'

Grizel stacked the plates in the sink and ran water over them. One of the many things Bone liked about her was her lack of fussiness about the house. If she didn't feel like doing dishes she didn't mind leaving them, and neither he nor Cha were chivvied to keep their own areas, his study and her bedroom, fit for inspection at all times. Grizel respected their privacy.

She spoke over her shoulder, turning off the tap. 'So you're saying that Kat went up to London—when was it?'

'Monday night.'

'Got in to see Winter at a moment's notice—'

'She probably was lucky there. The manservant believes an appointment had been made. Fleur had his telephone number and Kat must have found him at a loose end. You have to remember, fresh meat is always welcome to a moulting tiger.'

'Robert, you're a poet.' Grizel left the sink to press a kiss on his forehead; he turned where he sat and locked his arms round the slender waist. Both cats stalked off into the sitting room, recognising that the food-producing cycle had ended for the night. Bone heard Grizel's voice very oddly when she spoke again, for he had his ear against her ribs. 'So she pushes him into the pool—why doesn't he swim?'

'Because she's fed him sleepers in his drink and bashed his head on his marble poolside.'

'Is all this speculation or have you proof?'

'Not at the moment, but I have high hopes of Forensic. First, I have to find a wig.'

Grizel had opened her mouth for the astonished question consequent on such a remark, when they heard in the street below the arriving roar of a motorbike. They were looking at each other when, in the silence after it stopped, they heard a murmur of voices and then the quiet shutting of the front door. The bike zoomed off. Cha had returned, most probably by courtesy of Justin Rafferty, thought Bone—that boy is ubiquitous. They could hear her coming softly up the stairs, no doubt hoping they were both in bed and that the lights had merely been left on for her.

Bone looked sternly at Grizel.

'Your ball, I think, Kinloch.'

51

Biddinghurst was suffering from rapid change of mind.

In the course of a few days, its local celebrity and source of pride had been murdered, in grotesque circumstances, to their universal horror and indignation. He had then been exposed as a fraud, one who had grossly practised on their credulity and corrupted their young. Quite a percentage of the inhabitants now felt that the murderer, whoever it turned out to be, had only done everyone a favour. Wednesday morning brought the news that the Rector's daughter, rumoured to be in custody in Tunbridge Wells, was the one who had taken justice into her hands, and there was almost total sympathy and support. Kat Purdey, certainly, was not an appealing girl. She had kept her cool distance from all the world, and consented to involve herself in village activities strictly on her own terms. Until now, people had pitied the Rector for having a daughter so little use to him in the parish. Suppose she had indeed avenged the reputation of the village, so degradingly beslimed by re-

porters crawling everywhere, then Kat Purdey had up-
held the cause of morality as strongly as did her father,
though her method was characteristically extreme. Biblical mutterings about an eye for an eye, a tooth for a
tooth, were heard; though no one stopped to remark
that in this case the exchange rate was a little steep.

Heather Armitage, when she had fully digested what
the media had to say about Nigel's activities, on impulse
hurried out of her front door to collect the flower tributes left where her car had been parked. These she
thrust into her dustbin, lilies and chrysanthemums
crushed together with their poignant dedications addressed to Nigel. This was her sacrifice, because it had
given her real satisfaction to peep out of her front windows at these offerings on her drive. She saw them as
not just a tribute to Nigel but, in their way, recognition
of the trauma she had suffered in her horrid discovery
of the body. She crammed down the dustbin lid, shud-
dering at the recollection. Fate had forced her to witness
too many disgusting things of late. How that Wells pair
had deceived the innocent! The dear Rector had scarcely
been able to believe her warnings about Barbary and
the Rafferty boy.

Dolly Pike was on Heather's doorstep on Wednesday
morning, and had some trouble in getting her to answer.
Whether it was the stress of what she had gone through,
or leaving off her usual flowered bolero in the heat of
Tuesday evening, but the cold that had threatened to
ruin the fête for her had returned and she had recourse
to a powerful dose of the remedy that had worked so
well then. It was with her hair in disarray—for she had
checked that it was only Dolly on the step—and in her
quilted pastel-blue dressing-gown that she ushered Dolly
in, sat her down in the breakfast area of the kitchen, put
the kettle on and heard her news: Kat Purdey's arrest.
Her first thought was naturally to get dressed and hurry
across to comfort the Rector, but Dolly, with a kind
smile that was really almost a smirk, told Heather that

he had already left for Tunbridge Wells to be with his daughter. Dolly also had it on the best authority (Mary Markham's, but Dolly did not name her as she had been the one who emptied the Rector's small watering-can over the swooning Heather) that Sam Pearson, a well-known solicitor in Tunbridge Wells, had been called upon by the Rector to look after Kat's interests and be present during police interviews with her.

'Do you think she did it?' Dolly leant forward, her eyes alight.

'That is for the police to decide,' replied Heather repressively and, had she known it, inaccurately—the jury system, ancient bastion of English law, had slipped her memory.

Heather and Dolly put their heads together. Over tea and toast, Heather broke her promise to the Rector not to tell what she had seen Barbary and Justin up to when she called unexpectedly the evening before.

'Barbary Wells is no better than . . . After all, she's Nigel's sister. Tainted. And encouraging . . . having intimacies with people who do her garden! A gardener!' Heather recollected that Noah Pike was not perhaps actually a gardener but as sexton very near it, the holes he dug getting people popped into them rather than plants. She said quickly, 'Such a woman is *certainly* capable of anything, anything at all! I shouldn't be at all surprised if the police have got it wrong and it was her, after all.'

'You mean, stabbing poor Laurie?' Dolly was ready to credit Heather as another Miss Marple.

'Who knows? What I *do* know is that Barbary is very pretty in that film-star way of hers, and the police are only human. I don't know about the superintendent but that nice big inspector who talked to us could well have fallen for her tricks. You and I would have seen through them at once.'

* * *

Bone arrived at the Incident Room in the Old Rectory later than he had intended. He had rung the Chief with the glad news that their murderer, to all likelihood, was caught, and the Chief had displayed little enthusiasm. For one thing, Nigel's reputation had gone into such reverse, and the murderer was a motherless girl, daughter of a clergyman, so that Bone was made to feel he might have come up with someone less likely to attract sympathy. Bone, reflecting that if the Chief were to interrogate Kat personally he might change his mind, had to admit that the evidence so far might not carry the case; this, perversely, mollified the Chief.

Nor, this morning, was there anything fresh to help them from the interrogation of Kat. Bone had left this to Locker, whose case after all it was, although he expected what did happen: bolstered by the massive presence of Sam Pearson, a sort of Samuel Whiskers figure of a lawyer with an old-fashioned watch-chain draped across the imposing width of his waistcoat, Kat had refused to say anything at all.

'I pointed out that it wouldn't look good in court, and that old rascal Pearson—I know he's a friend of yours, sir, but—he just said, "My client's case may never come to court", and that young witch actually smiled.'

'Pearson needn't be too sure. London, after all, have matched her prints we sent them to those on the glass found by Winter's pool. What was she there for, that could be innocent? Yet we can't prove a thing. She might even cook up some story about going up to town to try and rustle up some money or help for Fleur. If Forensic, now, come up with anything on the gloves . . .'

Locker, grinning, laid a report on the table and Bone swivelled it round to read. 'I put a rocket up them and they called through half an hour ago. Threads caught in the ruching correspond exactly to those used on Heather Armitage's embroidered cushion. The only way she could have come by those is by putting it over that scumbag's face.'

Bone pictured Kat, fuelled by anger at Fleur's weeping confidences, crossing the deserted street of Biddinghurst in the first hours of that Sunday morning, wearing her customary black and Morticia's long gloves, to where she knew Nigel lay in the boot of Heather's car. Locker interrupted this vision of the Angel of Death in a much better casting than Fleur by adding, 'They'd dosed him with some of the Rector's Sereenox in his drink, same as she'd slipped Barbary in hers.'

'Another thing we can't be sure of, Steve. She was very careful to wash the glasses once she was interrupted.'

'Funny she didn't think to do that at Winter's.'

'I don't think it crossed her mind that anyone could connect her with Winter. It was just bad luck her father bought her those earrings.'

Locker was restless this morning, full of energy after a hearty breakfast in which he'd made up for the snack meals since the case started. He walked up and down the small room in his shirtsleeves. Wednesday had not let up on Tuesday's heat. 'I reckon she was beginning to think herself immortal. Nobody had tumbled to anything she'd done so far. She'd smothered one man and could be the one to've stabbed another, why shouldn't she drown a third?' He turned at the window and said, 'What I still don't understand is why. Why'd she do all those things with no personal motive? They'd none of them done a single thing to *her*. Would you murder for a best friend, sir?'

Bone laughed. He sat, and stretched his legs. 'I don't even think Fleur was a best friend. They're too unequal. And I doubt if Kat has one. No. What is true, Steve, is that people resent bad treatment more on behalf of others than they might do for themselves. I might murder for Cha or Grizel, I suppose—you might for Cherry or your children. Kat's at that age when people want to save the world, be doctors and nurses, sacrifice their lives. She got rid of people she felt were spoiling the place, deserved to go. She was doing a service.'

'I wonder who'd have been next if she hadn't been stopped.'

'We don't know she has been stopped. If we've a case and she goes inside, what about when she comes out and looks around for the next target? Don't chuck any litter about on that day.'

Locker paused in his pacing to look at his Super, hearing the tone more than the words.

'You're pleased with life this morning, sir. Did the Chief come out with congratulations?'

'He certainly didn't offer to step down and let me take over. No, it's Cha I'm pleased about. She got her GCSE results this morning.' Bone was calling to mind the shriek Cha had given, down at the front door as she opened the envelope, and the gallop, miraculously unfaltering, up the stairs to where he and Grizel waited. She had hardly remembered to give Grizel's letter of Biology results to her, so eager was she to spread her paper before them. 'Very good, and she's thrilled. She's done better than I'd ever have expected. We're going out to celebrate tonight.'

Indeed if they didn't, Bone thought, she would probably go off to celebrate with Justin Rafferty. Cha had informed them that Justin was once more staying with Grue's family. Mrs Grant, a social worker, had made room for him became his friend Phil needed the caravan for himself and his girl-friend who was coming out of hospital. He had also had a row with Phil, who had borrowed the motorbike, Justin said, to go and see his girl-friend in hospital, and now denied it just because he had bent a shin-guard. Bone had immediately thought that the one to borrow it was probably Kat, to get up to London on her errand of mercy to the world.

Grizel knew very well what Bone's opinion was of Justin, but her restraining influence kept him from saying it. Kat Purdey had accused Barbary of 'humping the gardener not an hour ago' and it had taken him a moment or two before he saw that this gardener could not be Laurie Scatchard but must have been Justin. No doubt Barbary had encouraged him and Justin was hardly to blame; Cha could choose worse boy-friends and, if he made a row about Justin, she very well might.

Besides, that morning, with her glowing face, she could do what she liked.

'That's excellent, sir. You must be very pleased. I know you said at one time that she wasn't much interested in her school-work. Hope my lot do as well when they come to her age. All they care about right now is kicking a ball about; and computer games.'

'Sounds a splendid preparation for a policeman's life,' remarked Bone. 'Let's go and see if the team's turned anything else up. I've asked Shay to order in some pastries and iced buns at elevenses to celebrate.'

Locker's eyes brightened and he followed Bone through with enthusiasm.

The team was in jubilant mood. The french windows which on Saturday night had let Fleur wander out of the party disconsolate into the long grass were wide again to let in the warm air of the August morning, and one of the team was straying on the trampled grass, enjoying the sun. Two others were hand-batting screwed balls of paper across the room, and Fredricks sat on the table beside a word-processor talking animatedly to a man with his hands poised over the keys. A group in the corner had got a cassette recorder and were playing a tape that seemed, appropriately, to be of birdsong.

As Bone's observation of all this was, itself, observed, the scene at once changed. The balls of paper were let fall to the floor and scuffed out of sight; the sun-worshipper came in quickly and sat down before a computer terminal, Fredricks pulled down her skirt and got off the table, the word-processor went into action. The activity in the corner, however, blamelessly continued, and Higg called out, 'Listen to this, sir. We found it in Nigel Wells's player. Isn't it pretty?'

He turned up the volume and liquid notes filled the air, making the typist pause, drowning out the hum of machines. Bone recognised a nightingale's song and was for a moment back with his first wife Petra, straying romantically by moonlight, straying abruptly into a patch of nettles which had instantly cooled romance. The bird sang with a quivering intensity, with energy and ease— energy that made the petulant shrilling of a telephone only a feeble interruption; someone snatched it off the hook. A more powerful interruption came on the tape itself: a distant drumming, heard under the birdsong, became a crescendo of battering hooves, louder and louder until they ceased for a moment, all in the room holding their breath until a thud, a creak of leather and a gathering of beats told that the unseen rider had cleared the jump and was away again. The nightingale sang serenely on as the hoofbeats faded into the distance.

'That's all there is, sir. We played it through when we first took it from Wells's place. It's a bit odd, somehow.'

Bone said, 'You mean, why didn't the nightingale stop when the rider appeared?'

'There's that too, I suppose, but I meant, why's it there at all? I wouldn't have put him down as one for natural history.' A general snigger showed what the rest thought.

Bone was silent for a moment. They watched him, waiting. He agreed. There was something odd about the tape. If Nigel had indeed been out recording nightingales, which was not a pursuit anyone would associate with him, then why include the horse, when the noise of hoofs spoilt the birdsong? Not many riders go at such a lick at night, either. You'd expect a few swearwords from Nigel in the foreground. Did Nigel get the subjects of his photography into the mood, all relaxed innocence in their decadent poses, by playing birdsong? But then, why hoofbeats? Some metaphor of sexual climax? The irrelevance of it aroused his curiosity.

'Play it, Sam. Louder this time.'

The nightingale sang, at a decibel level approaching Heavy Metal. The horseman approaching was the mutter of thunder in the background, the impact of its landing made Shay's coffee-mug rattle, but nothing else could be picked up beyond what they had heard before.

Hard on the horseman's heels they were interrupted. The doors had been left open in the heat and now the room door was thrust wide by a thin grey man who stormed in and pointed a shaking finger at the recorder.

'That's how he did it. The bastard. The filthy *bastard.* I knew there was something fishy about it.'

Reggie Merrick, in fine foaming form, was making everyone's morning. Bone spoke, soothing but authoritative. 'I take it you mean Nigel Wells. What was it he did?' As he spoke, a movement in the hall caught his eye. Jonathan Cade, come to give his statement of what he had seen Kat doing, was standing there with a face of intense interest.

Merrick's harsh voice insisted: 'The horseman. The ghost horseman that comes to Bidding Manor and jumps the gate there. It's an omen of approaching death for the owner. Graham—Graham Barnholt—rang me that day to say that Nigel had heard a nightingale and was going to take him out to hear it. I told him there couldn't be one this time of year. *There's* his bloody nightingale!' Merrick paused for breath. 'And the horseman, there on the tape with the nightingale . . . Graham collapsed right inside his front door. That porn artist! He knew Graham thought the world of him—"kindest man alive" Graham called him; Graham made the mistake of telling that bastard he'd left him the Manor in his will.' Reggie looked round. 'Can you *believe* in such a man? Couldn't wait to be Lord of the Manor. He knew—everyone knew—about Graham's heart. It's *devilish.* Lord of the Manor! Well, that bugger's in a warmer place *now,* you can be sure.'

Bone shook his head but not in disagreement. Nothing more likely than that Nigel, who clearly had tamed his conscience long ago, would arrange this lethal little affair. It wouldn't have been difficult to get a birdsong tape—Bone had seen them advertised—or to make one of his own, and then to overtape a horse jumping, perhaps with the help of a rider friend; and to precipitate a heart attack in a man already weak in health, already apprehensive of the legend. It occurred to him that this perhaps explained what Fleur had babbled in hospital about Nigel getting her to dress as a ghost at the manor for what he called 'a joke'. It was most likely a first attempt, which had failed, to give poor Barnholt a heart attack.

'Did you want to speak to us about something, Mr Merrick?'

Reggie actually smiled, as if suddenly infused with amiability by the discovery that Nigel Wells was even worse than he had imagined. 'Yes, I called to tell you that I don't now intend to sue you for wrongful detention. Sam Pearson will be keeping you busy suing you over the Purdey girl, I fancy.' He gave a last, triumphant glance round before turning smartly and walking out of the room.

A thought had occurred to Bone, and he voiced it aloud.

'If this Mr Barnholt fell dead inside his front door just after he thought he'd heard the horseman, the owner then became Nigel Wells. If the legend did its stuff, Wells should have heard the horseman too, and not just on tape.'

'He did, he did, his sister told me.' Jonathan Cade, in his enthusiasm, surged in from the hall. 'Miss Wells told me—when I was seeing her home, you know, after she'd been knocked down on Monday night and we got talking about Nigel and ghosts—he'd heard it quite plainly after Mr Barnholt had gone indoors; of course he couldn't have known Mr Barnholt was dead, so I suppose he thought it was Mr Barnholt's real warning.' He beamed at Bone. 'You know, a *perfect* example of a death warning!'

It was more than the team could take. A muffled explosion at the back of the room and someone bent hastily to retie trainer laces, several turned away as if silently summoned by their computer screens, and one went out into the garden and disappeared round the side of the house. Bone, whose expression was naturally bleak, did not sully it with a smile, though he guessed Jonathan was inured to open scepticism. Logically, he supposed, Barnholt ought to have heard a real ghost—if there were such a thing—and not just Nigel's faked tape. On the other hand, what if the faked sound coincided with the invisible rider?

The thing of most interest to come out of this was the simple fact: Nigel, Kat Purdey's victim, was by intent and result himself a murderer.

52

'When they're both new to it, neither of them can be top cat and they could settle together properly.'

Bone noticed that Cha spoke about the house they were viewing as if the future in it were assured and both cats would find their home and harmony. In this room Cha made straight for the windowseat, not more than a foot off the floor, and curled up there, hugging her knees and gazing dreamily out at the valley below and the hills blue with distance. Bone knew that sense of recognition in a place you had never seen before. He and Cha were sharing it here.

'We could easily get two beds in here, one for you and one for Grue . . .' Grizel was measuring the walls with her eye, and stretching out her arms so that the violet and green of her silk tunic made butterfly wings for a dazzling moment in the dimness of the room. 'And it won't look dark when we've painted it white—'

'Or black,' Cha interrupted without moving her gaze from the hills. 'This is my room.'

'Or black.' Grizel glanced at Bone, her eyes sparkling. 'It would look wicked in black.'

Bone did not disagree. He had already observed that the secret of Kinloch's managerial skills was to object only to the impossible. It seemed to work well with Charlotte, who saw her stepmother as an ally, not a rival. If he had tackled Cha over Justin the other night, there would have been a rumpus. As it was, she had promised not to ride pillion on Justin's motorbike without asking permission. Bone suspected that Grizel might easily accord the permission, but a principle had been established.

He must remind himself that Justin was not, so far as they knew, a murderer, and that he seemed genuinely fond of Cha. Bone vowed yet once again to make efforts not to be over-protective. Look what being over-protective had done for Kat Purdey.

Kat was on Cha's mind too. As they went down the wide, shallow stairs, tacitly united in the conviction that this was the house that had chosen them, she said, 'That girl you arrested. She's only a year older than me?'

'I suppose so. She's seventeen-plus.'

They went into the long sitting room that was begging silently for their furniture. Cha said, 'Do you get many murderers my age?'

Because it was a long habit with him to discuss any subject Cha brought up, he overcame a dislike of this one. 'Not a lot. Murderers aren't predictable, but they're not so often young. More of them lately, perhaps.'

'And then people say they don't know right from wrong and it's all the fault of society. Will she get life?'

The term sounded strange on Cha's lips. There was as much life ahead for her as there was for Kat, but how differently it might be spent. He looked at the poise of her head, confident without arrogance.

'I don't know, pet. As things are, we don't know if we've even a case. You could say, it hangs by a thread.' He was thinking of the thread from Heather Armitage's embroidery which had no way of getting on Kat's glove except when she pressed the cushion over Nigel's face. 'If it does come to court, a good lawyer could whip up a lot of sympathy for her. There are plenty who think justice belongs in private hands as much as with the police.'

Grizel shut a cupboard door, remarking, 'I'm sure I read about a man who got only nine months for killing someone he thought, and wrongly as it happened, had committed a crime.'

'And he said he'd do it again,' Cha chimed in. 'Everyone was on his side.'

'Except, I imagine, the family of the man he'd killed by mistake. What are you saying? That you'd have done what Kat Purdey is supposed to have done?'

Cha scuffed the toe of her sandal on the dust of the polished boards. 'Well . . . he *was* horrible.'

'And you'd smother all horrible people? The people you thought were horrible, anyway. How many steps are we away from Auschwitz?'

'Oh Daddy, don't be impossible.' She was not going to admit that she had taken his point and she moved off to peer, with Grizel, into the cavern of a brick fireplace. 'We could *barbecue* in here. Look, can we put a seat in at the side?'

'Why not?'

This might, or might not, turn out to be the perfect house that it seemed. Bone had learnt how seldom life offered perfection. There was even some danger in trying to get rid of the flaws.

Cha, already in possession of the room above, might not even stay in this house for many more years. While he did not precisely envisage her shacked up in another caravan with Justin Rafferty, Bone felt the poignancy of the mere thought; and then Grizel slid her arm into his.

'The nice thing about this house is that it's not too big and yet there's plenty of room. And I've seen just the right tree in the garden for the swing. Your son is going to love it.'